The Tysen Hotel

A Novel

Donna Gormly

iUniverse, Inc.
Bloomington

The Tysen Hotel
A Novel

iUniverse books may be ordered through booksellers or by contacting:

iUniverse
1663 Liberty Drive
Bloomington, IN 47403
www.iuniverse.com
1-800-Authors (1-800-288-4677)

ISBN: 978-1-4759-3361-1 (sc)
ISBN: 978-1-4759-3362-8 (hc)
ISBN: 978-1-4759-3363-5 (e)

Library of Congress Control Number: 2012910874

Printed in the United States of America

iUniverse rev. date: 7/5/2012

TO PAUL

MY HUSBAND, MY LOVE, MY FRIEND

AND FOR

TRISTAN AND AIDAN DORNFELD,

OUR GRANDDAUGHTERS

There are those who have supported me again and again as I made my tenuous way through the creation of "Tysen" and the characters who live there, those to whom I shall always be grateful.

I wish to thank Jane Roberts Wood who said, "Just write three lines and bring them to lunch"; Camille Daugherty, who read every version of every chapter and kept me going; The Twin Cities Inquiring Minds Book Club, who asked a question that changed my thinking and the life of a character; Dr. Lon Rogers, who diligently read two different drafts; and to my "other daughter," Patty Caudill, for loving the work and giving her morale-boosting support that meant so much.

I am indebted to my brothers, James and David Hodge, for reminding me of, and adding to, my remembrances of "Tysen."

To other family members who read and encouraged me: Leah, Harold, Bunny, James and Margaret Gormly; Analee, James, David and Della Hodge and Sandra Julien.

To my son-in-law, Tim Dornfeld, who promoted the manuscript to anyone and everyone and was the first to encourage me to self-publish.

To my son, Eric, who saw a change that needed to be made in the plot line and had the courage to keep pushing until I listened.

To my granddaughters, Tristan and Aidan, who make the sun shine every day.

To my friend, Patricia Knapp, for her reading and support.

To my sister, Debbie, my advisor, who is there to give advice on all things computer and otherwise and remains on stand-by even now.

To Beverlye Brown, for her incisive criticism, and always, always knowing.

To my daughter, Robin, for finally liking something I wrote, and for her constant reassurance and endeavors to get the work published.

And, finally, to Paul, without whom this book would never have been published. He is an excellent editor and my superb counsel. Thank you, my love.

In Memoriam: My Brothers
James Milton Hodge 1936-2012
David Alvin Hodge 1944-2012

For God hath not given us the spirit of fear;
but of power, and of love, and of a sound mind.

2 Timothy 1:7 (KJV)

Contents

Chapter One

Summer, 1950

The railroad tracks ran dead center through the middle of Tysen, holding the town together like a zipper running down the back of a skin tight dress. Without the railroad, the entire town would slide right off the shoulders, leaving a bare meadow of some two hundred acres surrounded by oak, maple, cedar, hickory, and at least ten other varieties of trees and heavy undergrowth in the middle of the Ozark foothills.

From any front porch, the townsfolk could not only peer into the windows of the passengers trains speeding by, they could view at least fifty percent of the population, who rarely sped anywhere. So, most everybody knew what everybody else was doing, and, as in any small town, if you hadn't seen it yourself, you could bet someone would call in ten minutes on the party line to tell you all about it.

It didn't take the sign in the front window of Johnson's General Store that read, "Pie Supper, Saturday, May 13, 7:30 p.m., Grade School Auditorium," to announce the Annual Pie Supper. Other than the Fourth of July picnic, it was the biggest social event of the year.

There was nothing in the air that Saturday evening but the sweet scent of jasmine and honeysuckle and the lush moistness of a Missouri evening, nothing to shine a lantern into the corners of the coming night. Nothing to tell a body that from Naomi Hollister's kitchen at the Tysen Hotel to the pulpit of the First Baptist Church, there were few who would be left unscarred in body or spirit by the conflict that would erupt that May evening at Tysen's Annual Pie Supper.

At quarter to seven, Naomi Hollister carefully held the pink hat box, tied with a large satin bow and a sprig of lilac, on her lap as Matt Neyerson eased the truck over the gravel of the grade school parking lot and stopped beside Loncy Oppenmeier's maroon Chevy. Matt turned off the ignition and pulled on the emergency brake.

"I appreciate you driving, Matt; I'd never be able to herd the truck and hold this pie at the same time," Naomi said.

"I'm just making sure nothing happens to that pie. Doc and I are both set on buying it."

Naomi, who owned the Tysen Hotel where Matt boarded, was famous for her cooking. She could make a pot roast or a meat loaf that would make a man's knees buckle. And her desserts were the talk of the county. Her apple-hickory nut pie always brought in the highest bid at the pie suppers. Most pies went for under five dollars, but her pie usually went for eight or more.

Naomi reached for the door handle, but Matt stopped her. "Naomi, wait a minute." She turned to him, the setting sun making a red-gold halo around the auburn hair that touched her shoulders. "You've got that little pucker between your eyes that says you're thinking mighty hard about something. You want to talk about it?"

She hesitated for a minute before answering. "I'm probably just borrowing trouble, but I've been worrying about Johnny and Ray all the way over here." Johnny was Naomi's adopted son who was dating Hope Howard, the preacher's daughter, and Ray Redeem was Johnny's best friend who was dating Alice Tolney, daughter of Webster Tolney, the town's ne'er-do-well, on the sly.

"Webster still not letting Alice date Ray?" Matt asked.

"Webster told Ray last week that Alice can't date until she's eighteen, but I don't believe a word of it. Webster's always got his own best interest at heart, and God only knows what it is this time."

Naomi looked down at the pink bow and picked at it. "And then there's Preacher Busby. He'll know the kids have planned to meet even if they don't come together, and that spells trouble for Johnny. You know Busby's rule about Johnny not taking Hope around Ray."

"That doesn't mean the kids can't all sit together in a public place," Matt reasoned.

She shook her head, disagreeing. "You think that, and I think that, but Busby won't. How the preacher can still be holding a grudge over something Ray did when he was a kid is beyond me."

"It's beyond me, too," Matt replied, "but I'm a Presbyterian; we've got a little more foot room than you Baptists do."

Naomi smiled. "Foot room is the word for it all right. Busby doesn't hold with a lot of things, and he 'specially doesn't hold with dancing." She looked down at her feet in her new white pumps. "He was always after me to give it up."

Matt grinned. "It must not have worked. I see you dancing around the kitchen to the radio like Ginger Rogers; you sure don't have Baptist feet."

"No, I don't, but don't tell Busby. It's none of his business what my feet are doing." They both laughed.

"Let's get out and get this thing started," Matt said.

She moved to open the door, but hesitated, turning back over her shoulder to say, "I want to thank you for loaning Johnny your car tonight."

"I never mind helping out Johnny," he said.

Naomi said, "Johnny hasn't had a man in his life for a long time. Having you at the hotel means a lot to him."

Matt touched her shoulder lightly. "It means a lot to me, too. Now, sit right there for a minute so I can come to help you down," he told her.

Matt came around the front of the truck and opened the door wide as Naomi stood up on the running board. He took the box in his right hand and, encircling her waist with his left arm, lifted a startled Naomi gently to the ground. Naomi wasn't a little woman, some five feet six or seven, but Matt was a head taller.

Naomi straightened her shoulders and her dress, looking around to see who might be watching. Matt just grinned as he carried the pie up the two front steps of the porch, settled it into her arms and watched her carefully tending it as she pushed through the swinging doors that led into the auditorium. Matt was quite sure as the doors swung to behind Naomi that nothing in the world smelled better than a lilac-powdered woman with a fresh-baked pie in her arms.

Matt pulled his cigarettes out of his pocket and looked around the parking lot. Clumps of men in threes and fours stood smoking and talking over by the yellow school bus parked beside the school, some leaning against its side. Matt stood where he was, thinking about what Naomi had told him over a cup of coffee last Sunday morning.

Naomi had been worried about Ray who had a fight at the tavern the night before. Ray hadn't had a fight since he'd been seeing Alice Tolney.

"He's been so happy. I don't know what got into him," Naomi said.

"Did he and Alice have a fight?" Matt asked.

"Not that I know of," she sighed, "and Johnny doesn't know either. Or at least he's not saying."

Naomi loved Ray Redeem almost as much as she loved Johnny. It was Ray who had taught Johnny to fish and to row a boat, taught him to swim on the Meramec River. Ray was about ten or so then, Johnny eight. Ray taught him to shoot a rifle, then a shotgun. They hunted squirrels and quail, and Naomi never worried about them. She just felt Ray knew what he was doing and that he'd take care of them both. Which he did. She also knew that Ray had earned himself a reputation fighting and then drinking, but Naomi understood why better than most folks.

Ray never involved Johnny in any fighting; if Ray were going to fight, he went his separate way. But the rest of the time, they'd fish and hunt together, or they'd drive down to the river for a swim. And they'd take in movies over in Meramec City and watch the girls. Ray ate dinner with them at least twice a week, and he put away enough of Naomi's desserts to start a bakery.

"I know he's had some problems, but you can overlook a lot," Naomi said, "when somebody's been good to your child."

"I like Ray, Naomi, you know I do," Matt said, adding a teaspoon of sugar and some cream to his coffee. "Fact is, most everybody does. He works hard at their sawmill." The Redeems, Jackson, the father, and Ray, the son, owned the largest sawmill in the county.

"Losing a mother is a terrible tragedy for an eight year old child," Naomi said.

"That's still the dangdest accident I've ever heard of, being struck by lightning while taking clothes off a line." Matt shook his head.

"Loretta was trying to get the clothes in before it rained," Naomi defended.

"I understand that, Naomi, but you don't stand out touching a clothesline wire strung on metal poles when you can hear thunder and see lightning. It's just not smart."

"She wasn't thinking, I guess. Poor woman," Naomi frowned. "I've never been able to get the thought of her just slumped there on the ground, face down, in a heap all alone, and having that little boy find her. Her hair was burnt off, they said. Her scalp was all black and her shoes, what was left of them, had been blown clean off her feet."

Matt could see the memory move into Naomi's hazel eyes. "Is that why you think he fights everything that moves?" he asked.

"He doesn't fight everything that moves," she bristled. "Not anymore, and he's been very sweet to the girls, he's polite to the women, and he's always been there for Johnny."

"I know that. Even so, Naomi, he liked to fight, and he liked to drink."

Naomi looked into her coffee cup. "He always rough-housed when he was little, but something changed in him when Lester was killed in the war; he went into fighting for real. He'd lost his mother, and then his brother was gone, too."

Lester Redeem was one of the first boys from Tysen to die in the war. All of them had mourned him.

"How old was Ray when Lester died?" Matt asked.

Naomi had to count back. "Not quite ten, I reckon," she told him after a moment. "I remember I had him here then as much as I could. Poor little thing. His mother was dead, his only brother had died doing battle, and his father didn't care about anything but his Bible and his sawmill."

Jackson Redeem was like a fortress after he lost Loretta; then, after Lester died, he just drew up the drawbridge and nailed it shut. It was like he quit seeing people as anything other than ghosts.

"As much as Jackson hates alcohol, I don't think he even noticed when Ray came home drunk and beat up. It's as though Ray isn't there, hasn't been for years. I believe," Naomi paused to think, "that Ray fought so somebody would know he's alive, and he made sure he knew it by the pain he felt."

"I'll give you," Matt said, "that he never really did serious damage, just a few bruises and bloody noses, until he got his first drink, but since then he's hurt some men pretty bad. Broken bones, a couple of concussions. That's just not right. If he starts in fighting again, he's headed for disaster."

"You're right, Matt, I know. I don't know what happened to set him off, but I know that he'd not been drinking. Bertie Reardon told me she was there at the tavern to bring Tom home and that Ray hadn't had a drink, just jumped up and went after three guys out in the parking lot and beat up all three."

Matt thought it over; until last Saturday it had been several months since Ray had had a fight. Then, out of nowhere, he cut loose again.

"I expect he'll tell us when he's ready," Matt said.

"You're right; I just can't help worrying about him, though. I'll just have to pray on it while I'm at church." She raised herself from her chair and patted his shoulder in thanks.

"Anytime," he told her, and watched her walk back toward her bedroom to get her Bible and her hat.

Matt spotted Doobie Pratt leaning against a large oak tree with a cigarette in one hand, slipping a bottle of Stag beer into the deep pocket of his overalls with the other. Doobie was taking in the crowd, wanting to know who arrived and who came with them. He looked about four beers into the evening, which was a little short of his usual pace by this time on a Saturday night. Matt liked Doobie; he never drank on the job, and he was reliable during the week.

While Doobie's condition, drunk or in some degree of sobering up, come tomorrow morning or any given Sunday morning, was entirely predictable, his location, on the other hand, was not. He had been found in the back of pick-up trucks as far away as Mahalia, some twenty miles to the southeast; he'd been found in the basement of the First Methodist Church spread out on one of the long tables used for dinners; he'd been found at one time or another in every front or back yard in town; and when he hadn't been found by noon on Sunday, he was usually curled up by his mother's tombstone in the cemetery behind the First Baptist Church, demanding that she tell him what it was really like in heaven and asking her to plead his case with the Almighty. Doobie'd never been a mean drunk, just a persistent one.

"Evening, Matt," Doobie said, patting his side to be sure his beer was steady.

Matt flicked a match with his thumb nail and lit his Camel. He pinched the match out between his fingers and dropped it to the ground. "Doobie," Matt nodded.

"I got me a feeling this is going to be some pie supper tonight," Doobie said, watching Wendell and Marie Johnson pull their Dodge into a spot near the front porch.

Matt took a deep drag and let the smoke trail out into the evening air. "Big crowd already. Guess we'll make a lot of money for those new school books."

"Looks like it." Doobie scratched his back against the tree, and then said offhandedly, "I hear tell Sample Forney's gonna be here tonight."

"Sample usually isn't one for pie suppers," Matt said.

"Well, he's coming tonight," Doobie said.

Sample Forney, the wealthiest farmer in the county, was six feet four and had to weigh 280. He'd put two wives in the ground and scared off a third. He was legendary for the size of his male appendage and the frequency of its use. The size the men knew about from working with him in the fields on the two sections of rich bottom land he owned. They'd seen him piss. Doobie told everybody that Sample's dick hung damn near to his knees and that when he pissed, it sounded like pouring water out of a boot, or a cow pissing on a flat rock. No matter how many times he said it, it always brought a laugh.

The frequency of its use, apart from the fact that Sample's wives were always pregnant, the men had learned from their own wives. Doris, Sample's first wife, once told Marie Johnson, who worked side by side with her husband at their General Store, that she tried to stay pregnant because that was the only time Sample would leave her alone. Marie couldn't keep such an item of information to herself; it was just too weighty. To lessen her load, she told Wendell and just one or two of her close friends who, in turn, passed the information along to their husbands.

"You think Sample is coming out tonight to scout for a wife?" Matt asked Doobie.

"Sample's already got a girl in mind. He's coming tonight to bid on Alice Tolney's pie."

Matt had just taken his last draw from his cigarette and choked. And I just told Naomi there was nothing to worry about, he thought.

"My God, Alice won't even graduate from high school until next month, and Sample's twenty five years older than she is." Naomi had more reasons to worry than she knew. There was trouble coming. "Besides, Alice is going steady with Ray Redeem." He dropped his cigarette on the dirt and ground it out with the toe of his shoe.

"I know that. I just said Sample was going to bid. I know as well as you do that Ray ain't about to let him have that pie without a fight."

"What makes Sample think Alice could possibly be interested in him?"

"It ain't Alice who's interested in Sample; it's her daddy." Doobie searched in his overalls for his beer.

"What are you talking about, Doob?" Matt asked. Sometimes, Doobie liked to elaborate, but there was almost always a seed of truth in his story.

"Webster Tolney thinks that if Sample marries Alice he'll be set for life. Fact is, Sample's willing to trade Webster some mighty good bottom land for Alice," Doobie said.

Matt stared at Doobie. "Webster is willing to trade him Alice for land?"

Doobie nodded. "Webster told me this afternoon at Harvey's Tavern. We was having a beer together. Said Alice would be better off married to Sample. Said Ray was a no good drinker and fighter, and he didn't want her with the likes of him." Doobie took a long swig of his Stag.

Matt's face was a map of unbelief.

Wiping off his mouth with the back of his sleeve, Doobie said, "If you don't believe me, ask Doc Barnes. When I told Doc, he said there's was no way in hell he'd let Webster do such a thing. Doc said he'd delivered that child into the world and if he had to, he'd take Webster out of it, and it would be the best thing that could happen for Alice and Evelyn." Evelyn, Webster's frail, much put upon wife, suffered equally from lupus and being married to Webster Tolney. "Doc was sure steamed up," Doobie said.

Matt stared out beyond the swings and see-saw and took his time lighting another cigarette. He just bet Doc was steamed up. Doc Barnes was sixty-two, stood no more that five feet eight, and had a bad knee; but when he was angry, you'd best not get in his way. Doc didn't hold a very high opinion of Webster in the first place, what with the way Webster treated Evelyn and Alice, expecting them to do most of the work and take care of him. Matt figured when Doc heard this, he had gone out to the Tolney farm and laid it all out for Webster. But as Doc himself always said, "If a jackass looks into a mirror, don't expect a prince to look back." Matt didn't know how even Doc could get through to a jackass like Webster Tolney, but he knew that Doc would have to try. And no matter what Webster said, if Doc were breathing, he would not be one to let Alice be bartered as chattel. Nor would Naomi. Nor, for that matter, would Alice herself. At least Matt didn't think Alice would.

Matt said, "I don't know why I should be surprised. After what he tried to do to Mary Jo."

"That's right," Doobie said.

Webster Tolney was always out for a deal. When his oldest daughter, Mary Jo, graduated from high school, he'd tried to trade her off to Wilber Little for a tractor and two cows. Wilber was well past sixty at the time. Mary Jo had the good sense to run off to St. Louis and not come back. But if he'd tried to auction off one daughter, why wouldn't he try to auction off her sister for an even better price?

Matt wished he had a beer himself, or a stiff drink of whiskey. "Webster doesn't have a scruple to be found when he thinks he's going to make a dollar. To him those girls are just livestock. I believe the son-of-a-bitch would sell his soul to Satan if he thought it would make him ten dollars."

"Probably would," Doobie agreed matter of factly.

They smoked in silence. After a few minutes, Matt asked, "Alice know about this?"

"I don't know about Alice, but I know that Ray don't. I saw him at work today, and he was just whistlin' away; you would've thought he had a big date or something. If he had knowed Sample Forney was coming to have pie with Alice, there wouldn'ta been no whistlin' going on, I can tell you."

Matt didn't comment. They both silently watched Rev. Busby Howard proudly maneuver his black, shiny Pontiac to a stop across the parking lot.

Matt said, "Preacher's new car looks like a good piece of machinery."

Doobie turned away from the Howard family. The last thing he wanted was another sermon from Busby Howard on what a fine Christian woman Doobie's mother had been and how disappointed she would be to see Doobie now.

Matt didn't cotton much to Busby Howard, either. Busby spoke about anything Biblical with a sureness that what he said came directly from God, and Busby rarely spoke about anything that wasn't Biblical.

The man was a pillar of Absolutes. Matt was always puzzled and put off by anybody who claimed to know the mind of God.

Then, there was Busby's approach to his sermons. There was all that hollering and Bible pounding. Busby didn't give a man room to pray, much less think. And a person could only take so many "God Loves You, BUT" sermons. There were too many "buts" in this world as it was. If God loves you, BUT, Matt didn't know how any of us could cope with all the contingencies.

"Johnny seems pretty crazy over that oldest Howard girl," Doobie said.

"Yep," Matt answered, "he seems to be."

"Hope is a right nice girl," Doobie opined before he changed the subject and reached for his beer. "You waiting for Doc?"

"Yep, Naomi is saving seats inside," Matt said.

"She's a good woman, Naomi," Doobie said, "raising Russell's nephew as her own when Russell ran off. She sure does dote on that boy, don't she?"

"She does that and with good reason," Matt said. Through the tall windows of the gymnasium, he could see Naomi talking to Maureen Fitzroy and Bertie Reardon. "I pity anybody who ever tries to hurt that boy. I'd rather fight a mother bear."

Doobie laughed. "Well, she's got fight in her, that one, that's for sure."

Chapter Two

Inside, Naomi had made her way toward the women who were standing near the stage, boxes in their arms, waiting to deliver them up to Maureen Fitzroy, the founding member of the Tysen Garden Society, who was chairlady for the pie supper committee this year. Naomi could see Maureen was printing Bertie Reardon's name and the kind of pie she'd brought on the sheet of paper secured against the clipboard she balanced on her left arm. Naomi could hear Bertie; she had a voice that carried like a bullhorn. Bertie was telling Maureen about her "new car"—a 1937 Ford Coupe with a rumble seat.

Bertie was Tysen's railroad mistress. The railroad station was the hub of the town, and Bertie commanded it like a ship's captain. She handled all the commerce for the railroad: the mail, ticket sales, shipping. Bertie was the connection between the railroad and Tysen, summer and winter. Naomi had heard about the car from Matt, and she knew she'd have to hear the story from beginning to end the next time Bertie stopped by for coffee. Right now, Naomi was more interested in seeing her pie safely up on the pie table that was already blooming with decorated boxes.

Throughout the auditorium, the women and girls were gathered here and there like bunches of wildflowers, decked out in their second-best floral prints, just a dress short of Sunday. The men off the farms came with their hair slicked down with Rose Hair Oil and all done up in bib overalls. Sharply ironed creases ran down the long sleeves of their clean blue shirts. White shirts were saved for the Sabbath. The younger men were in jeans and the townsmen in khakis, except for Brother Busby Howard, Loncy Oppenmeier and Wendell Johnson. They'd all be on the stage, which meant, for them, a white shirt, tie, and jacket.

The jacket wouldn't stay on anyone except the preacher after things got warmed up, but it made a good impression for beginnings.

The lights high overhead in the auditorium, that also served as the gymnasium, were on even though it wasn't dark yet, and Walter Pursey, the school handyman and janitor, had taken care of setting up all the folding chairs in two sections, leaving a wide aisle down the middle and narrow aisles along each wall. Women and children were clattering into chairs and already claiming seats for the men standing in the back of the room near the work-out mats, as well as those outside talking. The room brewed with the buzzing voices, a laugh percolating up here and there. The sound rose above them, pushing high overhead, gathering into a ball of chatter that floated just beneath the rafters; the feeling of anticipation kept it aloft and moving. Pie suppers were nights to feel young.

Loncy Oppenmeier was standing at the front of the stage tapping on the microphone. There was nothing that upset Loncy more than auctioneering with a bad P.A. system, and he took his auctioneering with the seriousness of a Divine Calling. Loncy had gone to the Missouri Auction School in Raytown, Missouri, which, as anybody who knew anything about auctioneering could tell you, was the best dang auction school in the whole country, and he did graduate at the head of his class. Why people from all over the state called for Loncy to auctioneer their sales.

He could auction anything from a prize bull to a mincemeat pie; he had a talent for rolling out words or slowing them down, just to let folks get the jokes. He was a born showman. To watch Loncy Oppenmeier auction was an entertainment in itself. He was reason enough to attend the pie supper.

Wendell Johnson, who was chairman of the school board, was in charge of carrying the pies to Loncy during the sale, bringing whichever pie that Maureen Fitzroy would choose to hand to him. Each box or hamper contained a pie, two small plates, two forks, a knife, a pie server, and napkins. When Loncy put the pie up for sale, the highest bidder won the honor of eating the pie with the lady who baked it. The young men, and the single older ones, fought over rights to the baker rather than the baked goods; married men knew to eat the pie of the one you brung. No matter how much you might be hankering for a piece of that pecan pie Jarvis Harper was eating, or the apricot cobbler Marvin Hanks was stoking away, you'd do well to eat your wife's apple pie and take home a happy woman. Otherwise, it'd be humble pie you'd be eating for a month.

Sometimes, the rivalries between the single men got pretty heated. There had even been a fistfight or two outside in the schoolyard after the supper when some young fellow had stepped in to ease a pie right out from under the wallet of another one. They'd had more than a few lively evenings here over the years.

Maureen called to Naomi over the top of Bertie's head right in the middle of Bertie's sentence, "Naomi, would you mind checking in the storage shed out back to see if we have another folding table out there? And don't you try to carry it in; one of the men will see to that." Naomi waved that she would, and Bertie went on talking as if she'd never been interrupted.

Outside in the twilight, Naomi was glad for a chance to have a few minutes alone. The soft evening air was a tease, and a reminder. It wasn't just Johnny and Ray Naomi was thinking about; it was Russell Hollister. Maybe it was the date, May 13. Russell Hollister had been gone twelve years today. Twelve years.

Seventeen years ago, Russell Hollister had brought her from St. Louis to Tysen a month after he married her, swearing eternal love and devotion. Brought her to his aging, deaf mother and her six-bedroom house which he said he wanted to fill up with kids. He had parked her there, right on the corner of Main Street and the spur road, and promptly took a job with the Missouri Pacific Railroad just as his daddy had before him, leaving her alone all week with his mother, coming home only on weekends. At least the first two years he came home on weekends. Then he came home every two weeks, then once a month. He'd been given longer trips, he told her, as though she couldn't read a railroad schedule and knew that from Tysen a round trip to the west coast, even if he had that route, wouldn't take two weeks, much less a month.

And the children never came. Which was a shame. Naomi loved children. Russell thought it was her fault, though Doc Barnes said he couldn't find a thing the matter with her. There wasn't money for a specialist, so Naomi just lived with it. There wasn't anything else to be done, and they finally quit trying.

Then one day, Johnny had been dumped with a sack of diapers, a blanket and two scraggly outfits in Mother Hollister's kitchen by Russell's brother, Grover, and his wife, Elvira, right before they just took off for California. Johnny was six months old. They said they were leaving for a vacation for a week, but two weeks passed, then a month, then two, and nobody heard from them, and there wasn't anyway to reach them.

Johnny became Naomi's Godsend. She had doted on him from the minute she saw him; he was the core that centered her life.

Then Elvira finally wrote. She said Grover had been killed in an automobile accident on Christmas Eve, and she was in no shape to take care of a child alone. They never heard from her again. Johnny was two.

When Johnny was five, Mother Hollister died in her sleep. Her heart, Doc Barnes said. Shortly after they buried her next to Russell's father in the Baptist Church cemetery, Russell packed a larger bag than usual and kissed Naomi goodbye. He promised to call that night from Saint Louis, carried Johnny on his shoulders to the train depot half a block down the gravel street, sat him down beside the train, swung up on the steps of the engine, and waved. No call came that night; Naomi realized it only after she'd gotten into bed and run the day through her mind. Well, she thought, he probably got busy and forgot.

The next week Russell's letter came, wrapped around a thousand-dollar check, saying he wasn't coming back and that she could have the house. Naomi was so shocked she didn't even cry, shocked that he really had left, and she was shocked that he had a thousand dollars to send. She never could figure out just where he got that money, but she had taken the check to the Tysen Bank the next morning and deposited it into a new account. She knew she had to do something to keep herself and Johnny in a state of repair, and she put considerable thought into just what it might be.

It took her less than two weeks to decide that since Tysen had a post office, a general store, a feed store, a telephone exchange, a funeral parlor, a school, three churches, a barber shop, a beauty shop, two taverns, a bank and a café, that it just stood to reason it could tolerate a small hotel. Russell had brought home a good many railroad men to layover and eat Naomi's cooking. She knew how to cook and clean and make things comfortable; she'd been doing it all of her life. The big house, with its two bedrooms downstairs and four up, made for a perfect arrangement. She and Johnny could sleep on the first floor, and the boarders could sleep on the second. She borrowed enough money from the bank to add a downstairs bathroom for Johnny and her so they wouldn't have to share with the guests.

She had opened her hotel, and she'd gotten by. In fact, she'd managed to put enough aside for Johnny to go to Missouri U. in the fall after he graduated from Meramec City High School at the end of this month. Johnny had his heart set on being a journalist, and if he wanted to be a journalist, Naomi would do anything she could to help him.

Twelve years today, she thought. Even so, why should the date bring him back? It never had before. She had a good life here. She had her son, she had her friends, she had her church. Life was good. She thought about Matt standing outside waiting for Doc. Yes, life was very good.

Well, now, she remembered, I need to check on those tables.

Doobie and Matt sat back on their heels waiting for Doc. Doobie wasn't about to go inside if he thought Doc could tell him what happened at the Tolney's. "Do you know what I heard over at Harvey's Tavern?" Doobie asked. He dropped by both taverns and the Talk of Tysen Café on a regular basis to keep abreast of the news. "Charlie Clark's home from St. Louis. Got back today."

Matt looked surprised. "That's pretty quick, isn't it? How long's it been?"

"Bout three months, I reckon."

"Why'd they let him go?"

"The docs at Arsenal Street told Charlene and Wyman that he'd probably be okay now that they'd run all that electricity through his head. Said he likely won't be acting out again." Arsenal Street was the way all folks referred to the Insane Asylum located on Arsenal Street in St. Louis.

"Acting out?" Matt asked. "They called what Charlie did 'acting out'?"

"Don't know what else you'd call it," Doobie said with a shrug.

Three months ago, Charlie Clark had slipped up on his sister, Annabelle, while she was in the barn alone milking. He'd run his pitchfork through her dress and pinned her to the barn floor. When she screamed, Wyman, and her brother, Carl, came running and it took both of them to pull him away. Carl finally got Charlie off her when he knocked him in the back of the head with a full bucket of oats. Charlie was out just long enough for Carl to sit on him while Wyman tied him up. Annabelle had been in shock ever since.

"I'd call it downright criminal; that's what I'd call it." Matt shook his head. "What are his folks supposed to do if Charlie starts 'acting out' again?"

"Hell, Matt, they're his family; they ain't gonna throw him out. Sometimes, I think all that education you got at Missou didn't do you a bit of good."

Matt had two semesters at the University of Missouri, but had to quit to take care of his mother when his father died. Of course, Matt knew that Doobie thought anybody who didn't say "ain't" was educated.

"Doobie, Charlie needs throwing out," Matt said, ignoring Doobie's comment about his education. "He raped his sister. Don't you think that calls for moving him to another place where he can't harm anybody?"

"Well, he don't have nowhere else to go, so they have to take him in. Who else wants him? Nobody around here; that's for sure. People are scared of him, and the insane asylum ain't going to keep him any longer. He ain't got no other place to go."

"That's about the size of it," Doc Barnes said, walking up to join them.

"You already heard about Charlie Clark?" Matt asked.

"Yep, I heard. I wish they'd kept him longer at the asylum, but there's not a thing I can do about it. It's the law. Wyman said Annabelle's so frightened she stays locked in her room. Somebody should shoot the poor devil and put him out of his misery."

"Well, now, fellas," Doobie said, "It ain't easy to shoot your kin."

Doc said, "Doobie, sometimes your kin are the only people worth shooting."

Matt laughed. "He's got you there, Doob."

Doobie shrugged and reached into his overalls for his beer.

The parking lot was full. People were parking out along the road. Matt spotted his own car with Johnny behind the wheel, an arm around Hope Howard's shoulder and Alice Tolney sitting on the far side of her in the front seat. They were pulling into the far corner, coming not from town, but up the Old River Road. Just coming around the bend behind them was Ray Redeem's truck. Oh, Naomi, Matt thought, I think you may have reason to worry.

Shifting attention away from their direction, Matt said, "Well, Doc, you still planning to steal my pie tonight?"

"It's not your pie, my friend, until the bidding is done, and tonight I plan to have me some mighty fine apple-hickory nut pie."

"How about a little wager?" Matt asked.

"Nope, not tonight; I'm saving all my money to bid on that pie." Doc rattled change in his pockets.

"It'll take more than that," Matt told him.

Doc patted the pocket of his seersucker suit coat. "I'm all covered, Matthew; you just better see how deep your own pockets go."

Matt didn't tell Doc that the pie he carried out of the hotel was going to be the same pie he'd carry back in, no matter what the cost. He didn't want to spoil his fun too much.

Johnny came up to them grinning.

"What'd you do with those girls, Johnny?" Doc asked.

"They're inside saving seats. I'll go find them in a minute," Johnny said, looking around the parking lot.

"Ain't two girls just a little more than you can handle, young Johnny?" Doobie asked.

"What do you know about it, Doobie?" Johnny laughed at him. "When was the last time you went out with a girl?"

"That'd be about 1946," Ray Redeem said as he came up to the group.

Doobie fake punched him on the shoulder. "If it ain't the man who handles the big saw," Doobie said. Ray fake punched back.

Ray ran the circular saw that was the heart of the Redeem Lumber Mill, the largest sawmill in the county. He mastered the saw in the same way he mastered any task he decided was worth the undertaking, and managing the saw was not a job for the faint of heart.

The mill was a pole-barn structure, standing some ninety feet long, sixty feet wide and twenty feet high; the roof and the far side were of corrugated sheet metal; the huge saw sat at its middle. The ends and the near side were open, and the men and the big saw blade, powered by a diesel truck engine, were protected from the sun and rain, but the heat and cold were part of their day.

Jackson usually supervised the rest of the business: he might be a ways off beyond the mill at the log pile, where some five hundred or more logs were stacked by size and cure time, marking logs for the next order. The Mueller brothers would then roll these onto the front-end loader of the tractor and move them to the skidway, a raised loading platform at the front end of the mill's trolley track. Regal King and Doobie were usually under the roof with Ray, though all the men would be at one time or another. Doobie was the off-loader, lifting the bark-covered slabs and then the rough-cut lumber from the end of the table away from the large whirring blade.

"Jackson comin' tonight?" Doobie asked.

Ray shrugged. Except for church and town meetings, Jackson Redeem, stayed pretty much to himself since the death of Ray's mother. "Martha baked a pie and told him he was coming whether he wanted to or not. She's been with us for so long now that I think it's easier for him just to do what she says. Could be he will. I never know."

"I gotta get inside to Hope and Alice," Johnny said. Then, as though the idea had just popped into his head, he asked Ray, "You want me to save you a seat?"

Ray shrugged, as though he couldn't care one way or the other. "Might as well."

"The preacher's inside," Matt cautioned. "Aren't you guys pushing it a little?"

"If Ray comes over to sit with us, we'd be rude not to offer him a place to sit," Johnny said.

Matt cocked an eyebrow at him.

"We'll be careful. I promise," Johnny told him.

Matt cautioned, "I want you two to take special care tonight. I know it's a public place, but you know how Busby feels about Ray."

Ray said, "Everybody in town knows how Busby feels about me, and everybody in town knows I...." Johnny put his hand on Ray's shoulder, stopping him, and said, "We'll be over on the left-hand side near the wall. You might want to come down the side aisle."

"I'll find you," Ray told Johnny. "I'll have a quick smoke and be there in a minute."

Johnny nodded and set off at a trot toward the lights that were spilling out onto the schoolyard; Ray lit a cigarette.

"We'd better move ourselves," Doc said. "I want to get myself dug in for battle."

"Well, get ready, you old son-of-a-gun, I'm coming after you tonight," Matt told him. "What about you, Doobie? You going to do battle over pie?"

"Not me, boys. I'm just going to stand by real quiet-like and hold the first aid kit. One of you boys is going to get mighty wounded."

"You might as well be the one to give first aid," Doc said; "you're the one carrying the alcohol."

"She's safe as can be," Doobie said, patting his pocket where Doc knew there must be a half pint of whiskey hidden along with his bottle of beer. The three of them, laughing, crunched over the gravel of the parking lot toward the auditorium. They left Ray smoking under the tree, following Johnny's progress through the window as he made his way down the aisle to Hope and Alice.

One Sunday night when Ray was thirteen, he and Shirley Hawkins had been sitting on the back row whispering behind the Baptist Hymnal. Nobody had heard them; they'd been quiet about it. But Busby Howard had seen them, and the Preacher couldn't wait until after the service to crack his whip, no, sir, not him; he had to make an example out of them. He had stopped his sermon, and, from the pulpit, ordered Ray to quit talking, come kneel at the altar, and pray for repentance. Ray stood up, looked Busby in the eye, turned on his heel, and walked out, leaving Shirley Hawkins with a flaming face and the church doors swinging shut behind him. Ray hadn't been inside the Baptist Church since.

Not even Alice could get him to change his mind; he told her he'd become a Methodist, he'd drive to the next town and become a Presbyterian if she wanted; he'd even become a Catholic, but he was through with the Baptists as long as Busby was their preacher.

And it was for being scorned in front of his own congregation, far more than Ray's fighting or drinking, that Busby Howard would never forgive him.

But Ray was not after Busby Howard's forgiveness; Busby Howard meant nothing to him, and Busby knew that, too.

Why had Doobie asked him if Jackson was coming tonight? Hell, he didn't know anything about Jackson; Doobie knew that. He and Jackson lived in the same house; they worked side by side at the same job, but Ray knew less of what Jackson was thinking than he did of what Webster

Tolney was thinking. His father had been a stranger to him since the day his mother died. Dear Lord, he missed her. He missed his brother, Lester, too. The ache never went away.

If it hadn't been for Naomi and Johnny, there would have been no one. And there were nights in the big house behind the mill, when the wind blew and the tree branches tormented his bedroom windows, that he was as alone as his mother's spirit that seemed to haunt the house. Jackson, reading his Bible in his room, never knew, never cared.

People used to say that they'd never seen anybody more in love than Jackson Redeem was when he married Loretta Marshall, and that he never got over it. They said it was a wonder the woman could walk 'cause Jackson wanted to carry her around like a doll. Not that Loretta would let him; she was a tiny little thing, not more than five feet one, but she had spunk, that girl. She'd just laugh and wave him off. "Go cut some lumber, Jack," she'd say, "and stay out of my hair. I can't tend to things with you underfoot." Then she'd gently push his big frame out the kitchen door. And he'd go and saw logs, counting the hours until he could come back for lunch.

The Redeems probably had the best marriage in the county. The only thing they had ever differed about was religion. Jackson loved two things: the Lord and Loretta, which brought him to some moments of trial and tribulation because Loretta had been raised a Catholic over in Meramec City, and Jackson, whose blood was pumped through his veins by a Baptist heart, worried about her soul. He knew, like everybody else, that Catholics worshiped the Pope; they even had saints. Saints, he'd think; how can she pray to saints? Brother Busby said Catholics were going to hell because they put the Pope in front of Jesus and worshipped idols.

Catholic or not, love her, he did, and he couldn't bring himself to pray to stop loving her, so he did the only thing he knew to do; he began a campaign to convert her. But no matter what he said to her, the best she would do was tell him she'd go to church with him and raise their children Baptist, which, he knew, was a sacrifice on her part. Given that she was willing to do that much, he decided to go against the Biblical injunction and be unequally yoked together with an unbeliever.

He still was always tormented by the thought that she wouldn't be with him in Heaven. How could he bear it if she wasn't there? Even worse, how could he bear the thought that she was being eternally punished in hell. Brother Busby told him that he wouldn't mourn for her in heaven, and he'd have no knowledge of her pain, but he didn't find that answer all that comforting. To him, there was no Heaven without Loretta.

He prayed every night for the Lord to speak to Loretta's soul, to lay a burden of sin on her heart and turn her toward the paths of righteousness. He knew better than to tell her he was praying for her; she'd tell him she could do her own praying, thank you very much. She did pray, he knew; she kept her rosary in the drawer of her bedside table, but she never used it in front of him. Not that he thought such praying did a bit of good.

She did keep her word; she went to church with him twice on Sundays and Wednesday night prayer meeting, and even went to the two-week revivals the church held twice a year, sitting quietly beside him in the pew, Lester sitting between them.

Then, one night right after Lester's third birthday when they'd been married four years, a miracle occurred right there in the First Baptist Church of Tysen. The visiting evangelist from St. Louis had preached a humdinger of a sermon on hell-fire and damnation during the last night of the revival and before Jackson even realized what was happening, Loretta had moved out of her seat during the fourth stanza of "Just As I Am," sobbing her way to the front of the church. Jackson, seeing Loretta on her knees crumpled at the front pew, crying into the preacher's white handkerchief, was moved by the Holy Spirit to shout. He danced a choppy war dance down the aisle to the front of the church, jerking his tall body back and forth, shouting, "Hallelujah, praise the Lord; Hallelujah, praise the Lord," again and again.

Neither the visiting evangelist, nor Brother Busby Howard, had ever seen anything quite like it; they were Baptists, not Pentecostals; both were taken aback. Southern Baptists rarely came forth with an "Amen"; they certainly didn't dance and shout. The preachers discussed it later at the parsonage over coffee and cake, still in their sweat-damp white shirts, exulting over their success, knowing there was rejoicing in heaven over another saved soul. In truth, however, they thought that Jackson should have contained himself a bit. His dance had unnerved them.

After that night, Jackson Redeem was the most contented man in Tysen. He'd never have to lose Loretta; they'd be together always. They had had Lester, and when he was seven, Ray was born. Loretta doted on them both; she was the one who fussed over them and spoiled them, not Jackson. His affection was like a stream rushing straight downhill to Loretta; he didn't know how to channel it any place else. Any affection the boys received came only in the overflow.

Out of nowhere the thunderstorm came, and Jackson's world washed away, changed forever. She was such a tiny little thing you wouldn't think the lightning could find her, but it did. Their eight-year old, Ray, was the one who saw it happen; he saw the flash in a puff of smoke and watched her go down. Ray should have come to the mill for him right then, Jackson always thought, but he stayed with her, stayed right there in the rain, holding onto her crying, "Momma, Momma, come back," like that would make it happen. Jackson had to pull him off the body and shove him to one side just to get to her, to lift her in his arms and cradle her against the rain, sheltering her blackened, hairless scalp with the shirt he tore off his body. He ran to the house with her, Ray and Lester following, Ray still sobbing, "Momma, Momma," and Lester with an arm around him, crying himself, his tears a part of the rain.

When Jackson got her into the house, he took her to their bedroom, calling over his shoulder for Lester to quick phone Doc Barnes, but Jackson knew she was dead. He laid her on their bed, went back to close the door to the bedroom and laid down beside her, pulling her into his arms. "Loretta, Loretta," he pleaded, "I can't bear it, I can't bear it." He kissed her scorched face again and again; then he'd pray, "Take me, too, Lord. Take me, too," and the bed shook with his sobbing.

The boys sat on the floor outside the door listening, Lester with his arm around Ray until Doc got there. Then they sat side-by-side on the flower-splashed couch in the living room and waited. Jackson had to be forced from the bedroom while Eugene Proutty came from the funeral home to take the body away. Jackson told Doc to tell Gene Proutty and the preacher to make all the arrangements.

Jackson went to the funeral parlor for the two days of viewing where he sat in a chair on the front row, staring at her body, not speaking, not moving, until Lester and Ray would take him home nights. He was like a stone through the funeral. Afterward, he didn't say a word or leave the house for two weeks. The neighbors brought in food and saw that the boys were fed for days, shaking their heads; they'd never seen a man so overtaken by grief.

Finally, after two weeks, Jackson got up one morning, dressed and went to the sawmill, moving like a robot. He'd talk to the boys when he had to or to buyers for lumber, but that was it. He ate and slept and did his work. That was all he could manage. Lester was left to take care of Ray the best he could, and Ray had to look after himself when Lester wasn't around.

After dinner, cooked by Martha Aikens who had been hired by Lester to come in every day to cook and clean, wash and iron, Jackson left the table and went to his bedroom every night. He wept and read his Bible; he kept looking for an answer. Busby Howard told him that he would see her again in heaven; he had something to look forward to. Jackson would just shake his head. Then Busby told him, "Jackson, the Lord giveth and the Lord taketh away; you can't question the ways of God; we see through a glass darkly; that's just a fact, you'll have to accept it."

Jackson was not ready to accept this fact; he didn't think he'd ever be ready. He needed answers. He needed a reason. He had to find out Why. Loretta was a good woman; she'd never hurt a soul. She'd done what the Bible had told her to do; she'd been saved and joined the Baptist Church. What more would the Lord want?

He prayed the prayer of the Psalmist: "My soul melteth for heaviness: strengthen thou me according unto thy word," but for months, no strength came. He wanted to be strong, but he wanted Loretta more. He spent hours looking for an answer in the Scriptures. Then, finally, late into one night, he read: "I had fainted, unless I had believed to see the goodness of the Lord in the land of the living. Wait on the Lord: be of good courage, and he shall strengthen thine heart; wait, I say, on the Lord."

Maybe that was the answer. He would take care of his business in the land of the living and wait for the Lord to tell him the reason, tell him what he should have done or needed to do. It took all that was in him to work each day and wait for a sign. But, he waited, and time passed. His boys had to take care of each other; there was no room in him for them.

Lester looked after Ray the best he could, but when Pearl Harbor was bombed, he said he had to go. There wasn't anything else he could do. He told Ray he'd write, packed up a few belongings and joined the

Marines. He came home for a week after boot camp, and then he was gone. Within six months, Lester was killed on Guadalcanal. Ray was alone. Jackson didn't notice.

His wife had been taken and then his firstborn son. He still was waiting on the Lord for courage and revelation. What was he doing wrong? What atonement could he make? His life collapsed into a hard kernel of need. He had to find the answer.

He worked at the mill, went to church, went into town on occasion on business, gradually began to show up for town functions, but he was always a man on a solitary mission. His body was moving through the day and getting to the end of it, but his vision was inward: He was on a quest.

Ray was a visitor in his father's life. They ate at the same table, slept under the same roof, worked along side each other at the mill after school and on Saturdays until he graduated from high school; then he worked there fulltime. He knew as much about the business as his father, and he was good at it. Jackson made him a partner six months after he graduated. The folks in Tysen all thought that was right nice, a father giving to his son that way. Ray was the only person to know that Jackson wanted Ray to be a partner because it took more decision making off his shoulders; Ray could see to things, sign checks and write up orders. Jackson could be there, but he wouldn't have to spend his time thinking about it. Ray could do that from now on.

They met and talked at the mill; that was their sole connection. Jackson barely noticed when Ray quit attending church. His own soul was too needy; he couldn't see to anybody else's.

Ray had learned when his mother died that there was no one left at home to love him other than Lester. That was when Naomi Hollister reached out for him, and when Lester was killed, Naomi and Johnny Hollister became his family. What he knew of love, of families, he learned from them, and he was mighty grateful for it.

Then, he met Alice Tolney. Ray knew from the moment he saw her that he'd been on a quest of his own, and he was finally standing on Holy Ground.

Ray crushed out his cigarette and moved toward Alice and the light.

Chapter Four

Inside the auditorium, the bright, overhead lights glared off the polished, hardwood floors. The room was almost full. A good many men were still clustered at the back. All eight members of Boy Scout Troop were lining up to march the American flag and the Boy Scout flag to the front of the auditorium for the Pledge of Allegiance. Across the hall, the Tonette Quartet, made up of the fifth and sixth graders, were in a huddle tuning up for their performance of "She'll Be Coming 'Round the Mountain," which would follow the invocation led by Brother Busby Howard.

In fact, tonight, Busby would deliver both the invocation and the benediction, which pleased him. He wouldn't say he was happy that the Methodist minister was in bed with the flu, but he wasn't sorry that he'd have twice the opportunity to pray over those non-members who would be there. You never knew when you'd reach a heart and spear another convert for the Baptists.

Matt saw Naomi about halfway down the room near the far wall sitting with Marie Johnson. She waved an arm at them. "Naomi has our seats," Matt told Doc, nodding in her direction. Matt lifted his arm to let her know he saw her.

Doobie said, "I'm going to stay back here out of the way." He knew Naomi wouldn't enjoy saving a seat for somebody who smelled like a tavern. "I'll just mosey on over with the rest of those fellas." Doobie headed toward a tight group of overall-clad men clustering near the back wall.

Doc suddenly nudged Matt in his ribs. "Matt, look over there."

Standing in the door, framed like a picture, were Matilda and Albert St. John; Matilda in her long blue crepe dress, rhinestone brooch pinned over her heart, and Albert in his tuxedo. The St. Johns dressed for every soirée. It didn't bother them a bit that no one else in town was decked out as they were; after all, a soirée was a soirée, and they weren't going to let their side down. They stood there until there was enough pause in the conversation and enough heads turned in their direction that they knew their arrival was duly noted; then they began their stroll down the center aisle, nodding and waving as they floated along, taking in the greetings as their just due.

Twice a month, Abe Carver, the school principal, rented films from St. Louis, set folding chairs in the gym, and Tysen went to the movies. The proceeds from the admission, twenty-five cents for adults, ten cents for children under twelve, went for new school books. The ladies of the Garden Society baked cakes and cookies to sell, and Wendell Johnson would bring over a cooler of pop from the general store that he sold for a dime a bottle. Wendell donated the profit to the school library. The first time Matilda and Albert had arrived for a Saturday night movie dressed for a ball, the citizens of Tysen were too dumbstruck to speak; they'd never seen a tuxedo outside a movie, and the only long dresses worn in the county were at proms and weddings.

Gradually, though, the citizens of Tysen had gotten used to it, and, now, it was part of the entertainment.

"All she needs is a crown," Doc said to Matt.

"She's a piece of work, all right," Matt said, "but she's got a good heart, and she always makes me smile."

Last Monday when Matt neared St. John's place on the Old River Road, he could see Matilda as soon as he turned the bend. She was standing beside the mailbox, holding her right arm straight out, waving it over her head from side to side with the regularity of a windshield wiper. She never trusted the mailbox flag.

She was wearing Albert's khaki pants pulled up high, cinched in well above her midsection by an old leather belt, the end of it flapping down around her right knee. The belt was also Albert's, he guessed, as well as the old white dress shirt she used as a blouse. The high black rubber boots all caked with mud (her Wellies, she called them) were her own, though she did wear Albert's when she couldn't find hers. She was topped off by a big-brimmed straw hat. Even at a distance, you couldn't miss Matilda.

She and Albert had lived in Tysen for four years now, and they both dressed for their roles as gentlefolk come to the farm. If Matt had known the term, he would have said they moved and spoke with an attitude of noblesse oblige, but his education hadn't extended quite that far. As it was, like everybody else, he just thought they were putting on airs. Not that they weren't nice enough people, but they weren't like anyone you'd ever known. They named their dog Amalgamation, for Pete's sake. Who else but the St. Johns would name their dog something you couldn't pronounce, much less knew what it meant?

"Ha-l-l-o-o, Matthew," Matilda projected gustily toward his open car window before the car came to a stop.

"Morning, Matilda. How's Albert?" Matt asked, braking softly beside her.

"Remarkably well this morning, I would say. He's walking off the acreage back behind the barn. He's thinking of putting in cotton."

"Cotton?" Matt was always amazed at just how Albert arrived at things.

"Yes, he's all enthused about it." Matilda was beaming; she loved to see Albert off on one of his projects.

Matt hesitated a moment before he said, "Matilda, cotton won't grow in Tysen; it gets too cold and the soil's not right."

"Oh, dear," Matilda replied, her smile disappearing. "Albert will be ever so disappointed. He's just finished reading a book on the great plantations of the South, and he has his mind set on planting cotton."

"Well, cotton is not the plant for the foothills of the Ozarks. Tell him to plant corn; he'll have something to show for it," Matt reasoned.

"Corn? Corn?" Matilda held the thought out in front of her and looked at it. "Matthew, corn just doesn't have the same caché as cotton, now does it?'

What in tarnation is "cash shay"? Matt wondered. "Well, I guess it doesn't, Matilda, but corn will grow, and if Albert wants a crop, he'd best forget about cotton and think corn."

"Well-l-l-l," she let the thought perk around in her mind for a minute, and Matt could see her imagining fields of waving corn tassels. She began to revive a bit. Then she rallied: "I know he'll be disappointed, but maybe I'll paint something for him, a pastoral scene, rows and rows of corn just waving in the sun. It will inspire him, and he can hang it in his gun room with his trophies."

Albert St John was a Lt. Colonel when he retired from the army, and after serving in France during WWII, he decided he wanted to retire to a farm and live the "simple life." Why they had chosen Tysen no one really knew. They just appeared one day in 1946 in a new station wagon with their wards, Penelope, who was ten, and Hampton, twelve, in the back seat, (they were the children of Matilda's dead sister) and announced to Marie Johnson when they stopped for groceries that they had just bought the Hallbrook place.

"Good idea, Matilda; you do that," Matt told her; then as he took his foot off the brake, he asked, "You and Albert going to the pie supper this weekend?" He wanted to change the subject. He didn't want to hear about Matilda's painting. She said she dabbled in it, but then she'd go on to talk about it as though they were going to hang her next canvas in the art museum in St. Louis. If he could just get her headed off in another direction, she would forget about the painting.

"We wouldn't miss it for the world, Matthew. It will be a lovely social outing; it will make a nice change from the movies." She beamed at him. "I'm baking my special rhubarb-cherry cobbler that Albert just adores."

"Rhubarb-cherry cobbler, huh? I just may have to bid on that myself." Matt hated rhubarb pie and why mess up good cherries, and he had a feeling that Albert felt the same way.

"Oh, Matt," she blushed with pleasure, "You don't have to do that. Albert's always in such a rush to buy he always overbids before anybody else gets a chance."

Matt believed Albert overbid so that Matilda wouldn't feel bad when nobody else rushed in to challenge him.

"Well, maybe this time he'll give the rest of us a chance," Matt said, knowing full well that Naomi was baking apple pie with hickory nuts, and he'd have to do battle with Doc and half a dozen other men.

"Not to worry. I'll tell Albert he must give others a chance. I do love the suppers; they're always a pleasant soirée," Matilda smiled. Matthew knew she meant that. The St. Johns seemed to enjoy the "soirées" of Tysen wholeheartedly.

Now here they were in all their glory, Albert carrying the pie box before him like a crown on a pillow.

"Speaking of strange," Matt said, "look over there."

Doc turned toward the nod of Matt's head. To the side of the cluster of men at the back of the auditorium, Webster Tolney was talking to Sample Forney.

"I see them," Doc said, his tone hard.

Matt searched for Johnny's head. He found him about halfway down the aisle near the wall. Ray had slipped in unnoticed and taken the seat beside Alice. Johnny had an arm around Hope, and they were both leaning in to hear what Ray was saying.

Matt felt uneasy. "Did you talk to Webster today?"

"Heard about that, did you?"

"Doobie told me."

"Doobie would." Doc shook his head looking at Webster. "For such a jackass, Webster is sneaky smart. Just like right now; he's trying to push Sample down Alice's throat in public where he thinks she can't make a scene about it," Doc said.

Doc turned to look for Alice and spotted Evelyn Tolney sitting on the back row alone. "Good God Almighty," he sputtered, "just look at that. That woman has lupus, and I told her this afternoon to stay in bed for two weeks, and here she is. Her blood pressure is so high she could work as a tire pump. Of course, Webster couldn't come without her; he probably wanted her to open the pasture gates to keep him from getting out of the truck, so he's propped her up and dragged her along. And would she have the gumption to say, no? Hell, no, she wouldn't. She'll just sit here and be miserable because Webster wants what he wants, and tomorrow she'll be back in bed for a month or more." Doc was so angry his face flushed bright red.

"Watch your blood pressure, Doc," Matt told him. "We need you around here." Looking at Sample and Webster, Matt said, "That's some pair. One wants land to fill up his greed, and the other wants a woman in his bed to satisfy his needs and to take care of his house and kids. Neither of them minds using Alice to get what they want." Matt's face was set in disgust.

Doc declared, "I don't care how badly Webster wants Sample to give him a parcel of land, he can't force Alice to marry Sample. Alice has more gumption than her momma, and she's crazy about Ray Redeem. It'd take more than Webster Tolney to make Alice give him up."

"I just hope things don't get out of hand tonight," Matt said, looking toward the stage where Busby Howard was surveying the audience, and Wendell and Loncy were laughing about something. Suddenly,

Busby's face clouded over; Matt followed his eyes and realized he'd seen Hope and Johnny sitting with Alice and Ray. Not good, he thought. He looked back at Sample and Webster. Not good at all. "Let's go sit, and it's probably best we don't mention any of this to Naomi for now," he said.

"Right," Doc said.

Matt and Doc made their way to the far side of the auditorium just as the first rat-a-tat-tat of the snare drum called the room to attention. Busby Howard, Maureen, Loncy, Wendell, and Abe Carver, the school principal, all took their chairs on the stage. Matt and Doc edged into their folding chairs, and the Boy Scouts marched their way up the aisle, followed by the Tonette Quartet playing, *America, the Beautiful.*

Busby rose and gave the invocation, strongly emphasizing the need for spiritual food being more important than the "celebratory delight in the delicious pies that our lovely ladies of Tysen have brought to us," and went on to close by sending out a plea that those lost souls in the audience might repent and believe so that they would not burn through eternity in the deep fires of hell.

Matt thought that was just the ticket to put a shot of joy into the celebration.

Abe Carver followed Busby and made all the announcements: school board meeting, PTA meeting, Boy Scout/Girl Scout meetings, and the need for volunteers to help replace shingles on the roof that were blown away by the big storm in April. Then he introduced the Tonette Quartet who struggled through *She'll Be Coming 'Round the Mountain* before they sat down with relief to the enthused applause.

Loncy took his place behind the microphone, and the audience settled back. He tapped the mike with the practiced fingernail of a man long used to public speaking. "Well, folks, we've got quite a turnout tonight, and I just want to tell you that I'm mighty glad to be here looking at all your smiling faces." He looked around the auditorium, stopping when he spotted Doobie. "I guess that leaves you out, Doobie." Doobie had the face of an old hound dog; it hung in little folds. A smile, if there was one, would be darn near hidden. Doobie was nudged from all sides by the men around him.

"What are you talking about, Loncy?" Doobie shouted toward the stage. "I am smiling."

Doobie's face moved in what might have been a smile; at least, his wrinkles rearranged themselves, and the crowd clapped.

"We're just glad you all are here," Loncy said, "even Doobie, smile or not. We've all got a lot to be thankful for. You know, I wake up every morning, open my eyes and say, 'Thank you, Lord, for another day to enjoy life with my beautiful wife, Lizzie'." Heads turned to smile at Lizzie who threw up her hands in a "he's too much for me" gesture, knowing she was helping Loncy along. "You know, I married Lizzie for her looks, but not the one she's giving me right now." The audience encouraged Loncy with a hearty laugh.

"Even with the look Lizzie is giving me, it's a wonderful thing to live here in Tysen. You know, I truly believe that country air gives more oxygen to the brain. Here in the country most folks have the sense God gave them. Has anybody told you about that city fella that bought that nice little place over near Meramec City last March and planted his potatoes around midnight because the Almanac said to plant potatoes by the dark of the moon?" It was an old joke, but like an old song, if it was done with style, it was worth hearing again and again.

Loncy knew that the crowd was warming up, so he eased gently toward the sell. "I know you didn't make this trip tonight just to listen to me. You're being polite and all, but I can see you've got your eyes fixed on the boxes and baskets that our ladies have worked so hard to make beautiful. You have my personal word that each and every one has a pie inside that is so delicious that it could make the angels sing *The Hallelujah Chorus*." He turned and opened his arm wide, moving it in the direction of the dozens of beautiful boxes. "Let's give these ladies a hand." The audience applauded with vigor; the show was about to begin.

"I'd be willing to bet that there are gentlemen in this audience who have their hearts set on buying a certain lady's pie." He let his eyes roam around the room and settle on Maurice and Modine Puckett. "Maurice, I know how much you enjoy Modine's blackberry cobbler, and, having put away a good share of it myself over the years, I can't say that I blame you. You may have to fight for it tonight." Modine blushed happily. Maurice nodded in agreement and held his billfold up for Loncy to see.

Loncy scanned the room quickly for an unmarried youngster, and his eyes fell on Johnny. "Now, Johnny Hollister, you're holding mighty tight to that pretty young lady's hand if my eyes don't deceive me. I heard tell she's a right fine cook, but I'm not so sure when you're with that particular young lady you'd know if you was eating sawdust."

Everybody laughed. Johnny blushed, but he didn't let go Hope's hand. "Preacher," Loncy turned to Busby, who'd been watching that very couple and quickly brought his attention back to Loncy, "I do believe that young man is smitten with your beautiful daughter. I'd keep an eye on him if I were you."

"Believe me, Loncy," Busby's smile was fixed, and his eyes narrowed even more as he took another look at Ray and Alice, "I always do." They had been holding hands, but Alice had slipped hers away when Loncy began his teasing. Ray was looking right back at Busby, but underneath he knew he'd put Johnny and Hope in a terrible fix.

Jackson Redeem had come in with Martha Aikens after Loncy had begun, and somebody handed Jackson two extra folding chairs that Jackson set up at the back of the room some ten rows behind Ray while Martha edged up the side aisle to slip her pie to Maureen. None of the young people had seen them.

"Okay, folks, let's start with this box all topped with beautiful flowers. What do you call these here flowers, ladies?" he asked, knowing full well what they were. "Daisies," came the chorus of feminine voices in front of him, in tones that said, "Silly man doesn't even know a daisy."

"Well, now, what am I bid for this garden of flowers, covering a –what kind of pie is this, Maureen? Pecan?"

Maureen nodded, smiling.

"Gentlemen, a pecan pie is a thing of beauty. The poet said, 'A thing of beauty is a joy forever.' Didn't know I knew that one, did you, Doc?" Doc shook his head, no, knowing full well that Loncy had a book of quotations for special occasions that Lizzie had given him to help with his auctioneering. "Doc thinks he's the only one knows any poetry around here, so I like to keep him on his toes from time to time. Now, back to what I was saying." He lifted the lid from the box and stood there beaming in wonder and admiration down at its contents. "This here pie is a thing of beauty all right, but I guarantee you that whoever buys this pie won't have it very long. It'll be a taste sensation that lucky gentleman won't ever forget.

"Just think, boys, one memorable pecan pie." He held the box up in one hand above his head, balancing it like a waiter's tray on the tips of his fingers. "Just shout right on out and don't be shy. Let's just start this beauty at two dollars. Two dollars. Do I hear two?"

"Two dollars," Albert St. John said.

"Albert's bid two dollars." Albert St. John always bought two pies if he could manage, Matilda's rhubarb-cherry cobbler, and one that he really wanted. "Come on now, boys, two dollars can't begin to touch this beautiful pie. What do I hear?"

"Two twenty-five," came a voice from a clump of men at the rear.

"Billy Sewell? That you?" Loncy knew it was. He knew every voice in the room.

Billy nodded. Billy had got wind that the pie was Josie Mallard's, and he had reason to know that Josey had gained the weight she'd gained because the woman not only loved to cook, she was danged good at it. She'd even taken a cooking class from some guy from France or Italy, or someplace foreign like that, in St. Louis one summer. She could cook a meal that a man could lust over as he'd once lusted over the breasts that had risen in full, round even mounds to float her summer peasant blouses out to a position that if he stood close enough, he could look down into the exposed valley of smooth white skin that dipped beneath the two. He thought he'd never get enough of Josie then, and, even now, he and Josie managed to swayback her mattress several times a month. He didn't mind extra flesh on a woman, and he'd come to like getting lost in all that softness. It was comfortable and hugely satisfying. But her cooking? That drove him to a different kind of ecstasy.

"Two fifty," Albert St. John responded.

"Three dollars even," Billy said, his voice gaining momentum.

"Come on, fellas, you can do even better. Do I hear three fifty?"

"Three fifty," Albert said, and Matilda nudged him in the ribs. He was looking too eager, she decided. Albert knew then that if Billy upped the bid, he'd have to let it go.

"Four dollars!" Billy said with finality in his voice.

"Four dollars? Four dollars? Do I hear a higher bid?"

Heads turned to see if anyone else would speak.

"Sold to Billy Sewell for four dollars! Good for you, Billy. You're the lucky man who is going to share this pie with Miss Josephine Mallard. After the bidding is over, Billy, you just come right on up here and claim Miss Josie and her pie." There were several sets of lifted eyebrows among the ladies, but Billy sighed with satisfaction and leaned back against the wall. A pecan pie of his own, shared with Josie, of course, and then a little bedtime exercise that topped off their satisfaction better than whipped cream on a chocolate sundae.

Loncy knew the bidding had started at a goodly price, and it kept right up. Johnny paid $6.85 for Hope's lemon meringue, and that was $1.35 more than he had planned on, but he couldn't let her eat pie with anybody else, not even Billy Easton, his good friend, who'd bid against him.

They had raised more than $275 dollars by the time Loncy got to the last four pies. Wendell handed Loncy Naomi's pie and said quietly into Loncy's ear, "Let's see what kind of rise you get out of Matt and Doc; they both are craving this pie—not that I can blame them. Naomi is some kind of cook."

Loncy said out of mike range, "Let's see which one places his stomach before his wallet."

"I'm not sure with Matt it's his stomach he's thinking about," Wendell told him.

"How's that?" Loncy asked, not quite hearing.

"Nothing," Wendell said, shaking his head. "Just thinking out loud. Go on and see what kind of trouble you can start between the two of them."

Loncy turned back to the audience, Naomi's pie box in hand. He stood there surveying it, turning it to look at every side, savoring, taking his sweet time. "Now just look at all the work some lovely lady has put into this; it's worth buying just to have the box. But I happen to know what's in this box. A little bird just whispered to me that inside this very box is an apple-hickory nut pie." Loncy wanted everybody to know what was about to happen because every soul in town knew that Naomi could go into business selling that pie alone, and they also knew that there was a yearly battle between Doc and Matt. Last year neither of them had won, so they went home equally put out, but this year the fight was on. Each had been swearing vengeance and victory. Loncy took his time admiring the box.

Both Matt and Doc had straightened up in their chairs and were looking determined. One of the men from the back of the room called, "Hey, Loncy, you gonna eat that pie yourself or auction it off?"

Somebody yelled, "Yeah, come on, Loncy, you're slowing down. We want to get to these pies before they get stale."

"Now, folks, somebody said time is a relative thing; said if you sit on a hot stove for a minute, it seems like an hour, and if you sit with a pretty girl for an hour, it seems like a minute." Everybody laughed, and Loncy decided to slide in one more just to see Doc squirm a bit because

Loncy could see that Doc was tasting the pie already. "You know, now that I'm getting older I decide how long a minute is by what side of the bathroom door I'm on." That one brought the guffaw he was looking for. Nate Daniels yelled, "Glad I'm not that old, Loncy." Nate was eighty-two. Another laugh. The audience was primed to watch Doc and Matt go at it.

"The next thing I know, Nate, you'll be telling me those aches in your joints come from lifting 100 lb. bales of hay with one hand."

"No, they don't. They come from that fifty pound bass I pulled out the Meramec last Saturday." He held out his arms as wide as he could and smiled a beatific, toothless smile.

Everybody laughed, including Loncy. "Okay, folks," Loncy said, happy that he'd revved everybody up, "let's get to this pie. Who's going to start off the bidding?"

Neither Doc nor Matt wanted to be the one to start; neither wanted to set the original bid.

"Come on, come on. Where are all you anxious men who couldn't wait for me to get started?"

Doobie Pratt shouted from the back of the room, "Five dollars!"

Ray Redeem called, "Five fifty." Both were giving Matt and Doc a hard time. Jackson Redeem didn't realize until he heard his son's voice that Ray was there. He stretched a bit to see where he was sitting.

Johnny chimed in with a six-dollar bid, and Naomi leaned forward in her seat to give him a "stop that now" look. Johnny just grinned back at her. Then, he remembered: he and Ray, without thinking, had just drawn more attention to the four of them as a group. He shot a quick glance at Busby Howard and saw that they were the focus of his attention.

Busby's disapproval was oozing out of his pores, not that anybody really noticed except Johnny, Hope, Naomi, and Helen Howard, who was holding Hope's three year old sister, Grace, on her lap. Helen was a weathervane to Busby's moods, and she knew a storm was coming. Hope and Johnny were in for a lecture at the very least; at the very most, Helen didn't know what he would do. Both of them had openly disobeyed his direct order: Hope was never to associate with Ray Redeem. Johnny had promised her husband to abide by that rule, and now he and Hope were sitting right there in the open with Ray and Alice. Of course, that might just be coincidence, she thought, giving them the benefit of the doubt. Ray hadn't come with them. Maybe she was making more of this than she should be. She knew, though, that she wasn't making more of it than Busby would.

Doc couldn't stand it any longer. It was time to jump in and do some serious bidding; the guys would stop as soon as he and Matt truly began to bid. They just wanted to get them on out of the gate and into the race.

"Six twenty-five," Doc said.

"Six fifty," Matt responded immediately.

"Six seventy-five."

"Eight dollars," Matt bid, hoping the jump would serve notice to Doc.

"Eight fifty," Doc countered. Neither looked at the other as they bid.

"Nine dollars," Matt replied evenly.

"I hear nine dollars; nine, nine, do I hear nine-fifty? I got nine, I got nine, do I hear more?" He paused, looking out at Doc and Matt. "Doc, you gonna let this beautiful pie go?" There was a short silence. "Okay, nine dollars once, nine dollars twice..."

"Nine fifty," Doc said. His face was beginning to redden.

"Ten dollars," Matt said with determination.

"I got ten, I got ten. Do I hear more?"

"Ten fifty," Doc said between clenched teeth. Doc had never bid more than seven-fifty for a pie in his life. There was a collective intake of breath in the audience; nobody could quite believe it. Every person in the room knew Doc Barnes, and they knew that as much as Doc loved to eat, there were limits to what he would spend, and this bid for Naomi's pie went well beyond his limit.

The room was totally quiet. Loncy said, "Doc Barnes bids ten fifty. Do I hear eleven?" They were all waiting for what Matt would do. Ten fifty was the most ever bid for a pie at any pie supper in memory. Just as Loncy started to open his mouth, Matt said, "Twelve."

Doc threw up his hands in defeat, and Loncy shouted, "Sold to Matt Neyerson for twelve dollars, one apple-hickory nut pie and the right to eat it with the lovely Naomi Hollister."

The crowd burst into applause, and Matt stood up, bowed, and then offered his hand to Doc. "Shake hands with me, Doc, and I'll take you back to the hotel for a piece of this with a cup of Naomi's coffee." He looked at Naomi. "If she's willing, that is."

Naomi smiled and nodded, Doc stood up, and the men shook hands. "I'll be saving for next year," Doc said. "I'll be here waiting for you," Matt replied. The crowd applauded again.

Every one settled in to finish off the bidding for the last three pies. They felt the entertainment was over for the evening, and they wanted to get on to eating and socializing, swapping pieces of pie when they could.

Wendell delivered a cream-colored hatbox to Loncy that was tied with slender pink ribbons, holding a nosegay of wildflowers. "Just look at this, folks. Some lovely lady has done herself proud with this box."

Ray looked at Alice who colored slightly, but he knew she was pleased. He wished he could hold her hand, but this wasn't the time; besides, he had to concentrate on bidding. There were several young men there who thought Alice was mighty pretty, and they really didn't care if she could bake a decent pie or not. They didn't know that Ray had staked a claim.

"Now let's start this one off with a bang, gentlemen. Remember, we are raising money for the school tonight and we are coming down to the finish. How much am I bid for this pretty as a picture box that has in it…." He paused and held the box up to his nose, exaggerating taking in a deep breath. "Unless my nose deceives me, there's a peach pie under this beautiful lid. I don't know about you, fellas, but I am especially fond of peach pie. In fact, if the rules and Lizzie didn't forbid it," he looked at Lizzie, and she gestured him away with a get-out-of-here wave of her hand, "I'd take this one home myself." Loncy got the laugh he wanted. "Now, what am I bid?"

"Five dollars," Ray said firmly.

Heads turned in Ray's direction. Some of the ladies smiled at him.

"Five dollars. Now, that's the way to start. I got five dollars," Loncy said pointing a finger at Ray, "from Ray Redeem. Do I hear six?"

Webster Tolney, who had been so busy talking to Sample Forney that he hadn't recognized Ray's voice earlier; he hadn't realized the bidding had begun on Alice's pie either. Suddenly, he pushed himself away from the workout mats that had been holding him up and followed the direction of Loncy's finger to find Ray sitting beside Alice. Well, I'll be damned, he thought, right here in front of the whole town when I told everybody that I'd chased off that no good drunk and that he wouldn't be bothering my daughter again. So what is that son-of-a-bitch doing sitting there beside Alice? And actually bidding on her pie? His anger began to push out of his stomach and move toward his head and his fingertips. He took another step out from the wall.

Evelyn, who was sitting beside Bertie Reardon on the back row, had quickly turned to find Webster when she heard Ray bid. Bertie had sat down beside Evelyn because she thought Evelyn was looking really poorly. When Ray had bid on Alice's pie, Evelyn's head had spun round, and her body had gone board stiff; her elbows were pressed tightly against her sides, her hands knotted together in her lap like a ball of yarn. Her face was so pasty Bertie thought she might faint. Bertie turned quickly to see what she was looking at.

Webster, with his face all flushed, stared across the room. Bertie followed the spark in his eyes and found Alice and Ray. She had heard those kids were keeping company; she thought they made a right cute little couple. She'd also heard that Webster didn't cotton to Ray. She snorted under her breath. As if Ray would pay any attention to what Webster, or most anybody else for that matter, would tell him when he had his mind set on something. Whatever was going on here surely was upsetting Evelyn.

Bertie looked back at Webster. Just looking at Webster Tolney always made Bertie feel better about marrying Tom. She'd rather be with Tom, even if he was on a piddly little railroad pension and drunk half the time, than be tied to a man like Webster. Of course, Bertie wouldn't have stayed tied to Webster; she'd have kicked him out long ago. She could take Tom; she was used to him, but Tom never tried to tell Bertie what to do or how to do it. No man was about to do that! And Webster was a weak, bullying sop, as far as she was concerned. Then Bertie saw Sample Forney. Jesus, Mary, and Joseph, she thought. The rumors are true: Webster does want to trade Alice to Sample! She shook her head in disbelief. It was beyond her ken.

Matt and Doc, too, had turned to see what Webster was up to. Webster was saying something to Sample Forney. There was Sample, all six feet four of him, standing straight as the new flagpole, at least a head taller than Webster, and Webster talking up toward Sample's ear. Sample's dark hair was slicked back with Rose Hair Oil, and his belly pushed against the front of his overalls. Both thumbs were hooked into his straps, and he looked directly at Loncy. Sample had not missed the fact that Ray Redeem was there. He'd searched for Alice and found her as soon as he came in; Ray hadn't slipped down the aisle without his notice either. "Six dollars," he said, hardly raising his voice, but there wasn't a soul who didn't hear the deep, flat vibration of it.

Ray's head whipped around to look at the back of the room, followed by Johnny, Alice and Hope. None of them had known that the Tolneys and Sample Forney were there.

They thought Evelyn was home in bed with Webster looking after her. Johnny saw the tips of Ray's ears turning red; that was always Ray's first sign of anger.

Webster continued to glare at Ray and Alice, his face bunched together in a frown, his eyes narrowed. Alice raised herself enough to find her mother who was steadfastly staring at the floor. Alice dropped back into her chair.

Hope felt the swirl of all the emotion and tightly clutched Johnny's hand. She knew that her father was soaking all of this in from the stage; there was no missing it; an angel might as well have descended with trumpet in hand to make the announcement. Johnny, feeling Hope's fingers tightened on his, felt his stomach starting to hollow out just thinking about what he might have to pay for this. The preacher was not a forgiving man; forgiveness was an article of his faith he seemed to ignore. But right now, at this moment, Johnny had to stand up for Ray. He couldn't worry about what the preacher might do later.

"I got six dollars from Sample Forney at the back of the room," Loncy said. Heads swiveled round to look at Ray.

"Seven dollars," Ray said without looking at Sample. The heads swiveled toward the back of the room.

Hope whispered to Johnny, "Can't we do something?"

"There's nothing we can do, but hope Ray outbids him," Johnny told her.

"I got seven dollars from Ray Redeem. I got seven, I got seven; do I hear more?"

"Eight dollars," Sample said. Heads turned so completely in unison that later Matt would think he'd actually felt a breeze from the movement.

Nobody else had even bothered to bid. This was a two-man duel, and it wasn't over a peach pie.

"Nine," Ray said.

"I've got...," Loncy began.

"Ten," came evenly from the back of the room.

"Twelve," Ray said, and his voice was getting harder.

"Fifteen."

"Twenty."

"Twenty-five." Sample's eyes hadn't moved from Loncy's face. He didn't even look down at Webster who kept slamming his fist happily into his open palm after each of Sample's bids as if Webster were landing a personal victory.

"Now, wait a minute, boys," Loncy interrupted. "Take a second to think about this. This is one fine peach pie, I know. But I know neither one of you fellas wants the responsibility of paying for all of the fifth and sixth grade primers." He laughed at his own joke. "You are going to be buying books for the whole dang school if you don't stop. Now, why don't you think for a..."

"Thirty," Ray said, raising up slightly from his chair. Alice grasped Ray's hand; she wanted to keep him in his seat. Hope had taken her other hand, and Johnny was holding Hope's. Johnny looked toward Aunt Naomi; she was chewing her bottom lip. Doc's forehead was puckered in a frown, and Matt was looking solemn. They knew, just like Johnny, there wasn't much they could do to head this off. They'd just have to watch to see how it played out.

"Fifty," Sample said. His expression hadn't changed, and his voice was the same even, flat tone he used when he began.

Ray let go of Alice's hand to slip out his billfold, holding it down at his side, and quickly counting his bills. "Sixty seven dollars," he challenged, bidding every dollar in his wallet.

"One hundred dollars," Sample said.

Ray jumped to his feet with such force he pulled Alice up with him. She let go Hope's hand just in time to keep from pulling them all to their feet like some child's game of Crack the Whip. The two of them stood there looking back at Sample Forney.

"My Gawd," Doobie Pratt said and didn't even think about reaching for his bottle.

"What was the bid again, Sample?" Loncy asked, wanting to be sure he'd heard correctly.

"One hundred dollars," Sample said, looking directly at Ray for the first time.

Ray's ears were bright red, and his body was so tight he looked ready to spring.

He turned back to Loncy. "Will you take my I.O.U.?" he asked Loncy. "You know I'm good for it."

Loncy's expression said he wished like blazes he could do something. "I know you are, Ray, but the rules state all bidding has to be in cash or certified check. There's nothing I can do about it." He looked out over the audience; then he took a deep breath and said, "Going once, going twice, going three times, and sold to Sample Forney for one hundred dollars."

There was complete quiet in the auditorium. What on earth had just happened here? No one had ever, ever paid $100 for a pie.

Loncy, trying to mollify everyone concerned, said, "Now, folks, just think how many books and supplies all this generosity will buy for our kids here at Tysen School. They're gonna be mighty happy about this." He looked over the audience, and he urged, "Let's give Sample and Ray a round of applause." He began clapping with vigor into the microphone.

Slowly, people began to clap, but the applause was light and hesitant; they weren't sure whose side they were taking, and they would rather not have to go up against either one.

When the applause began, Alice sat down and pulled on Ray to sit with her, leaning toward him to whisper, "Ray, it's only a pie. I can eat a piece with him, and then the four of us will go to Meramec City. I'll just take a few minutes."

"I don't want you eating with him," Ray told her, not bothering to sit or whisper. "I don't want you that close to him, and I don't want anybody thinking you are having something to do with him."

"Shhh," she said. She knew everyone was watching. "I'm not having anything to do with him," she told him. "You know that."

"They don't," he said, moving his head to indicate the crowd.

"It doesn't matter what they think," Alice pleaded.

"It does. It matters a lot to me what people think about you and Sample Forney. He just paid $100 for your pie. Everybody in the county will have heard about this by noon tomorrow." Ray pulled back from her. "Don't you care what I think?"

"You know I do." She reached out to put her hand on his arm, but it might have been made of marble for all the give it had to it.

"Then don't eat pie with Sample Forney," he said between clenched teeth.

Loncy tried to drag the attention back in his direction. "Folks, we still have these two fine pies to auction off. Let's keep in mind this is all for a good cause. That's why we're here tonight, so bid up on these great looking pies, and we can all get to eating."

People didn't know whether to look at Loncy or Ray and Alice, but those close enough strained to overhear every word so they could pass on the information. Sample didn't bother to look in their direction. He didn't care what they were talking about; he had bought Alice's pie, and he would be the one to eat it with her.

Alice pulled on Ray's hand. Ray sat down, but he was rigid, staring straight ahead. Alice tried again. "Ray, this is hard. Momma and Papa..." Tears were pooling in her eyes.

"Alice," he cut her off, "let's make this simple. Do you love me or not?"

"You know I love you." Tears were beginning to run down her cheek, and she dropped her head, hoping no one saw. Hope pressed a handkerchief into her hand without interrupting them. Johnny's knee was jerking up and down, a sure sign he was worried.

"Then don't eat pie with Sample Forney."

Alice bowed her head farther and tried to wipe her tears away.

On the stage, Wendell handed Loncy Myrtle Bullock's pie. Regal King snapped it up with no contest for five dollars, and then Wendell bought the last pie, Marie's blueberry cobbler, for six.

"That's it, folks," Loncy said, thinking this was the toughest auction he'd ever called. "We've done a mighty fine job for the school tonight. As soon as Maureen can, she'll let you know just how much money we've raised. Let's give ourselves a big round of applause."

The applause seemed more a sigh of relief than a sign of exuberance.

"All right, now, you gentlemen come up and claim your pie. You fellas just form a line, and Maureen will be happy to take your money. You folks have done a right fine job tonight; give yourselves a hand." There was a light smattering of applause.

Loncy went back and sat down next to Wendell; his shirt was wringing wet. Wendell patted him on the shoulder. Busby Howard sat staring stony-eyed at his daughter.

The children bounded up like paper wads shot from rubber bands, but the adults slowly eased themselves out of their seats.

A few of the men closest to the stage moved in Maureen's direction as she began to disperse pies. Some hung back to watch Sample Forney who had started up the aisle. He walked straight toward Maureen without turning his head, stopping just behind Maurice Puckett to wait his turn. Maurice walked off with Modine's pie, and Sample moved to the front of the stage. "I'll take my pie now, Missus Fitzroy," he said. Maureen looked toward Alice, whose head was still bowed, and decided to give the pie to Sample. She'd let them work it out. He counted five twenty dollar bills into her hand. Maureen thanked him and looked down at the money for a minute as if it wasn't real before she carried it to the cigar box on the table and checked Alice's name off her list. Alice still hadn't moved away from Ray.

Carefully, lifting the box topped by Alice's ribbons and flowers, she brought it back to the edge of the stage and held it down to Sample. He took it from her in both hands, holding it like glass. He nodded his thanks, turned, and started back down the aisle.

The attention was so focused on Sample that nobody had noticed that Busby Howard had come off the stage until he moved rapidly around Sample down the center aisle toward Hope and Johnny. He'd stopped at the end of their row. "Hope," he ordered, "come out of there right now."

Johnny could hear Hope's intake of breath. He knew she was scared. Hope thought it better to make God angry than her father. Johnny followed her to the end of the row to meet him.

"Sir...," Johnny began.

"Not a word from you, young man." The preacher's face was as hard as Ozark flint stone. "Get out of my way; I'm taking my daughter to sit with her mother, and you are to stay away from her. Far away from her," he glared at Johnny.

"Daddy, what about my pie? Can't I eat with Johnny?"

"No, you can't eat with Johnny. If there's any eating to be done, Johnny can do it by himself."

"Daddy," Hope pleaded, still not moving, "you don't understand."

"Shut up," he said, and he grabbed her wrist hard and yanked her toward him; he managed, in fact, to catapult her right into Naomi who had appeared from the mouth of her row, followed by Matt and Doc. Both men steadied Naomi on either side to keep her from falling.

She righted herself and began, "Pastor, wait."

"Sister Hollister, I don't need to wait; my daughter is not eating with your son," he said, jabbing a finger toward Johnny. "He's taken my daughter out with that no-good Ray Redeem. He knew the rules, and he gave me his word he would follow them."

Naomi took in a quick breath; the preacher had just publicly insulted Ray and jabbed a finger at Johnny. She could feel her anger rising. "I'm trying to tell you," she made another attempt, "these kids haven't done anything wrong; you're mistaken about all of this."

"I'll be the judge of that," the preacher said, "and I'm not talking about this now. I'll discuss it later." Dismissing Naomi, he turned on his heel and started walking back up the aisle toward Helen, jerking Hope along like a recalcitrant mule, Hope looking back over her shoulder at Johnny.

Naomi was just plain floored. Never had she heard such a thing. The Preacher had attacked Johnny, turned his back on her, and walked away! For a second she was speechless; then she dug her heels into the floor runner, took a deep breath and said loudly to his retreating back, "You're dang right we're going to talk about this, Busby Howard. In fact, you can bet your life on it. Nobody treats my son this way."

"More like betting his soul's salvation," Doc's said in an aside to Matt. Matt nodded in response; in another situation he might think this was funny, but for now, he was keeping a worried eye on Naomi.

Never before had anyone in that auditorium ever heard Naomi Hollister say "dang." They stopped in stunned silence, not because of what Naomi had said, but because of the anger it took to force her to say it.

Naomi turned to Johnny and put an arm around his waist. "Don't you worry, honey," she told him, "we'll get this all worked out."

"I don't know, Aunt Naomi," he said, looking after Hope like she'd been loaded on a Campbell moving van and was being driven off to live in California.

Naomi gave him a quick squeeze. "Don't think about it now. Right now we've got to see to Ray."

Johnny gave a last look toward Hope, who was wiping tears away. Her father's face was frozen into a hard mask. He knew it was useless to try and talk to Busby now, and Johnny knew Ray needed him. The four of them, Johnny, Naomi, Matt and Doc, looked over toward Ray and Alice.

Sample Forney had stopped to wait until the exchange in the aisle was over; then he said, "Excuse me, Missus Hollister," as though he were stepping around them all on the sidewalk, and moved toward Alice, stopping at the row where she and Ray were huddled at the far end against the wall, talking.

From the back of the room, Webster Tolney came forward in a trot, skirting between people standing in the middle aisle, looking across the row of chairs at Alice and Ray.

"Webster, no," Evelyn weakly called after him, and when he didn't turn, she pulled her body out of the chair and moved with effort across Bertie to follow him. He stopped beside Sample.

"Alice, get over here," he commanded.

"Just a minute, Papa," she said; her voice was trembling.

"You'll do what I tell you right now." Webster's words were so angry they came out in a gargle.

"Leave her alone, Webster," Ray said without even turning to look at him. "She'll come when she's ready."

"Don't tell me what my daughter is going to do, you no good drunk," Webster shouted at him.

By this time, all movement in the room had come to a halt. The audience was one collective ear.

"I don't need your help, Webster," Sample said evenly.

Webster flushed, but he couldn't just back down now. "That's my daughter he's talking about, Sample, so it's my fight, too."

Evelyn had woven her way unevenly up the center aisle, around people who were rooted like posts, to stand behind Webster and pull gently at his sleeve. "Webster, please," she said quietly.

He shook her off. "She'll do what I tell her when I tell her to," he said, but with Sample's disapproval he wasn't quite so forceful.

"She'll come in a minute, Webster," Evelyn said placating him, "just let them finish talking."

"I'll handle this, Webster," Sample said, ignoring Evelyn. "You just let it be."

Webster moved back a step or two telling himself that as long as he didn't leave the spot, he hadn't given in. He'd just stand right there and make his presence known.

Sample spoke to Alice as though Ray hadn't risen at the opposite end of the row and placed his hands on her shoulders. "I've brought your pie, Alice. Where would you like to sit?"

Alice looked at Sample and then back at Ray.

"What are you going to tell him, Alice?" Ray asked, looking down at her.

"Please, Ray," she whispered, "everybody is watching. Just let me do this, and then we'll work everything out. Sample has already bought the pie. I have to eat with him." She stood and unsteadily began to move toward Sample.

Ray grabbed her wrist. "No, you don't," Ray said. "He can eat with your folks. You don't owe him a danged thing." They were slowly inching closer to Sample who was just outside the row, Alice barely moving and Ray holding her back.

Sample was standing in the aisle holding the pie toward Alice like a gift. "Don't see that she's got any choice Redeem. I just paid $100 for the privilege."

"It ain't pie you're after Sample, and you darn well know it."

"It's pie I bought, though," he said.

Webster, who had been squirming inside his overalls, just couldn't stay still any longer and dashed back to stand beside Sample. "He paid for it fair and square, Ray. There ain't a thing you can do about it."

Ray ignored Webster. "I'll pay you for the pie, Sample. You can keep the thing and take it home; you don't need Alice to eat it with you."

"You're wrong about that, Ray. For one hundred dollars, I need Alice to slice it, serve it up right nice, and sit down and eat it with me for as long as I want to eat. That's what I need, and that's what I'm going to have. Ain't I Alice?"

Alice wanted to be anywhere but in this room; she felt every eye was locked on her. She looked from Ray, to Webster, to Sample, and then, finally, to Evelyn. "Momma?" Her question was pleading and teary.

Evelyn said, "Oh, Alice, honey, I...I...I...." And with that, Evelyn Tolney closed her eyes and sank to the floor.

"Momma," Alice screamed, pushing between Sample and Webster, hitting Sample's arm so hard that the pie flew out of his hands and did a 180° flip to land up-side-down, instantly becoming peach cobbler on his boots. Ray followed Alice before either man could move. It had all happened so quickly. Webster and Sample stood there staring down at most of the pie on Sample's feet and the rest splattering Webster's pant legs and the floor.

Alice slipped to the floor, sliding Evelyn's head on her lap; Ray knelt beside her. "Momma," Alice said, "say something."

"Let me through," Doc was saying loudly, making his way through the clumps of people who were trying to see what had happened. He knelt beside Evelyn, automatically putting his fingers to her pulse; her eyes fluttered open. "Can you hear me, Evelyn?" he asked. She didn't blink. He lifted her arm into the air slightly and let it drop. It fell lifelessly beside her body. "Blessed Jesus," Doc said. "She's had a stroke. Ray, carry her to the car for me, will you? I've got to get her to the hospital in Meramec City in a hurry."

Johnny, who had come up beside Ray, said, "You need any help?"

"No, I can get her," he replied. "She don't weigh more than a sparrow." With that, he swooped Evelyn up while Alice clung to her limp hand, and they ran toward the door, Doc in the lead.

Suddenly, Webster, who had been standing there as though it was somebody else's accident, came to and bolted after Ray, skidding his way through the peach pie, shouting, "Put her down. Put her down. Don't touch her."

Johnny and Matt were beside Webster in an instant. Matt said, "Let him carry her to the car, Web. Doc needs the help."

"I don't want him to touch her," Webster shouted.

Doc shouted over his shoulder, "Shut your mouth, man, and let me do my job, or you'll have a wife to bury before morning. Now get in your truck and follow Alice and me to the hospital."

Webster stopped dead still, looking dazed. She'd done it, again, he thought. Evelyn'd gone and messed up his entire plan. It was just like Evelyn to up and get sick. Just like her.

"Webster," Matt asked, having to shake his arm to get his attention, "do you want me to drive you to the hospital?"

Webster kept looking after the procession as people parted and held doors to let them through, not answering. He just couldn't get over it. How could she?

Matt thought he was in shock. Johnny said, "I'll do it, Matt. I want to go be with Alice anyway, and Ray can bring me home in his truck."

Matt nodded, "Okay, son, you do it."

"You ready, Webster?" Johnny asked.

Webster looked beyond Johnny at Sample. "Sample?" he questioned.

"You got a ride. You don't need me; I've got chores at home," Sample told him, his face hard, his lips barely moving.

Webster looked lost. Turning back to Johnny, he said, "I guess you can do it then."

"I'll be home when I can, Aunt Naomi," Johnny told her.

"Be careful, and will you call me as soon as you know anything?" Naomi asked.

"Yes, ma'am," Johnny said.

Busby Howard emerged from the crowd, Hope following several paces behind him. "I'll follow you to the hospital, Brother Webster," Busby told him, draping an arm around his shoulders. "I know you'll want me to sit and pray with you."

Webster nodded as though Busby was making sense to him.

"Daddy, can't I go with you to be with Alice?" Hope pleaded, coming closer. "She'll need me; you know she will."

"No," Busby said, his tone pushing her aside. "I want you to walk straight home with your mother and sister." He turned away from her. He didn't even look at Johnny.

Johnny looked over his shoulder at Hope, and she formed the words, "I'll see you tomorrow." He nodded and took Webster's arm, guiding him toward the door. As they eased their way through the wake created by Doc, Johnny said, "I'll need you to get your keys out for me, Webster."

Both Busby and Sample began making their way to the door leading to the parking lot. Busby had reason to go, and Sample had no reason to stay.

Nobody noticed Jackson Redeem, senior deacon of The First Baptist Church of Tysen and father of Ray Redeem, carefully watching.

Matt found Naomi beside him and, without thinking, put an arm around her. They stood there until Johnny and Webster went through the doors. It wasn't until after they went out of sight that Matt let his arm drop away. Then Naomi turned to Hope just as she burst into tears. Pulling her to her breast, Naomi said, "Don't cry, honey; we'll sort all this out somehow. You just go on home and try to get some sleep; you'll see Johnny and Alice tomorrow."

"But, Naomi, you know my dad." She sobbed away into Naomi's shoulder, soaking thoroughly the floral print of Naomi's new dress. "He doesn't change his mind when he decides he's right. Now, all this has happened to poor Evelyn. And Alice? What about her? What are any of us going to do?"

"Well, right now, we're going to get your eyes dried." She pulled her hanky out of her black patent purse and wiped the wet cheeks in front of her. "Why don't you go find your momma and help her home with Grace? You can always come by and talk to me tomorrow—or anytime you need to. You just remember that."

"Yes, ma'am, I will," she said, kissing Naomi on the cheek and clutching her wet hanky as she went off to look for her mother, knowing that there she would find a parent who understood. Even if her mother might not act against her father, Hope knew she would want to be on Hope's side. Naomi could see, across the room, Helen holding Grace in one arm and opening her other for Hope.

Loncy spoke through the mike at the front of the room. "Okay, folks, we've all suffered a bit of a shock here, but we know that Evelyn is in good hands with Doc. He'll do everything for her that should be done, so the best thing that we can do is to get back to the pies that we've all been looking forward to. Come on, men, let's help our ladies get things going."

The men began moving chairs, forming groups, and the women slicing and serving pie. Matt helped the men, and Naomi went to see if Maureen needed any help with tallying the proceeds. By the time Maureen and Naomi finished, and Maureen gave the total of $467 to Loncy, people were chewing and talking in every corner of the room. They had a lot to hash over; it had been the most excitement any of them had witnessed in years—and not because it was the largest amount ever raised at a Tysen pie supper.

Naomi found Matt with Wendell Johnson who was offering him a bowl of Marie's blueberry cobbler. Matt was declining, saying, "I'm saving up for Naomi's pie."

"You know full well you can eat that cobbler and still have room for my pie. That way you can save a little extra for Doc; he's going to need it. He won't be making it back in time tonight to get any," Naomi said.

"I'll save him two pieces for tomorrow," Matt said.

They sat long enough for Matt to finish the cobbler. Then Naomi scooted her chair back and said, "I'd better be getting on home. Johnny will call as soon as he gets a chance, and I want to be there when he does."

"Come on; I'll take you; I can pick up my car in the morning," Matt told her, scraping the last bite of cobbler from the bowl. "Good cobbler, Marie; Wendell is a lucky man."

"Tell him that," Marie, said, laughing. "Will you call me, Naomi, when you hear?"

"Course I will," Naomi told her. Marie and Lizzie Oppenmeier were Naomi's closest friends.

Matt collected Naomi's pie from the table, and together they left the auditorium and climbed into the cab of Naomi's truck for the ride home. Naomi settled the pie back in her lap, and Matt drove.

"Who would have thought all this would have happened this evening?" asked a depleted Naomi.

"That's a lot of excitement for a body to go through in just a few hours," Matt told her.

"Let's just get on back to the hotel, and I'll make us some coffee. We'll have a piece of pie and wait for Johnny's call. I'm just about done in, and I could use some peace and quiet."

"Sounds good to me," Matt said. The hotel was a haven for both of them.

Matt drove down Main St., passing the post office, and Naomi could see the light was on in the hotel kitchen. "Matt, I'm getting to be an absent-minded old woman. I've left the kitchen light on again."

"There's nothing old about you, Naomi, and I probably did it myself."

Naomi liked that Matt didn't think she was old. "Maybe it's Willie. Could be he didn't go to St. Louis." Willie Newman was Naomi's other full-time boarder.

"That doesn't seem likely," Matt said. "I certainly hope not; I don't want to share this pie with anybody but you."

"You have to save two pieces for Doc," Naomi reminded.

"I'll do it, though he'd better get over here tomorrow, or one of them may be gone. A man only has so much will-power." Matt slowed to turn into the driveway.

"Don't bother to take the truck to the back; we'll park here in front. Johnny won't be needing the space since Ray will be dropping him off."

Matt opened the screen door for Naomi, and they stepped into the entryway and went directly into the brightly lit kitchen to the left. Naomi couldn't help but fuss at herself for running up the electric bill. It wasn't the first time she'd done it either. She shook her head at her absent-mindedness. Putting her purse on the sideboard and the pie on the table, she turned to start the coffee. Matt went to the china cabinet for cups and saucers.

The flame blazed up yellow and settled into a blue dance under the percolator. Naomi washed her hands and came back to the table to cut the pie while Matt set out the plates, putting the forks and the napkins to the left side of each. The aroma of the brewing coffee swirled up into the room, and the sound of the flame and the fragrance of the perking coffee were comforting.

"You want ice cream with that?" Naomi asked, setting a good size piece of pie at his place.

"No, ma'am, I don't want to spoil perfection." Matt went to get some milk for the coffee, poured two cups, added the milk, and the two of them settled themselves into their accustomed spots, Naomi with her back to the sink and Matt directly across from her. Matt took one enormous mouthful of pie and began to chew as though he were eating manna on a flaky Crisco crust. When he had swallowed, he reached across the table and covered her hand with his. "Lady, you make my heart sing."

Naomi laughed. "You sure it's not your stomach that's singing?"

Matt looked at her a long moment. "That, too," he said. "But about my heart, I mean that; I've just been a long time saying it."

Naomi felt a sudden catch in her own heart, and her cheeks blazed. She was flustered and she thought unprepared, until she realized she'd been waiting for just this.

They leaned toward each other over their pie and coffee, and Matt's lips touched hers in a kiss so fulfilling that she knew she was completely in love. When they slowly parted, she said his name, and it was a prayer of thanks.

Matt turned her hand palm up to meet his. They just sat there, caught in their new love and the warmth of their hands, palm to palm.

There was a movement in the hall. Naomi looked up into the archway, and the blush in her cheeks blanched to white. Matt could feel her hand grow cold as he held it.

"What is it?" Matt asked, and he turned quickly to the doorway.

Russell Hollister was standing there.

"Hello, Naomi," Russell said.

Naomi gripped Matt's hand in a spasm; both she and Matt were slack-jawed. Several seconds passed before Naomi, not sure of what she was seeing, could ask, "Russell?"

"Yep, it's me."

"Where did you come from?"

"California."

Naomi had meant where was he in the house that they hadn't seen him, but she decided not to explain that now.

"How did you get here?" Naomi asked. There were no cars out front to announce him.

"I got them to stop the 7:45 Express for St. Louie," Russell told her. "I used to work with the engineer."

"Oh," Naomi said, still dumbfounded. The wind was knocked right out of her.

"I've come home," Russell said, as though it was perfectly natural that he should appear in the archway after all these years.

"I see that," she said, "but why?" Of all the things Naomi had never imagined, not since the day Russell left, was his coming home again. His leaving had such a finality, and she had come to comfortable terms with her life without Russell. She felt shell-shocked. Tonight had been enough to set a body in a whirl, and, now, here, big as life, was Russell Hollister, standing in the doorway of the kitchen he'd left twelve years ago, and she had no idea what to say to him.

"Hello, Matt," he said and stepped toward the table. It was not until Matt started to stand to shake Russell's hand that she realized she was holding onto Matt like a lifeline. She reluctantly released her fingers, and they slid away into her lap.

"Russell," Matt said, not a happy man to be greeting Naomi's runaway husband. Not now at any rate. Not when they'd just begun. "How are you doing?"

"Getting by, I guess. How about you?"

"Fine. I'm just fine," Matt said. There was complete silence except for the grandfather clock in the hall.

Naomi sat there, staring at Russell, looking as though if she stared long enough he might go away as quickly as he'd come.

Finally, Matt said, "Aah, take a seat, Russell. Would you like some coffee or a piece of pie? Naomi baked one for the pie supper tonight."

If Russell thought it strange that Matt was offering him pie in his mother's kitchen, he didn't voice it. He lowered himself into the chair, and a small sigh of relief blew out though his lips when the chair took his weight. "That sounds mighty good," he told Matt. "I thought that was where everybody had gone. I saw a sign in Johnson's window." Russell sat down across the table from Naomi.

"I'll fix it," Naomi said, pushing her chair back before Matt could voice any objections.

Naomi thought if she could just move a bit and do something normal, life might right itself some. As it was, she couldn't quite grasp it: Russell's sitting at the table getting ready to have pie didn't seem real to her. Matt was real to her, real and solid. Not a ghost who'd suddenly appeared, like Russell.

Even when he'd called this home, Naomi remembered, Russell had come and gone, always the visitor, never settling in long enough to leave his dent in the easy chair, or his side of the bed. He was always shifting, always moving, like those little balls of mercury that spill out of a broken thermometer and splash and dance around. Yes, that was Russell, all splash and dance.

"You still delivering mail, Matt?"

"Yep. You still with the railroad?"

Russell shook his head. "Nope, I quit the railroad not long after I left." He didn't look at Naomi as he said it.

Naomi set his coffee cup in front of him and began to slice a piece of pie. Russell picked up the bowl and spooned two teaspoons of sugar into his cup, setting the sugar bowl back in the middle of the table before he began to stir in a gesture as natural as if he'd done the same thing that very morning.

She poured more coffee for herself and Matt, automatically passing Matt the milk pitcher. She still wasn't ready to talk.

Matt said, "What are you doing now?"

"Not anything right at the minute. I'm just sorta resting for a bit."

Naomi had been slowly redrawing the picture of Russell that had been in her head. Now, almost all his hair was grey, and it was sparser on top. He was thinner, much thinner; his face was gaunt. Maybe it was the light, but he looked a little jaundiced. She sat down with her own coffee and stared into the cup. What in the name of all I hold dear is he doing here, she asked herself? She didn't know what to say, what to ask, so she just sat there holding onto her cup.

Matt pulled a Camel out of his pack that was beside his coffee cup and offered the pack to Russell. Russell shook his head "no."

"When'd you quit smoking?"

"'Bout six months ago. The doc in California said I'd feel better if I quit."

"I guess we all would," Matt said and exhaled up toward the light. "But I'd sure miss it."

"So do I," Russell said.

As the smoke floated downward, he began to cough. It began in that light tickling push of a cough; then it moved on down into his chest with all the crack and rattle of a storm. Each cough was louder than the last, each intake of breath a needier eating of air. He bent at the waist, his upper body contracting, holding his handkerchief to his mouth, spitting into it, his forearms resting on his knees.

Matt ground out his cigarette in a single motion and moved quickly to hold Russell, afraid he might fall from his chair. Naomi's chair fell backward onto the linoleum as she rushed to the sink for a glass of water. She grabbed a dishtowel to replace the handkerchief, sliding it under his face and putting it in his hands. When she took the handkerchief away, she could see the phlegm mixed with blood.

As the coughing began to ease, Russell, with effort, gradually brought himself upright and rested against the back of the chair. He kept wiping his mouth, making sure it was clean. Naomi held a glass of water to his lips, and he sipped at it.

When he seemed rested a bit, Naomi, jolted out of her trance, asked, "What is it, Russell? T. B.?"

He shook his head, no. She and Matt waited until he could speak. Finally, he said, "I've had bronchitis for a couple of weeks. I've coughed so much that sometimes I bring up a little blood."

Naomi looked at Matt over Russell's head. "I guess we need to get him into bed for the night." Naomi didn't know what else to do; sudden arrival or not, the man was ill and needed a place to sleep.

Matt nodded.

Russell tried to grin. "I'm a rundown old fart who's pushed too hard. Just need to rest a bit."

"Looks like it's hard for you to breathe," Naomi said, watching the strained rise and fall of his chest.

"Oh, I just get winded with the coughing, that's all."

"You better have Doc take a look at you tomorrow," she told him.

He nodded. "I will," he said, "first thing."

Matt asked, "Where did you put your suitcases? I'll carry them to your room."

Russell didn't protest. "They're in the living room. I was in there waiting for you," he told Naomi.

"You gonna be able to climb the stairs all right if Matt and I help you?" she asked.

"I can manage these steps just fine. I've just been working too hard. Maybe lifting a few more beers than I should and not getting enough sleep. It takes a toll after a while."

Matt asked Naomi, "Where shall I put his bags?"

Naomi thought a minute. "Put him in the bedroom between you and the bathroom; he'll be close if he needs to use it during the night, and he can call you if he needs help." Upstairs, there were two bedrooms on one side of the bathroom, and two on the other. Matt and Willie Newman each had rooms at opposite ends of the hall, giving them more privacy.

A month after Matt moved in, Willie Newman took up permanent residence as well. Willie, section foreman for the railroad, had been burned out of the railroad section house. The section house sat smack up against the track where the track curved just west of town. A freight train came through one windy night, and the sparks from the engine set the thing on fire. The house burned to the ground in less than thirty minutes. It was cheaper for the railroad to keep Willie at Naomi's than to rebuild the house. For Naomi it was a stroke of luck.

Neither Naomi nor Matt entertained the thought of Russell sleeping in his old bedroom with Naomi. For all Naomi knew they had never been divorced. But divorced or not, she was not going to share a bed with Russell Hollister. Legalities not withstanding, Russell had made his bed miles away from Naomi for twelve long years, and the bed he slept in under this roof was not going to be the one he slept in when he left. And another thing, this might be his house under the law, but, sick or not, he wasn't about to move her out of her bedroom, and he certainly wasn't going to move into it with her.

While she hadn't voiced it, Matt was sure Naomi felt this way, and, for his part, Matt was not about to let any man, including Russell Hollister, get near Naomi.

"Why don't you sit right here for a minute, Russell, and I'll take these bags on up?" Matt wanted to give them some time alone.

"I think I'll do that," Russell said, relieved that he could rest a bit more before starting the climb. "Naomi," he asked, "could I have a spot more coffee?"

Still trying to absorb the situation, she picked up the pot and brought it back to the table, pouring each of them a half-cup before setting the pot on a silver trivet that had belonged to Russell's mother. She settled into her chair, and they looked at each other over the coffee pot, the empty pie plates, and all the distance and time.

"I see by the sign by the door you've opened a hotel," Russell said.

When Johnny was twelve, he decided they needed a different sign than the placard Naomi had tacked beside the door. It had taken most of his summer vacation to sand the board he'd selected and paint "THE TYSEN HOTEL" in block letters in bright blue. Johnny had thought blue would be just the thing against the white of the house. He'd attached a chain to the sign and hung it like a picture to the right of the front door. Naomi prized it more than a Rembrandt, and for all of a week Johnny thought he might become a carpenter.

"I had to do something to feed Johnny and me," Naomi said with asperity.

Russell blushed. Changing the subject quickly, he asked, "Why is Matt here so late?"

"He lives here. He moved in four years ago when Beth Lynn died."

"I didn't know. I'm sorry to hear that; I always liked Beth Lynn."

"We all liked Beth Lynn," Naomi said. "Matt took it mighty hard."

"Looks like he's beginning to get over it," Russell said dryly.

Naomi gave him a long, hard look. "That wouldn't be any of your business, now would it?"

Russell shook his head. "No, it's not." He looked down at his cup. "You're right. Of course, you're right."

After a pause, Russell said, "You haven't changed much, Naomi. You don't look any different than the day I left."

"You need to put on your glasses, Russell. I'm older, I've put on some weight, and my hair is starting to turn grey." She took in again the age lines around his mouth and eyes, the sag just under his jaw. He was too thin, and his color was off. He had never been heavy; he'd been slim and graceful. Now he was drawn and bony. Doc would definitely have to look him over.

"We've got a lot to talk about, Naomi."

"Yes, we sure do, but whatever you have to say will have to keep until tomorrow. We've all had a long day, and I'm not up to hearing it tonight. It's time we all got to bed."

He nodded. "How's Johnny?" he finally asked.

"He's just fine." Naomi's faced tightened.

"He probably won't remember me."

"He remembers you." There was a hard crust around the edges of Naomi's voice. How could Johnny not remember him, Naomi thought. He'd cried every night for a month when Russell left and waited each day for the train to come in, just hoping Russell would step off.

Russell nodded. "I guess he does. How old was he again?"

"He was five."

"How old is he now?"

"Almost eighteen." Naomi realized that Russell didn't even know how long he'd been gone.

Matt came back down the stairs. "Russell, you ready to turn in?"

"Yep, I am." He looked around the kitchen. "This is the room I thought about most. I missed it."

Though he had protested earlier, he let Matt take his arm on one side, and he grabbed the banister with his other hand.

Chapter Six

Later, in bed, Naomi lay awake from all the coffee and the buckshot of events that had peppered her. She had never lived through a night like this one; the whole night was like Alice's peach pie turned upside down on the floor. She stopped herself. Not the whole night. Tonight, Matt had said he loved her. Not exactly in those words, but that's what he meant. Matt loved her. She could feel his strong hand holding hers and the sweet softness of his mouth, and in those minutes in the warmth of the kitchen and his nearness, Naomi had felt a happiness she had never known.

And, then, right then, with five minutes of happiness to her name, there was Russell. Russell.... After twelve years, he had walked in just like he owned the place.

Twelve years, twelve years, began clicking through her brain like the sound of the train hitting the expansion gaps on the rails. Where did they go? She lay there staring at the reflection on the ceiling light from the moonlight outside. Time. Time had a way of storing a thing in the back of the attic and quietly cob-webbing it over. You'd forget about it. If you'd bump against such a boxed-up memory when you went up for winter blankets or to sort through Johnny's old clothes, you knew you didn't want to look inside. You didn't want to brush it off, have the cobwebs clinging to your fingers, all sticky, tangling you up again. If you left it there long enough, there was always the chance it would crumble into dust in whichever trunk or box was handy when you stuck it back out of sight in the first place. Now, tonight, Russell had come home, and there she was in the attic again, examining all the boxes.

She sat up in bed and reached for the pull on the lamp on the bedside stand. Slipping out of bed in her bare feet, she crossed the room to the dresser and dug underneath her flannel nightgowns in the bottom drawer. It was here that she'd kept their wedding picture. She took it back to bed to study it.

There they were: she in a pale rose suit and matching hat, Russell in the same navy-striped suit he'd worn the night she met him, looking scrubbed and a little surprised. There was no crystal ball there, nothing to tell her why they had parted. Nothing to tell her why they had come together.

Russell always said they'd danced their way into marriage. And she guessed he was right. They were fitted for each other on a dance floor; people would stop to watch them two-step or waltz, and Russell could tango. She'd never met anyone else who could tango. He could lead her over polished wood with such ease she felt like she was floating over time. They'd become part of the rhythm, matching step for step, hearing the heartbeat of the music; Naomi was sure it must be love.

She wished she had a picture of them dancing to the band in the Odd Fellows Lodge Hall. That's where they'd met. She'd gone to the lodge hall with her friend, Sarah Morgan, whose father was a member. Russell had come with Sarah's brother, George. The two of them, Russell and George, pumped gas at Mr. Morgan's filling station on Hampton Avenue.

When they married, Sarah and George stood up for them at City Hall, and that night they'd all gone dancing at the Starlight Roof atop the Chase Hotel. They'd danced until midnight, sorry when the band stopped playing.

Maybe that was it: the band stopped playing.

They'd quit going out after they'd moved to Tysen. Russell was too tired when he'd come in from a railroad run. Then she joined the Tysen Baptist Church, where Brother Busby Howard put a damper on dancing, though her feet never stood still; they still danced their way around the kitchen to the big band music that came out of St. Louis on Saturday nights.

Brother Howard, unlike her minister in St. Louis, would exhort them from the pulpit to pledge never to dance again. Dancing, he insisted, caused John the Baptist to lose his head, and that was reason enough for all good Christians never to tap a toe. If John the Baptist's bloody head on a platter was not reason enough, then they were to remember that dancing led to Impure Thoughts!

In spite of all Brother Howard's pleadings, Naomi could never bring herself to sign the pledge. She could promise not to drink, not to smoke and not to curse, but she could not promise never to dance again. That would be asking more than she was willing to give. You might as well tell a body not to listen to music of any kind, because even in church, with the first note of the piano, her right foot usually kept up a pretty good beat.

When Russell first left, she would lie in bed at night thinking, listening to the sounds of the katydids and the owls during the long stretches of silence between trains. Sometimes there was the lonely call of a coyote or hunting dogs barking at a coon. Then the blasting insolence of the train whistle would fill up all the space in the room and in her head, and the fierce, pulsing motion of the train, usually a freight, moved the house, made it clutch in a tremor and, finally, release as the train moved on through. There was always, after the last vibration of the train had faded away, a silence louder than the noise of the train before the night sounds came moving back again.

In the hours between trains, she'd ask herself again and again why he'd gone, or where he'd gone. She never thought about his coming back. There was a certainty to this thing that had happened to her. Then, one morning, she realized that she had known his leaving would come. What she hadn't known was that she'd been waiting for it. That surprised her.

She was used to being alone in her bed; she'd been married to a railroad man. When he was home, he seemed more of an interruption than a help; he took up so much space and so much time. Their routine, hers and Johnny's, had to be measured to his. So she wasn't at a loss by having him gone. She had Johnny to care for, Johnny to fill her life and her heart. Naomi was sure that God sent her Johnny to fill up the empty rooms inside her. He was her son as surely as if she had carried him to term and given birth right here in her bedroom in this house. Johnny was her life then and now.

Russell had never even known she was lonely, and there had never been a way to tell him how she felt. Had she tried, she knew that he would have given her that puzzled look he gave her when he met a thing for the first time that was totally foreign to him. He would look at her the way he had when she told him she missed the sound of the streetcars and traffic in St. Louis and the smell of gasoline fumes. She'd been a city girl all of her life; it took time to make the quiet a part of her, to include the loudness of it. She had to learn to sleep through the sound and movement of the trains passing just across the gravel road from the house. It was several years before she let her weight be held up by the quiet and could float above the sounds that broke through it at night.

Russell had never really been there even when he was home, had never really known her. She hadn't known him either, it seemed. But there was the finality of it, his being gone, that caused her to feel uneasy. It was one thing to live without a husband when you knew he was coming back, and another when you faced all the days and nights knowing you weren't attached to a man, had the wall of his name to stand behind. That there would not be a husband who would be coming back to share things, somebody to ask what he thought about getting a deeper well dug or putting in a new septic tank. Those were powerfully big decisions to make on your own.

It had never occurred to her to divorce Russell. If she'd been asked about it and had to think it through, she might have said it wasn't necessary; she wasn't looking to marry somebody else. Or she might have said it somehow kept her safe, and she didn't even know from what. Besides, she wasn't a woman who'd been brought up to get a divorce. A woman got married and stayed married; she was in it for the long haul.

If Russell had wanted a divorce, Naomi knew he'd have probably gone ahead and done it. So it wasn't even something she gave much brain time to. She had her life in Tysen, she had friends here, and she had Johnny.

She didn't think about it much, nor did anybody else in town. Naomi was just Naomi. She was Naomi Hollister who used to be married to Russell Hollister before he left. She was a part of them, as outsiders usually weren't. Probably because, without his knowing it, he'd left her in their care.

But it was her house now, hers and Johnny's; it had been for twelve years.

They had painted it and repaired it and planted the gardens and put up wallpaper. She and Johnny had mowed and trimmed the yard and the trees, cared for the roses and kept up the flowerbeds. It wasn't Russell. When had it ever been Russell? Had he been here to help dig the new well or re-gravel the driveway? And now he just waltzed right in here as though he'd left last week and expected what? Life was going to pick up where he left it? Well, she could tell him that would happen when hell froze over, and not a minute before.

What was it he'd said? He said it was the kitchen he'd missed. Not her or Johnny. No, it was this house. But whose house was it really? He had said in his note he gave it to her. Surely, that held some weight, even under the law. It was too much, too much to think about now. Ray, Sample, Busby, Johnny, Hope, Evelyn, Doc, Alice, Webster, and Russell. The day had been too long, and her mind began to buzz and darken. But her last thought before she fell into an exhausted, dreamless sleep was of Matt, strong, secure, helping Russell up the stairs to bed.

Chapter Seven

Sample Forney sat at his kitchen table in the dark, drinking a cup of strong heated-over coffee that Wanda Puckett had made at dinner. He hadn't turned on the light in the kitchen; he could see anything he needed by the hall light that Wanda had left on for him. Wanda was sixty-seven and took care of the kids and the house since Ella Sue ran off. The coffee had a bite to it; he liked it that way. He had thought the remains of Alice's pie would be on his table beside his coffee, not splashed all over his boots and pants and still on the floor of the school auditorium. Damn Webster and his interference, and double damn Ray Redeem for getting in his way.

Webster, that greedy fool, should have told him about Ray; he'd kept that mighty quiet. He had let Sample think that Alice had put him off because she was too young to know better. Now, it was Sample who knew better, but Alice's wanting Ray didn't change his mind none. It was what he wanted that mattered.

He sat there, holding his cup in both hands, his forearms on his knees, going over what had happened with Ray and Alice at the pie supper and Evelyn's crumpling like an empty feed sack. She might well die and that wouldn't be good. If she died, Alice wouldn't stay.

He knew what people said about him in town, but he didn't care what they said, and he didn't care what they thought. All he cared about was Alice Tolney.

Sample wanted Alice in a way he'd never wanted a woman before. He didn't want Alice for birthing. He'd had two other women for that. He didn't need any more children; he had four boys and two girls. The girls weren't important; when they were old enough, he'd portion them off to men who'd be willing to trade something worthwhile for them, and four boys were enough to run the farm after he was gone. They'd do it; he'd see to it. Children weren't important anymore. He wanted Alice for himself, and he wanted her slim and beautiful, kept just the way she was now. He wanted her in his bedroom every night, just waiting for him, just to use for his pleasure.

Sample had been fixed on Alice since the summer she turned fifteen. Even before Ella Sue ran off. He'd watch her long, tan legs in her shorts swing down from the step of the truck. Then, she'd reach over the gate at the back of the truck for Webster's lunch basket, and he could see the push and lift of her breasts against the front of her blouse. The summer sun shone through the soft cotton. For the last two summers those breasts had been straining just a little more and a little more, and the sun made twin haloes around the curves. Alice was a beauty, and she was young and untouched. He'd watched her these last two years just ripening like a smooth plump tomato tugging down the vine or a peach weighting the limb, both ready to burst their skins.

He knew Webster had seen him watching, and after Ella Sue left, he wasn't surprised when Webster had come up with a plan. Webster told Sample, if he was interested, that for 100 acres of Sample's bottomland, he'd talk Alice into marrying Sample when she was eighteen next August. That was in February. Sample pretended to think it over for several weeks, long enough that Webster started pestering him about it, but there was never a doubt in his mind that he wanted Alice; he just didn't want Webster pushing for more, and he wanted Webster thinking that he was the one getting the bargain. He was willing to pay a lot for Alice, but he wanted Webster and Evelyn to keep their distance.

Sample hadn't been worried that Alice wouldn't marry him. He knew what money could do, but he didn't know until tonight that Alice wanted Ray Redeem. Now, it would be harder to convince her to choose him instead. He could do it, he knew he could. Evelyn's illness could work to his advantage, and he planned to use it, even if he had to move them into his house and hire a nurse for long enough to convince Alice he meant business. There was little Alice wouldn't do for her mother; everyone in town knew that. She was the one who took care of her, not Webster. He'd see to it that Webster kept Ray away long enough for Sample to have a clear field. Ray Redeem was a tough kid, but he was no match for Sample. Alice wasn't going to belong to anybody but him.

All that beauty, all that young, soft skin. He could feel the very softness of her skin as he sat there. He wanted to touch her, to rearrange her arms and legs, to pose her, admire her, to run his hands down over her breasts and feel the nipples against his palms, to stroke over her navel and move slowly beyond to the triangle of hair, pushing her legs apart. He turned his calloused hands over, palm up, and studied them. These hands would touch Alice's body where no other man had touched her. He could feel himself hardening, pushing against the leg of his overalls, and he moved his hand toward the buttons on his fly, fixing his eyes blankly at the wall above the kitchen door at the two rifles and the shotgun in the gun rack mounted there.

Chapter Eight

Brother Busby Howard could think of nothing but Johnny Hollister and Ray Redeem while he was driving to the hospital; he had no room at this moment to consider the Tolney's tragedy. He was ablaze with anger and indignation. After all, he had been betrayed! Betrayed by Johnny Hollister. Betrayed by his own daughter! And in front of the entire town! How could he expect his flock to heed his word if his first born child made mockery of his beliefs and spent time in the company of such a reprobate as Ray Redeem? Ray Redeem who drank and fought, and had actually, actually, walked out of the church with Busby's words pounding against his back. Walked out as if those words had no meaning, no power.

Here Hope and Johnny Hollister, a boy who had given Busby his word and his hand when he agreed to Busby's rules, had set out deliberately and openly to conspire to disobey him, and, even worse, to disobey him publicly. Busby had to do something, do something quickly; the members of his church had to be sure that his stand was just as steadfast as it always had been despite the actions of Ray Redeem and Alice Tolney, and certainly despite the actions of Hope and Johnny. "Oh, Lord," he directed, "tell me how to punish these sinners! Tell me what to do. I need to know now how to uphold myself and my ministry!" He exhorted God again and again, as though he were saying the rosary, though that thought never crossed his mind.

Then, just as he turned off Route 66 to enter Meramec City, it came to him, came as clearly as he could see the lights of the hospital just ahead. The Lord had struck down Evelyn Tolney as a direct result of the wages of the sin of Ray Redeem, Alice Tolney, Johnny Hollister and Hope, his own offspring. They had brought about the wrath of God, pulled it right down from His heavens, and caused it to strike an innocent God-fearing woman like Evelyn, hurt her husband, and caused embarrassment to Sample Forney.

And Busby knew what the Lord wanted him to do: Tomorrow morning, he would preach on this. He would stand before his congregation and denounce these people in the name of God. Ray Redeem would not be in church, but his father would be. Jackson Redeem, his senior deacon, never missed a Sunday. Jackson would have to do his duty this time. He'd realize Ray had to be punished. Jackson would have to lay his grief down long enough to take Ray in hand and make a stand for the Lord. If Busby presented it to him in just that way, Jackson would see the need for it. It was just too bad that Alice Tolney couldn't be there to hear it, too. He'd just have to speak to her later.

And Naomi Hollister. She'd truly let the Lord down. He wouldn't have believed that she could stand up for her nephew, right there in public, after what she'd witnessed last night with her own eyes. The woman wasn't blind; she knew what Johnny had done. She certainly had to know that he was far more responsible than Hope. Johnny Hollister had been the one to lead Hope astray; he was the one with the sinful, rebellious friend, not Hope. Hope would never have done this on her own.

Now that he thought about it, he realized Naomi had probably known about them all the time and hadn't put a stop to it, hadn't even come to him to tell him. That meant she bore the responsibility, too. This woman, who had been chairlady of the Lottie Moon Christmas Offering for the past ten years and was the best alto in the choir, would have a lot to answer for when she stood before Her Lord. Sin, he thought, could creep into hearts without warning. It just proved a Christian had to be on constant lookout, couldn't stop for a minute. Satan was everywhere.

Busby had never doubted the rightness or the righteousness of his calling Ray to account for whispering to a girl while Busby presented the Word of God to the sinful. Ray was distracting from Busby's work. Busby could see that, even though the other members of the congregation hadn't been aware. That's why he had to stop Ray right there, make an example of him.

When a man's been called to the service of the Lord, it was necessary to offend people who did not share his beliefs or behave as Christians should behave. He came to realize early on that taking up the Cross was not for the faint of heart. If he had to offend or wound, it was his burden to bear.

He didn't just limit his mission to members of his congregation. When he had refused to remarry Rosemary Hoffmeister, Helen's life-long friend who had driven all the way from St. Louis just so Busby could marry her, he told Rosemary he couldn't. Rosemary's husband had divorced her and run off with his secretary, and Busby told her he couldn't marry a divorced woman. Rosemary was crushed and burst into tears, but Busby knew he was in the right; he stood solidly on the direct Word of God. They were his sword and shield. He had opened his Bible and pointed out the scripture to Rosemary; it was right there: I Corinthians 7:10-11: "And unto the married I command, yet not I, but the Lord, Let not the wife depart from her husband: / but if she depart, let her remain unmarried...."

Helen had tried to plead Rosemary's case to him in their bedroom while Rosemary and her fiancé, a nice widower she'd met at work who had two children, sat huddled on the couch in the living room. Busby had had to remind Helen that The Word was The Word. When Helen told him that Rosemary hadn't done the departing, Bill had, Busby said Helen was splitting hairs.

Rosemary had driven away from the parsonage to return to St. Louis unmarried, hurt, and angry, and Helen had gone to the bedroom and closed the door. When she came out to prepare dinner, her eyes were puffy, and her nose still red. They'd never heard from Rosemary again. Helen hadn't spoken to him, except in public, for almost a month after that.

Dealing with the non-members, though, was easier than dealing with his members. When the Bradley's sixteen year old son, Bobby, had been killed in the automobile accident near Havana, the Bradley's, who knew full well that Bobby hadn't made a profession of his faith and accepted Jesus Christ as his Savior, had pleaded with the Preacher before the funeral to tell them that they would see their beloved Bobby in heaven. Bobby Bradley had been one of those hold-outs who sat on the back pew through every invitational hymn with his eyes steadfastly boring a hole in the floor. It didn't matter how many verses of "Just As I Am" or "Almost Persuaded" they sang; Bobby remained firmly planted. Nothing Busby could say had ever moved him to the front of the church to make a profession of faith.

Hard as it was for them to hear, and, as he told them, for him to say, according to the scripture, Bobby would spend eternity in the fires of Hell. He had opened his Bible and read to them from Mark 16:16: "Whoever believes and is baptized will be saved; but he that believeth not will be damned." When Connie pleaded, "Surely God will accept him; he was such a sweet boy and he never hurt a soul. He wouldn't even go hunting because he didn't want to kill an animal. Why, he sat with his grandmother every day, holding her hand before she died. He was a good, good boy. Surely, God would take a good boy." Busby had sadly shaken his head, wishing for the first time that he could tell her there was some hope; they were good Christian people. The visit had shaken him mightily.

After meetings such as the one with the Bradleys, he would often be visited at night with flurries of self-doubt that sent him into severe nausea and stomach cramps. He would wrestle with his pillow and try to find comfort in the fact that he'd remained steadfast in his faith. He was lonely then. Helen went on quietly breathing beside him. He couldn't tell her; he couldn't tell anybody. He was their leader, and right was right.

In the mornings, when the sun came through the ruffled curtains above the sink, and he held a cup of fresh morning coffee in his hand, he felt more sure; everybody must face doubts, he would tell himself; it's a test of faith. After blessing the breakfast and eating his fill of Helen's biscuits and gravy, he had the strength to hoist his mantle of righteousness around his shoulders and go forth into the world to preach the gospel. After all, Busby Milford Howard was called to be the Gate Keeper of the Lord. He'd tell them: "For wide is the gate and broad is the road that leads to destruction, and many enter through it." He was trying with all his might to save his people from eternal damnation; surely they understood that.

Busby would have to admit that most of the time he liked wearing his mantle in Tysen; it marked him as the leader of his community. In small Missouri towns, most of the folks knew that the Trinity was made up of God, the Father, God, the Son, and god, the Baptist preacher.

The preacher got his messages straight from the Lord and could pass on His information directly. Something, Busby felt, the Lord often didn't seem inclined to do for others.

Busby knew he was no ignoramus; he was proud to say he had spent six entire months at the Moody Bible Institute in St. Louis, proud even though he'd received it at the hands of the Methodists. He told his congregation that he believed that deep down Dwight L. Moody had really been a Baptist; Moody just hadn't known it. He also said he forgave Moody for being sprinkled instead of immersed.

After six months at The Moody Bible Institute, the Lord made it known to him he'd had enough education; he was to go forth and preach the Gospel, using his own good sense and the King James Holy Bible. "Too much education," he would intone on Sunday mornings, "can blind us from the Truth." Busby had decided to "forego blindness for the path of the Lord." He had left education in the ditch with the oxen, and he declined on Sundays to get either of them out.

It was through the Moody Bible Institute that he had developed a fondness for certain words that he used regularly from his pulpit. He would say, "I don't want to be like one of those 'erudite' preachers, all 'sounding brass and tinkling cymbals'," and then he would crash thunderously away for the next thirty minutes. He liked the sound of "efficacy," and would try to use it at least twice during any baptismal service. "There is no efficacy in this water," he would say, putting his hand into the baptismal pool and holding it up so that the water could run through his fingers. "I don't care what you've heard from those sprinklers across the way." The First Methodist Church sat diagonally across the road from the First Baptist Church. When he referred to the Methodists, they were "sprinklers"; when he referred to the Catholics, they were "fish eaters." Busby always made sure they knew exactly which group he was discriminating against.

Busby's beliefs were defined by a set of "Don'ts." He liked his members to know what was expected of them; he didn't want them to have to think about Biblical passages or other religions and be confused. Thinking led to questioning, questioning led to doubt, and doubt led straight down the slippery slope to Hell.

The members of the First Baptist Church of Tysen knew the Truth; they had the Way to Salvation. Busby and his followers found great comfort in Absolutes; they didn't have to worry about falling from Grace. They were Baptists: Once Saved, Always Saved. And it was so much easier for Busby to tell people what Not to do than what To do. There was greater room for variety if a person had to choose a path of action. Not choosing simplified one's life; it closed it off from all those troublesome possibilities.

Now here he was, parking in the hospital lot, about to give comfort to Webster and hold Evelyn's hand, even if she couldn't feel it. He took his King James Bible from the dashboard, where it always rode with him, and holding it in his right hand like a sword, he marched across the blacktop, pushed open the double doors, and strode toward Webster Tolney.

Chapter Nine

In the bathroom the next morning, Naomi's hazel eyes took a last look in the mirror over the sink and reached for the two tortoise shell combs beside the soap dish, sliding them, one at a time, above her temples, pulling her curly, auburn hair back to get it out of her face. It had grown down just beyond her collar. She needed to have it cut. Thank goodness there was enough curl in it she didn't need a permanent; that saved money. She'd have to call Dell over at the beauty shop soon, but she'd think about that later in the week. This morning there was Russell and Matt and Johnny.

And today was Sunday, and for the first time in years, she wasn't going to church. She had everything she could deal with right here at home; she had her own ox to get out of the ditch. Besides, she wasn't ready to face Busby just yet; she wasn't sure just how she wanted to handle it. To her thinking, Busby Howard was being much more of an ass than an ox, and if he was in a ditch, he could just blame well stay there. It gave her a moment's pleasure to think he'd miss her voice in the choir. Naomi knew she had the best alto voice in town.

She adjusted the collar of her starched print dress, fluffed her hair a little more, touched her lips with a pink lipstick, and took one last look in the mirror. Right now there was plenty to face in her own kitchen. Matt would be up soon, then Johnny; she would have to explain to Johnny about Russell. If that weren't enough, sometime today she had to find time to get to the hospital to see what she could do for Evelyn. Alice would be needing some relief, poor child, and she would certainly need a friendly face.

When she opened the bathroom door, the fragrance of lilac talcum and Palmolive soap floated out before her on the warm, moist air lingering from her bath. She started down the hall toward the kitchen, stopping at Johnny's door, opening it for a peek, and saw he was curled up in a ball sleeping soundly. He'd slept like that since he was little, all tight and protected, especially when he was tired or upset. Well, there was no reason to wake him; he'd had a long night. Heaven only knows what time he got in. She could smell coffee and knew Matt was already in the kitchen. Matt, she thought, and in spite of all the turmoil and the problems, her heart felt lighter.

When she came through the archway, Matt was pouring cereal into a bowl. "How long you been up?" she asked him. The clock over the refrigerator said 7:10. "You should've wakened me."

"There wasn't any need. I know how to pour Rice Krispies." He smiled at her. "Sit down and let me pour you some coffee."

"Don't you want something more than that?" she asked, looking over at his cereal bowl.

"No. Just have this coffee and sit with me for a few minutes before everyone gets up." He put the cup in front of her.

She took a sip of coffee and looked directly at Matt for the first time through possibility. There he was: sturdy and dependable, intelligent and caring, and she knew he'd be there no matter what. It was a blessing to know that about a man. There was a man who knew how to listen, knew when to put down the newspaper. He was a rarity, Matt was.

They sat quietly until Naomi sighed and said, "I don't know what to tackle first."

Matt reached across the table and took her hand. Here she was, with her hair pulled back from a face that could let you in and welcome you home. He wanted to hold her and tell her everything would be all right, but he couldn't do that just now. He'd have to wait.

"It'll come to you," he said. "Do you know what time Johnny got home?" Matt had seen his car parked behind the hotel.

"I'm not sure." She sipped her coffee with her free hand. "I wonder how Evelyn is doing? I guess we'll know when Johnny gets up." Lifting her chin with a touch of defiance, she said, "I'm not going to church this morning."

"I guessed as much," he said.

She frowned. "My heart's not right for church. I need to go see Evelyn later this morning, and I have to think about Russell. I don't know what to make of his showing up like this."

"I know you don't." He tightened his grip.

"Matt," she began again, "about Russell…."

He interrupted her, "It's all right, Naomi. Let's just meet things as they happen."

She turned her hand palm up to meet his. It felt warm and safe.

"If I just knew why he's come back…." She looked down into her coffee cup and chewed lightly on her bottom lip. "What if he's thinking of moving back in?"

"He may well be," Matt said with his usual directness; he released her hand and got up to get the coffee pot. "You want some breakfast now?" he asked.

She shook her head. "I don't know anything about him anymore. Course, I probably never did. Do you know I don't even know if we're married or not. Until now," she shot Matt a shy glance, "it didn't matter."

"You never heard a word from him?" Matt brought the pot to the table and set it on a hot pad.

"Not a word." Her eyes darkened. "What if we're divorced and he wants this hotel? I don't have a leg to stand on."

"I don't think that's it." Matt filled both cups just full enough to leave room for cream. "For one thing, the hotel brings in money, and from the look of him, I wouldn't say he has much. Even if he was well, Russell doesn't know a hen from a rooster when it comes to running a hotel. So I don't think he's here to make changes."

"Just his being here makes changes," Naomi said. "And, Matt, what if I'm not divorced? I'm not sure which is worse."

He smiled, but his eyes were bothered. "I'm not either." He put his hand back over hers. "But we'll meet it together."

They heard Johnny's door open. "I'll be there in a minute," he called to them and headed for the bathroom. Johnny always heralded his coming; it was as if he wanted to be sure someone would be waiting for him.

Naomi took in a long breath and set her shoulders. "Well," she said, "I guess it's time to pull myself together," and she began to take her hand slowly from between Matt's. "We're out here, honey," she called down the hall.

"I've never seen you not together," Matt said, and he let her hand slide away after squeezing it gently.

All this time, she thought, and this man has had his khakis planted in my kitchen chair. It was just short of a miracle.

By the time Johnny came into the kitchen, Naomi was frying bacon. "How many eggs do you want?" she asked over her shoulder, watching the bacon so it didn't get too crisp. "Matt, you sure you don't want some bacon and eggs?"

"I'm sure. I'm happy with my coffee," Matt said, smiling at her.

"Two," Johnny said.

"Tell us about Evelyn," Naomi said, keeping an eye on her cooking while she looked at Johnny over her shoulder. Her boy looked so tired this morning, but what could she expect after last night.

"Doc said she's had a stroke. She's paralyzed on the left side of her body, and she's can't talk very well. I can't understand her, but Alice seems to be able to."

"Oh, my," Naomi said, flipping bacon grease over Johnny's eggs, "poor thing."

"Is it permanent?" Matt asked.

"Doc doesn't know yet. He said to tell you both he'd come by as soon as he can get some rest and goes back and to check on Evelyn."

"What time did Ray bring you home?" Naomi asked.

"About three, I think."

"Were you able to see Alice?" Naomi placed a plate filled with two eggs sunny-side-up, six pieces of bacon and four slices of buttered toast in front of him.

Johnny nodded. "I saw her. Ray stayed in the truck most of the time. He wanted Alice to know he was there, but he didn't want Webster or the Preacher to go off on her because of him. I'd go in from time to time to check on her, and we stayed until they let her go in to be with Evelyn."

"Was the preacher there all the time?" Naomi wanted to know.

"He was there," Johnny said looking glum.

"Did he say anything to you?" Naomi could feel herself bristling.

"Nope. He just looked through me like a window."

"Give it a little time, son," Matt said. "There's a lot going on right now."

"He's not a man to change his mind." Johnny looked forlorn. "I don't know what I'm going to do."

"We'll think of something," Naomi told him. "Just don't give up hope." Then the three of them realized what she said, and they all laughed. "Well, you know what I mean," she said. "Now, eat your breakfast and stay strong."

The thought of being shut off from Hope was no easy row for Johnny to hoe, but Aunt Naomi was right, he had to eat and stay strong. Actually, little stopped Johnny from eating. He scooped up a large forkful of egg and began to chew. When he swallowed, he said, "I thought Willie went into St. Louis for the weekend."

"He did," Matt said.

"Who's upstairs? I heard someone in the bathroom a minute ago."

Naomi and Matt exchanged glances. Carefully, Naomi said, "Honey,....Your Uncle Russell came back last night."

His fork stopped midway to his mouth. "What?"

"Your Uncle Russell. He was here when we got home."

Johnny stared at her for a minute; his eyes registered confusion. He put his fork back on his plate. "Why did he come back?"

"We don't know yet," Naomi said, watching the questions running behind Johnny's eyes.

After a minute or two, Johnny said flatly, "We don't need him here. I want him to go." His fists were clenched on either side of his plate.

Naomi couldn't have agreed more. She said, "We don't know that he's staying. He isn't well, and he's probably come home for a rest." Naomi was trying to keep her voice even; she didn't want Johnny to know how upset she was.

"Home? This is our home, Aunt Naomi. It doesn't belong to him anymore. He gave it up when he left. When you leave people you're supposed to take care of, you don't have any rights anymore." He suddenly slammed both fists against the table, and the knife and spoon jigged beside his plate. Johnny certainly knew about being left. His jaw was set tight. "What are we going to do about it?"

"I don't know what there is to be done."

"He just can't come back and live here."

"I don't have any choice about that, honey. It's his house."

"We're the ones fixed it up and made it a hotel."

"He owns it, Johnny. I don't have legal claim to it," Naomi said.

"He doesn't own us. He left us, remember? We didn't leave him. He doesn't have any claim to this house or us."

From the doorway, Russell said, "You're right, Johnny. I don't have a right to claim you or Naomi. I was just hoping to stay here for a spell. It's the only home I know."

Johnny looked at the man standing in the doorway, tall, skinny and pale. He wouldn't have recognized him if Aunt Naomi hadn't already told him who he was. "You said in the letter you sent that the house was Aunt Naomi's. Do you remember that?"

"Yes, I remember that. It is Naomi's, but that doesn't mean I can't be here, too."

Johnny challenged him, "Are you back to stay?"

"I don't know yet," Russell told him.

"Why not?"

"Johnny," Naomi interrupted, "not now. There's a lot to talk about. Let Russell have some breakfast. He hasn't had his coffee yet."

Johnny knew from her tone that he'd better let it rest, but he wasn't happy about it. He stared at his plate; his eggs were cold and unappetizing.

"Sit down, Russell," Naomi said. "I'll get you some bacon and eggs. Johnny, you want some fresh eggs?"

He shook his head without looking up.

Russell looked more rested this morning; it showed in his face and the way he moved. Frail as he looked, Russell moved with a kind of grace and ease that few men possessed. Naomi had forgotten that. He came across the kitchen floor as if the old linoleum was polished hardwood. She watched him sit before she carried his coffee to him and watched him pour cream into it. Until that moment she'd forgotten he was left-handed.

"I'm going to make you some biscuits and gravy," she told Johnny. "I know full well you're hungry and you'll eat those. So will Matt, won't you, Matt?"

"Never turned down your biscuits and gravy yet, and neither has Johnny." He put his hand on Johnny's shoulder; he was like a colt, ready to buck, but he didn't shake Matt's hand off. "Russell will probably have some of those, too."

Johnny looked at Matt and then Naomi with an expression that clearly asked, "Why are you being so nice to this man?" Both Naomi and Matt kept neutral expressions.

"Actually, Naomi," Russell said, "I'd rather have that than the bacon and eggs, as long as you're fixin'. You got any of that blueberry jam you used to make?"

"There's some down in the cellar." She came around the table to stand behind Johnny and put her arms around him, giving him and the chair the tight squeeze. She kissed the top of his head before she asked, "Johnny, honey, will you go down and get me a fresh jar?"

Johnny stiffened in protest; he didn't want Russell having any of Aunt Naomi's jam or anything else she'd brought into being. Reluctantly, he pushed back from the table. "Yes, ma'am," he said, but he still didn't look at Russell, and his jaw was set.

Naomi caught him around the waist when he stood, looking up at him. "You going to eat some of my biscuits?" He nodded and ducked his head a little so she could plant a lopsided kiss on his cheek, but he sent Matt a look before he left saying watch Russell while I'm gone.

Matt nodded.

Naomi busied herself with flour and lard. "He's protective of me, Russell," Naomi said as she worked the dough. "We're the only family we've got. Not that Johnny hasn't been enough. He's the joy of my life; I'm grateful to God that I've got him."

"He is one fine boy," Matt said. "All that's due to Naomi." Matt wanted his stand on the issue made clear.

"I can see he is," Russell said.

"You're going to have to give him time, Russell," Naomi said. "You can't expect the boy to welcome you with open arms. In fact, you are going to have to give us all time. Things have changed a lot since you were here. We've all changed a lot."

Russell nodded. "I can see that, too. I'm not trying to make trouble for you, I promise. I haven't been feeling too well, and I'd like to stay here for a bit and use the upstairs bedroom if you'll let me. I don't have any money for board; there isn't any way I can pay you. But I was hoping that you would feed me until I'm feeling better and get on my feet. I'll pay you back then. But I want you to know now that I won't go back on my word to you; it's your house; I gave it to you. I don't want you to worry about that."

Naomi could feel her shoulders ease; she hadn't realized how tight she'd been holding herself. She said, "I know what you said in your note, but it is your house in the eyes of the law. You have every right to stay here, and, of course, I'll feed you. What kind of person would I be not to feed you?"

"Everybody's not like you, Naomi." He paused a minute. "I know there are things you'd like to know right now, but I'd like to rest a few days before we talk, if I could."

"I guess I can wait a few days, Russell. I've waited twelve years." She turned back to the stove, and both men reached for their coffee cups to fill the silence.

Naomi was sliding the biscuits into the oven when Johnny came back. "Johnny, your Uncle Russell's going to stay in the upstairs bedroom for a while. He hasn't been well, and he's come home to mend. You and I will talk later, all right?"

"Yes, ma'am," Johnny said. He wasn't appeased, but he knew that was as much as he was going to get, and those biscuits were beginning to smell mighty good.

Naomi brought two dozen biscuits to the table, golden brown and looking as if they might take wing and float right off the plate. She set a butter dish with fresh butter next to the biscuits, emptied the jam into Russell's mother's Depression glass jam server, and finished by filling the gravy boat with sausage gravy and put it where the three of them could get to it. The men set about eating. Biscuits, sausage gravy, fresh butter and blueberry jam: those were things men would stop quarreling to eat.

There was a knock on the screen door, and Bertie Reardon said, "Hello in there. Got an extra cup of coffee?"

There wasn't any putting off Bertie, so Naomi said, "Come on in, Bertie. We're just having breakfast. Have a seat; I'll pour you a cup." Naomi was thinking that all of Tysen would know by noon today that Russell was back.

Bertie talked her way to the table. "I just came over to find out if you were going over to the hospital to see Evelyn this morning and if I could ride along with you. I was sitting with her last night at the pie supper and watched her go through all that. I've been feeling mighty bad for her all night; I didn't get much sleep."

Naomi said, "I'll be going over in an hour or so, and, of course, you can go with me. It'll be nice to have the company. Here's your coffee; take my place."

Bertie lowered herself into place before she looked across the table at what she had thought was a weekend boarder. She sloshed her coffee onto the oilcloth, just righting her cup in time. "Dear God in Heaven! Russell Hollister, is that you?"

"It's me, Bertie. How in the world are you?"

Chapter Ten

"Well, I guess you were surprised when Russell turned up last night," Bertie said first thing as she was climbing into Naomi's truck for their ride to Meramec City.

"Yes, I was," Naomi said. She busied herself with starting the truck and backing out. Naomi was not about to discuss Russell with Bertie, or anybody else for that matter.

Bertie had been so taken by the fact that Russell was there she had forgotten to ask about Evelyn. She had spent the time while Naomi changed for the hospital pumping Russell about why he'd left, why he'd come back, and whether he was going to stay or not. Russell told her he'd come back for a visit to see what the old town looked like. When she wanted to know where he'd been, he said he'd been traveling most of the time and hadn't settled down anywhere special. He said he'd just lived the life of a railroad man, and Matt sat there listening, knowing Russell was telling Bertie what he wanted the town to hear.

"Tell me about your new car," Naomi said, and Bertie was thrilled right down to her bony little behind, which she settled into the truck seat as though she was taking up residence.

Bertie always sat with her knees apart like a man's, even in a car. They looked like tent poles stretching out the fabric of her dress that fell to mid-calf. She wore brown oxfords and brown ankle socks day in and day out all summer long, and there was a six inch patch of white leg exposed between skirt hem and stocking top. (In winter she added brown cotton hose under her brown cotton socks.)

The ends of her short, grey, bristly hair with its bowl cut were usually sticking out under the brim of her blue and white railroad cap, which read, "Mo-Pac." She had left the cap at home today out of respect for Evelyn, but her hair was bristling as it always did. Bertie's front tooth had been chipped when Naomi first met her, and it left her with one front tooth slanted diagonally and just half as long as the other. Bertie never seemed to mind her chipped tooth any more than she minded wearing her gold wedding band on her thumb. Tom Sr. won it off a man in a poker game and used it at their wedding, telling her he'd have it sized first chance he got. That was twenty years ago.

"It's a coupe with a rumble seat. Looks like new. Tom Jr. got it from a friend in St. Louis and drove it out last weekend."

"Who's going to drive it?" Naomi asked.

Everyone in Tysen knew that Bertie hadn't gotten behind a wheel since she'd taken out both pumps at Billy Sewell's Sinclair station. Bertie had both kids in the front seat of the car and her groceries in the back. Bunny got a gash in her forehead from the dashboard that required six stitches, Tom Jr. was knocked unconscious by a large flying can of Campbell's pork n'beans, and Bertie had broken two ribs when she collided with the steering wheel.

"Tom Jr.'s going to teach Bunny. Gives Bunny and me some freedom. We won't have to wait on Tom no more."

"I'm happy for you, Bertie," Naomi said. Bertie had had to work hard to support the family. Naomi knew that Tom Reardon, Sr. was not a man to depend upon unless it was to put his posterior on a bar stool at Harvey's Tavern or Wel-Come Inn. He was at Harvey's Tavern more often because it was closer to his house. Bertie was afraid that some Friday or Saturday night she wouldn't be there to walk him home, and she told him that if he was going to get himself liquored up, the least he could do was not cross the railroad tracks. She had visions of his body being cut in two by a fast-moving train. Said she'd dreamed about it, half of a man's body on either side of the track; said she couldn't see the face, but it certainly favored Tom's backside.

"You have Tom Jr. drive you by the hotel the next time you're out driving," Naomi told her.

"I'll do it," Bertie said, satisfied with Naomi's response. Then she changed the subject. "Has Maureen said anything to you lately about me joining the Tysen Garden Society?"

Maureen hadn't, but Naomi didn't want to come right out and say so. She said, "I haven't had a chance to talk with Maureen except about pie supper business, and you know how busy she always is. It's hard to get a long conversation out of her."

Maureen and Patrick Fitzroy had five children of their own and took in four foster children from the Catholic orphanage. They were good people, even though they were Catholics, people always said. Maureen was President of the Tysen Garden Society; she could grow tulips like a Dutchwoman, and her roses were the envy of the county.

More than anything, even more than having a coupe with a rumble seat, which gave her a definite status, Bertie wanted to be invited to join the Tysen Garden Society. Not that she could grow a cactus; she just wanted to be asked to join. She didn't want to be excluded. She'd done her best to woo Maureen and any other of the women who were officers in the club, and she just couldn't figure what was keeping her out.

Bertie knew it wasn't because she was Catholic, since the Fitzroys, children spit polished and shined, attended mass regularly, even when they had to drive to Havana three Sundays out of the month. The traveling priest came to Tysen the second Sunday of each month to hold mass; he didn't have a permanent parish; he drove from one parish to another, able to give communion out of the trunk of his car if necessary. Bertie went each second Sunday, but she rarely made it to Havana the other three; she figured communion once a month should cover it.

Bertie hadn't always been a Roman Catholic; she'd tried the Baptists, the Methodists, and spent one revival with the Pentecostals, but she'd finally settled on the Catholics because they were the only ones in town who would let her drink. She didn't even mind confession; it was good, in fact, to get things off her chest and be forgiven, even when the priest wasn't too happy with her and gave her what Bertie thought was way too much penance. It was a dang sight better than having the hell scared into you by Busby Howard every weekend, and she hadn't had to sign any pledge about cussing or anything else for that matter.

So she wasn't left out because she went once a month to worship idols and light incense to pray souls out of purgatory, as the Baptists were always saying Catholics did. It had to be something else.

Bertie worked for a living, but Naomi worked for a living, so did Marie Johnson and half a dozen other women. Tom Sr. drank, but so did Maurice Puckett. Maurice popped the bottle cap off as many beers as Tom, and Modine Puckett was vice president of the club. Bertie had never been able to sort out just why she hadn't been asked to a single meeting in the last five years that the club had been the social hub for the women in Tysen. As far as she could see, there was no blame good reason.

Of course, Wanda Mallard and her likes wouldn't be asked. With one blonde daughter, one redhead, and one brunette, and not a husband in sight (though two of them had the grey cat eyes of Teeler Hawkins who'd boarded with the Mallards for fifteen years), Wanda would not be a likely candidate. Bertie, on the other hand, was a woman who served a purpose in Tysen; she kept things moving. Without her, where would they be? Maybe they didn't think she could be interested in gardening since she had never grown flowers or vegetables—only a few spindly watermelons. But the Garden Society had projects other than flowers, and she'd just have to convince Maureen and Modine and Naomi that she could certainly spearhead something. After all, she might not drive a car, but she could deal with a railroad, and that was definitely worth their taking a good long hard look at. They needed her in the Garden Society; she was sure of it.

Bertie sat quietly for a few minutes staring out of the windshield; then she drew in a deep breath and soldiered on. "Did Doc say Evelyn's going to get better?" Bertie asked Naomi.

"Doc doesn't know yet." Naomi kept her eyes on the road, the steering wheel firmly in her hands. The way she felt this morning, she needed to hold firmly to what was right in front of her.

"The poor thing hasn't had much of a life has she?" Bertie asked, but it wasn't really a question.

"No, not with Webster, she hasn't. But she has that sweet Alice," Naomi said.

"And she does hear from Mary Jo," Bertie added.

Naomi must have looked surprised.

Bertie laughed. "I bring the mail in, Naomi, and I'm there when Jake sorts it. I know Mary Jo sends letters to Alice care of General Delivery, and Jake holds them for Alice to pick up. Mary Jo arranged it with him before she left."

"I didn't know that," Naomi said. Matt, of course, hadn't said a word.

"I don't tell everything I know, Naomi," Bertie let out a guffaw, "just a lot of it. But the mail, I take very serious."

Naomi reached over and patted her arm, thinking, there's a good woman under all that loud talk and roughened skin. She was going to have to have a word with Maureen Fitzroy about a membership for Bertie in the Garden Society.

Chapter Eleven

There were very few cars in the parking lot of the Meramec City General Hospital, but it was eleven o'clock on Sunday morning, and Meramec City, like Tysen and every other town in Missouri, was filled to overflowing with Baptists. Unless both legs were broken or your mother was dying, you'd best be in church, or you'd have a member of the home visitation committee calling, Bible in hand, come Sunday afternoon to see what dread disease had kept you from where you were rightly supposed to be.

Naomi looked for Doc's car, but didn't see it; he was probably at home getting a little rest. She didn't see Webster Tolney's truck either. She reached for the pink roses she'd cut from the bushes in the back yard and wrapped in wet newspaper to keep fresh, and the two women walked through the swinging doors at the front of the hospital to be encased in the odor of antiseptics.

Wilma Hoops, the nurse on duty at the front desk, said Evelyn still couldn't have visitors except family. Wilma would tell Alice they were there, and they could just have a seat down the hall in the waiting room. "If you'll give me those roses, I'll see they get put in water," Wilma said. Naomi thanked her, and she and Bertie headed down the hall. Everybody knew where the waiting room was. Meramec City had the only decent hospital for miles around; they had all used it at one time or other.

Not that people ran to the hospital for treatment all that often, but life sent you, or one of the family, there a time or two. It was inescapable, unless you were a Christian Scientist, and there weren't any of those that Naomi knew lived hereabouts. Of late, more women were coming here to have babies, but a lot of them still delivered at home; it was cheaper that way. Mainly, people came here for emergency treatment and short stays for illness. They went home for long illnesses and to die. Nobody wanted to die in a hospital.

The waiting room was sparsely furnished; it held two couches and half a dozen chairs, backs all squarely against walls. A sleeping woman in a crumpled, much-washed print dress hid in the corner of one of the couches toward the back of the room, head bobbing back against the wall; there was a narrow rivulet of drool creeping its way toward her chin. She was alone except for one man who was sitting straight-backed on a hard plastic chair. Naomi and Bertie lowered themselves onto the couch directly across from him, settled into place, and put their purses on the floor beside their feet. As they raised their heads, both women stopped short. With his hands placed solidly on his knees, wearing ironed overalls, hair neatly combed, Sample Forney sat staring straight at them.

Naomi and Bertie looked at each other; neither knew what to say.

Then, by way of a greeting, Naomi asked, "Have you heard anything about Evelyn this morning?"

"Webster said she was better." Sample's voice was, as always, low, deep and flat. There was no emotion in it, no rise and fall. Just a one-note cant.

"Is Webster in with her?" Naomi asked.

"No. Had things to tend to at home, stock and such."

"Who are you visiting?" Bertie asked, knowing full well why he was there.

"Nobody," he said, without offering an explanation.

"Well," Bertie said, "you don't come to a hospital to see somebody who's well, generally speaking."

He didn't have time to respond. Alice walked through the door into the waiting room looking so tired she was almost in a stupor. It took her a minute to recognize Naomi and Bertie who were sitting almost directly in front of her. "Oh, Naomi," she said when she saw her, managing to get to the couch before she sank to the floor in front of her, putting her head in Naomi's lap and starting to sob.

"Honey, honey," Naomi said, patting her back and pushing her hair off her forehead. "Bertie, reach in my purse there and get me some Kleenex, would you please?"

Bertie fell to shuffling through Naomi's purse, pulling out a neatly folded stack of Kleenex and handing them to Naomi who put one in Alice's hand for her nose and pulled off another for her eyes. "It'll be all right, honey. Just think, she made it through the night."

"I know, but she can't move her left side, and she can't talk except the tiniest bit. What if she stays that way?"

"Now, honey, you have to trust that she will get better. You know Doc is the best doctor anywhere as far I'm concerned. And we're all praying."

"Yes, we are," Bertie agreed and patted her awkwardly, but gently on the top of her head.

"Everything is such a mess right now," Alice said, the tears still streaming.

"I know it is. But things have a way of righting themselves." Naomi hoped as she said it that it was indeed true. "How's she doing right now?"

"Doc's in with her; he just got back. He told me to wait out here, and he'd be right out." She raised her head to look around the room, and Naomi felt her body stiffen when she saw Sample Forney. "Where's my papa?" she asked Naomi.

"He went home to take care of the stock," Naomi told her.

"When's he coming back for me?"

"He left me to bring you home," Sample interrupted. "He said you'd be needing to come and help out around noon and told me to bring you along. He said you could drive back after lunch."

Naomi felt Alice's shoulders jerk.

"I told him I'd wait until you were ready," Sample said.

Alice pushed up from the floor and smoothed her skirt. "I have to see Doc, and I may need to stay with Momma," she told him.

"Your dad said to tell you the nurses can take care of your momma. He said you can come back after you'd cleaned up things at home. He was dead set on it," Sample told her.

"I bet he was," Naomi said under her breath.

Before Alice could respond, Doc came into the room. There were circles under his eyes, and he was limping from his bad knee, but he'd gone home to shower and change and had gotten some breakfast.

"How's Momma, Doc?" Alice asked at once.

"She's holding her own. She seems more alert than last night, and she's trying to form some words, but she's very confused by what's happened."

"Can you tell anything about the outcome yet, Doc?" Naomi asked.

"There is some improvement, as I said, but we'll have to wait and see how much. At any rate, she's going to be a long time recovering from this, and it's going to take a considerable amount of nursing and care."

"What about talking?" Bertie wanted to know. "Is she going to be able to talk all right?"

"It's a bad stroke. Sometimes a person's speech comes all the way back, sometimes partly, like with her now. There's a likelihood she'll not have the same mobility on the left side, but nobody can say for certain; we'll just have to wait to see."

Alice started to sob again. Doc put his arms around her and held her. "Alice, we'll do everything we can to help her. Don't give up hoping for the best."

She nodded against his shoulder.

Sample stood up, and Doc saw him for the first time. "What are you doing here?" Doc asked. "Where's Webster?"

Sample said, "He went on home to take care of the stock. He left me to look after Alice." He was staking his claim so that Doc would know.

"That sounds about right," Doc said in a voice almost as flat as Sample's. "Webster asked me to come get Alice when you said it was all right for her to leave for a while."

"Well," Doc said, "that sure was thoughtful of Webster, thinking about Alice's need to rest." Doc knew full well that Webster wanted her home to help put food in his mouth. Webster couldn't take it upon himself to open a refrigerator or light a match to a burner. He wouldn't know how.

"We can take her home," Naomi said. "There's no need for Sample to do it."

"I give Webster my word, Missus Hollister. I can't go back on that."

Doc looked at Sample and then at Alice; she was so tired she was swaying slightly. "I want you to go home and try and sleep some." When she started to protest, he said, "You can come back later today, but you won't be much good to your momma if you don't rest now. You'll be all right with Sample." Doc stared hard at Sample over the top of Alice's head. "And you tell your daddy I said you were to rest, you hear me?"

She nodded.

"Is there anything I can do for you, honey?" Naomi asked, coming up to put an arm around her. Alice put her head on Naomi's shoulder, saying into her ear so Sample wouldn't overhear, "Can you call Mary Jo for me? I want her to know about momma. If you could set up a time for her to call me at the hotel, I'd sure appreciate it."

"Course I will, sweetheart. Don't you worry about a thing." Naomi patted her on the back. Alice slipped a piece of paper in her pocket with Mary Jo's number on it before she moved away.

While Alice was talking to Naomi, Doc eased over to Sample who was still standing in front of his chair. "Sample, you take good care of this girl. And don't you tell me it's none of my business."

"You're right, Doc; it ain't."

"I'm making it my business, and I'm telling you, as God is my witness, I love this girl, and I don't want anything more upsetting her."

"I ain't gonna upset her. I'm just helping out her daddy."

"Yes, I see that," Doc said, looking him eye to eye. "Alice," he said turning toward her, speaking so they could all hear, "I'll call you in an hour to let you know how she's doing. You'll be home and have had a chance to take a bath and get yourself something to eat by then."

Alice came toward him to give him a kiss on the cheek. "Thank you, Doc, and thank you for taking such good care of Momma last night."

"It's all right, honey, you go ahead with Sample; he'll take you right home. I'll take care of everything here just like you'd want me to." He squeezed her shoulder, and Alice knew that Doc would call Ray. She gave him a soft smile, which slipped away as she turned to Sample.

"I'm ready," she said, sounding, like somebody about to be taken prisoner, but just too tired to resist.

Sample held the door for her. Alice walked through without looking at him, and the two of them headed down the hall that led to the parking lot. Naomi felt a wash of disgust. It was in the way Sample looked at Alice. It tainted the very air around him.

She turned back to Bertie. "Let's go, Bertie, so Doc can get back to his work," Naomi said; she could feel her need to move away from this room. As Bertie was gathering up their purses, Naomi said softly to Doc so she wouldn't remind Bertie about Russell, "Come on by when you can so we can talk. I need to go over some things with you."

Doc nodded. "You save me any pie?"

"There's a big piece in the fridge with your name on it."

"I'll be over this evening. Maybe with a piece of your pie and a cup of your coffee life will turn right side up again."

"I hope it helps, but things are looking a mite bleak just now."

"You're right about that. You two want to see Evelyn before you go?"

They both nodded.

"Well, just remember, you can touch her, but don't say much; she's mighty confused. When you do speak, speak slowly, and one at a time." They nodded again to say they understood. Doc continued, "It may do her good just to know you're here. I'll take you in, but you'll have to leave after ten minutes, all right?"

They walked quietly into the room where Evelyn Tolney lay staring straight up at the ceiling, IV bottles dripping fluid into both arms. Naomi went to the far side of the bed and Bertie to the near. Evelyn's right eye moved to Naomi, and she tried to say something, but only the right side of her mouth moved; neither of them could make out what she said.

Naomi touched the back of her hand, being careful not to disturb the needle in her arm. There was a box of tissues beside the bed, and she pulled one out, wiping the spittle from the side of her mouth. "Just hold on, honey; just hold on. You're getting better; Doc told us so." She picked up Evelyn's hand and held it between both of hers. "We're all praying hard."

"We sure are," Bertie said from the other side of the bed, holding Evelyn's left hand even though it couldn't feel a thing.

Outside, Sample held the truck door open for Alice. On the passenger's seat was a box of Whitman's Samplers.

"You left your candy in the seat," Alice said eyeing the box.

"That there candy's for you."

"You mean to give to my momma?"

"They're not for your momma; they're for you," Sample said.

Alice didn't know what to say, so she said nothing. She knew she shouldn't be rude. Sample was driving her home because her father had asked him to. If she had known that Sample had directed Webster to go home, telling him that he'd take care of Alice, she wouldn't have been in the truck in the first place.

But she didn't.

She lifted the cellophane covered box, sat down in the seat, and placed the box on her knees. She wanted it as far away from her as she could get it. The box weighed her down as heavily as a fifty-pound sack of chicken feed.

Chapter Twelve

Johnny was lying on his bed staring at the ceiling—*Joseph Pulitzer, His Life & Letters*, face down, on his chest. He couldn't concentrate on the book. He kept thinking about last night. He felt so bad about Evelyn. They didn't dream that Evelyn, or Webster, either, for that matter, would be there. Alice told them that Doc put Evelyn to bed, and Alice left home thinking Webster would be at home with her mother; otherwise, she'd never have left her. Alice doted on her momma, and Evelyn depended on Alice for the love and care she never got from Webster.

Johnny hadn't set out to disobey Busby, either, but Alice had come to Hope and begged Hope to double date with her and Ray, so that Alice could slip out and see him. Johnny had tried to talk Hope out of it; but when Ray came to him to ask, too, Johnny knew he couldn't turn Ray down. He certainly couldn't go to Busby to plead their case. He didn't know what to do. He'd given Busby his word, and Johnny had never broken his word before.

He'd finally decided when he and Ray met down at the river last week. It was the first flat out favor Ray had ever asked of him. How could he refuse? Even afterward, though, he'd gone over it and over it in his mind. In fact, he hadn't thought about much else. He knew Aunt Naomi had probably guessed what was bothering him so; she could almost always tell. But she hadn't asked him; he knew she wouldn't. He wanted to tell her, but he couldn't. This was his decision; he couldn't put it off on Aunt Naomi.

Johnny and Ray had sat side by side, dangling their legs off the low bridge at Harris ford on the Meramec River; they each held a pole and line. They were using crawdads for bait. The water rushed under them with enough force that pebbles did a jig on the river bottom. Just beyond them the river deepened sharply. Every kid in the county knew not to dive off this bridge; it was too shallow up river, and they could be grabbed by the current and sucked right under in the deep water just a few feet down river. It wasn't a wide river, just a treacherous one after a rain, its bottom changing depth with each downpour. But the bridge was fine for fishing, especially when you didn't want to take a boat out. Neither of them had felt like troubling with that. They weren't even fishing, really; they just wanted something to fill in the gaps. Neither spoke.

Ray had taught Johnny to fish from this bridge, a can of freshly dug worms between them. He'd also taught him to swim at the swimming hole around the bend up river. He'd been a good teacher. He'd never just tossed Johnny in; he'd put an arm out flat in the water, told Johnny to stretch out over it and to grab on if he got scared. Johnny was eight, Ray ten. Ray pushed off and Johnny followed. He'd kept Johnny afloat over his arm for long enough for Johnny to kick his legs and slap his arms into the water in what Johnny thought was a swimming stroke; then Ray said, "Now, just do what I'm doing; I'll be right here beside you. I ain't going to let you drown."

He wouldn't drown; Ray had told him so, so he set about to swim; in a month, there was no keeping him out of the water. By the end of the summer Ray had taught him to grab the bag swing the older boys had thrown over a limb of a large cottonwood tree on the bluff further up the river and run with it. He learned to swing far out over the clear, rushing water, to let go at the peak of the arc, and drop through the air, then hit the surface of the river, going down, down into the ever cold blue of it. When he felt his body slow, he'd do what Ray had taught him to do: begin to blow out, watch the bubbles, stretch his arms upward toward the light, kick his legs and shoot through the surface into the world of air.

Ray made him swear he'd never jump unless Ray was there until the two of them decided Johnny was old enough to be on his own. Johnny promised, and he'd never broken it. They'd made the same kind of deal when Ray taught him to hunt and to drive. "Remember," Ray would warn when he got ready to leave, and Johnny would cut in, "I know, I know; not unless you're there."

"Damn straight," Ray would say.

Ray had never broken his word to Johnny, nor, to Johnny's knowledge, had he ever lied to him. No matter what anybody said about Ray Redeem, Johnny knew Ray was a man to trust. Even drunk, he was a better man than most men Johnny had known. Even fighting mad. Ray had his own rules for fighting: he never fought anybody smaller than he was, and he said he tried never to fight anybody drunker than he was. Johnny wondered just how he sorted that out after he'd downed a six pack or more.

Ray had been there for him even before Matt. Matt Neyerson was a good man; Johnny loved him. But Ray was Johnny's closest friend, and he knew Ray Redeem as nobody else knew him, and he was not about to let Ray down.

The fishing lines tugged outward from the bridge by the pull of the water, their corks moving left, then right, bobbing with the current. A bobwhite called its name from a tree somewhere off to the left of them. Breaking the silence Johnny said, "Did you hear about Bert Snyder's dog?"

"Nope," Ray said absently. Then after a minute, "Which dog?"

"The one that got most of a hind leg cut off by a mower a couple of years back."

"Bummer?"

"Yeah, that's the one."

After a minute Ray asked, "Well, what happened?"

"Bert decided that he should do something to put the poor old thing out of its misery since it had one leg gone and the others were getting so arthritic he or Doreen had to carry Bummer under the porch when it rained or got cold. He was going to shoot him, but Doreen told him he couldn't do any such thing since he knew perfectly well he couldn't hit the Welkes' red barn on a clear day. He hasn't made a decent shot since the gas water heater blew up in his face and singed off his eyebrow and burnt his left eye. She didn't want him just wounding the poor thing; she said that wouldn't be humane. Bert would just have to think of another way."

"Thinking's never been Bert's long suit," Ray said dryly. It was the longest statement Ray had made since Johnny had picked him up in Aunt Naomi's truck. Both of them were still looking out at the water.

"Well," Johnny went on, "he came up with the idea that he could tie Bummer to that pole he stuck in the yard last year when Doreen wanted some place to hang clothes nearer the house—"

Ray interrupted. "Why did he just put up one pole?"

"I don't remember," Johnny said. "He hurt his back or something. You want to hear this story or not?"

"Yeah, sure. Go on."

"Okay, he decided to tie Bummer to the post and tie a stick of dynamite to his back leg. He said he figured it would be quick, and there wouldn't be enough of Bummer left to bury. That way he'd be taking care of everything at once."

"This is supposed to be humane?"

"We're dealing with Bert here."

"John, is this one of Doobie's tales?"

"No, I swear this is true."

They sat in silence listening to the push of the rushing water against the low bridge; then, Ray couldn't resist asking, "So what happened?"

"First, Doreen sent the kids over to Johnson's Store for a Baby Ruth and an RC Cola to get them out of the way. Then Bert gets Bummer all tied up to the post, ties the stick of dynamite to his leg, tells him goodbye, pats him on the head, lights the fuse, and runs back to stand on the porch with Doreen.

"When Bummer sees this fizzing thing shooting sparks around his back end, he starts making like a greyhound after a rabbit. Doreen said she didn't know a dog with only three legs could move that fast. He pulls so hard on the rope his head slips out of the loop, and then he makes a beeline for the front porch and darts under it, getting as close to the house as he can. Bert jumps off the porch, takes a quick look under, sees he's not going to be able to get him out in time, grabs Doreen, and they both run into the yard and wait. When the blast comes, it takes off the entire porch. They just sorta stand there and watch splintered boards landing all around them. The only thing left was the first step to the porch."

Ray had started to laugh. "What happened to the dog?"

"What dog?" Johnny asked.

Ray looked at him for a second, and then they both broke into a fit of laughter.

When it had died away, Ray asked staring out at the water, "You know why I wanted to see you, don't you, John?"

"I think so," Johnny said, watching the cork bob in the water. He knew this was hard for Ray; he was one proud son-of-a-gun.

"You know I don't drink anymore, and I've quit fighting for the fun of it."

"I know that," Johnny said.

"I had to shut those guys up in the bar last Saturday night. They were talking about Alice and that Sample was after her. I couldn't let her be talked about like that."

"I know you couldn't. You did what you had to do," Johnny said.

"Johnny, man, I love this girl. I've never loved anybody like this in my life, and Webster has cut me dead off."

"I know."

A whippoorwill sounded across the water, and a moist breeze blew across their faces.

"I just have to see her; I feel like I can't breathe when I don't."

Johnny nodded, knowing Ray would sense the motion.

"I hate to ask you this; I just don't know what else to do," Ray said.

Johnny waited; he could feel what it was taking for Ray to say this. The muscles in his jaw were so tight Johnny didn't know how he was getting his mouth open to talk.

Slowly, Ray went on, "Alice says she's in a prison, and I'll make it worse if I come back to her place and try to take her out."

"Hope told me Webster threw you out and then told Evelyn he was going to see to it that Alice married Sample. I told Hope you'd never let that happen."

"You can bet your life on that," Ray said, his voice hard. He was quiet for a few minutes.

Johnny asked, "Did you tell Alice what the fight was about?"

"Nope, I just told her some other guys started it," he said; then suddenly jerked his head toward Johnny. His shiner was still riding his cheekbone. "You didn't say anything to Hope, did you?"

Johnny shook his head. "I didn't say a thing to her. I told you I wouldn't."

"I don't ever want Alice knowing those guys were making jokes about her and Sample Forney. Damn this town; everybody knows everything. I should have killed those sons-of-bitches." Ray's free hand was making a fist and the other was clamped tightly around his fishing pole.

Johnny waited a minute before he said, "Now that'd solve everything." He yanked on his pole, thinking he had a nibble, but there was nothing there. "Aunt Naomi would be baking cakes with files in them."

"Have her do that chocolate one with the pecans on top," Ray said, grinning and shifting to pull a foot up and lay his arm over his bent knee. "Damn it, John, Webster's using Alice. She'd do about anything to help Evelyn, and he knows it. It really worries me."

"What can you do about it?"

"The only thing I know to do now is to try to see her as often as I can to keep her spirits up and me on her mind. I don't want Webster to guilt her down into the ground. She's got to know I'm with her even when I'm not," Ray said. He looked at John. "Right now she wants to go to the pie supper with you and Hope and have us all just sorta meet there. That's why I wanted to see you."

"Hope told me, and she wants to do it. She wants to stick by Alice. She said it wasn't Christian to turn her back on her best friend, whether her daddy agreed or not. And you know she likes you. She said you were the only person she ever knew who had walked out the door of the church rather than down to the altar because of something he believed," Johnny said.

"She's mighty brave about this; I know Busby scares her sometimes."

"Busby scares everybody but you, Ray."

Ray smiled. "What about you, John?" Ray asked. "I know Busby doesn't scare you either, except about Hope."

"I don't want him to stop me from seeing Hope, but you'd do it for me; I don't see how I can do less."

"I'm not going to forget this."

"You've got nothing to forget," Johnny said.

Ray nodded; he knew. After a bit he said, "I don't know how you put up with Busby."

"Same as you with Webster."

Ray liked Hope Howard; he thought she was a special girl, but he knew it would take somebody like Johnny to measure up to the law laid down by her father.

"Seems to me, John," Ray said, "we had an easier time of it before Alice and Hope."

"Yep," Johnny said; then he grinned, "but before Hope, I spent a lot of time hanging out with you, and you are plain butt ugly and smell like fish."

"Well, I am butt ugly, but I haven't touched a single fish today." Just then his line jerked and his pole dipped close to the water.

"I think you're about to," Johnny said.

Johnny heard Ray's truck pull up in the backyard. He knew the sound of that engine; it ran smoother than any truck in town. The door of the cab shut solidly, and Ray appeared at his window. "Let's take a ride over to the gravel company in Havana. Jackson wants to order two truckloads." He'd never heard Ray call Jackson, "Dad"; he had called his father Jackson for as long as Johnny could remember. It was Ray's way of putting distance between them. "He's going to lay it on the back road down to the hen house next week."

"How you going to order gravel on a Sunday?" Johnny asked.

"I'll just scribble a note to Corky and stick it in the mailbox."

"Couldn't you just call him in the morning?"

"Sure, but then I wouldn't have something to keep me busy. I can't just sit at the house, and it's better I stay away from the mill. This ain't no morning for me to be working around sharp moving objects. I'd probably lose a hand or an arm."

Ray was proud that all of his extremities were intact. The most he had suffered at work was a couple of bad cuts. Most of the men at the mill had lost a finger, some two.

Jackson had cut the tip off the middle finger on his right hand, and his trigger finger next to it was cut clean off at the second knuckle. He was still known as one of the best shots in the county, working the trigger of his hunting rifle with the stub of what was left.

"Hell, John, the mood I'm in I might even lose something worse."

"Wouldn't be that big a loss, would it?" Johnny asked, throwing the paperclip he'd been using as a bookmark at him.

Ray grinned and said, "A loss to the world, my man. A loss to the world."

Johnny told him, "Aunt Naomi's gone to see about Evelyn. She'll be getting back before too long. I've been laying here just waiting to hear what she has to say."

Ray's smile vanished. "I've gotten you in one big mess, haven't I?"

"I knew what I was doing. None of us knew Webster and Sample would be there, and we sure didn't know that Evelyn would have a stroke."

Johnny knew that Ray was as anxious as he was to know what Aunt Naomi had found out.

"Come on, John. We won't be gone long, and it's better than just sitting here waiting. It'll make the time pass. Then we can both come back and wait."

"You're right," Johnny said, pulling on his sneakers, and tying each one in three expert moves. Then he called down the hall. "Matt?"

"Yep?" Matt called back from the kitchen.

"Will you tell Aunt Naomi I'm going to run over to Havana with Ray, and I'll be back in thirty minutes to an hour?"

"Yep. You boys be careful; you've had a hard night."

"Right," Johnny called before he shut the door and slid out the window, dropping the short distance to the ground. It never occurred to them to use the back door at the end of the hall.

They moved across the yard with oiled joints and strong muscles. The climb to the seat of the truck was an act of grace, and neither of them knew it. Ray turned the key in the ignition, backed out of the yard and swung onto the spur road heading to Route 66, where he'd turn west toward Havana. The windows were open, and the air was early summer sweet and smelled of home. Ray eased the truck lovingly over the railroad tracks and rolled on toward the highway, passing the sign that announced: "Tysen, population 232."

They picked up speed, curving with the road, taking the rolling of the Ozark foot hills with the knowing of their childhood, gliding past large oaks and sycamores, letting the cool Sunday morning breeze flow in from the rolled down windows and the side vents tilted toward them. Ray put a Camel in his mouth and rasped a match against the side of the small box with his right hand, cupping the flame from the wind, steering with his elbows. John was washed over with the tang of sulfur and the bite of cigarette smoke. He felt too worn out to bother with one himself.

"Doobie Pratt came by this morning to borrow a chain saw," Ray said.

"Why'd he want a chain saw? It's his day off."

"He said after all the goings on last night, it seemed too much trouble to go back to the tavern to get drunk, and since this is the first Sunday he can remember not having a hangover, he thought he should do something to mark the occasion."

Johnny laughed. "Doobie probably doesn't remember what Sunday looks like."

Ray rested his left arm on the open window and sighed. "Sunday's always been the longest darn day of the week."

"Sunday seems softer and quieter than other days," Johnny said. He looked out the window at a small field of grain that was just beginning to get a good start; the breeze was tilting it back and forth.

"John, my boy, did anyone ever tell you, you think too much?"

"Yeah, you do. All the time."

"It'll drive you to drink, son; it'll drive you to drink."

"That might be," Johnny told him, "but I don't know how to stop it."

"Could be a real problem for you," Ray said.

"It already is," Johnny said. Then they rode along in silence looking ahead through the windshield for the two miles it took to reach the highway.

When Ray pulled up to the stop sign all geared to turn west onto Route 66, he had to wait for a truck coming from the east that was slowing to make a turn onto the spur. It wasn't until the truck turned directly in front of them that Ray and Johnny recognized Sample Forney sitting proudly at the wheel and Alice Tolney in the passenger seat beside him. For an eternal two seconds, Alice and Ray stared, startled, into each other's eyes; then the truck swung past them and headed in the direction of town and the Tolney farm.

"That son-of-a-bitch! That son-of-a-bitch"! Ray shouted. "Did you see him? Did you see him? Sitting there like he owned her? Like she was supposed to be in there with him? That's the most unbelievable God-damned thing I ever saw." He glared at Johnny. "And Alice! Can you believe that? She was letting him drive her like that didn't bother her one little bit." Ray screamed the last sentence and banged on the steering wheel with his fists. The burning tip of his cigarette flew off and sparks showered across the knees of Johnny's jeans before it landed between his sneakers, and Johnny crushed it out with his toe. More quietly, Ray asked, "What in Christ's name is she doing in there with him?"

Before Johnny could open his mouth to answer, Ray turned the wheel so sharply that the truck spun against the gravel on the shoulder, and they had reversed their direction, gravel flying from behind his right rear wheel.

"Ray, buddy, you can't do this," Johnny said, talking loudly over the wind flying through the windows.

"Yeah? What's going to stop me?"

"You know Alice doesn't want to go anywhere with Sample."

"Then why's she in there?"

"I don't know, but you chasing her down and getting her all upset after the night she's had isn't going to help her a bit."

"Her being with him just ain't right; you know that."

"Okay, you're right. But your chasing them down isn't going to help matters."

"I'm not gonna let that asshole take her alone to the farm. There's no way that's going to happen." He pushed harder on the accelerator.

"She's not going to be alone," Johnny told him.

"Yeah? How do you know? Somebody make you God this morning?"

Johnny could see Sample's truck up ahead; they were really gaining. Ray was racing against time, and Sample was trying his best to slow down the clock; he was enjoying himself. It didn't take a genius to see it would just be seconds before Ray got in front of Sample to cut him off.

"Webster's at the farm, and so is Cloris West."

Ray's foot eased a little off the accelerator as he turned to look at Johnny. "How do you know?"

"Millie Mueller told Matt this morning that she'd overheard it over at the telephone exchange when Cloris called Alvin to tell him that she was going to stay at the Tolney's longer than she'd thought. She was going to make enough food for Webster and Alice for lunch and supper. Slow down a minute, will ya, so I can tell you this?" Johnny yelled. Ray slowed a little more.

"Cloris told Alvin she'd left his lunch in the refrigerator, and he was to go on and eat. She had gone over to feed Evelyn's chickens and water her flowers and fix some food for the family. Alice isn't going to be alone with Sample. Now, let's just let her get on home; she's got to be worn out."

"I just want to be sure he never lays a hand on her. I'll kill him before that happens. I'll by God kill him."

Johnny knew he meant it; he could feel a knot starting in his stomach. Ray wasn't an angry fighter. Through any fight, other than the one he'd had when they talked about Alice and Sample at Harvey's Tavern, he'd never seen him mad. Even then, he wasn't out to kill somebody. Calculatingly sober or drunk on his rear, Johnny had never seen him more than a little ticked off.

Ray reached for another cigarette.

This time Johnny reached for one, too. He'd taken to buying his own, though he hadn't told Aunt Naomi yet. Johnny waited a minute, letting the silence give some bumper room, before he said, "Just don't be going off half-cocked; you've gotta think this through. Alice is not going to be doing anything to hurt you. We'll know a lot more after we talk to Aunt Naomi."

Ray had slowed to ride Sample's bumper. Alice turned to look over her shoulder toward them. Johnny could tell from there how white and drawn her face was. Ray looked at her for a several seconds. "Maybe you're right, I'll wait and hear what Naomi says." Johnny and Naomi, the only two people he'd trusted—before Alice. Without Alice.... Well, he wouldn't even think about that.

He put his foot on the accelerator and pulled out and around them, cutting paper-thin close to the side of Sample's truck. Johnny turned to wave at Alice as Ray went beyond them and swerved back onto his side of the road; she lifted her hand in a motion that looked to Johnny like pleading, but he decided not to say that to Ray who stared at the road as though if he took his eyes away from the blacktop, it would disappear, and he'd have no map to find his way home.

"Let's go have some of Aunt Naomi's coffee," Johnny said, and Ray inhaled on his cigarette and nodded his head. The distance broadened between their back bumper and the front bumper on Sample's truck. Johnny turned once and could barely make out that it was Alice in the seat beside Sample when Ray followed the last curve in the road that would bring them into town.

Chapter Thirteen

Matt poured himself another cup of coffee and carried it and the Sunday paper out to the front porch. An occasional car or truck bumped over the railroad tracks heading toward the river. The stores were all closed, and most everyone was still at Sunday dinner or napping. It was the soft, quiet part of the day that Matt loved; Matt wasn't bound by sermons on both ends of Sunday.

Directly across the track from Matt was the tiny, white Catholic Church; to the right of it, but sitting half-way back on the lot, was Proutty's Funeral Home. For reasons known only to Eugene Proutty, he displayed his big, black, always-polished-and-ready-to-go hearse on Sundays in the driveway of the funeral home, front end forward. Matt had known Eugene Proutty since they were children, and Eugene had always been into death. Matt always thought Eugene was more comfortable around a corpse than a living person.

The sign above the door of the funeral home was in script: "**We Welcome the Dead at All Hours.**" Nobody in town, including Matt, had the vaguest idea why the sign in the first place, or why Eugene had chosen old English script. Matt's best guess was that Eugene had seen something like it in one of the old horror movies he was always going to see.

On the other side of the funeral home, George Wilson sat in his accustomed spot on the front porch of his white house which bordered the road, staring out at the railroad tracks over his black nose cone, looking almost like Death itself. Poor George, the cancer had almost eaten his nose away before the doctors took off the rest of it. His wife, Estelle, made him a nose cone that he wore where his nose should have been. Most folks just pretended it wasn't there, but it was darn hard trying to look him straight in the eye and hold a conversation. George passed his days and many of his nights just sitting there waiting for the trains, talking to folks who came by.

The breeze slipped lightly through the tall oaks in the front yard, and now and again a squirrel knocked an acorn to the ground in a soft bounce. Matt could hear the Mallard's dog barking from the other end of the block, and a mockingbird took a run at being a whippoorwill.

He sat in the swing at the far end of the porch, spread out the Sunday paper and began to read. This was his favorite spot to sit when he was alone. He could check out the town without being completely checked out himself. The lilac bushes in front of the porch gave some protection.

The front page news told him they weren't making much progress on the Brinks robbery in Boston; they still hadn't arrested the robbers. It had been almost four months now. The robbers had taken over three million dollars. Three million dollars! And they actually got away with it. He was still shaking his head over that one. They were robbing armored cars here at home, and overseas they were working toward signing the Warsaw Pact, the East European mutual defense agreement. It was a lot to think about.

There was a lot to think about here at home. He, Matt Neyerson, was in love with Naomi Hollister, and it had just crept up on him, crept up so slowly that he hadn't felt it coming, and, then, all of a sudden, there it was. He'd only realized it about a month ago, watching Naomi cook chicken and dumplings late one afternoon. He'd lifted his cup to sip some coffee, and Naomi turned from the sink laughing about something Bertie had told her, and Matt had thought, I love this woman. I love her, and there's no place on earth I'd rather be than in this kitchen hearing Naomi laugh. It gave him quite a start.

Even then, he was cautious about approaching Naomi. They'd been good friends for such a long time. He knew Naomi was fond of him, but fond didn't constitute love, that's for sure. He'd always been fond of Naomi, but he hadn't dreamed of loving her.

After Beth Lynn had died, Matt had moved himself and his clothing into the back upstairs bedroom of the hotel. It was the largest and airiest of the four bedrooms; Naomi had insisted he take it. She'd asked him if he wanted to bring any furniture, but he'd said, no; he wanted to leave it at the house. His room at the hotel was homey, but not frilly, and it was comfortable enough that he didn't have to come downstairs for anything but meals if he hadn't a mind to.

The pain of losing Beth Lynn had been so much bigger than anything he'd ever known. He couldn't talk about her; he was afraid he would have been washed away in the grief; and there would be nothing left to hold to if the dam broke. It had taken Beth Lynn so long to die, and she'd done it in every room in the house, moving her frail body from kitchen chair, to couch, to bed. There wasn't a place that he could sit or stand or breathe without remembering. They'd had no children, and the house was too haunted for him to live in alone. That's why he'd moved to Naomi's. That's where, after a while, he'd begun slowly to let himself mourn, where he came to realize it was safe to mourn.

On the nights when he couldn't sleep, he'd slip quietly downstairs and sit at the kitchen table, staring out the front windows toward the railroad tracks. The nightlight on the front porch of Johnson's Store cast light enough to see by, even if the moon wasn't out. Sometimes, he sat there till the nightlight went out, and the early dawn light came through the kitchen window, falling first into the sink, then down to the floor, inching its way across to the braided rug under the table, giving the room the pearl glow of early morning. In the quiet, he often thought he could hear the dew slipping down blades of grass; he came to listen for it. Then, before there was any other movement in the house, he'd go back to his bed for an hour and wait for Willie Newman to begin mumbling in his bedroom and bumping his way down the hall to the bathroom. After Willie lumbered back to his room and closed his bedroom door, Matt would kick back the covers, put on his robe, grab his razor and begin to push forward into his day.

Some nights, though, when he was loneliest, Naomi would come down the hall from her bedroom as if the loneliness had seeped under her door and called her. She'd appear in the doorway, knotting the belt of her washed out blue chenille robe, her red hair all a tumble, and ask, "You watching for trains?"

"Yep," he'd say.

"Want some coffee?" she'd ask, and he'd nod his head. Then, without turning on a light, she'd move to the kitchen range, and the blue flame would whoosh up around the old stainless steel coffee pot she kept in action most of the day and had left ready for morning. In cold weather, she'd stick a log into the pot bellied heating stove she'd left stoked that sat to the left of the sink. In the winter, the heating stove often did double duty; while it heated the kitchen, Naomi would often simmer vegetable soup or stew on its top. The kitchen was a comfort place, made fragrant by burning logs and slow cooking food that made you hungry even when you hadn't been.

Some nights they'd talk quietly, counting off the hours by the quarter as the grandfather clock in the hall chimed. If he wanted to come down and sit and read the paper or a book, she just let him be.

They talked when he felt like it. Sometimes, they talked about the weather; sometimes the gossip. No matter what they talked about, she understood; she'd lived alone with her own thoughts long enough. Others, they'd just sit there, the only sound other than the clock, the light clink of their cups against saucers or a match striking to light Matt's cigarette.

After a year or so he came to think of the hotel as home; he spent as much time in the kitchen as Johnny did, probably more. Willie Newman would come in evenings in time for supper. They'd listen to the radio or play a little pinochle until time for bed, Johnny sometimes there and sometimes going off to see Ray. On weekends, Willie used his railroad pass to ride into St. Louis to see his lady friend, Lenore, and have Sunday dinner with his sister. They had the house to themselves, then, Naomi, Johnny and Matt. Matt always thought of Willie as boarding; he, Naomi and Johnny lived there; the two of them had taken him in as family. Last year he'd sold his house, furniture and all, to the Muellers who'd been renting it. He knew he'd never go back.

But it had taken almost three years before he could drive his whole mail route without the memory of Beth Lynn haunting him at some point along the way, only in the last year had she stopped coming. Before that, she'd come in the mornings when he pulled out of Tysen and began his drive down the Old River Road toward the St. John's. The scent of her would sit in the seat beside him until it brought her fully back, and with her, the long, sweet spring nights when the lilac bush sent its fragrance into their bedroom, or the winter nights when the cold wind stung snow against their windows and gradually painted the two of them into their muted, soft world. He best liked those nights when the moonlight slipped easily into the room and he could see her. He'd had to teach her, slowly, carefully, about making love. He'd been the only man she'd ever been with.

He loved everything about his closeness with Beth Lynn, the smell of the shampoo she bought at Johnson's store, the lilac talcum she used after her bath. He loved the length of her beside him, the feel of her, the taste of her. And the tiny catch in her throat when he entered her. He loved it all. It was with her he found that it's what you do after making love that's as important as what you do when. He would lie beside her, running his hands through her hair, gently pushing it back from her face, or he'd place his thumbs in the tired muscles of her shoulders, circling softly, until her breathing changed and she left him in sleep. Then he would slip his body in behind hers, cover them both, surround her with an arm, cup her breast in his hand, and fall asleep. That final closeness that cemented the earlier need, that was like a closing prayer, a kind of Amen.

Matt had known love. He just hadn't expected to know it twice, and he just wanted to be sure he didn't lose a good friend if Naomi didn't feel the same way. He exhaled a deep contented sigh out into the Mayday perfect. Naomi loved him, too. He'd seen it in her eyes, and now she'd told him so. He was a blessed man.

He was reaching for the sports page when Russell came out onto the porch, cup of coffee in hand. He'd gone up to his bedroom to take a rest after Bertie and Naomi drove off.

"Mind if I join you?" he asked Matt.

"Nope," Matt told him, though he'd have rather had time to finish his paper alone. Matt rose from the swing. "Let's move on over to the table and chairs; it'll give us more room."

Russell settled into the chair on the far side of Matt and looked out over the town. He took it in slowly, counting off houses, turns in the road, the curve in the railroad track, the trees and telephone poles. It was all there, just as he remembered. He turned to Matt, satisfied. "Heard from Naomi yet?"

"Nope, but it shouldn't be long. Doc may not let anybody in, and if he does, he won't let them stay long. Want some of the paper?" Matt held out the front page.

Russell shook his head. "I just think I'll just sit here and look around a bit."

"It hasn't changed much since you left," Matt said, and laid the paper down on the porch.

Eugene Proutty came out of the back of the funeral home; he lived in two rooms he'd built on behind, waved a white cloth at Matt and Russell, and began dusting off the hearse that he always kept spit-shined. Eugene thought the hearse worked to emphasize Busby Howard's sermons, added a visual aid for those driving by before and after church.

Russell said, "Good Lord, Eugene is still into death, isn't he?"

"Hasn't changed a bit," Matt said. They both watched Eugene wiping off bits of dust here and there.

"How many animal burials did we go to when we were kids?" Russell asked, putting his feet up on the porch railing.

"I don't rightly remember," Matt said. "More than we should have. We probably helped feed his craziness."

"Probably did," Russell said. "But he did put on a rip-snorting funeral with all his preaching and crying."

"Yeah, but how many times can you bury the same dead squirrel?" Matt asked, shaking his head.

"Gene wanted to do it until the poor thing rotted," Russell said.

"I think he liked them better that way."

"Boy, those things really did stink, didn't they?" Russell asked.

"They did that," Matt said. Both men laughed.

Russell looked across at George Wilson. "What's that on George's face?"

"Oh," Matt glanced over toward George, "guess you wouldn't know that George got skin cancer couple years back, and they had to take most of his nose off. Just left him with two holes in his face. He won't go anywhere except to the doctor when he has to. Estelle made him a nose cone so it would cover the worst of it. That way she could get him to sit outside."

"Is it terminal?" Russell asked.

"Don't know for sure; don't think anybody does. They don't talk about it much."

"Guess none of us really wants to know we're terminal, do we?"

Matt said, "We all know it, Russell; we just refuse to believe it."

After a minute Russell said, "You'd think God would have a better plan than have a person die all eaten up with something, wouldn't you?"

Matt's voice was low when he said, "Yes."

Russell took one look at him and said, "Matt, I'm sorry. I just wasn't using my head. Naomi told me about Beth Lynn, and I'm mighty sorry."

Matt lifted his right hand from the chair arm, moving it slightly back and forth, telling Russell not to worry about it.

Russell rushed to change the subject. "Tell me about what's going on around here." He grinned, "What's Mary Jane Hawkins been up to?"

Like every other boy in Tysen anywhere near their age, Matt and Russell had been initiated into sex first by Mary Jane Hawkins, who would take two boys at a time to the bottom of the small hill behind the Baptist church, lie down flat on the ground, pull her dress up to her waist, and say, "Who ever gets these pants off me will be the first one to ride, and quit just standing there gaping, I ain't got all day." Mary Jane, who was larger and brawnier than any of them, more often than not, bullied them into sex, and she charged them a nickel. But in spite of it, the sight of a female's panties, much less what was beneath them, made them decide that a little bullying might show them in the flesh what they'd been having wet dreams about. After the first time, it didn't take too much bullying. Except for Eugene Proutty, whose eye she blacked when he refused. Eugene ran home, told his mother that Purvis Land, the town bully of Matt's day, had hit him. Then Eugene steered clear of Mary Jane Hawkins.

Matt grinned. "She married Seth Parker about ten years ago, and they have four kids, one right after the other."

"You don't mean it." Russell was genuinely surprised. "I wonder how she got old Seth to marry her? You don't suppose she threatened to beat him up, do you?" Russell asked. Matt laughed. Russell continued, "Wonder if she's charging him a nickel a throw?"

Matt said, "I think it's probably cost Seth a lot more than that." They both laughed.

Russell began to sing:

Mary Jane is a friend of mine.
She will do it anytime.

Matt joined him, and together they sang:

Once for a nickel, twice for a dime,
Fifteen cents for overtime.

Russell punched Matt lightly on the shoulder when they'd finished; it was a gesture that Matt found bridged a good many years. Matt and Russell had fished for their nickels in their overall pockets during the same sessions. They had been equally embarrassed and equally eager, and they both remembered it as a major rite of passage, though neither of them would have called it that.

"How's Josie Mallard?" Russell asked, caught up in their youthful sexual initiations.

Matt grinned. "Josie's Josie; she's not going to change," Matt said. "Except to gain a pound or two, maybe. She never lets them get to her, no matter what they say about her. And she still has that same slow 'I've got your number smile'."

"She's a rare one, all right," Russell said. "And was she a beauty!"

They were quiet for a minute remembering; both acknowledging, in their silence, the fact that they'd each been a willing pupil of a tender and skilled teacher.

Matt didn't know exactly what had gone on between Russell and Josie, but Matt had truly learned about sex from Josie, whose mother, Wanda, ran the boarding house. Wanda had taken in male boarders, primarily Teeler Hawkins; but there had been others, those who had come and gone who had responded to Wanda's hospitality. Josie, who had witnessed more through a hole in the wall of her bedroom covered by a picture of Niagara Falls than Matt had even read about, began teaching him in the back of the feed store after hours. He was fifteen, she was seventeen. She was beautiful then, slim, long brown hair half way down her back. Sometimes, even now, when he went into the feed store, the smell of grain brought a soft brush of remembered lust.

He still had a soft spot for Josie, who now weighed more than two of the one-hundred-pound sacks of grain they had used for their bed. When they'd meet outside the post office, she'd give him a grin and a wink before she hoisted her way inside. Josie never pretended to be anything other than what she was. Which had earned her a dubious reputation in Tysen. Josie wasn't bothered in the least.

"How about Myrtle Bullock? She still being serviced regularly?" Russell asked.

"Twice every week. Course the servicer has changed; she got a newer model, but they kept it in the family. Hubert King turned that task over to Regal King when Hubert married the Widow Tulliver," Matt told him.

Myrtle Bullock was a woman who'd dealt with livestock all of her life, and servicing was a very important part of the business. Make no bones about it; it was a very important part of Myrtle's personal business as well. Her husband had done a fine job in the bedroom. Then one soft

April morning, while the birds sang and warm breezes pushed the sweat from his face, he reached behind his moving tractor for the lever to raise the discs, and his seat gave way. He fell backwards into the path of the discs and became more of a part of his land than he had ever planned

Shortly thereafter, Hubert King became a frequent visitor at Myrtle's farm and did the honors for years until he married the Widow Tulliver; then Hubert told Regal that as much as he'd like to, he just couldn't keep up both ends.

Regal had stepped right up and said he'd be happy to take over his uncle's obligations if Myrtle cottoned up to it. Myrtle said she cottoned; she most definitely cottoned.

Their arrangement was the widest known secret in town, and not a soul dared mention it in public. They especially didn't want Busby Howard to get wind of Myrtle's weekly activities; Myrtle was the best pianist the Baptist Church had ever had, and they knew Myrtle well enough to know that if a word were said to her, she'd have no trouble walking across the street to the Methodists who would rejoice and greatly benefit from the Baptists' loss.

When Busby Howard drew a bead on fornication from the pulpit, ne'er a head turned in Myrtle's direction. It was their duty to keep Brother Howard in the dark on this one. They just decided to live and let live, not judge and be judged, and lifted up their voices joyfully in song to the rhythm of Myrtle's busy fingers running up and down the keyboard.

"If I remember correctly about Regal," Russell said, "he wouldn't mind taking up the task."

"Not even a little bit," Matt responded.

"At least Myrtle could sing you one pretty hymn for a job well done. You might feel so good you'd join in on the chorus," Russell said.

Matt, still in the mood for singing, threw back his head and began to sing in his clear baritone, "Glory, glory, hallelujah."

Russell's tenor joined him. "Glory, glory, hallelujah." They sang the entire *Battle Hymn of the Republic*, added *The Old Rugged Cross,* and went on to *In the Garden.* You would have thought it was church on Sunday evening. Both of them with their heads thrown back, singing up into the air, tapping out the beat with their toes and with their fingers on the arms of their chairs.

The last words were still resting in the oak tree in the front yard when Ray's truck came flying across the railroad tracks, past the hotel, and turned to park in the back. "That was one quick trip," Matt said. "I wonder what happened to bring them back so soon?" At that moment Sample's pickup came into view, slowing to roll carefully over the tracks. Sample raised his hand in a stiff wave to Matt and Russell, and Alice just sat there, looking straight ahead, wide-eyed and worn.

"Now we know what brought them back," Matt said.

"We do?" Russell asked.

"It'll all be clear to you shortly, Russell. If you came back for peace and quiet, you may have to find yourself another town."

Chapter Fourteen

Busby Howard usually tried to take a nap on Sunday afternoons after dinner. Today, he took two Alka Seltzer and sat behind the desk he put in his bedroom so he could work on sermons at home when he could get away from his office at the church. He opened his Bible and prepared to summon his eldest daughter. He was tired, but this couldn't wait.

He'd felt a definite let down when the congregation assembled in front of him at 11:00 o'clock this morning. Naomi wasn't in the choir, and Johnny wasn't sitting with the young people. Naomi never missed church; Johnny either, for that matter. Their absence dulled the edge of the sword he was wielding for the Lord. He would have drawn more blood if he'd been preaching to the lot of them. Well, he'd just have to deal with Johnny and Naomi later. Alice could wait until her mother got a little better, but she wouldn't escape either.

He had not told Hope about his sermon; he'd not even told Helen, but he did tell Helen to make Hope sit with her in church services; he didn't want her back there with the young people. He wanted Hope near the front so the congregation would see he did not spare his own child. He certainly wouldn't spare Johnny Hollister.

He had stood before his members armed with the heat and passion the Holy Spirit had supplied him, and he laid out God's message. Holding his Bible high above his head, he put the blame for the dreadful happenings of last night directly on "those young people here and absent this morning, and an adult member of this congregation who publicly defended them, as well as conspired with them, as they lied and deceived. Those are the people who must face the fact that God punishes us for our sins, a punishment He sometimes visits on those close to us to bring us fully to acknowledge the error of our ways. It is those people who are directly responsible for the condition Evelyn Tolney finds herself in this very morning as she lays unable to move in the Meramec City Hospital." At that point a gasp came from the congregation. Busby felt in that gasp that every person there above the age of accountability, the age at which Baptists could be saved, witnessed the Truth of his words.

Looking often at his daughter, he made sure that every member knew their pastor's stand for God was stronger today than it had been yesterday, even though he'd been sorely tested. He shook the church from rafters to basement. He was on the Lord's side. Where were they? Busby Howard knew that he must truly place the fear of God in them. He had done his duty, he was sure, even though Hope hadn't lifted her head.

Now, he heard Hope come down the hall and stop outside his closed door. He let her tap lightly and made her wait as he opened his Bible to Exodus 20:12, placing the red silk ribbon along the spine of his King James Edition and leaving it open in front of him on his desk.

Hope stood outside her father's door, her chest a tight knot. At that moment she wanted to be anybody else's daughter. In church that morning she'd sat in the pew next to her mother, her hands clenched in her lap, feeling her heart pounding. Her father believed that God sent Evelyn Tolney's stroke because of her. She could hardly breathe with the unfairness of it. Hope spent the forty minutes of her father's sermon with her head lowered and her eyes fixed on the faded blue carpet under her feet. His words rained on her like fire, and there was no place to go. She was frozen with anger and embarrassment. It went on and on and on, and there was nothing to do but endure it. And there was the fear. With God, there was always the fear. God was cruel; she had learned that. All those armies wiped out, cities destroyed, people turned to salt. An eternity spent in fire if you didn't believe the right things. There was no way out.

Her father, too, could be cruel; she'd learned that as well, but this was cruel beyond anything she could have imagined. How could her own father shame her in front of everyone? She wanted her mother to do something, to make him stop, but her mother couldn't help; nobody could when her father made up his mind. Oh, her mother was angry with him all right, Hope could tell that, and she would talk to him about it after church, but it wouldn't change a thing. The most Hope could count on was that her mother would hold her later and would listen. Listening was the only salve Hope would get for these wounds.

Even in such an assault as her father leveled upon her and her friends, even in the midst of her anger, it would never have occurred to Hope to rise as Ray Redeem had risen and walk out of church. As angry as she was, her fear nailed her to the pew. You couldn't walk out when your father was Busby Howard, when your father was the right hand of God.

Now he waited on the other side of the door. She knocked again.

"Come in," Busby said sharply.

She reached for the doorknob. She knew she had disappointed him, had shamed him in front of the entire town, but she hadn't meant to. He had told everyone in church that she was a sinner and to blame for Evelyn's stroke and that God was angry with her. While one half of her thought that couldn't be true, the other half felt it had to be; her father had said so. He was the one that God spoke to.

She had tried to pray, but she didn't know what to say because she couldn't say she was sorry for helping Alice and Ray. She certainly couldn't say she was sorry for standing up for Johnny. She knew God was going to punish her if she didn't ask for forgiveness, and she couldn't ask for forgiveness when she didn't think she'd done anything to be forgiven for. She was so frightened that her teeth felt locked together, as though they really couldn't open when she spoke.

She might even go to hell for loving Johnny Hollister, but she didn't know how to stop. More than that: She didn't want to stop. Johnny Hollister had the sweetest smile Hope had ever seen, and his eyes were blue-green and clearer than the Meramec River. She had known she loved Johnny since the moment in Sunday school when he had reached under her chair for the red lettered edition of the King James Bible, the one her father had given her on her thirteenth birthday, and handed it to her for the Sword Drill, the Sunday test of how many Bible verses you could find and how quickly. When the tips of his fingers had touched the back of her hand, Hope had felt tiny shocks in parts of her body she barely knew were there. It had astonished her and pleased her, maybe even frightened her a little. She hadn't realized until that very minute that she could feel tingly and dizzy because she'd been touched by a boy. No one had told her.

No one in her house ever talked about such taboo things. The word "sex" was never, never mentioned. Her father didn't allow words like "pregnant" or "breast" or any reference to body parts that could be related to having babies or what led up to it. Monthly periods were certainly never mentioned in front of him, and her mother had told her about menstruation in hushed tones and said that she was never to talk about her "monthlies" to anyone. Kotex boxes were hidden away in her dresser drawer, and her mother told her not to use Tampax; they could injure her permanently. She was never told by her mother about having intercourse; her mother just referred to it as "what happens with a man after you're married." She said she'd explain it before Hope's honeymoon; Hope wouldn't need to know before then.

The fact that her body fell open like a book that Johnny Hollister had taken in his hand was brand new and exciting. Being around Johnny was always like riding a roller coaster, but sitting all snuggled in the curve of his strong right arm never made her feel sinful, not when it was happening, even when his hand slid down to her breast. The sensations it brought about were so pleasurable. She never let him go farther than touching her breast. They had a rule about how far he could go, and he always kept his word.

It was not until she was at home in bed and she could hear her father cough in his bedroom that she felt the stomach clench of guilt. What if he knew what she and Johnny were doing? What if he knew that they kissed until their lips were almost raw from kissing and still they didn't stop? What if he knew that Johnny rubbed the nipples on her breasts that brought about quick, spurts of feeling between her legs? What if he knew that they laid close together in the backseat of Matt Neyerson's blue Chevy? It never bothered her that God knew about that; God was far away; God dealt with things when you were dead. She worried that her father would find out.

Now here she was, hand on the knob, and she felt the weight of punishment would crush her right through the parsonage floor and into the basement. She pushed open the door and waited in the doorway until her father lifted his head from reading his Bible and looked at her. Her father's eyes were like hard brown rocks. He could give her a beating with those eyes, make dents in her very skin; he had before, and there had been nothing as serious as this. He nodded with his head toward the chair across from him, and Hope walked to it and lowered herself, holding onto the wooden arms for support; her knees wobbly, perspiration trickling down between her breasts and her legs.

He waited a moment, clenching and unclenching his lips; it was his habit when he was truly angry. He said it kept him from saying something he might regret as a Christian. Then he tapped his Bible with his index finger, drawing her eyes down to the page. He quoted in his sermon voice, "Honour thy father and thy mother: that thy days may be long upon the land which the Lord thy God giveth thee." He stared at her, waiting for her to say something.

She said very softly, "Daddy, I truly didn't mean to hurt you or mother. I promise I didn't." Her throat was so dry she could barely speak.

His eyes never changed. "You've disgraced me."

"I didn't mean to disgrace you, and you know I honor you."

He was silent for what seemed to Hope like an eternity just looking down at his Bible; then he said, "You've disobeyed me so that the whole town would see. Just how do you figure that's honoring?"

"Daddy, I didn't set out to disobey you. It is just that Alice is my best friend, and Ray is Johnny's...."

Busby interrupted, "You know full well that I forbade you to have anything to do with Ray Redeem," he said between clenched teeth. "He's a drunk and a fighter, and he is not fit to be with Christian young people. You knew when you set out to help them that you were doing wrong, and you certainly knew you were disobeying me."

"But, daddy, Ray's changed. He..."

"Ray Redeem hasn't changed," his eyes were blazing now; "he's still the same Godless drunk he's always been."

"But he isn't; he truly isn't," she pled, "and he doesn't fight anymore either, and he wants to marry Alice."

His tone was icehouse cold now. "I don't want to hear anymore about Ray Redeem. He's not fit for any decent young girl to marry. Alice ought to know better than that."

"Daddy, please, she loves Ray."

"Young lady, you listen to me; the Bible says: 'Be not unequally yoked together with unbelievers: for what fellowship hath righteousness with unrighteousness? And what communion hath light with darkness?'"

"Ray believes...," she began to explain.

His upper lip curled back. "Since when have you become an expert on believers? I'll tell you who's a believer and who isn't. You're not qualified to know."

Hope dropped her eyes.

He went on. "I'm so ashamed of you, young lady. You are supposed to be an example for all the young people in this town. Now just look at what you've done. Look what you've caused. Why if you weren't my daughter, I wouldn't even like you. I wouldn't want to have you around." His face was solid; there was not a flicker of tenderness in any line or crease; there was no giving there.

Tears were seeping out of Hope's eyes. She didn't know what to say. If she weren't his daughter, he wouldn't even like her? He was stuck with a daughter he didn't even like? Wouldn't that mean he didn't love her? Had never loved her?

"You need to know right here and now that you've been on your last date with Johnny Hollister."

Even bewildered as she was, the cry came from her before she could stop it, "Daddy! No, please."

"You are not to have anything else to do with him. Not ever."

She was pushed against the hard back of the chair by the thought. All she could think to say was "What about my birthday and what about the prom? I have my dress and everything. Can't we please just go out this weekend? Then I'll never see him again." Hope would be seventeen on Friday, and the Junior/Senior Prom was Saturday night. She and Johnny had had such big plans. She'd been excited for months. Hope was a junior, and Johnny a senior. Her father had reluctantly agreed that she could go to the prom as long as she didn't dance. He hadn't noticed she hadn't promised.

"I said 'not ever,' and I mean just that, and I don't want to have this discussion again. You can just forget about it; there will be no prom for you, and no birthday celebration either. You've got a lot to make up for, and, frankly, at this moment, I'm not happy that you were born."

His words struck her chest with the force of a boulder, and they caused such pain she couldn't stop the tears.

"Here," he said, as though the very sight of her disgusted him, "wipe your face," and he threw his handkerchief across the desk at her.

She pressed the handkerchief to her face with both hands and doubled her body into a wadded ball.

"Stop that right now," he barked at her. "That's not going to help one bit, and you look a mess. Sit up. Behave yourself." He'd turned his face away from her toward the window. "You make me sick."

She pulled herself erect and held her body tightly to try to stop her sobs. Her life was crumbling. There was nothing out there, nothing to look forward to. Johnny would go away to college, and she would only see him during summer vacations; then finally, he would graduate, and then he would just go away.

Her mother would be of little help to her; she was afraid of Busby, too. If Johnny were gone, she didn't know how she could live. She certainly didn't know how she could die. Her father was what she feared here, and God was what she feared if she died. There was no way out; no way at all. Not in this life or the next.

She had to try one more thing, asking softly, a small catch still in her voice, "May I see him just to tell him?"

"No, you may not." The pelting continued. "I'll tell him. I've got quite a lot to say to that young man."

Hope flinched. She could just see her father shouting at Johnny. She wanted at least to warn him, to let him know somehow.

"Another thing: Alice Tolney won't be seeing Ray Redeem again. Webster and I talked this over last night at the hospital. She's not going to have much time for seeing anybody; she'll be spending most of her time taking care of her mother."

"Won't somebody come in to help her?" Hope asked. "Does she have to do it all alone?"

"She'll have help until school is out. Webster said after that he figured Alice could take care of her mother on her own. They can't afford a nurse, and Alice is young and strong. She's perfectly capable of taking care of Evelyn. It's what she owes her parents."

Alice would have all that to do without help, Hope knew. Webster wouldn't help her; she'd never be free. If Evelyn didn't get well, Alice's life was like a jail sentence.

"Will she be at school tomorrow?"

"I don't know when she'll be back. Doc'll have to say."

"May I go to the hospital tomorrow if she isn't?"

"You can go over on your lunch hour, but I want you on that school bus after school."

"Yes, sir."

"And you just remember: you are never to shame me again as long as you live. Do you understand me?"

She felt as if she were stepping into quicksand. "Yes, sir," she said, looking him clearly in the eye. She did understand him. Oh, yes, she understood him.

But she still hadn't promised.

Chapter Fifteen

It must have been twenty minutes or more after they drove in the backyard that Matt and Russell heard Johnny talking in the kitchen. "Johnny," Matt called in, "there's chocolate cake in the cake container on the counter."

"Any pie left?" Johnny called back.

"Only the piece for Doc that's in the refrigerator, and if you touch that, he'll break your arm and not set it."

Russell grinned.

"Guess I won't take the chance," Johnny said. Matt could hear him go on talking softly and quickly to Ray.

"When you get finished eating, you boys might want to come out here with us. Naomi should be getting home any time now, and she'll have news. Might as well tell us all at the same time."

"We'll be out after we finish this cake," Johnny called. His voice went down several notches , and Matt could hear Ray join in.

Just as Matt was trying to decide if he'd interrupt them if he went in for more coffee, he saw Wendell Johnson driving his new black Plymouth across the track down at the far end of town followed by Loncy Oppenmeier in his Oldsmobile. They both turned to come down the street toward them and pulled to a stop in front of the hotel. They were dressed for Sunday evening services: Baptist Training Union at 6:30 p.m. and song service and preaching an hour later. Wendell taught the adult men's class, and Marie taught the young people. Loncy led the singing for the evening service, and Lizzie kept the nursery. They'd all be heading back to church before too long.

The quartet came up the steps, the men herding the women by their arms. "Russell," Loncy said, "we just had to come over and see for ourselves if it was really you." Russell stood up and shook hands with the men and kissed the women on the cheek. If Marie and Lizzie didn't seem quite as enthused as their husbands about seeing him again, Russell never let on.

Matt went to get some folding chairs so they could all sit and to get something cold for everybody to drink. In the kitchen, Ray was looking glum, and Johnny was none too cheerful himself. "Will you young fellas grab those folding chairs from the closet and take them out to the porch? The Johnsons are out there and so are the Oppenmeiers. I'm going to pour some of that iced tea Naomi has in the refrigerator and carry it on out there."

"Why's everybody here, Matt?" Johnny had heard them come up on the porch. It wasn't the habit of folks in Tysen just to drop by on a Sunday afternoon. Most everybody had full days on Sundays, and they did their socializing before and after church services.

"I guess they heard about Russell, and they want to know what Naomi learned about Evelyn."

Ray's eyebrows shot straight up in question marks. "Russell?" he asked.

Johnny slapped his forehead. "What with everything else, it just went right out of my mind. Uncle Russell was here in the house when Aunt Naomi and Matt got home last night."

Ray stared at him. "Just like that?"

"Yep."

"Is he staying?"

"Can't say."

"What do you think?"

Johnny shrugged. "I just want him gone. He's not a part of this family. We sure don't need him."

Matt listened without interrupting.

Ray thought about it for a minute. "What did Naomi say?"

"She hasn't said too much, but she's upset; I can tell. She can't figure out why he's come."

Matt was settting glasses on Naomi's large round Coca-Cola tray. He said, "Russell told Naomi and me he hadn't been feeling well, and he just wanted to come home and rest awhile."

"Do you believe him, Matt?" Ray asked.

"Don't have any reason not to. The man is feeling poorly; you can tell that by looking at him." Matt broke ice cubes out of trays and clinked them into tall glasses. "Guys, can you get those chairs on out there for me? Those folks would probably like to be more comfortable."

They pushed their chairs back and headed for the closet. "You okay now to go out there?" Johnny asked Ray.

"Yeah, but I still say Sample Forney better be watching himself. I'm not taking anymore from him or Webster without a fight."

"As long as you don't want to go a round or two on the front porch," Johnny said, holding out two folding chairs.

Ray jabbed him on the arm and took them; Johnny grabbed the other two. They held the door open for Matt who carried the large tray loaded with five, tall glasses of iced tea, the sugar bowl, spoon and napkins.

"How you boys doing today?" Loncy asked, getting up to unfold the chairs they were carrying. "You both had a pretty big night last night." Marie reached over and patted Johnny on the arm. "From what I hear a long one," she said.

"Yes, ma'am, we did," Johnny answered for both of them. Ray set up the other two chairs and held his peace. Everybody settled in; the boys each hooked a hip over the rail of the porch.

"That was quite a job you did carrying out Evelyn," Loncy told Ray.

Ray shrugged, "She's not very heavy. Not much of a load."

Nobody mentioned Sample Forney or Alice.

Johnny said, remembering, "Uncle Russell, this is Ray Redeem." Ray stood up to shake Russell's hand.

"You're Jackson Redeem's boy?"

"Yes, sir."

"You were just a little thing when I left. Guess you don't remember me?" Russell asked.

"No, sir." Ray wasn't feeling especially friendly toward Russell, but this was Naomi's home, and she didn't take to rudeness.

Matt had distributed all the glasses and was passing the sugar bowl to Wendell as Naomi and Bertie pulled the truck into the driveway. When Naomi saw the group on the porch, she turned off the ignition and didn't bother to pull around back.

Now, that's strange, Naomi thought. Marie and Lizzie both knew she would call them with the news about Evelyn; she'd told them she would. She certainly couldn't fathom why they'd drive over in such an all fired hurry to see Russell. After all, they hadn't been all that happy with him when he took off. Not that a son of Tysen wasn't always a son of Tysen, as long as he hadn't murdered anybody, and even that depended on the circumstances. "Are you all having a party without us?" she asked, as she and Bertie came up the steps.

"No, we just come by to see Russell and thought we might sit a spell until you come home and told us about Evelyn," Loncy said.

"Bertie, why don't you fill them in on what Doc said while I go inside for a minute to see about some cake for everybody." Naomi knew Bertie would love telling, and it would give Naomi a minute to run a brush through her hair and freshen up.

"We'll help," Johnny said, and he and Ray were on their feet.

The three of them disappeared into the kitchen.

Russell was watching Matt as Matt's eyes followed Naomi. It became clearer and clearer with every gesture that they made that Matt was in love with Naomi, and Naomi was in love with Matt. Naomi Hollister, his wife. He hadn't thought those words in a long, long time. His wife. Well, his wife was still a very attractive woman; yes, she was, and she deserved a good man in her life.

Bertie told them everything Doc had told Naomi and her, and she told them about seeing Evelyn and Alice. Then she quietly added what she knew about Sample Forney. Marie gestured with her head toward the kitchen; and the rest of the group nodded. They could hear the voices from inside, though they couldn't make out what they were saying. They'd all wait till later to have their say about Webster and Sample.

Inside, Naomi washed her hands and talked as she sliced cake.

"Did Doc say when they'll know just how bad it is?" Ray asked.

"No, he doesn't know yet, but he did tell Alice that Evelyn would need a lot of care."

"Did you see Hope?" Johnny needed to know.

"No, honey, I didn't, but I'll tell you what; if you two will just wait until everybody leaves, we'll sit down here and talk. I do have some information to pass on, and we don't need to share it with anybody else. They won't be here long."

Ray couldn't wait. "Naomi, do you know how come Alice was riding in Sample's truck?"

I should have known they'd know, Naomi thought. "That was all Webster's doing. He had to go on home to feed the stock, so he called

Sample to come drive her home. She wasn't happy about it. Go on, you two, we'll finish this later like I said. It'll all keep."

Johnny looked at Ray like "see, I told you; she wouldn't have been there on her own." As they went toward the back porch to wait out the crowd, Naomi heard Ray tell Johnny, "I may have to take care of Webster before I go after Sample." The screen door shut on Johnny's reply.

Naomi carried the sliced cake out onto the porch, Matt holding the door for her.

The group settled in to eat. Russell said, chewing a large bite, "Naomi, you're still one fine cook."

There was an awkward silence. Lizzie wondered if Russell thought about Naomi's fine cooking when he climbed on the train the day he left. He probably didn't think at all, she thought. Probably thought, too, that she'd always be there just waiting for him. Just like a man to think whatever world he left would stop in place, frozen, 'til he came back and breathed life back into it. After a long moment, Wendell took up the slack and said, "She sure is." Everybody assented.

Bertie finished her cake, said goodbye, and hustled off the porch to go give her family the news. Brown puffs of dust sent smoke signals from her heels as she moved across the street.

The men turned to talk of Russell's travels and the railroad and who was dead and who had left town. Nobody asked Russell why he had left. Marie and Lizzie would have been antsy in their chair with curiosity if they hadn't had so much else on their minds. Wendell and Loncy didn't seem all that curious about what had made Russell leave; they just figured he had finally come to his senses and come home. Lizzie told Marie that it seemed to those two like Russell had just gone out for cigarettes or a paper and been gone for twelve years. Now he was back, and that was that. Of course, Wendell had said to Marie, though she didn't tell Lizzie, that Russell's return might pose a few problems. Marie had nodded; at least, he hadn't been so blind he hadn't noticed what even Naomi and Matt had just begun to realize.

The Johnsons and the Oppenmeiers weren't there because Russell Hollister had decided to come home; they would have seen him soon enough. Russell was just their excuse. They were there because Naomi Hollister was their good friend, and Wendell and Marie doted on Johnny. The Oppenmeiers had called the Johnsons after they got home from church and asked if they could come by around 3:00 for a talk.

The Oppenmeiers needed to know if the Johnsons were thinking like them, thinking that the preacher had gone too far.

The four of them had decided that while in the past they'd always stood square behind their preacher on doctrine, this time, in their opinions, Pastor Busby Howard was just flat out wrong. No matter what he'd said in his sermon that morning, it didn't seem to any of them that the Lord had singled out those four young people and held them responsible for Evelyn's stroke. "That stroke was no doing of the Lord's," Wendell had said, and Loncy had said, "Amen."

Lizzie said, "He should never, never have said what he did about Naomi; it just isn't right. Even though he didn't mention her name, everybody knew who he was talking about." All four heads shook in agreement.

There were those folks who would side with the preacher and agree with every word that came over the pulpit; that was their right. The Johnsons and the Oppenmeiers respected Busby Howard, but he did not strike fear in their hearts, and while they felt sure that the Lord inspired him again and again, they believed fully that Busby Howard was not the only person in Tysen in tune with the Lord. He was a good man, but nobody was perfect. This time, Loncy had said, he'd missed the mark. Wendell decided not to tell Loncy something he'd learned in studying to teach the men's Bible class: that "missing the mark" was the definition of sin.

Now, on Naomi's front porch as the men talked on, Marie and Lizzie exchanged glances; they had been designated by their husbands to tell Naomi what had happened before someone else did; they also wanted her to know what they thought about the preacher. Marie, touching Naomi's arm, asked, "Naomi, would you get your upside-down cake recipe for Lizzie and me while we're here?"

The women eased out of their chairs and into the kitchen. Once in the kitchen, Marie said, "Let's sit down for a minute. Why don't I get us all another glass of tea, and we can talk a minute without the men?"

Naomi sat down with a sigh. "You all talked me into it. It's been a long day. Poor Evelyn; she looks just awful. I hope and pray she comes around. It sure doesn't look good right now."

Lizzie said slowly, "I know you've had a long day and last night was such a scene, and then to come home to find Russell here after all these years, you must not know if you're coming or going."

Naomi took a long sip and sighed gratefully. "I don't; I really don't."

"Well, I hate to have to add to your plate when I know you've already got more than you can say grace over, but there's something we think you should know about," Lizzie said. Marie nodded in agreement.

"What in the world is it?" Naomi wanted to know, looking worried. "What's happened?"

"It's Busby Howard," Lizzie said. She paused a minute and took a deep breath, "He preached a sermon this morning about what happened to Evelyn last night."

Naomi looked relieved. She had thought it was something bad. "I suppose everybody wanted to know about how she was. He was at the hospital with Webster most of the night."

"Well, yes, they did want to know how she was, but that wasn't exactly what Busby preached about." Lizzie stopped to clear her throat.

Naomi looked puzzled.

"He preached on why Evelyn had the stroke," Lizzie continued.

"He preached on high blood pressure?" Naomi asked.

Lizzie shook her head. "Not high blood pressure." She took a deep breath and swallowed. "Busby said that Hope and Johnny, along with Alice and Ray, brought about Evelyn's stroke."

Naomi wasn't sure she had heard right. "He said what?"

"Busby said God struck down Evelyn because the kids had sinned; they had lied and deceived God."

"They'd deceived God? How could anybody deceive God?" Naomi asked.

"Well, that wasn't really clear to me," Lizzie told her, "but Busby was preaching right at Hope, and he said right out that they'd deceived him, and they'd deceived God."

"God caused Evelyn's stroke because they deceived Busby Howard?" Naomi asked.

Lizzie nodded. "He said God sometimes punished the innocent in order to punish the guilty."

Naomi looked a question at Marie; not that she doubted Lizzie; she just needed more confirmation. Marie nodded.

"Why would God punish the innocent to punish the guilty?" Naomi asked. "That doesn't make sense. And who is Busby Howard to say those children are sinners? There is no way on this earth he can know what's on God's mind. Sometimes, Busby thinks he's more than mortal." Naomi's sigh was full of concern; the young people shouldn't be treated this way.

"He was on a real rampage," Lizzie said, "shooting hell fire and sparks all over the congregation."

"Lizzie," Marie cautioned.

"Well, it's true," Lizzie said with more than a little asperity. "And that's not all."

"Not all?" Naomi didn't know what more there could be.

"He said anybody who knew anything about it and didn't tell him was responsible, too." Lizzie blushed when she said it.

Naomi felt like she'd been slapped across her face. "He means me," she said dumbfounded. "He was preaching about me as well as the kids. He believes it's my fault, too, that Evelyn is paralyzed in that hospital bed."

"I'm afraid so," Marie said quietly. "We're awful sorry he said that, and we've come to tell you that we think he's done a wrong thing."

Lizzie reached over and took Naomi's hand in hers.

Naomi said, almost to herself, "He said all this from the pulpit without saying a word to Johnny or me. After all these years we've been faithful to that church. I've rarely missed a Sunday in the choir, and Johnny never misses." The women nodded. "I've cooked enough meals there to feed three counties." They nodded again. "And he doesn't do me the courtesy of coming to me first?" They shook their heads.

"This is going to break Johnny's heart. He loves that church. You remember the Sunday that Johnny was baptized down at the river before they built the new baptismal pool in the sanctuary?"

"Uh-huh," Lizzie said.

"We sure do," Marie agreed.

"I knew Busby was mad when he wouldn't listen to me last night, but I never dreamed. Never." She shook her head; there was too much to sort out all at once. She didn't know which piece of string to try to unknot first.

Lizzie said, "We knew you'd find out first thing tomorrow, and we didn't want somebody telling you about it, and you not be prepared."

"The thing is, Naomi," Lizzie went on, "Busby truly believes what he's saying and that makes him a hard man to convince, and you know how he is about Hope, and even about little Grace. He expects them to toe the line. If they stray, he's failed in some way. We think he's trying to make sure the congregation doesn't look on him as a failure."

"But that doesn't make it right, Lizzie," Naomi said.

"Oh, honey, we know it don't. That's why we're here. We just wanted you to know we don't agree with him. We love you, and we love those kids; that includes Ray. They've just done what kids do."

"He made Hope sit up beside Helen, and he preached right at her," Marie told her.

"Dear Lord," Naomi said. "Poor little thing." There was silence in the room. Nobody knew what to say. Finally, Naomi said, "How am I going to tell Johnny?"

They shook their heads.

"I'm not so worried about Ray; he knows how to deal with Busby, but Johnny and the girls?" Naomi shook her head.

"You'll figure something out, and we'll help in any way we can," Lizzie said.

Marie patted her shoulder. "Surely, it will all blow over soon. Maybe Busby will realize the kids were just helping out their friends. Maybe he'll forgive them and won't hold it against you."

Naomi said, looking into her watered-down glass of tea, "The real question now is: How can I ever forgive Busby Howard?"

Chapter Sixteen

When the Johnsons and the Oppenmeiers had no more than turned the corner, making their way toward church, Russell said he thought he'd go lay down for a spell. Naomi told him to rest, that she'd call him later for supper. They weren't having much, she said, just ham sandwiches and some coleslaw; they'd have the rest of the cake for dessert. That suited him just fine, and he left Matt and Naomi in the kitchen.

Matt would have noticed that Russell was looking mighty peaked if he hadn't been taken up with the drawn expression on Naomi's face. "What is it, Naomi?"

"Everything," she said, and began to cry, the tears flooding her face, running into the corners of her mouth and dripping off her chin. She covered her face with her apron. Matt had never seen her cry before, not ever. Finally, she was able to say, "I'm sorry, Matt. It's just I'm tired, and hurt, and madder than I've ever been in my life, and I don't know how in the world to handle all of this."

He knelt beside her chair and put an arm around her, "Don't cry. We'll work something out. Whatever it is, there's got to be something we can do. Just tell me what's wrong."

She put her head on his shoulder and sobbed wetly into the collar of his blue denim shirt.

That's how Doc found them when he came through the front hall and into the kitchen, stopped short by the sight. Matt looked up at him, and Doc mouthed, "What?" Matt shook his head that he didn't know.

"Naomi," he said softly, "Doc's here."

She wiped away her tears with the apron she'd forgotten to take off earlier and lifted her head. "Sit down, Doc," she said. "I'm sorry; I didn't mean to let go like that."

"Whatever it is, Naomi," Doc said, "it must be something damned important."

"Where are the boys?" she asked, taking a last dab at her eyes and looking down the hall toward the back porch.

"Still out back, I think," Matt said. "You want me to check?"

She nodded.

Doc moved across the room to pour himself a cup of coffee. "You want some more tea?" Doc asked her over his shoulder.

"Please," she said, her voice still wet.

"They were in Johnny's room; they're both sound asleep," Matt said as he came back into the kitchen. "Each one spread out across Johnny's bed."

"Good," she said. "They need the rest." Naomi was calmer.

Doc had his head in the refrigerator looking for his pie.

"It's back behind that gallon of milk where I hid it," Naomi told him.

"Enjoy that, Doc; I saved you two pieces," Matt told him.

"I intend to lick the crumbs off the plate," Doc said.

Doc placed the pie on the table, sat at his accustomed place and cut into it with the same care he'd use in surgery.

Naomi asked, "Evelyn any better?"

Doc was intent on swallowing. "Lord 'a mercy, that's good," he said before he turned his mind to Evelyn. "Not yet; change will come slowly. We should know more in the next couple of weeks." He went back to his pie, forked up a king-sized bite and said as it made its way to his mouth, "Now, Naomi, what's got you so upset?"

When she'd finished telling them, Matt said, "Damnation!" something Naomi had never heard him say before, and Doc slammed his fist on the table, "Why that narrow-minded, bigoted, son of seven fathers. That megalomaniacal, egotistical, solipsistic jackass."

"I don't know what you just said, Doc," Matt told him, "but I bet I agree."

Naomi said. "I just can't fathom how Johnny's going to deal with all this: to find out he and his friends have been denounced in church and held responsible for Evelyn's stroke. What on earth will that do to him?

And Ray and Alice? Then there's Hope." Tears came back in her eyes. Neither of them had seen her look so defeated.

Doc said, "You've got to keep in mind, Naomi, that they're young, and they've got far more bounce to them than we give them credit for. They've all got fight in them. We know for sure Ray does."

"Fight is something I do have, Doc." Ray was standing in the archway. "What is it I need to fight about?"

"Is Johnny awake?" Naomi asked him.

"Still out like a light. What are you talking about? Last night?"

"Naomi is talking about this morning," Matt said. "Seems Busby Howard is out to make examples of all of you. Spent his sermon on it. He accused the four of you young folks of bringing on Evelyn's stroke. He even…." Naomi kicked him under the table and shot him a look. The last thing these kids needed was to deal with her problems. They had enough to balance.

"He what? That's crazy even for Busby," Ray said.

"The fool's made all kinds of crazy accusations," Doc said.

"Do you know he made Hope sit with her mother at the front of the church and proceeded to preach right at her. She really got the brunt of it since nobody else was there," Naomi told him.

"That's just like him. He's so damned—sorry, Naomi— filled up with himself he can't see anybody else. I don't give a whit what Busby says about me; he's been after me since I walked out on him, but I do care when he goes after my friends. This is too much; I'm going to have a talk with the preacher."

"You'll just make things worse," Naomi told him. "I want your word that you'll stay away from Busby. I mean it! There's too much at stake for Hope and Johnny. I want you to promise me." Naomi looked so upset that Ray walked over to kneel beside her.

"If it means that much to you, Naomi, I'll give you my word," he said.

Matt said, "It'll be dealt with Ray, you don't have to worry about that."

"This is gonna hit John hard," Ray said. "Busby'll make sure that Hope doesn't have anything else to do with John, you can bet your life on that, and he's shamed him in front of the whole church." Ray shook his head. "John wouldn't be in this fix if he hadn't tried to help me and Alice. Hope either."

"Now, stop that. You can't take all the blame for this," Naomi told him. "Johnny and Hope knew what they were doing."

"I shouldn't have asked them to take the risk," Ray said. "I know what Busby is like. He's used me as his best bad example all these years. He wasn't gonna let that go."

"What does your daddy have to say about Busby being after you?" Doc asked.

"Jackson never talks to me about much except work." Ray's face was tight.

"I imagine," Doc went on, "that he might have something to say about this."

"If he does say anything, he'll probably side with Busby. Don't see why things will change any now."

"Don't count on it, son. He might surprise you," Doc said.

Ray didn't look like he held much hope of that.

Doc said, "Ray, about Alice, remember that she's is mighty worn out right now. You be there for her, but try not to push anything. Alice's got a big job in front of her."

"I wouldn't do anything to hurt Alice, Doc. I love her and I aim to marry her. I can wait." Ray was certain, standing there so solid in his jeans and t-shirt, that his loving Alice took care of everything.

Doc had given enough doses of discouraging news in the last few days; he wasn't about to burst any balloons just now with a dose of realism, so he just said, "I know you're both set on being together, but right now she's mighty scared about Evelyn. Just go easy. We'll know more about Evelyn's condition in a week or two."

"I'll go easy with her, Doc, I promise, but I can't say the same for Sample Forney or Webster if they start something again. Sample better keep his distance from Alice. Webster don't need to think that he can wedge him in there while Alice has her back turned taking care of her momma. I ain't standing still for that."

"Well, stand still long enough that Alice knows which end is up, okay?" Doc asked.

"I can do that," Ray told him, "at least, I think I can."

Naomi broke in, "Alice said for me to tell you that she'd be in touch with you as soon as she could, and for you to remember what she'd told you."

Ray grinned. "Yes, ma'am." It was the first time he'd look happy since last night.

"I take it you don't have any trouble remembering just what it was Alice told you?" Matt teased.

"Nope, not a bit."

"I called Mary Jo from the hospital. She'll call there early in the morning. You want something to eat?" Naomi asked him. "You haven't had much today."

"No, thanks. I think since John is asleep, I'm going to go on home, but will you tell him I'm at the house if he needs me?" Naomi nodded. "And tell him I'm sorry, Naomi, please. I'm so sorry. I wish I could take it all back somehow."

"I'll tell him, but I want you to quit blaming yourself. Now, you take some cookies home with you; you'll want something to eat a little later." She put half a dozen cookies into a brown paper sack.

The aroma of the cinnamon and raisins on the seat beside him and the thought of talking to Alice lifted his spirits. For a few minutes, with the pine-scented wind blowing into the cab and the response of the truck to his hands, he almost felt happy; then he thought of what Aunt Naomi was about to tell John.

In the kitchen Naomi said, "I'm not going to gain anything by putting off telling Johnny. I'll be back to fix us some supper in just a bit. You'll stay won't you, Doc?"

"When did I ever turn down a meal here?"

"Never," Matt said.

Doc ignored him. "Go tell Johnny and take your time. Matt and I are fine right here. Besides, I want to tell him what happened when I went to talk to that fool Webster Tolney last week." When Naomi hesitated, Doc said, "Go on now; Matt will tell you later, and Johnny needs you."

She nodded and started down the hall.

Matt asked, "What did happen at Webster's, Doc?"

"I went upstairs to check on Evelyn, gave her some more cortisone, and told her she wasn't to get out of bed. Then I went back down to the kitchen to tell Alice about her momma. Alice was just taking a peach pie out of the oven, and I could tell she'd been crying. I got her to sit down and talk to me."

"You didn't sample any of that peach pie, did you, Doc?"

"Sample it? Hell, no, I had three pieces." Doc frowned at Matt. "You want to hear this story or not?"

"I do," Matt said, and laughed.

"Alice was all upset about Webster. She told me that Ray came out to pick her up for a date, and Webster threw him off the place, telling him never to come back because Alice was never going to marry him; Webster had other plans."

"That must have gone over real good," Matt said.

Doc nodded. "Webster shouted, Ray shouted, Alice cried, Evelyn cried; and then Webster tried to push Ray out the door."

"Ray wouldn't stand for that," Matt said.

"No, not normally, but Alice asked him not to hit her daddy, and he didn't. He just banged the screen door so hard a hinge came loose, and he must have scattered gravel all the way to town."

"Did you get a chance to talk to Webster?"

"I did. I went right down to the field where he was playing at plowing, and I talked. Did Webster listen? Hell, no, he didn't."

Doc Barnes had driven slowly over the rutted path that led to the field where Webster was plowing, turning over the old earth, exposing the new. It was almost too late to put in corn, but it would still be ready for picking in time if he got it planted in the next week or so. He spotted the old Case tractor coming toward him, slowly advancing down the row, its red faded to a crusty brown. No more than half the field had been plowed, and it was almost noon.

Webster scooted a hand toward Doc in a shallow wave, and Doc let the car roll to a stop and turned off the engine. He would just sit there a spell, enjoy the breeze coming through the windows and wait for Webster to inch his way toward the road. He could still taste Alice's peach pie; the memory floated lightly on his tongue.

Webster finally came to a stop at the edge of the field some twenty feet away from Doc's car and turned off the ignition; the engine chugged on for several seconds before it coughed and died. He slid his lanky body off the metal seat and let himself drop to the ground behind a light cloud of smoke put forth by his Lucky Strike. Webster must smoke three packs a day, Doc thought, as he opened the door and got out of the car. I've never seen the man without a cigarette at the corner of his mouth. Webster's overalls were hitched up high on his shoulders. They were always too big for him; he seemed to have airshafts on both sides under his arms, and the overalls floated along with him, rather than rode next to his body. He looked like a man put together by hinges, and he moved as though he needed oiling.

"Morning, Doc," Webster said, nodding at him.

"Morning, Web. Getting ready to do some planting?" Both men looked out at the half-plowed field.

"Yep. Thought I'd put in a little corn."

Doc nodded. "Think it'll come in in time?"

"Ought to." Webster examined the sky from beneath the bill of his Case gimme cap, looking at it as though it determined the time it would take to plant. "I'll have it in the ground by tomorrow evening."

Doc doubted that tomorrow's sun would set on a fully seeded field.

"You out making calls?" Webster asked, still looking at the field.

"Yep. Came by to check on Evelyn."

"Think she's any better?" Webster let the smoke drift out of his mouth. The ash on the tip of his cigarette burnt grey and curled slightly downward. Doc couldn't help watching it grow and hang there past the point of logic.

"Bout the same," Doc said.

"When you think she'll be back to herself?" Webster looked in Doc's direction.

"It'll take time for her to improve some. Alice's going to bring her in to see me at the office in a few days. I want to give her a good going over."

"Won't be too costly, will it?" Webster took the cigarette from his mouth for the first time since he'd climbed down from the tractor. "Times ain't good now."

"No, they aren't. They're bad for a lot of people."

"Yeah, Doc, but Evelyn's sicker than most women; she never seems to get no better no matter what she takes. Seems like a waste of good money most times."

Doc could feel his jaw tighten. "It'll cost what it'll cost, Web. She needs seeing to."

"Don't do more than you just have to, Doc. If I had enough money wouldn't be so bad." Webster had let his cigarette fall to the ground, crushing it under his work boot and reached for another one from the bib pocket in his overalls. He struck a match with his thumbnail, ducked his head to get to the flame, inhaled deeply and took the cigarette from his mouth to flick a piece of tobacco from his tongue.

"Hell, Webster, who do you know has enough money?"

Webster said, still appraising the field, "Sample Forney, for one."

Blessed Jesus, Doc thought, will the man never stop pissing in the wind? "Sample does have money; he's made it from his land. He's a hard man, but I'll give him this: he's sweated damned hard for what he's got."

"If a man had just a piece of what Sample has, he could make himself some real money." He rolled the cigarette to the other side of his mouth. "It would give a body a real start." Webster looked off over the field toward the grove of trees on the other side of his property line as though he envisioned owning it and all that lay beyond toward the river.

"You got something in mind, Webster?"

"Just thinking bout making some improvements hereabouts."

"What kind of improvement?"

"Thinking about adding some land, putting in some more crops."

"Land's expensive. How you going to manage that when times are hard?"

"A fellow can always make a deal."

"Webster," Doc couldn't wait any longer, "are you actually thinking about trying to trade Alice to Sample Forney for some land?"

"What are you talking about, Doc?"

"You never could keep you mouth shut, man. Did you think the men in the tavern you were spouting off to wouldn't say anything? The whole town probably knows by now."

"The whole damn town can go to hell as far as I'm concerned. Ain't nobody's business but mine." His face set hard. "It ain't none of your business either."

"I'm making it my business. Alice isn't a piece of your property. You're actually talking about selling your youngest child to a man who will use and abuse her, and you damn well know it. How can you even think about it, much less try to force Alice in his direction? Have you lost your mind?"

"Nothing wrong with my mind, Doc. Sample ain't gonna hurt Alice none. He'll give her a good home, and she'll have everything she needs. And as I said before, it ain't none of your damn business."

"Bull shit! It is my business. I brought the child into the world, and I've got an obligation to care about her. And as far as Sample goes, you're the one who'll have everything you think you need, and you don't care what you have to do to get it."

Webster pulled his skinny body up to his full five feet seven inches and brought his anger with it. "I got a right to have something before I die. Alice owes me," he spit out; then added as an afterthought, "She's owes her momma, too. We already lost one daughter."

"Lost, hell. You drove her away. And you're going to drive Alice away from here as surely as you're puffing on that cigarette. If she has any sense, and she does, she'll run like crazy just like Mary Jo."

"I won't let her run; she ain't eighteen yet. I can keep her at home till then. She ain't thinking about nobody but herself. She just wants to hang around Ray Redeem and get herself all messed up so that nobody else will have her. It's better that she has a good solid husband that don't spend his time running around drinking and fighting."

"No, Sample doesn't drink or he doesn't fight, but he's put two wives in the grave and run off another one. Sample thinks of women the way he thinks of a field: you plough 'em and plant 'em. You want that man to climb in bed with your little girl and use her the way he's used the others?"

Webster didn't answer; he looked out at the field, his face rigid, his cigarette smoldering.

"Hell, Webster, the man is built more for a brood mare than a young girl like Alice."

"All that's talk, Doc. There ain't no truth in it," he said, still not looking at Doc.

"You know it's true. I know it's true. I've seen with my own eyes what's happened to the others. You can't do that to Alice."

"I can do what I damn well please. And I will. Nothing's going to happen to Alice. I will see to that."

"Now, that's just talk, Web. There won't be a thing you can do. And you know it."

Webster turned to look at him, "Now, I got me a field to plow. You best go where you're needed."

"You're a damn fool, Webster. You go ahead and plow your field, but I'll tell you this, you put your hand to this plow and there is no turning back; this is one time you are going to reap a helluva lot more than you sow."

As he backed his car into a small clearing to turn around, he glanced over at Webster Tolney who had turned his tractor to start plowing back across the field. Doc's anger felt like a heat field around him. He'd been foolish to try. There was no talking to Webster Tolney; it was more senseless than talking to Doobie Pratt past seven o'clock on a Saturday night.

"Doc?" Matt asked, jarring Doc back to the present.

"Oh, sorry, Matt," Doc said. "The long and short of it is he didn't pay attention to a word I said. You can't reach the bull-headed son-of-bitch by talking to him. We're going to have to find another way."

"We'll all put our heads together, Doc. We'll tell Naomi, and then we'll all work something out," Matt said.

"I told Alice at the hospital not to let Webster try to sway her by telling her that Sample could help her mother more than Ray. I don't think she knew that the Redeems are every bit as well off as Sample Forney," Doc said.

"Alice wouldn't care enough about money to even think that way," Matt said.

"No, but her daddy might try to twist things so that Alice thinks she'd harm Evelyn by marrying Ray. I wanted her to know what Ray has to offer her momma, and to not forget it."

"I see your point," Matt said and went to the stove to put on another pot of coffee.

Naomi wished the hall were longer. Not that it would make any difference if it ran from here to the river. She still wouldn't know how to tell Johnny he'd lost his girl, and, even more, though he wouldn't grasp the fullness of it for a while, he'd been deprived of solace in the one place other than home he'd found it since he was a baby. How could he go back to Busby Howard's church and feel comfortable? And would he even know how to stay away?

Johnny had always been a child of faith; he'd seemed born with it. Naomi thought this was a special gift to make up for what had been taken away. To Johnny, God was as real as the wind. Church was his other home; the people there had made up the rest of his family. Like Naomi, they'd always been there.

She closed her eyes and prayed, "Help me, Lord"; then she turned the doorknob and quietly opened the door. Hope and Johnny were sitting on his bed, their arms around each other. Hope was sobbing, her head on his shoulder, and Johnny's face was buried in her hair. It would be months before Naomi would find out that Helen Howard had helped her daughter to slip away from Training Union so that she could tell Johnny what Busby had said. Hope, like Ray, had come through Johnny's window.

Neither of them saw her. Looking at them, Naomi was relieved. Right now, Johnny needed Hope more than he needed Naomi. And, Lord knows, Hope needed him. Let them talk it out and work it through the best they could. Naomi would always be there; she'd be standing by. He'd need her later. She wondered as she looked at them where Hope would turn.

Naomi closed the door silently and had turned back toward the kitchen when she heard Doc say from down the hall, "Great Caesar's Ghost! Russell Hollister. When did you get back in town?"

Chapter Seventeen

Naomi drove Russell to see Doc Barnes on Monday. Doc had looked Russell over when he sat down across the table and knew why Russell had come home. After they'd finished their coffee, he'd said, "Russell, if you'll stop by the office tomorrow, I'll give you something that will help with that cough." Russell had thanked him and said he thought that would be a good idea. Naomi was busy stacking dishes in the sink, but Matt saw the contract that Doc had just sealed with Russell: come see me tomorrow, and I won't say anything until you're ready.

Naomi knew Russell needed some medicine other than what he had; she could hear him coughing even from downstairs in the middle of the night. She knew that cough must shake his bed; it rattled through the halls and down the stairs, and she was surprised the men slept through it. You could run a train over Johnny when he slept, but she thought Matt or Willie would have been jarred by the sheer force of it.

She dropped Russell off at Doc's office and went on to the hospital to see Evelyn. Alice was there, sitting beside her mother, holding her hand. She motioned Naomi outside so they could talk.

"I talked to Mary Jo just a little while ago, and she said she would be out weekends to see Momma. She'll come when Papa's at home and spend the nights with her. "

Naomi voiced concern. "Are you sure your daddy won't see her? It might upset Evelyn if he starts in on Mary Jo."

"Papa won't be here on weekends. He's already told me he'd have to work weekends at Sample's to make up for time lost."

That's Webster, Naomi thought. He never lets anyone get in the way of his going after what he wants. But she said, "It will be especially nice for your mother to have both of her girls here with her. It will be good for you, too, honey."

Alice smiled. "Yes'm, it will. I talked to Ray earlier, too. We'll work something out so we can see each other; we just have to be patient." There was pink in her cheeks again.

"That is good news," Naomi said.

Alice blushed nicely. "You can go in and see momma if you want. I'll just run across the street and get a soda if you're going to be here for a few minutes," she said.

"Take your time; I'll be right here." Naomi waved her along and quietly slipped into the room. She picked up Evelyn's right hand, and Evelyn opened her eyes. She focused in on Naomi, and tried to move her face in what Naomi thought was an effort to smile. Her lips lifted on the right side, but the left side just couldn't manage it. "I came by yesterday, but you were sleeping," Naomi told her. Evelyn moved her head slightly and made two sounds that Naomi swore came close to "I know."

Naomi patted her hand and said, "Good," which she thought would cover whatever Evelyn was trying to say. "Alice ran over to get a soda pop; she'll be right back. I know you're right glad that Mary Jo is coming to see you."

Evelyn tried to move her head up and down. Naomi said, "Now don't wear yourself out trying to talk, we've got all the time in the world. Doc said things are looking real good; you just need to rest. He should have you home in a few days." Naomi felt pressure on her hand again.

They sat there in silence for half an hour, Naomi holding Evelyn's hand.

When Alice came back with her coke, she was smiling, and Naomi thought she'd probably called Ray. Alice went to the other side of the bed and began smoothing the hair off Evelyn's face. "We need to brush your hair, Momma," she told her and reached into the drawer for the brush she'd brought from Evelyn's dressing table. "Do you think you'd like a little soda pop?" Evelyn tried to move her head from side to side, but was too tired out; she closed her eyes as Alice ran the brush through her hair.

"I'm going to go now," Naomi told her softly. "I'll be back tomorrow."

"Give my love to Johnny, and thank him for coming to the hospital with Ray," Alice said.

"Course I will," Naomi said and left with a wave.

When she picked up Russell, she noted he had several bottles in the brown paper sack Doc had given him. They didn't talk much until Naomi turned off the highway and headed down the blacktop.

"Naomi, I know you have a lot of questions, and you have every right to answers."

"Yes, I certainly do, but you're not well, and I've got my hands full. I need to get rid of some of this other load before we get into all that."

Russell wasn't sure whether to be more concerned or relieved. "How was Johnny this morning?"

"He didn't have much to say," Naomi said. "He gets that way when he's thinking. He'll talk when he's ready."

"I guess it kind of runs in the family," Russell tried at a smile.

Naomi kept her eyes on the road.

After a few minutes, Russell said, "I've always thought it strange that bad things seem to come in bundles; we never get them one at a time."

Naomi shot him a quick side-glance. It had never occurred to her that Russell would think about such things.

"You'll handle it, Naomi. You could always handle everything."

She felt a shock of surprise. "Why in Heaven's name would you think that?" she wanted to know.

"Because you always did," he said matter-of-factly.

She took her eyes from the road for a minute to look at him. "Russell, what you saw on the outside was all you ever wanted to see."

After a pause, Russell said, "That's probably true, Naomi. Of both of us."

They finished their trip in silence.

Chapter Eighteen

No one in Tysen would have known that Naomi Hollister had gone to see Busby Howard the Wednesday after he'd denounced them all from the pulpit if Essie West hadn't been sweeping the front steps of the Methodist church and seen her come out Busby's office door at the side of the Baptist church. That was about quarter past ten. By noon, it was all over town, but Naomi's face wasn't telling anything, and Naomi wasn't the sort you asked about her business until she got ready to say. All they knew was that, come Sunday, Naomi wasn't sitting in the choir, Johnny wasn't among the young people, and Busby Howard mentioned Evelyn Tolney only to say that Sister Tolney was improving and that Doc Barnes said there was some chance she'd be able to come home in another week if she continued the way she was going. The members of the congregation were to keep her on their prayer lists.

All Naomi had told Matt and Russell Wednesday evening when she was browning the pot roast for dinner was that she'd seen Busby Howard, and she wouldn't be going to church for a while. Matt told her to do whatever she wanted; she already knew how he felt about Busby. Russell nodded and kept his mouth shut.

She told Johnny that she'd been to see Busby, and she'd had enough to say for both of them. There was no need for him to go plead his case, if he had that in mind; she'd already done it, and there was no moving Busby. She said she didn't want Johnny to have to take any more insults by going to that man, and that Busby would not be coming to talk to Johnny, either; she'd taken care of that as well. When Johnny had protested that he needed to go and try for Hope's sake, Naomi told him that for Hope's sake he'd better leave well enough alone. Naomi hadn't been able to move the man one whit, and there was no use in trying to change a donkey's mind, even if that donkey was dressed in a suit and tie and holding a Bible in its hand.

Naomi worried about the consequences for Hope. Johnny was about to go off to Mizzou, and he'd be caught up in another world. But Hope was caught here for another year, and Busby Howard was not one to spare the rod if he felt he was divinely inspired to use it. "Don't go pressuring Hope, honey. You think about what she has to live with before you think of what you want for yourself. You both got a long way to go yet. And I can tell you that Busby, short of being struck blind on the road to Damascus, will not be changing his mind."

On Sunday morning Naomi read her Bible, prayed in her bedroom, and went into her kitchen where she spent the morning cooking for Alice and Evelyn. She made it clear she wasn't doing it for Webster; Webster could starve if she weren't a Christian woman, and even then, she had to remind herself that she was.

Johnny had been all set to do battle with Busby, but when Aunt Naomi asked him not to for Hope's sake, he felt as penned in as one of Myrtle Ballard's prize bulls. When he told Ray he felt like he'd just hit his head on a brick wall instead of his fist on Busby's jaw, Ray said it was the Wailing Wall and he'd been there a few times lately himself. John should line up beside everybody else and have himself a good cry. Johnny couldn't summon what it took to laugh, even though he had to admit Ray had gotten off a good one.

He was cut off from Hope. There were no more lunches at the same table and no meeting at their lockers. Too many tongues were ready to report to Busby if they spoke a word to each other. The most they could do was exchange glances across the classroom or as they passed in the hall.

Graduation was three weeks from Friday; then what would they do? Summer was short, and Johnny would be leaving after Labor Day. He would have to think of something; he just didn't know what.

Nothing was easy now; everything had changed.

At Johnson's General Store, where Johnny worked after school and on Saturday, everybody kept saying they'd missed him at church for the last two Sundays and wanted to know when he'd be back. Johnny missed them, too, and he missed being in church. Aunt Naomi had told him he shouldn't miss church just because she did; he had every right to go if he chose to. But how could he go back to church with Hope feeling all uncomfortable because people would be watching them and Busby Howard in the pulpit thinking Johnny had led his daughter into sin and half the church agreeing with him? Even more, how could he go back to a church where the preacher posed as God?

Yes, he had taken Hope where he promised he wouldn't, and no matter how he sliced it, Johnny knew that he'd do it again; Ray was his friend.

At night in his room, when he tried to read his Bible, he couldn't keep his mind on it. If he just let the Bible fall open to a verse, a Baptist device for divining God's answer to prayer, it always fell open to the Song of Solomon, and reading that didn't help him feel at all holy. In fact, all he felt when he read Solomon was that he wanted very much to be holding both Hope's breasts "like clusters of the vine" in his hands. Then, he was torn between needing to pray and wanting to squeeze Hope's nipples.

When he could wrest his mind from Hope, he was fervent in begging God to show him what to do.

He'd never expected Doobie Pratt to deliver the answer to a prayer.

Chapter Nineteen

Hope had been very careful not to mention to Johnny what her father had said about Naomi; she knew Johnny well enough to know that would set off sky rockets. Johnny didn't get angry very often, but when he did, you'd better look out. She knew he'd do battle for his Aunt Naomi at a moment's notice; he loved her fiercely.

So Johnny still didn't know about Busby's condemnation of Naomi when he borrowed Willie's truck on Monday afternoon to go to the sawmill. Willie never minded; he said it needed some driving now and then 'cause he didn't drive it enough. Getting into the truck reminded Johnny to tell Aunt Naomi that Willie had called and said the railroad wanted him for a month or two in St. Clair, but to hold onto his room for him.

When he pulled up, the Mueller brothers were helping Doobie load newly sawed railroad ties onto one of the long, flatbed trucks. Jackson was directing a loaded gravel truck toward the back road. Johnny guessed Ray had called the gravel company that morning. Regal King was working with Ray at the big saw. The sharp whine of the saw shot biting spears of sound out through the trees.

Johnny waved at Ray and went over to give the Mueller Brothers and Doobie a hand; they still had at least a third of the ties to load. The three of them lifted ties and slid them onto the truck bed while Doobie filled them in on what he'd heard at the Talk of Tysen Café that morning. Seemed that Wyman Clark had had to hit Charlie with a ball bat last night to keep him from getting at Annabelle and Charlene. Wyman had thought he had Charlie tied right tight to the bedpost in Carl's room, but Charlie broke the bedpost off and slipped the knot over it, and Carl had slept right through it. Charlie had made straight for Annabelle's room. Wyman heard Charlene screaming to get in there quick. He picked up the ball bat that he'd set by the bed, ran down the hall in his BVD's, rushed into Annabelle's room, came at Charlie from behind, and knocked him out cold. Doobie related all this with much satisfaction.

"Charlie should be back at Arsenal Street," Hance Mueller said, referring to the mental institution in St. Louis the way everyone did. "It ain't right, having those women tormented like that. It must be dang hard just to try to get through the day at that house."

Doobie said, "They won't take him back on Arsenal Street, Wyman told me, and nobody else will have him. When they try to get him to take his medicine, he bites, and he's so damn big, it takes three of them to hold him down. Wyman said short of caging him, they didn't know what they was going to do."

Joe Mueller said, "I said all along they should shoot him enough to cripple him. Keep him in a wheelchair that way. Might be best for all concerned."

"I don't think it's legal yet to shoot somebody because they're crazy," Johnny said.

"Don't have to be legal, and it's a dang sight better than having him rape somebody else," Joe said.

"What are they doing with him the daytime?" Hance Mueller asked.

"Carl takes him along with him. Carl's almost as big, and he guards him with a shotgun. Course it's hard to get your chores done when you're hauling a shotgun around and trying to keep an eye on your brother who's tied to the nearest fence post or whatever," Doobie said.

"Yeah," Johnny said, dryly, "that might slow you down just a bit."

They picked up another tie and swung it up onto the truck. Johnny was getting the hang of it. He hadn't worked at the mill very often. Just to help Ray out once in a while. Ray had stopped the saw and walked up to join them.

"You and Ray have a few worries of your own just now, don't cha?" Doobie asked Johnny.

Johnny grunted an assent, pushing at the tie.

"How's Naomi taking it all?" Doobie asked Johnny when, with Ray's help, they'd gotten the tie in place on the truck bed. "I've always been very fond of Naomi; she never treats me like a drunk."

"She's doing okay, I guess," Johnny said; "I haven't talked to her much since Saturday night. I know she was awful mad at Busby then. Today, she's been busy taking Russell to see Doc Barnes and going to the hospital to visit Evelyn."

Doobie nodded. He'd heard, of course, that Russell was back in town, but that wasn't what was on his mind at the moment. He said to Johnny, "I figured you'd be pretty steamed up about what Busby said." Doobie, who'd heard it at breakfast that morning at the Talk of Tysen Café, had told Ray about Busby's tirade from the pulpit and included the part about Naomi. Ray had let loose a stream of curse words so coarse the saw couldn't have cut through them.

Ray shot Doobie a keep quiet look, which he chose to ignore.

Johnny said, "I don't care what he says about me," something that wasn't completely true; Johnny cared very much what he said about him. "But I don't like what he's said about Hope and Ray and Alice."

As they were lifting another tie, Doobie said, "I was thinking more about what he'd said about Naomi."

"About Aunt Naomi?" Johnny asked, stopping dead, causing Ray and Doobie to juggle with their hold on the tie. "What do you mean?"

"Doobie," Ray said, trying to change the subject, "John and I can finish loading these ties, why don't you go help Jackson for a while?"

"Wait," Johnny ordered Doobie, "I want to hear what Busby said about Aunt Naomi, and who he said it to."

"He's gonna find out sometime, Ray; I might as well be the one to tell him," Doobie justified.

Ray shook his head in aggravation. "Go ahead then; you've already started it."

They put the tie down.

Doobie launched in. "He said it in church on Sunday, same as when he said things about all of you. Said she was responsible, too, 'cause she knew about it and didn't stop it. I thought you knew that."

The color was slipping away below Johnny's collar. "Hope didn't tell me that."

It was one thing to attack him and Ray, even Hope and Alice; they had been a party to what had riled Busby so, but Aunt Naomi? Aunt Naomi? How could anybody attack Aunt Naomi; she'd never hurt a soul in her life.

"Now, John," Ray told him, "Hope just didn't want to upset you anymore than you already were, and I just found out this morning after I got to work."

"I'm not upset with Hope or you," Johnny said. "I know why she didn't tell me, but there's no way that I'm not going to have this out with Busby Howard. I told Hope and Aunt Naomi I wouldn't try to talk to him 'cause she said it would just upset things more, but Busby can't do this. No sir. Not this. Nobody can talk about my Aunt Naomi and think I'm just going to stand by. I don't care if he is Hope's father and the preacher."

Ray knew that when Johnny used that quiet tone he would do whatever he had set his mind to. "John, let's take some time to think about this, and then if you're still set on it, I'll go with you. I've been Busby's punching bag for years; I'm used to dealing with it," Ray told him. They'd all stopped loading ties.

Johnny shook his head, no. "I'm not going to be Busby's punching bag; you can count on that."

Ray understood that, and he was worried for Johnny for just that reason. Tysen was a Baptist-heavy town, and there would be some that would stand against the preacher, but a good many that wouldn't, a good many who believed every word he uttered might as well be printed in red in the King James Version of the Bible. Johnny had always been a church-going kid, living right and doing good. The folks in Tysen would have a tough time with this one if Johnny went after Busby. They loved Johnny, but Busby held the tickets to heaven. It would cause quite a quandary.

"You know what you're always telling me about not going off half-cocked, John. You gotta take it easy, son; here's the time to practice what you preach," Ray said.

"I'm damn fed up with preaching just now, and I sure as hell don't feel like practicing it."

Neither Ray nor Doobie had ever heard Johnny Hollister curse. They were just short of astonished.

"I can understand that," Ray told him. "Couldn't have said it better myself. But you need to think what you want to say. You gotta think about Naomi and how she'll feel about all this."

Before Johnny could answer, Doobie said, "Here comes Jackson."

Jackson Redeem was fifty-two; his hair was graying, and his face had been left too long in the sun and wind. His back, though, was steel-rod straight, and the mill had fine-toned his muscles so that his body was stronger than that of most twenty year olds. Standing side-by-side, he and Ray looked like a bulwark.

Jackson had been given a lot to think about this past weekend, all that business at the pie supper made him wake up and look around, and, then, sitting in his regular pew, listening to the preacher take after Ray and the others, he'd heard something besides the echo of his own sorrow and the feel of his own searching for the first time in years. It was faint, but it was there.

Jackson had wondered why Busby pointed a finger at Naomi and not at him. Maybe it was because the preacher knew that Jackson and Ray shared little by way of conversation other than business. When the preacher had asked Jackson to talk to Ray about walking out of church that time, Jackson had said, "Ray and I didn't have much to say to each other when he was a little boy; I don't rightly see how I can start asking him questions about what he does now that he's almost grown."

Jackson couldn't be persuaded to move from that position, though the preacher couldn't figure out why. Jackson wouldn't have told him, even if he'd asked, even if Jackson had really understood it himself. Truth be told, after what happened to Loretta, Jackson had never tried to win anyone over to his beliefs. And after he'd lost Lester, he didn't want to take any chances by reminding God that Ray was still very much alive and very healthy.

"You boys can quit when you've loaded these ties," Jackson told them. "Ray and me'll haul them into town tomorrow." He nodded at Johnny. "Johnny," he said by way of greeting.

"You doing all right, Jackson?" Johnny asked.

"Fair to middlin'," Jackson said.

Doobie, never one to hold back, said, "Jackson, we was just talking about the preacher's sermon yesterday."

Jackson studied Doobie for a long minute.

Doobie pushed on, "What'd you think about what he preached?"

Just when they all thought he wasn't going to answer, he said, "I guess the preacher has a right to say what he believes."

"But do you go along with what all he said?" Doobie never knew when to stop.

Jackson had been mulling over the preacher's sermon, going over it and over it, like Loretta working her way through her rosary beads back when she was a Catholic, but he hadn't figured on talking about it. Finally, he said, "No, can't say as I do."

"You going to tell him that?" Doobie asked.

"I'm thinking on it."

Ray asked, much to the surprise of Johnny and Doobie, since they'd never heard the two of them talk about anything other than business, "Will you all talk it over at the next deacon's meeting?"

"It might well come up."

"Will you let me know if it does?" Ray asked.

"If I'm able," Jackson said, meaning that he'd tell Ray if he didn't think the information should stay just among the deacons. Jackson looked across the pile of ties toward the Mueller brothers and Regal King who had moved off down toward the mill.

"Gotta go to work with the boys," he told them and headed toward the saw shed. They watched him go down the hill and into the shed, flipping on the switch that would start the sharp, slicing twang of the blade. That saw was a living thing to Jackson and the men who worked it; it had power and might.

You had to respect it.

Chapter Twenty

Sample Forney had gone back to the hospital on Monday afternoon to pick up Alice. He knew she hadn't been glad to see him, but she came along without any fuss, even though she hadn't a word to say all the way home. That was all right, Sample thought. He could wait. When he pulled his truck up in front of the Tolney's picket fence, Webster came out the front door like he'd been waiting for them, which he had, and invited him in for supper. As usual, Webster hadn't felt any need to go to the hospital that day. After all, Alice was there, and he had work to do.

Alice heated up some of the food the neighbors had been bringing by. Sample and Webster sat at the table and smoked, and when she tried to tell Webster about Evelyn, Sample took it for granted that she was talking to both of them.

But she had eaten in silence while he and Webster talked about the acreage Sample had planted with corn, and, just as silently, she cleaned up the kitchen. Then she kissed her father's cheek and said, "Good night," which she directed into the air, somewhere between Webster and Sample. Just as she started up the stairs to her schoolbooks, Webster stopped her by saying, "Alice, Sample's sure been helping me out; you keep that in mind when he comes to get you in the afternoons and thank him properly, hear?"

She'd said so softly Sample could barely hear it, "Yes, Papa." Then she'd turned to Sample and said looking someplace over his left shoulder, "Thank you." The "thank you" was all he needed for encouragement. He had time, and as time passed and the burden of taking care of Evelyn increased with every day, he knew he could convince her that her folks, especially her mother, were truly in need and that it was her job to help them. And the best way to help them was by letting him help her.

Sample had always been good at helping folks to see what would be best for everybody all around; that's how he'd managed the transactions with his farm and had built it to the largest one in the county. He didn't think any man had ever lost out on one of his transactions; he always gave equal value or more for what he got. No man had ever thought him easy, but no man ever thought him unfair. Webster would get everything he'd been promised.

Alice would just have to know her place in all this, that she was the one who could make it all happen. When she came to understand that, she'd see he had big plans for her, too—but that would come later. She would never be wanting for anything, not as long as she belonged to him. With Alice, too, he truly believed he'd be giving equal value for what he bought. And he'd be getting it.

Upstairs in her room, Alice turned on the desk lamp and looked down at the stack of books Hope had brought by for her along with her homework assignments. She sank into her chair, slid her geometry book out of the pile, and reached for the pad and pencils she kept in the top drawer. There was enough work in front of her to keep her busy for at least two hours, and she didn't want to get behind. She opened her book and stared at the first problem, wishing she could call Ray, but there was no way that was possible. She'd have to wait until she got to the hospital tomorrow; she could call on the pay phone there.

She tapped her pencil eraser against her front teeth as she began thinking through the first geometry problem; she was good at math, but she had to work hardest at geometry. Just before she slipped away into the world of Euclid, she saw the box of Whitman's Samplers she had left on her desk the day before. She couldn't throw them in the trash yesterday when her papa and Sample were standing right there in the kitchen, so she'd carried them upstairs. Sample's Samplers, she thought, and she shivered. She lifted the package, touching it only with her thumb and index finger, and dropped it into the wastebasket. She was having nothing to do with Sample Forney. Not in this lifetime.

Chapter Twenty-One

It was five o'clock on Wednesday, ten days after Busby's pulpit proclamation, when Johnny Hollister threw open the door to Busby's office at the church without knocking. He knew Busby was alone; he'd checked the parking lot before he came in.

Busby was too surprised to be indignant. Johnny was the last person he'd expected to come busting through his office door. He'd made it perfectly clear to Naomi when she appeared unannounced last week that her nephew was never to come anywhere near his daughter, and he wouldn't discuss Hope with him. Period.

Of course, that bull-headed woman probably never told her nephew what he'd said. It would be just like her. She had stood across from him, arms folded, looking him straight in the eye while he delivered the Lord's own truth to her, never once interrupting. When he finished, she unfolded her arms and opened her mouth, and her words came at him like buckshot. The rounds she fired scattered and spewed around the tiny room with such force they seemed to jiggle the heavy objects and dance the papers right off the desk. He'd never witnessed anything like it. And what was worse, there was no stopping her once she began. Every time he'd begin to open his mouth to interrupt, she'd slap his desk with the flat of her hand. No living soul had ever come at him as she had. She'd had her say all right, and his ears and his pride were still stinging.

How dare that woman attack him? How dare she tell him that he had no heart and little soul? How dare she say that he spent too much time with both feet in the Old Testament, and that it was high time he tried a few steps into the New One?

Now, here was Johnny Hollister in the church office, busting right on in without knocking. Then, looking at Johnny framed in the light streaming in behind him in the open door, Busby had an epiphany: The Lord had presented him, Busby, with the opportunity to let Johnny know that he wasn't going to shame Busby and his family and not have to atone for it.

"Come in, young man; I have a few things to say to you," Busby began, standing up so Johnny wouldn't be looking down on him. "And let's get something straight from the beginning; you and Hope are through, so there's no use begging to see her."

Johnny's blue eyes grew so dark they looked black. "That's between you and Hope, 'cause for my part, I'm not begging for anything. And you'd better get something straight; I didn't come here to talk about Hope, and I didn't come here to listen to what you have to say about anything."

Busby was startled enough that he blanched, but he pulled himself together and drew himself up to his full 5' 9". "You change your tone if you have anything to say to me," he ordered Johnny, "and take a seat in that chair." He pointed toward the old wooden chair that was on the other side of his desk.

Johnny didn't move and his eyes could have drilled holes in an oak two by four. "You might as well sit down and listen, preacher, because neither of us is going anywhere until I'm through."

Busby suddenly realized that Johnny Hollister with his height and brawn could, indeed, overpower him. Still he would keep his dignity. "Say it then, and get it over with. I've got church business to attend to," Busby told him.

"I know you had a right to be upset with me because I took Hope out with Ray and Alice. I should have come to you and told you when Ray started dating Alice, and the four of us wanted to do things together. When I gave you my word, I never dreamed anything like that would happen."

Busby started to interrupt, but Johnny held up his hand.

"I'm not here to argue with you; what's done is done. Ray's my friend, and no matter what, I'd do it again. I am here to tell you this: None of us, not Ray, not me, not Alice, and certainly not Hope, caused Evelyn's stroke. If anybody was responsible for that stroke, it was Webster Tolney, driving Evelyn the way he does. And I don't even know if that's so. I could have put up with anything you had to say about Hope and me because Hope wanted me to; I could even keep my mouth shut about Ray and Alice.

"But nobody is ever going to get by with saying what you had to say about my Aunt Naomi. If I'd known about it, I would have been here sooner, but nobody told me that part until today." He took a deep breath and leaned forward, placing his hands on the desk. "Aunt Naomi has never done a bad thing in all the years she's raised me. She's the best mother any boy could hope for, and she's the best friend and neighbor anyone could have. And you stand in the other room there," he jabbed his finger back toward the sanctuary, "and say from the pulpit that she's responsible for Evelyn Tolney's stroke."

"Young man," Busby began loudly, rising from the chair, "You've gone too far."

"No, sir, you have. As far as I'm concerned, God doesn't work the way you say He does, and I'll tell you this," Johnny leaned in so his face was just inches from Busby's, "if He does work that way, I don't want to have anything to do with Him."

"That's blasphemy," Busby yelled."

"Maybe. Maybe not. I'm leaving Tysen. I'm going to Missouri U. in September, but even if I weren't, I wouldn't be back in this church. You've soured me on anything you'd ever have to say again. I don't want any part of the God you preach about, and I don't want any part of you."

Busby shouted at Johnny, spewing saliva into his face, "You'll burn in hell for all eternity, Johnny Hollister, in a fiery hell where you'll beg for water on your tongue."

Johnny leaned back and looked long at Busby's red face. "Then God's worse than Hitler, preacher. Once the poor Jews were dead, at least they weren't tortured anymore.

"And I think you'd better prepare for a big surprise, Busby. Some of the very people you call sinners may have a front row seat in Heaven. I'd be looking toward my own backyard, because I'm telling you right now that you have committed the biggest sin I've ever known any person to commit." Johnny's eyes locked onto Busby's. "May God have mercy on your soul."

With that, Johnny turned his back on Busby and was out the door, leaving a funnel of motion in the spot where he'd been standing. Busby kept staring at the empty space as though some evil spirit still whirled within it. How had he been so wrong about Johnny Hollister and his aunt?

Busby sat back down. May God have mercy on my soul? My soul? Sometimes, he thought, closing his eyes and taking in a deep breath, Satan can fool us all. He put his head in his hands; he had to brace himself to go home to dinner with Helen and his daughters. Hope would be there, and he really didn't want to look at her. He didn't like her right now, and he didn't want to be reminded of what had just happened. He thought about dropping by the Johnson's and having dinner with them. They had to come to church after dinner for prayer meeting, and he and Wendell had deacon's meeting after. He thought it over and decided he'd better not; the Johnsons might want to talk to him about Johnny; they were overly fond of that boy.

No, he'd better get on home. With dinner and prayer meeting after, it was going to be a long night. He closed the side door to the church and started toward his car. Charlie Clark was standing still as a fence post at the edge of the woods behind the church. Busby stopped with his hand on the car door. How in the very name of what is holy did that crazy man get away from home?

"Charlie?" Busby called hesitantly. Charlie looked at Busby, then turned quickly and disappeared into the grove of red oaks and cedars.

Busby slid into the car seat and laid his Bible on the dash. He kept watching the edge of the woods as he turned the key in the ignition. I'll have to call Wyman, he thought. The Clarks are going to have to keep a closer watch on Charlie. If Wyman doesn't take better measures to keep him home, Charlie might hurt somebody bad sometime soon, and Busby didn't want it to happen to any of his church members.

Chapter Twenty-Two

Johnson's Store had been more fertile in gossip in the two and one half weeks since the pie supper than Jenny Majors was in giving birth every year for the last five years to twins. The first week after Evelyn's collapse, every customer who pushed open the swinging front doors of the store wanted an update on her condition. That was only fitting. In the second week, when Doc made it clear—and the word spread faster than a summer cold—that Evelyn would, with time and proper care, gain back most of her faculties, the people of Tysen gave a sigh of relief so great it could have lifted the railroad tracks in a ripple before they settled back into place. Now, they were guilt-free to run into the storm the preacher's sermon had created; there hadn't been so much excitement in years.

They all had learned right quickly that Naomi and Johnny had been to the church office separately and had it out with Brother Busby. That was followed by the monthly deacon's meeting. The board of deacons, who met with the pastor, was made up of Wendell Johnson, Loncy Oppenmeier, Otis Callum, Holland Dample, and Jackson Redeem. The five men had worked together for the last four years, and, for the most part, business of the church seemed to be handled without much strife. Then came the first deacon's meeting after Busby's sermon of condemnation.

It didn't take long for Wendell Johnson and Loncy Oppenmeier to take the preacher to task. They'd done a lot of thinking and a lot of talking between the two of them. They told the preacher that, in their opinion, the kids didn't mean any harm and Naomi was totally blameless. Loncy had gone so far as to say that the preacher, too, had a daughter, and asked him if Naomi were to blame, just who else might be to blame? That made the preacher so angry that the red shot up his collar and into his face with such a rush that Wendell told Marie later that he thought another stroke might be in the offing.

On the other hand, Otis Callum and Holland Dample were shocked by Loncy and Wendell. Holland came loudly to the defense of the preacher; he might as well have been carrying pipes and drums, banging out the Battle Hymn of the Righteous. Busby, he told them, was a man chosen by the Lord. Who were they to question him? He looked hard at Wendell and Loncy, who looked right back. Wendell retorted that as far as he knew each human being had a right to question. After all, what did Holland think they were, Catholics?

Otis Callum couldn't have agreed with Holland more. Otis had long held to the belief that the earth was flat because the Bible clearly stated that it had four corners. He and his wife, Agnes, believed every word in the King James Bible just as it was written, knowing, too, that anything printed in red came straight from the mouth of Jesus. Why would God take time to dictate to all those holy men if He didn't mean every Word He said?

Agnes, if anything, was even more steadfast in her beliefs than Holland. It was well-known she kept their bedroom window open all year round because she wanted to hear the trumpet of the Lord when the Second Coming occurred. She knew her name was written in the Book of Life, and she wanted to be first in line, just in front of Otis. Her last words after she settled her head just so into her pillow so her curlers wouldn't pinch were "Lord, let this be the night."

For Otis and Holland and Agnes, anything less than a concrete explanation of the inexplicable would shake their whole belief system, right down to the very four corners that held up the earth. Of course, they were staunch supporters of Busby's. He was a fundamentalist just like them, and he preached the word of God. After all, who better to state the word of the Lord than a preacher who agreed with them?

So there were two against the preacher and two for, and then there was Jackson Redeem. Jackson, so far, hadn't said a word except to open the meeting since that was his job as chairman of the deacon board. But he was usually last to speak to any issue. Even then, he always took his time and weighed his words. Busby felt sure that, like always, he'd have the support of Jackson. Here was a man who'd never let him down. Jackson had heard him mention Ray from the pulpit before, if not by name, by action, and everyone in the church knew who it was, and he'd never had a word to say to the preacher about it.

Jackson, who had been staring at the table in front of him, letting the talk filter in, lifted his head and looked round the room, first at the deacons and then the preacher. Busby let out a breath of relief that it had come back around to Jackson. Then, Jackson said, "I've done a lot of praying and thinking about this." The preacher nodded, and the men waited.

Jackson continued, "As far as I can tell, nobody done nothing directly to Evelyn; she's just been sick and overworked a long time. Those kids, mine included, didn't have a thing to do with her stroke. They didn't even know she'd be there. She should've been home in bed where Doc told her to stay, but she wasn't. That wasn't her fault either. Fault is a mighty hard thing to assign. I think we'd better leave that to the Lord. If we start dealing out fault, then we all, myself included, better look to ourselves." He looked around the room at each of them and ended eye to eye with the preacher.

The room was so quiet they could hear the crunching of tires on the gravel outside.

The preacher was wordless.

The silence grew, bringing the walls in closer and closer, and, finally, Loncy took a deep breath and posed the question to Jackson, "Do you think anything can be done to straighten all this out? Folks are mighty upset."

"I just don't know. It's gonna take a mighty amount of thought and prayer," Jackson told him.

"Why should anything have to be done?" Busby fumed. "I preached the sermon, and I still stand behind the Word of God."

Wendell spoke up. "The issue here, preacher, is that not everyone in this room, or in the church for that matter, agrees that what you said is the word of the Lord." Busby started to cut in, but Wendell held up his hand. "Not a soul is free from misinterpreting now and again. Even you. You're only human, Busby. Even the apostles were only human. I hope you'll take some time to think this over and see if you think that in this case you might have been just a little too close to the subject to hear the Lord's voice clearly."

"I don't need any time. Right is right; I heard the Word of the Lord," Busby declared.

Otis and Holland murmured their assent.

Loncy said, "I agree with Wendell, and I think it might be a good idea just to give it some time, let it all settle for a few weeks. Might be the Lord has something else to say to you, to all of us. Maybe have some redirections on the subject. Naomi and Johnny Hollister are fine people. I, for one, want to see them back in church."

There were many members of the church who, like Wendell Johnson and Loncy Oppenmeier, thought Busby Howard had crossed a line, though not many of them would stand up and say so without a lot of support. There were others, like Otis and Holland, who believed that whatever the preacher said was right. They didn't like room for doubt. Doubt was a frightening thing; it made them think, and they couldn't afford that.

"Nobody's keeping them out of church. They're the ones deciding not to come," Busby said, his face bright, angry red.

Jackson spoke up. "You remember when Persimmon Hollow Church split right down the middle over that six dollar rug Effie Calendar wanted to put in front of the pulpit? The same could happen to us, and over much bigger stakes. I think maybe we should all go home and do some thinking and praying. We can wait till next month's meeting to talk about this. It ain't something to try to settle in one night."

Nobody in the room was pleased, but at the moment, it was the only option that let Busby, Otis and Holland think that with prayer, and right thinking, the others would come round to a different point of view.

"Let's close with the Lord's Prayer," Jackson said and bowed his head and began to pray. The others joined in, Busby last of all. Busby Howard had been met for the first time since he'd come to Tysen with opposition. Now, three of his deacons disagreed with his stand, and, if he had it right, some of the other folks in his congregation could actually be thinking he was in the wrong.

It was a force he had never reckoned with. He felt assaulted.

Chapter Twenty-Three

Russell knew it had to be soon, today or tomorrow at the latest, that he tell Naomi. He'd been home four weeks come Saturday; time was getting shorter and shorter. Every night, the stairs to his room grew steeper and longer; he had to rest at least twice on his way up, leaning against the banister until he caught his breath. When he did, even above the rasp of his breathing and the groan of the stairs, he could hear Naomi and Matt sitting at the kitchen table, talking softly: "He must be really sick. I can tell by Doc's face that it's bad." He was going to have to tell them what was going on. Naomi hadn't asked since that day in the truck.

He hadn't wanted to say anything before Johnny's graduation; he thought he should wait. Bad enough that the boy had not been able to take Hope to the senior prom and had had to go alone. If he hadn't been Senior Prom King, he'd have stayed home, but Russell had heard Johnny tell Naomi that he had to go through with it; he just didn't have to stay around and dance after the coronation. So he'd gone, been absolutely miserable, and come home early.

Yesterday had been graduation. Naomi told Russell she'd been planning Johnny's graduation party for six months, and now he wasn't up to having it. So the graduation party last night had been a small dinner for Johnny, Naomi, Matt, Doc, Ray, Doobie, the Johnsons, the Oppenmeiers and Russell, and everybody had worked real hard at having a good time. Dinner was delicious, the cake decorated with "Congratulations Future Pulitzer Prize Winner," and the gold Bulova watch Naomi gave Johnny was a beauty. The rest had given him money for his college fund. Johnny couldn't have been nicer to everybody, but

Busby Howard had dug a hole in the festivities as deep as the Meramec River after a hard rain. Everyone was glad when it was over.

Now there was nothing to keep Russell from telling Naomi why he'd come home, and, of course, she'd ask why he'd left in the first place. Telling Naomi why he'd left was what he dreaded most of all.

Doc had told him yesterday he had two to three months, and there wasn't anything that could be done except to keep him as comfortable as possible. The cancer was spreading from his lungs to his other organs like a spider spinning out her web, threading them together with an inescapable, consuming deadliness.

In California, the doctors had given him six months. At first, he was going to stay there. Just let the sunshine sink into his frail bones day after day, stringing each day together like sandy beads. Then, the hunger to be where he could feel time began to gnaw at him. He wanted to know the hour of day by the feel of morning air, or the heart beat of the trains, or the sound and smell of suppertime from the kitchen.

He wanted to go to Tysen. He knew there wouldn't be time to feel the snowflakes against his face, but he needed the taste of apples that came in from the big tree behind the house, let the blackberry cobbler fresh from his mother's oven, filled with biting sweetness and warmth, topped with tablespoons of thick cream, lay on his tongue. More than anything, he wanted to hear the voices of people he knew, people who knew him. And he wanted to see Naomi, to make amends if he could.

So he'd come home.

The first week he was back, he soaked in what he had always known, letting it soothe the hurt some; then he began to take in the changes. The town was the same, but not. The house was the same, but not. Naomi was the same, but not. And Johnny. Well, Johnny had grown up and become a man. Naomi had done a fine job. And he didn't blame Johnny a bit for not wanting him there. He had every right. Russell had deserted them.

Then there was Matt. Russell had never thought about another man in Naomi's life; that had come as a surprise. He didn't know why he hadn't thought of it; she certainly was a fine looking woman and some man was bound to want her. He'd actually forgotten how pretty she was.

That first week, he'd walked down to The Talk of Tysen Café, but the walk was a bit long for him and the talk wore him out. He'd taken to sitting on the front porch each morning with a coffee cup that Naomi would come out and fill from time to time and check to see if he needed anything.

He and George Wilson, sitting catty-cornered across the track from each other every morning, George not wanting to go anyplace, and Russell still wanting to go everyplace. He'd like to walk over and see if George were up for a little conversation, but it was too far by way of the street, and he was too unsteady to manage the gravel and the train rails if he went straight across the track. George had taken to waving to him, though. It was as though George knew. Maybe he could sense the cancer.

Russell heard the screen door slide open, and Naomi came out and sat down beside him, coffee cup in hand. "I need to get off my feet for a few minutes," she told him.

"That screen door's opening real smooth," Russell said. "It used to have quite a squeak to it."

"I had the hinges changed. After Johnny got big enough to run in and out so much, I just couldn't tolerate the noise. It was just creak, creak, creak all day long."

Naomi waved at George; he didn't wave back. They sat there silent for a spell until the squirrel set up a chatter in the tall oak in the front yard. Russell looked up to try to find it. "I had a bag swing in that tree when I was a boy," he said, as though he hadn't told her a dozen times when he first brought her here to live. He and Naomi and his mother would sit on the porch in the evenings, and Russell would say he had the swing, and his mother would tell the same story about how he'd tried to jump from the limb onto the swing and broken his leg. And how Doc, brand new and shiny out of medical school, had come over and set it.

Naomi looked out at the railroad track; it was shooting sunrays that made her blink and turn toward Russell. He was just sitting there, looking into the glare as though it didn't bother him a bit. "It's time to talk, Russell," she said, gathering her courage to hear what he was going to tell her.

He guided his coffee cup to the arm of his chair; then, he said, "I don't know where to start."

"Start on why you came home; then it might be easier to say why you left." Naomi looked off toward Johnson's Store, giving him a chance to speak out of the spotlight of her eyes.

The words came as if he were squeezing them through a small opening in his throat; they were new and tight. He'd never actually said it aloud. "It's cancer, Naomi."

She hesitated until she thought her voice wouldn't stick in her throat. "I thought as much," she said, still looking at Johnson's Store.

"They tell me I don't have much time." The breeze swished the leaves and carried the fragrance of the honeysuckle blooming on the trellis the Muellers had put up in the side yard between the two houses. Naomi's heart contracted in the ache of the sweetness of it, of the briefness of it. Was Russell thinking that? How could he help it?

"I didn't want to die across the country with nobody left but strangers. I wanted to come home."

Of course, he was dying, she thought. Any fool could tell that by looking at him. Why does it take us so long to admit to ourselves that we know what we know? She cleared her throat. "Did Doc tell you how much time?"

"Anywhere from two to three months."

There was a quiet spell between them; then Naomi said finally, "It's not right for anybody to die someplace all alone."

"It's all right then that I came, Naomi?"

"This is your house, and as far as I know, we're still legally married."

Russell smiled. "Well, I never got a divorce, and if you didn't, I guess we are." More silence. "I haven't been much of a husband though, have I?"

"You haven't been *any* of a husband for the last twelve years," she said.

"I was never a very good one; I'm sorry for that."

"It's a little late for being sorry," she said.

"It's late for most everything," he said, looking off down the railroad tracks.

"Yes, I reckon it is." She sighed. "I'm truly sorry you're dying, Russell. I wish I could change that, but I can't. Anymore than I can change all that's happened between us, but I can tell you that it's fitting that you came home now. This is where you should be."

Russell felt a great flood of relief to be wanted, not to be turned away.

"But," Naomi continued, "that doesn't change my needing to know why you left me. I've spent years wondering about all the things I've never understood. What I want to know most, Russell, is how could you just all at once take off and leave me and Johnny? I need to know the truth; was it something I did? Was there another woman?"

"No, Naomi; there was nothing you did, and there was never another woman."

"Not in all these years?"

"Not in all these years."

"Well, what then? What other reason could you have?"

Russell paused. "It was something I needed that I couldn't explain. I'm not sure I even knew it myself until it began to happen."

"Until what happened?"

"I guess it all started the weekend I had a short layover in St. Louis, and I went over to the dance at the Odd Fellows Hall to see Mr. Morgan and ask him if he'd heard from George lately." George Morgan had bought his own filling station in Florida, and Sarah had married and moved to Minnesota. They hadn't seen much of them after Naomi and Russell moved to Tysen, and when George and Sarah moved away, the correspondence had dwindled to an occasional trickle at Christmas or Easter.

"Mr. Morgan wasn't there that night, but Oscar Sudmeyer was."

"Oscar Sudmeyer?" Naomi questioned. "Oscar Sudmeyer who used to bring his sister to the dances?"

Russell nodded.

"He never brought a girlfriend, did he?"

"No, he always brought Maxine. Oscar was a fine dancer, Naomi. He and Maxine practiced at home all the time; they said they wanted to be another Fred and Adele Astaire. Anyhow, Oscar and I got to talking that night. He'd sprained his ankle pretty bad, so he asked me if I'd dance with Maxine and practice for a dance contest they'd entered, and I did. She wasn't much of a looker, but she was some kind of dancer."

Naomi remembered Maxine, whose poor face was a map of acne scars. She couldn't really be jealous of Maxine, but she couldn't help but ask, "Better than I was?"

"I didn't say that, Naomi. No woman I knew was a better dancer than you, but you weren't there. It just gave me somebody to dance with."

"No, I wasn't there," Naomi flared. "I was here. Taking care of your mother, and the house and Johnny." Cancer or no cancer, Naomi just couldn't keep that in.

"I didn't ask for that first layover; it was business," Russell defended himself. "I didn't stay on purpose. But after I went and danced that first night, I did begin asking for them so I could dance in the contest. We won it, by the way."

"Well, that's right nice," Naomi said, not hiding her sarcasm.

"It felt right then, like I should be there." Russell went right on; he had to tell the whole thing now. "After the contest when I had a layover during the week, I'd go over to their house, and we'd all practice together. Oscar would play the piano for us until his ankle healed, and then Maxine played the piano for Oscar and me. We'd make up routines. We'd have a great time."

Naomi just looked at him. Russell off dancing, having a great time on weekends with Maxine and Oscar Sudmeyer. It was something she could never have imagined.

Russell implored, "You know how great it feels to dance, Naomi; you always loved it, too. I think that's the reason I married you."

"That's true, I did love it. Still do, as a matter of fact. But I didn't leave home or you over it," she flared.

"No, you didn't." He studied the new paint on the porch floor.

"If you loved dancing so much, why did you move me to Tysen? I loved St. Louis."

"Momma needed us."

"You mean Momma needed me." Naomi stared hard at him.

"I didn't think about it that way, Naomi; I promise I didn't. I went to work for the railroad and hated every minute of it, but it was just expected of me. That was my part to do. And I guess I just expected you to be willing to do what had to be done here."

He had done that, Naomi thought. "Why didn't you tell me you hated it?" she asked.

"It wouldn't have changed anything."

"We would have thought of something," she said, wondering as she said it, just what that would be.

"There wasn't anything else to think of. What other jobs were there around here besides farming if you don't own a business? And, Naomi, I felt right dancing. I felt really at home with something for the first time in my life. And then this great opportunity just dropped out of the sky. It was like it was meant to be."

"What opportunity?"

"Oscar's Uncle Claude came to town for a visit one weekend. He was head camera man at the MGM Studios. Oscar asked him to watch the routine we'd put together, and Claude really liked it. He said he could get us both auditions for the new musical they were casting if we'd come to Los Angeles in two weeks."

"He wanted you for the movies?" Naomi was not sure she understood any of this.

"Well, not Maxine. Because of the acne scars and all, but Claude said she could come along, and he could get her a secretarial job at the studio. Anyhow, I had to decide right then and there. Claude told me he thought I could dance almost as good as Fred Astaire and Gene Kelly, and he was sure I would make the cut."

Naomi was slack-jawed.

"I'd always wanted to dance for a living, Naomi; I just never had the nerve to tell you. Even when I was a kid I wanted to dance like Mickey Rooney, but I just thought it was some kind of crazy dream like wanting to pitch for the Cardinals. Then, I thought if I told you I was going to try out for the movies, you'd think I'd lost my mind. So I just packed up and took off."

"Dance?" Naomi was saying, trying to get her mind around it. "You left to dance?"

"Yes," he nodded.

"And you couldn't tell me that?"

He shook his head, no. "How could I tell my wife I was leaving her to go try my hand at dancing in the movies?"

Of all the things she could and did imagine, never, never in her wildest dreams could she have come up with this. Naomi was wordless; she just sat there staring at him.

Russell went on, "I guess, truth be told, I didn't want to tell you either. You'd taken one look at Johnny and fallen in love with the boy. I knew you wouldn't come with me, even if I'd asked you."

"You could have asked; we might have come. You could have given me the opportunity to make up my own mind."

Russell drew in a deep breath before he said, "Okay, here's the truth of it. I didn't want to take you, and I didn't want to take Johnny. And when Mama died right at that time, it seemed like a double sign. I just knew I had to go."

Naomi was staring at him. "You didn't want to take me or Johnny? I always thought you loved Johnny just like I did."

"Not like you did. I never really wanted children of my own, even though I said I did, and he wasn't even mine."

"He was mine," she said, her motherhood deep in her eyes.

"Even more than I was," Russell said flatly.

Naomi couldn't deny the truth of that, but she hadn't known that Russell knew it. "Yes," Naomi admitted to him, "even more than you were, though I'd never stopped to think of it just that way. I needed him more than I needed you."

"I didn't need him, and I really didn't want him. And I knew you'd never forgive me for that either."

"No, I wouldn't have." Another surprise. Russell hadn't wanted Johnny. He'd never let on to her, not for a minute. He'd always said he wanted children.

"You had what you needed in Johnny, and I wanted what I needed."

"I could have dealt with it all better if you'd just told me, if you hadn't just walked away and left me not knowing anything. That was cowardly, Russell."

"You're right; it was, but I had a chance, and I took it."

"So we danced our way into marriage, and you danced your way out of it."

"That's about the size of it." He wished he had a good, hot, strong cup of coffee just now, but Naomi didn't seem prepared to move. She just sat there staring straight ahead.

Finally, she asked, "What happened when you got to Los Angeles?"

"You want some coffee?" he asked.

She shook her head. "No, I want to hear about Los Angeles, and I'm not moving until I do."

"Okay. I did get parts in the chorus in five or six movies. They were churning out musicals at MGM. Even had a couple of small roles with one or two speaking lines."

"Well, I never," Naomi said. "It looks like I would have seen you in one of them over in Meramec City."

"You weren't looking for me. Besides, they had me all made up, and I generally looked like everybody else in the chorus."

"Where did you live?"

"Maxine, Oscar, and I got an apartment together. I got a job as a bellhop at the Beverly Hills Hotel, and the money was good there. Great tips. Gene Kelly hired Oscar as a kind of jack-of-all trades to work for him, and Oscar loved it. Nights when everybody had finished at the studio, Oscar and Gene and some of the other dancers would come down to the hotel after hours, and we'd all horse around together. Dance and sing. Drink more than a little."

Gene? Naomi was thinking. Gene? He called Gene Kelly, Gene? She barely knew what to ask next. Finally, she did ask, "You ever think about coming home?"

"I felt guilty about leaving you; I did. But I was doing something I really wanted to do. I wasn't riding the same train, bound to the same tracks day after day, riding from here to there and back, over and over, just looking at life through a window, not really going anywhere."

"You left me and Johnny, and you went somewhere." It was a statement, not a question. Naomi was looking at the railroad tracks as if they could fill in even more of his story.

"Yes, I went somewhere. Even after the movie parts didn't come anymore, just being at the hotel with all of them, being that much a part of it, was something special to me. I was happy; I was finally off the train. And I got to dance with some of the best: Gene Kelly, Gene Nelson. Once or twice I even got to dance with Fred Astaire. Oh, he was something, let me tell you." He sighed happily, remembering. "I was happy. Really happy."

Naomi swung toward him in a movement that sent sun sparks flying from her auburn hair. "You were happy?" she queried, drilling him with her eyes. "Well, what about me, Russell? Did you ever wonder how I was? If I was happy?"

Russell came out of his reverie like a man shaken out of a dream. He was in Tysen, dying, and he was now faced with the wife he'd left, with the life he'd left. He had nothing in him to soften the truth as he knew it. "You had Johnny, Naomi. I knew you loved Johnny."

"Yes, I had Johnny, and you left us with a $1,000 to make a life with."

Russell looked down at his shoes. The boards of the front porch were freshly painted brown; everything about the hotel was well kept. "I knew you'd be all right, Naomi; you always had what it took to take care of things."

She shrugged that off and pushed on. "Didn't it occur to you that I'd wonder if you were dead or alive?"

"I'm ashamed to say it didn't." Russell looked hang-dogged. His chin kept getting closer to his shirt.

She could feel the anger fill her mouth, pushing against her teeth, ready to spill out over her tongue. She said between clenched teeth, knowing the Muellers could hear every word if she raised her voice, "You should be ashamed. All this tells me is that you never really thought of us at all. Couldn't you even think to tell me whether we were divorced or not? That would have been the least you could have done."

"I never thought about divorcing you," he said. "It never occurred to me."

"It never occurred to you?" she asked indignantly.

"It just wasn't something I ever thought about doing."

Was the man shell-shocked? "You never thought about it? You never thought about it? Did you ever think that I might like to know? That I might want some other life besides being married to you? That there might be things that *I* would need? That I might not be thrilled at sitting here waiting out my life wondering whether you were dead or alive? Whether I was a widow or divorcee? Or by some chance still married?"

Russell felt like he'd been peppered with a shotgun. He said, "I never thought you'd care one way or the other; you had Johnny, and I believed he was what was truly important to you." He hesitated, "For the most part, I was thinking mainly of myself."

"Well, amen to that." Naomi shook her head. It was beyond her.

"I just knew I couldn't stay, Naomi. If I had waited, it would have been too late to dance. But, you're right, it was selfish. It was very selfish."

The mockingbird, agreed, setting up a chatter in the oak tree.

George Wilson got up to shuffle his way inside. They both watched him labor from his chair across the porch and over the doorsill. It took him some time. When the screen door slammed behind him, Naomi asked, "What happened to Oscar?"

"He had a heart attack and died last year," Russell said.

"Did the two of you live together all that time?"

"Yes. Maxine married a camera man after we'd been there a year, and they moved to San Diego. We didn't see them very often. It was just Oscar and me." Russell looked far off down the tracks, wishing for a train that wouldn't be coming. "I miss him."

"I can see how you would," Naomi said, "living together so long and all."

"It was more than that," Russell said quietly.

Willard Moseby's pickup slowly crossed the tracks, bales of hay loaded in its bed. He waved at them, and Russell waved back.

"Naomi, I don't know how to say this to you. I don't know if you'll understand."

Naomi took offense. "Well, I'm not stupid, Russell."

"No, of course not, but you're not a worldly woman." Taking a deep breath, he said, "I loved Oscar. I was in love with Oscar."

There was silence: no birds, no dogs, no train, no human voice. The very wind waited to breathe. Then, Naomi's face jolted with recognition.

"O-o-oh," she said, breathing out as though she'd been punched in the stomach. Her face lost color, and her hands made fists in her lap, pleating up her skirt. For a minute, she couldn't draw a breath. It seemed like forever before she gulped in a swallow of air.

After that—silence.

Naomi's mind was whirling. She'd lived with him, slept with him. How could she not know he was…different? But she hadn't known. There was nothing to tell her. They'd made love. Not often, but she thought he was tired from working so hard. He was always so-so-so—normal. There was never anything about him that would point to his being….

Finally, she managed to say, "Did you always know you were that way?"

"No, I didn't know. I thought I was just like everybody else."

"You didn't know when you married me?"

"I didn't know until I met Oscar."

"I wish you had known sooner."

"I do, too." He paused, "But if I had known sooner, you wouldn't have had Johnny or Matt."

Naomi knew that was true, but he had a nerve trying to try to trade tit for tat. It didn't even things out, and it didn't lessen the shock. "Set that aside, Russell. If I'd known sooner, I'd have had the right to choose. You robbed me of that."

Russell's head sunk lower. "I did; you're right." He was getting more and more tired, and his voice was just above a whisper. "But, most times, I'm not sure we know ourselves well enough to choose. Even when we have the facts. I didn't. I think we lie to ourselves more than we know."

"I don't know." She shook her head in puzzlement. "I don't know." She, too, looked tired. "Let me just sit here and get my wind back."

"Can't we just be us? Friends, I mean?" He leaned in her direction, imploring. "I meant it when I said I love you. I'll always love you, Naomi. You are very dear to me."

"You're going to have to give me some time to get used to this. I have to sort out quite a few things." She chewed her bottom lip; then, she sighed and leaned back against the chair. She'd changed; Matt had changed; Johnny, too. Everything was different, which wasn't all a bad thing, but there would be a lot of getting used to. This certainly would, she knew. But she also knew that judging wasn't hers to do. There was too much judging going on around her; she was thinking of Busby. She rose; she had to move, to do something. "I'm going to get that coffee now."

He nodded and exhaled, putting his head back to rest.

When Naomi came back, Russell's color was putty, and he was sunk back, looking small and brittle. She put the cup and saucer in his hands which trembled so his fingers knocked against his cup, rattling it in the saucer. He was dwindling away right in front of her, his edges blurring.

Her heart clutched. He was sick; he'd come home to her. She and Johnny and Matt, they were all he had.

How could she stay angry at a dying man? A man she'd once loved? A man she'd shared her life with? In spite of the pain he had caused her, she was here because of him, had Johnny because of him, even had Matt because of him.

She took the cup from his hand, steadying it as he took a sip, then set it back in the saucer and placed them on the table.

Russell said, "I'm sorry for the hurt, Naomi. With all my heart, I am. And I'm grateful to you for taking me in."

"You came home, Russell," she said. "You're sick; I couldn't turn you away."

They sat in the silence in sadness and a kind of peace neither of them had felt for a long time.

"Rest for a bit," she told him, "it will take a little time, but it'll be all right."

Russell's body relaxed in relief. He could really come home now. She heard him whisper, "Thank you. Thank you," and he closed his eyes.

"Tonight, when Johnny and Matt get home, we'll move you downstairs into Johnny's room so that you don't have to climb the stairs, and I can be closer to you."

His eyes opened; his voice was quiet and worn. "Won't Johnny mind?"

"Of course, not. Just because he's mad that you left, doesn't mean he's not glad you came back, no matter what he says. For the most part, he's just defending me."

Russell's lips rose at the corners. "He does a darn fine job of it."

Naomi told him, "I won't tell the others, the part about you and Oscar; that's yours to do if you choose. But I want you to tell them about the dancing; that's too good to keep."

He lifted a hand out toward Naomi who reached over to gently clasp it, lowering it softly in hers back to the arm of his chair. That's where Johnny found them, their fingers entwined, when he came home for lunch from Johnson's store.

Chapter Twenty-Four

"It's all right, son," Russell told him, seeing the look on Johnny's face. "I'm not stealing her away."

Johnny opened his mouth to say something, but Aunt Naomi shook her head slightly.

"Come help me set the table, Johnny," Naomi said. "I lost track of the time."

Johnny followed her into the kitchen and over to the sink where Naomi set the cups and Johnny began to wash his hands. Under the sound of the water, Naomi said, "Honey, Russell doesn't have long to live, and it's up to us to make him as comfortable as possible. What he did or didn't do isn't all that important now."

"But...," Johnny began.

"It's something we have to do. We need to do."

Johnny's honey-colored hair fell across his forehead; there were puckers between his eyes. "How much time does he have?" Naomi knew his heart was bigger than his anger, not that he'd let all his anger go; he had a storehouse full. Russell had come back and caught the brunt for all the desertion Johnny had had to deal with. His mother's, his father's, even the death of his grandmother.

"He says two to three months or so. I doubt it will be as long as that."

"What's wrong with him?"

"Cancer."

"Can't they do something?"

"No, it's all been done. Now it's up to us to make him comfortable. Doc will keep him on medication to ease the pain."

Naomi watched Johnny's face. There was little guile about Johnny; his eyes were weather signals, his face open and readable.

"Will he go to the hospital?"

"No, he'll stay here with us."

"Until he dies?"

"Yes."

Johnny looked into the sink at the swirling water going down the drain. "I've never watched somebody dying before."

Naomi dried her hands on her apron and put her arms around his waist, holding him tightly; he hugged her back, putting his chin on the top of her head. She said, "You've had an awful lot to deal with this summer, sweetheart, and this won't be easy." She could feel his heart beating, this, her boy, her tall, healthy young man, her son. "We'll all just have to help each other through it."

"I'll do whatever you need me to do," he said.

"I'm going to ask you to do something that won't be easy for you." She looked up into his face. "It's too hard for Russell to get up and down the stairs now, and I'll need to be close to him in the night as time goes on. If you're willing, I'd like you to move to one of the upstairs rooms and let Russell use yours for awhile."

Johnny's room was his sanctuary, and he required a sanctuary, especially when he needed a familiar space to grieve about Hope and be angry at Busby and worry about Ray and Alice. And, as he had for years, to think about his future at Mizzou. Naomi wasn't asking a small favor, and she knew it.

"If you agree, we'll move all of your furniture upstairs with you. Russell won't be using that. You take some time and think about it if you need to."

He shook his head. "I don't need time. I'll move."

Naomi gave him a squeeze. "Thank you, sweetheart."

He kissed her on top of the head. "I'd do anything in the world for you."

"What do you think keeps me going?" She smiled up at him, but there were tears in her eyes. They'd both had a tough summer, and it was barely June. "We'd better get some lunch on the table," she told him, giving him a little pat, "or you won't be back to work on time."

Johnny started setting the table and Naomi began making ham salad sandwiches from leftover ham she'd cubed last night. "There are chips in the pantry, honey. Would you get those for me?"

"Sure." He started toward the pantry and stopped. "Aunt Naomi, I've quit my job at Johnson's."

Naomi quit stirring the mayonnaise into the mixture of cubed ham, diced hardboiled egg, celery, onion and dill pickle. "What?" Johnny had worked at the General Store since he was twelve.

"I quit my job. I just can't be there anymore. Everyday people come in asking me when they're going to see me at church." He didn't tell her they asked when they'd see her, as well. "And it's really hard when Hope comes into the store. Everybody knows we're not supposed to talk to each other, and people stare at us, watching how we are with each other." Johnny went into the pantry for the potato chips. When he came out, he said, "Ray's been wanting me to work at the mill with him and Jackson. It'd be more money, and that would help with tuition and board this fall."

Naomi knew working at the mill might pay more, but she didn't like him around those saws. She'd seen the fingers of men who'd spent any time around a sawmill. But Ray would be there, she reminded herself. He'd never let anything happen to Johnny. "If it's better for you to work at the mill now, then I think that's the best thing for you to do. Just be careful, please. You can't type without fingers."

"Count on it." He held them up and wiggled them at her. They both laughed.

"Can I get in on the joke?" Russell asked, coming into the kitchen.

"Aunt Naomi's worried about my career as a concert pianist; she doesn't want me sawing logs when I go to work next week at the sawmill."

"You changing jobs?"

"Yep, I can make more money there."

"Sounds good to me." Russell lowered himself into a chair at the table.

Naomi put loaded plates in front of them. "Now you two start eating your lunch. I'll sit as soon as I pour the tea." When she put her head down to reach for the tea in the refrigerator, she thought, this is the first conversation Johnny has had with Russell since he came home.

"Russell," she said, coming back to the table, "We're going to have a moving party tonight. Johnny and Matt are going to take Johnny's things upstairs and bring yours down."

"You okay with this, Johnny?" Russell asked.

"Yeah, I'm okay with it. It's just a loan until you're better, though."

"Right. Until I'm better." Russell swallowed hard; then he said, "I appreciate it." He wanted to reach over and pat Johnny on the shoulder, but decided against it.

"Thank Aunt Naomi; she engineered the whole thing," Johnny said, but his voice was soft when he said it.

Russell nodded.

"You two eat," Naomi told them. "We've all got work to do when Matt gets home this evening."

Doc dropped by that evening for coffee and conversation and to take a look at Russell. When they invited Doc to help with the move, he said he'd supervise Johnny and Matt.

"Supervise is just another word for sitting on your fanny, Doc," Matt told him, carrying a rocking chair down the stairs. Russell often sat up nights in this rocker; Matt had heard the hypnotic sound of the rockers meeting the braided rug on Russell's bedroom floor. He'd fall back asleep and wake again several hours later, and the sound would still be there. Matt wondered if Russell couldn't sleep or if he felt he needed to stay awake to soak in the night.

"You're going to have more than enough help," Doc called in to him. "I saw Ray earlier, and he said he was coming over for some of Naomi's chocolate cake. With three of you working, I'd just be in the way." Doc took a seat on the front porch next to Russell.

Matt knew Doc couldn't do any real moving; his arthritis and his bad knee wouldn't let him; Matt just wanted to devil him a little. He walked to the porch door. "I guess since you're not helping, you'll not be wanting cake, right?"

"Have you taken leave of your senses, man? If Naomi's baking, I'm eating. Besides, I am helping; I've giving you the benefit of my years of experience."

"Moving furniture?" Matt asked.

"No, not moving furniture," Doc told him. "There's an art to not moving furniture, and I'm practicing it. Besides, Russell needs me to keep him company; the two of us will just be sure that you take care of business."

"What business are you guys taking care of?" Ray wanted to know coming around the side of the house.

"Well, son, here you are, right on time," Doc said. "Just head back toward Johnny's room, and I'm sure they'll let you know."

Naomi came out of Johnny's room with a box filled with odds and ends and called to him, "Oh, Ray, would you help Johnny lift the mattress off his bed?"

When Ray raised his eyebrows in a question, Doc said, "She'll explain it all to you when you get back there." Naomi juggled the box a bit, righted it and brought it on down the hall to the stairs.

"Remember, Ray," Doc called from the porch, "four layer chocolate cake with a chocolate icing chock full of pecans. It's going to melt in your mouth." They could hear Doc chuckle and a raspy laugh came from Russell.

"You two kibitzers quit bothering my help," she called out to them. Doc heard her laugh. That was a sound he hadn't heard for days.

When the rooms had been sorted to Naomi's satisfaction, Naomi cut generous slabs of chocolate cake, gave them all large glasses of iced tea, and sat down on the porch to rest. Johnny and Ray took theirs upstairs; eating in his room would help Johnny to lay claim to it. He'd chosen the room next to Matt's, which looked pretty much like his room downstairs, except it was set up in reverse, and the walls were painted green instead of blue.

The greatest difference from Johnny's point of view was that it would be harder to climb in and out of the window, though it could be done. The limb of the large oak was close enough that it provided solid footing to begin a climb down, and with a little jump, he could grab the lowest limb to begin a climb up. It wasn't that he needed to slip out; he could go anywhere he wanted, but he liked the idea of having private access to the outside. He had always been able to climb in and out of his bedroom window and sit outside in the cool of the night; it made him feel free, and freedom was something Johnny cherished—more than even he realized.

Naomi, Matt, Doc and Russell sat on the porch in the cool evening, listening to the cicadas sing.

"How were things out at the Tolney's today, Doc?" Naomi asked him.

"Evelyn's managing to get from the bed Webster and Sample put up in the living room to the kitchen table for meals with the help of a walker and somebody beside her. She's improving slowly, but she's improving."

"Sample still out there trying to make points?" Matt asked.

"Is a pig pork? Now he's announced to Webster that he'd pay for any medical expenses that Evelyn has. Webster told me that today. Told me not to worry about my bill." Doc shook his head. "Now when did Webster ever worry about my bill? I do think though," Doc went on, "that Webster's just about licked Sample's boots clean. He knows that if Alice marries Sample, the debt will be wiped out. Sample's there almost every night for dinner."

"How is Alice holding up?" Naomi wanted to know. "I haven't had a chance to talk to her in a couple of days. It's a lot having her mother to care for much less having to deal with Webster and Sample."

The plow lines between Doc's eyes furrowed deeper. "I wish I knew," he said. "I don't know what Webster's been saying to the child, but he's been riding her. I've watched her around Sample. For the most part she treats him like a piece of heavy furniture that somebody moved into her way. Since she can't move it, she just tries to maneuver around it. But I can tell you she's not happy about having to do it."

"Problem with that," Matt said, "is that Sample isn't just going to sit there forever and be moved around. One of these days, he's going to expect payment for all this great kindness he's doling out. We all know 'pie is never free,' and Sample's already paid $100 for his."

"Seems like Sample is already collecting at a right smart rate," Russell interjected.

"That fool Webster should know better than to make any deal with Sample that he couldn't be positive he could deliver. Forney is not a man to be shortchanged," Matt said.

Naomi gave a shudder and glanced uneasily through the screen door at the staircase.

Matt touched her arm. "They're upstairs with the door shut and the radio on; they can't hear. You want your shawl?"

"No, I'm all right, thank you, Matt. I'm just worried."

"We all are, honey," Matt said, and no one thought the endearment out of place. He put his hand on top of hers, and Naomi felt the strength of it. It calmed her a little.

Russell asked, moving his head in the direction of the stairs, "Ray and Alice able to see each other any?" Russell had become as caught up as the rest of them in the lives of the two young men who were out of hearing at the top of the stairs.

Doc said, "I haven't seen them together yet, but if I were a betting man, I'd say that they were managing it. Alice has a developed an interest in taking long walks a couple of times a week when her mother takes her nap after lunch. I've seen her head into the Oppenmeier's woods just across the road from the Tolney's mailbox. Now just how far she walks, I couldn't say, but she's generally carrying a lunch basket big enough to hold lunch for more than one slim girl, and those woods do back up to the Redeem's property."

"Webster hasn't noticed these long walks, has he?" Naomi worried.

"Webster's working over at Sample's every week day, and then he brings Sample home to dinner every evening," Doc said. "I think the only two people to notice Alice out walking at that time of day, if she's careful, would be Matt and me, and neither of us would be telling anybody except the people on this porch."

Matt nodded. He'd noticed, too, and had told Naomi.

Naomi still wasn't satisfied. "I just want them to be careful. Sample may be determined to have his pie, but Ray is just as determined that he's never going to get it. Nothing has ever scared Ray, except losing a person he loves, and Ray truly loves Alice."

Doc said, "Right now, I don't think Sample is even considering Ray; he thinks Ray is out of the picture. He's working on Webster and Evelyn every day, and Alice knows it. She sees her mother, who never did stand up very well to her father, too weak and sick to even try right now. There's nobody to stand with Alice. That's an awful load for one young woman to carry."

"I wish Mary Jo could stay here to help, but she'd lose that good paying job if she had to take off. She just can't take the chance," Naomi said.

Matt wanted to take the worry off Naomi's face. "Let's let it rest for tonight. Anything interesting happen today, Doc?" he asked. Matt had usually had something happen on the mail route or Doc did while he was making rounds

"Matilda St. John wanted me to examine her two Guernseys," Doc told him, chewing contentedly on a large bite of cake.

"Why on earth would she want that?" Naomi questioned

"Seems the cows haven't been giving down milk as they used to."

"Why didn't she call Doc Funk?" Russell asked him.

"Matilda thought since she caught me driving down the road that I might do her 'this one little favor that would just take an ever so quick run back to the barn,' and she wouldn't need to call Doc Funk over from Meramec City. She also told me it ought to be easier to examine an animal than a person. She said, 'Not quite so complex, I would think'."

Naomi laughed; she could just hear Matilda. "Did you do it?"

"I didn't examine the cows, but I did examine Matilda."

"You examined Matilda?" Russell asked.

"I asked her some questions, Russell." Doc looked at him over the tops of his glasses. "I didn't physically examine her."

Russell grinned. "I figured it would be quicker than trying to explain the difference between a person and a cow."

Doc took another bite of his second piece and made loving murmurs before he swallowed. He continued, "I asked her if there were any changes that might affect the cows, and she said Albert had moved them out to the back pasture because he felt it was better grazing land. I told her that shouldn't make any changes in milk production. Then she told me that Albert has been going after the cows on the Harley that they got for Hampton last Christmas." Doc did an almost perfect imitation of Matilda: "The military academy won't let him keep it on campus, you know. Far too much noise. So Albert decided to put it to some use."

They all began laughing. "Did you tell her that Albert has been scaring the milk right back into those cows?" Matt asked.

"I did, and she said she wouldn't think a little thing like that would bother them when it was so much more convenient for Albert to go for them on the motorcycle than to drive the truck where there were no roads."

"What did you say to that?" Naomi asked him.

"I told her that cows generally were not given to that kind of speculation."

They settled into another hour on the porch, Russell resting his head back against the pillow that Naomi had brought out for him, thinking how right it had been to come home. Doc finally roused himself, saying he had an early call and had to get on back home. He drove off with a wave, and Naomi and Matt helped Russell into his downstairs room and into bed as easily as though they had been practicing. Naomi left the light on in the bathroom and told Russell to call her if he needed anything. Then she shut the door softly, and she and Matt went back out to the porch to sit in the swing.

Chapter Twenty-Six

Hope Howard was thankful she didn't have to share a room with her younger sister. The parsonage had four bedrooms, and her little sister, Grace, slept in the room across the hall. Her room was her one refuge. Her father spoke to her only when it was necessary. Then his voice, which usually rose and fell in a softer, slower cadence than his pulpit voice, was flat. It was a constant reminder of what she had done. Even if his voice hadn't been a register for his emotions, his eyes would have told her over and over again.

Hope felt like some ghost who used to live there. It had been four weeks since Evelyn's stroke, and her father hadn't relented at all. If anything, he was more like cold, hard stone than ever.

Even her mother, who always privately took her side, said that Hope would just have to wait until her father got over this bad spot, that everything would be better then. Just now, her mother said, she had all she could handle. What with the goings-on at the pie supper and Evelyn's illness, and Naomi and Johnny's not attending church after her father's sermon, her mother said she was just about at her wit's end to know how to keep her father calm. If that weren't enough, he had been taken off guard by the deacons at their last meeting. He had never for a minute thought they would disagree with him, and then they'd gone and left everything open. Everybody in town was discussing the situation; her father, her mother said, had never been so shaken.

In her room, she built a fortress wall, using Dickens, Jane Austen, the Brontes, and Steinbeck. They knew her; her family didn't. The rest of the time she felt weighed down by her father's unending disapproval, his downright dislike of her. Every breath was a lonely one. More than anything she wanted to be free, as far away from her father as possible. In the weeks apart from Johnny and the weeks of her father's shunning, she had come to hate him, hate him even more than she feared him. Oh, she knew she was supposed to love him; he was her father. But she hated him more, and she wanted to leave his house and never, ever have to obey him again.

So at nights she escaped as soon as she could to her books. She supposed she should be grateful that her father never had stopped her from reading; he'd stopped her from everything else. She was free to read what he called "acceptable books" as long as she did her daily Bible study. What he would never know was that lately she'd simply been moving the red, silk ribbon bookmark of her Bible from one chapter to the next on a daily basis. Hope found Dickens far more comforting than Matthew, Mark, Luke or John, and she never read Revelations. It was worse than a horror movie.

Every night since the deacon's meeting, she could hear her parents talking after they went to their bedroom next to Hope's. Her father would be going over and over the meeting. He kept telling her mother what Wendell Johnson and Loncy Oppenmeier had said. He'd repeat that he never expected that those men would turn on him like that. Then, he'd get even more worked up, saying that he didn't deserve this kind of treatment; after all, wasn't he doing the Lord's work? And Jackson, what was wrong with him, he'd ask her mother, that Jackson didn't see that he had to say what he'd said? He couldn't believe they'd put off settling this thing until next month's meeting. By this time, he'd be pacing, and his voice would grow louder and louder.

She would hear her mother murmur something. It was more a soothing sound than words, kind of a "there, there" she did with her voice. Her father would say that at least *she* understood, and after her mother had coaxed him to lie beside her and told him about some incident of the day that had nothing to do with Evelyn's stroke or deacons' meetings, he would finally drift off to sleep. What he didn't seem to notice was that her mother never, by anything she said, directly agreed with him. Hope would fall to sleep trying to hold onto that fact.

Then, this morning, her mother had been on the phone with Maude Elkins, who called every day to relay the latest gossip, and Hope had heard her mother ask when Johnny had quit his job at Johnson's Store and gone to work for Ray Redeem? Hope felt the last bit of air push right out of her lungs. At least, she'd been able to look at Johnny when she went into Johnson's; even if they couldn't speak, her mother usually sent her over at least once a day for bread or bologna or something. She knew he was there, right down the road. Now what would she do?

She had to talk with Alice. Hope had finally been allowed to go to the Tolney's on Mondays and Wednesdays to help Alice with the chores. Much better to be with Alice than at home; she could talk to Alice. After hearing her mother, she could hardly wait to get there.

Alice was sitting on the front porch steps waiting. Jumping from the steps, Alice ran to open the car door, saying, "You'll never believe it; you'll never believe it," and launched right into telling Hope how Ray and Johnny had finally worked out a plan for all of them to meet.

She explained it had begun when she and Ray left notes for each other under a large rock across the road from the Tolney's mailbox. She took a walk most days while Evelyn took a nap after her lunch, and she'd go check the mail and pick up Ray's notes and leave him one.

Last week Evelyn was doing well enough that on Tuesday and Thursday, Alice had slipped off to meet Ray, going through the woods on the Oppenmeier's land that fronted the road across from the Tolney's mailbox. She took the path that led through the large stand of trees to the Redeem's property, and she and Ray had eaten lunch on Flat Rock overlooking the creek. They'd only had an hour or so, but at least they could see each other and talk.

Ray said it was perfectly safe. Flat Rock was the spot where they always had the church picnics. Nobody came there except for a party. It was an easy place to find, but impossible to see from any road. The only direct path came down from the Oppenmeier's farmhouse, and they never came down on weekdays; Ray said he was sure of that. Hadn't he lived next to them all of his life? Hope and Johnny would be safe there, too. They could all go to lunch on Mondays and Wednesdays.

It was a perfect plan, Hope thought. There was no reason that her father would be out at the Oppenmeier's. He only came on church picnic days, and he had far too much to do to be out roaming around the country.

Even after she got home, Hope's heart was still lifted in her chest and was beating out a fox trot. At dinner she could barely sit quietly. She was glad her father had taken her mother and sister to a revival meeting in Havana that evening. She hadn't had to go because of band practice; she played the clarinet in the school band. Her mother didn't need to drive her because Billy Easton picked her up, and she rode with him to Meramec City.

Billy had graduated with Johnny, but he was going to summer band practice to keep his hand in. He was going to major in music at college. At least he was going to Drury College in Springfield; he wasn't going off to the Baptists. Billy made her laugh, and she was thirsty for laughter.

Thank goodness, she thought, she'd been able to spend the evening with Billy; she was afraid her father might have seen the happiness in her face. By morning, she'd be better prepared to hide it.

Johnny, Johnny, she kept thinking. She couldn't wait to see him again.

Chapter Twenty-Seven

Doc had always been a frequent guest at Naomi's, but after Russell told the family and Matt his prognosis, and they moved him into the downstairs bedroom, it was easier for all of them if Doc dropped by each evening to check on Russell, bringing whatever medication he needed to keep him comfortable. Besides, Doc liked the company. He'd always been the closest friend of both Matt and Naomi; he was practically a member of the family. Now, he was the keeper of the pain.

Their evenings on the porch became their ritual, their comfort. They would sit out there after dinner, Naomi, Matt, Russell, Doc, and Johnny, when he was home. Usually Ray as well. There was no more choir practice for Naomi, no church group get-togethers for Johnny; neither he nor Ray were dating, at least not that anybody was supposed to know, and Ray had given up taverns and fighting. Sometimes, the boys went off in Ray's truck to a movie in Meramec City or Havana, but just as often they sat on the porch banister, bracing themselves against a pillar.

The steam of their anger against Russell was pretty well spent when they'd learned Russell was dying, and Naomi had told Johnny to remember that without Russell they'd never have known each other, and she wouldn't have had Johnny as a son. He still hadn't been pleased with Russell's leaving the way he did, but as the days passed and Johnny came to know Russell more and watched the way that Aunt Naomi and Matt and Doc treated him, Johnny began to soften. And when Johnny softened, so did Ray. Then the two of them learned something about Russell they hadn't known; Russell could be funny. His stories about dancing in the movies were more entertaining than going to one. They, too, came to know he hadn't come home to set them all mourning; he'd come so he wouldn't be alone.

Now, they all took part in caring for Russell. He had come home to his family and they had taken him in: his family, tenting each other up with their nightly talks on the porch, their voices tethering them to each other in the moonlit nights.

Summertime in Tysen had always meant open windows all day and evenings on the porches with handheld fans on Popsicle sticks at the ready. Usually, after sundown there was a breeze making its way across the night blooming jasmine, male cicadas whirring their love song that came in waves, louder then softer then louder, and pitchers of iced tea or lemonade sweating on trays on a wicker table or the porch floor amongst the chairs that could withstand all summer weather. Neighbors were careful to keep to the walk or the street, unless they were invited up, calling a greeting or standing a minute for a word about the weather or some local news.

"People generally have a sense of propriety and good taste about illness," Doc said one evening toward the last of June. Millie Moffatt who ran The Taste of Tysen Café had just walked by on her way home after closing up. She stopped long enough to be neighborly, but not so long that she'd tire Russell out, and when she left, she didn't tell Russell to get better soon or she hoped he'd be up and about before too long. She just said, "I hope your day wasn't too uncomfortable, Russell," and he had assured her it hadn't been. "Good," she said. Then with a wave she went on her way. Everybody in town knew Russell was dying; there wasn't any reason to pretend he wasn't.

"Generally," Matt agreed, "they do. Of course, some don't have the sense of a goose." There was gravel in Matt's voice. Doc and Naomi looked at him.

Russell grinned. "If you're saying, Matt, I'd just as soon go ahead and die as have Busby Howard come by here again, I'd say, you're dang well right."

"Busby Howard came here?" Johnny asked, standing upright.

"When?" Naomi asked, her voice rising.

"Yes," Johnny echoed, "when?" He moved to stand beside Naomi's chair.

Ray put his glass down on the rail, and Doc put his macaroon back on the plate.

"I probably wouldn't have brought it up, but Matt came home just as he was leaving, and I think the Muellers might have heard some of it, as well as a few other folks, so you would have found out about it mighty quick anyhow. It was when you were out at Evelyn's this afternoon, Naomi. I think he'd been waiting until he was sure you'd gone."

"What did he want?" Ray asked.

Russell grinned. "To check on the state of my soul. He said he wanted to know that I'd been sincere about the profession of faith I'd made when I was a boy. Said he knew I'd not attended church all that often when I worked for the railroad, and he knew I was always one for dancing, but I was to remember the Baptist motto: 'Once saved, always saved.' He told me, 'Baptists don't believe in falling from grace; we leave that to the Methodists. Your mother was a fine Christian woman, and she would want me to come to see if you are ready to meet your Maker, being that you're dying. All you need to do is to rededicate your life to the Lord'."

"Well, wasn't that kindly of him?" Doc asked, biting fiercely into a new macaroon he took from the platter; then asked Russell while he was chewing, "Did you ask that 'fine Christian man' why he made his visit when Naomi and Johnny were away from home?"

"No, but I did tell him that the state of my soul was between me and the Lord; he needn't worry about it."

"What happened then?" Ray wanted to know, wishing he'd been there to hear it.

"It was about that time that Matt came home." Russell grinned with pleasure and turned to Matt. "Matt got a little riled this afternoon."

When Matt had seen Busby on the porch, he had steamed up the sidewalk from the post office and taken the porch steps two at a time, demanding, "What're you doing here, Busby?"

"What do you mean, what am I doing here?"

"Just that. Why are you on Naomi Hollister's porch?"

"This is Russell Hollister's porch, if I remember rightly," Busby had said indignantly.

"You got that wrong, Preacher," Russell had said. "I gave this place to Naomi when I ran out on her and Johnny. She just took me in and let me stay here out of Christian charity. For that matter, it's Matt's porch, too; he pays rent."

Busby ignored Russell's comment. He spoke to Matt: "I came here to see Russell; I'm certainly not here to see Naomi or Johnny, or you, for that matter."

"I'm sure we're all grateful for that," Matt said.

Busby brushed aside that comment as well. "I'm here on the Lord's work, seeing to a very ill man."

"Did the very ill man ask you to come?" Matt asked him.

"No, but he doesn't have to ask; he's on the church rolls. If I didn't check on Russell, I might have let a dying soul slip out of my grasp and slide right down to Hell."

"Busby, the sorriest thing about you is that you are so all-fired sure that you are right and that the rest of us are so all-fired wrong." Matt's voice was rising. "God in heaven, man…."

By this time the Muellers had come out of the phone exchange, leaving the phone ringing away inside, and the Johnsons had been called out onto the porch by the Pucketts who had been buying salt pork and beans and were just going out to get into their truck. Even Bertie and Tom Reardon had come outside the railroad station. Nobody moved closer, but the voices of Matt and Busby were loud enough by this time so that there was no need.

"I don't answer to you; I answer only to the Lord," Busby said defiantly, his chin set. "*I'm* the pastor of First Baptist Church of Tysen."

"You're no pastor; you're just a preacher, just a loud-mouthed preacher. You've never been a pastor in your life. It's 'Feed My sheep,' Busby, not have them follow you over some dang cliff. Now, you've hurt people I love, and I'm not going to stand by with my mouth shut. So get yourself off this porch, and don't come back here until you can apologize to them."

"And with that," Russell concluded, "Busby turned tail and walked past Mueller's and the Reardon's and high-tailed it into the post office, where Jake Weaver was probably the only person not to hear. Millie Moffatt was even standing out in front of the Talk of Tysen with Matilda and Albert St. John who had just come out of the feed store. I would imagine that there's nobody in the county who won't know by tomorrow morning." Russell looked highly pleased, and Matt looked just a tad sheepish.

"Got a few things off your chest, did you, Matthew?" Doc asked, grinning at him.

"I guess I did."

"You don't look sorry about it, Matt," Ray said, smiling.

"Can't say that I am." Matt looked at Naomi. "You mad at me?"

"Course I'm not mad at you," Naomi said, flushing a nice shade of pleasure pink.

Ray said, "I wish I could have been here to see it."

"I probably shouldn't have got so riled up, but I just couldn't stop myself. I've had all I can take of that man," Matt said.

Johnny, going back to his seat on the porch rail, knew just how he felt.

They all sipped their tea with a sense of satisfaction.

Chapter Twenty-Eight

June began to smell like growing rows of staked tomatoes, green beans, corn stalks, bell peppers, cucumbers, strawberries and beds of mint. Tiny points of asparagus pushed through the surface and took a breath. Miniature apples and peaches promised to ride down the limbs of trees in orchards and yards, and Doris Ettleman's pear tree, always the best bloomer in town, looked to outdo itself this year.

In the woods, the sweet fragrance of moss and dogbane, of aster and honeysuckle, cast a spell around Flat Rock. The cold, spring-fed creek chasing itself downhill over the pebbles, through watercress and around an occasional boulder, sounded like a love song to the four young people who came twice each week to eat lunch together. Nothing had ever tasted as good as the thick-sliced ham sandwiches and Alice's oatmeal cookies, washed down with a thermos of sweetened iced tea.

After lunch, Ray and Alice would take off walking in one direction beside the creek, and Johnny and Hope would walk in the other. If Doc had seen them, he would have said that was the way they were heading into the future, too.

Ray and Alice waded barefoot and began to plan their life together. Johnny and Hope didn't think past the end of August. They were happy to eat ham sandwiches and hold hands. The summer was still ahead; life was good; something would work out for everybody. Didn't it always?

At the Tolney's, over dinner, Sample Forney had seen Alice's face relax more and more the last week or so, and her eyes had begun to look brighter. Time, he thought; time was helping. He'd been right just to bide his time. He kept bringing little gifts that he hoped would please her. Once he'd brought a basket of apples he knew she liked for baking. She thanked him, but didn't bake a pie, at least not one he saw, though the apples disappeared. Another time, he'd offered a box of candied dates, and she said she'd put them right into a batch of oatmeal cookies for her momma to enjoy.

Then came the day he'd boldly bought some cornflower blue dress material that he knew would match Alice's eyes. He'd had Wendell Johnson cut it, rather than Marie; he didn't want any female eyebrow-raising. "Cut enough for two dresses," he told Wendell, who measured the material without looking at Sample. "Good weather for the crops," Wendell had said as he cut. Men know how to do business, Sample thought.

When he had come in for dinner and handed the package to Alice, explaining the dress material was for Evelyn, she had said, "That's right nice of you. Momma needs a new dress." She turned from him, walking over to her mother who was sitting in the rocker by the kitchen window watching them, and laid the material in her lap.

"There's a little more there than she probably needs," Sample told her. "Maybe you could find a use for the rest of it yourself." Alice looked down at the shiny blue cotton that shimmered like silk. The color is beautiful, she thought, and how she would love a new dress, but not from him. She wanted nothing from Sample Forney, not even if it came as surplus with a gift for her momma.

"Momma loves blue," she told Sample to avoid answering him.

Evelyn was rubbing the tips of her fingers over the cloth. She looked up at Alice and smiled a lop-sided smile. "Sing," she said, and pointed to the material. "Sing."

"Sing 'Alice Blue Gown'?" Alice asked her.

Evelyn nodded.

Alice took Evelyn's hands and waltzing them slowly back and forth began to sing:

In my sweet little Alice Blue Gown,
When I first wandered down into town,
I was so proud inside,
As I felt every eye,
And in every shop window, I primped, passing by.
A new manner of fashion I'd found,

And the world seemed to smile all around.

Evelyn tried to join in and sang a word here and there with Alice.

'Till it wilted, I wore it,
I'll always adore it,
My sweet little Alice Blue Gown.

That was the first time Alice had heard her momma try to sing in months; she had sung only a few words, and her voice had wavered, but Evelyn was smiling.

Alice knelt to hug her. "Oh, Momma, it's so good to hear you sing again." Alice felt such a rush of happiness that she had forgotten about the extra material; she'd even forgotten Sample was there. But when she turned and saw him, she was so full of the sound of her momma's voice that she would have been grateful to any person who'd made her sing again, and said, meaning it, "Thank you, Sample. You've made Momma very happy."

Well, now, Sample thought, she took it. And she called me Sample. I knew it! I knew it! I knew I could make her see what I could buy. Now that she wasn't seeing Ray Redeem anymore and was home every night, he knew he would have a chance.

Things were right on track, as far as Sample was concerned. She was there tending her momma, not going anywhere, and he was there as well. Things were going along just fine.

Alice, though, dancing around the kitchen table while she hummed another chorus, held the dress material in her arms and danced right by Sample's chair without seeing him.

Chapter Twenty-Nine

In town at Naomi's, Russell was holding on as well as could be expected. He did seem to grow thinner by the day in spite of Naomi's effort to cook any dish that she thought might tempt him. Russell said he just didn't have much appetite, and Naomi told him she understood and would go promptly back to the kitchen to try to think up something else that would tempt him to force down three or four bites.

She had moved his chair to the far end of the porch where he was shaded by the big oak, and he could set a coffee cup or a plate on the railing if he had a mind to. She'd added soft cushions and a large, padded footstool that had room enough for his legs as well as his feet. There was always a throw on the arm of the chair in case the evening air was a little chilly for him.

Busby Howard had not been back. Naomi had seen him drive up to Johnson's Store and even driven in front of the hotel, but he never so much as turned his head in her direction. Helen Howard, though, always managed the tiniest wave to Naomi when she drove by alone. Then she would pretend to smooth her hair just in case someone had been watching.

Helen couldn't phone, though she would have liked to. Everyone in town would know that she was talking to Naomi behind the preacher's back. That would be disloyal to Busby. Helen longed to sit in Naomi's kitchen and have a nice cup of tea with her and tell her she didn't agree with Busby and she was so sorry he had done and said what he had. But there was no possibility that she could do that. Just like the phone call, everybody would know the minute she set foot on Naomi's front porch—or back porch, for that matter. There were no secrets in Tysen;

someone else always knew. So secrets spread like poison ivy, depending on who knew and how much the person in the know itched to tell.

There were very few people in Tysen who could keep from scratching.

Busby began to think that it wasn't such a bad idea that the deacon's meeting had been postponed. He had believed that Naomi and Johnny probably wouldn't be coming back to church while he was there, and after his visit to Russell, he was certain of it. He was counting on the fact that the church had moved right on without them during these weeks, and that by the time Russell died, the rest of the congregation would realize that the Hollisters were not necessary members. In fact, the more he thought about it, he thought it was the best plan the deacons could have come up with.

The only thing in June that caused much of a ripple in Tysen was that North Korea decided to cross the 38th parallel and invade South Korea. The Rockwell brothers, John and Walter, were called up almost immediately, and Parcel Jones, who lived just east of town, got his draft notice the week following. Ray hadn't passed his physical when he went to sign up for the draft because of the broken eardrum he'd got in a fight, and Johnny had a college exemption. They'd all had to go sign up for the draft when they were eighteen; President Truman had signed the Selective Services Act two years before. Some folks agreed with President Truman's decision, and others didn't, same as always, but the draft had become a fact of life.

Johnny told Ray sometimes he felt like going to college gave him special privileges, and that just wasn't right. Ray had said that it did give him special privileges, and he should damn well be glad of it. Ray didn't want to see another brother blown to bits. "You'll be of service to the country being a journalist; you won't be any good to anybody getting yourself killed," Ray said. "Besides, you want to be the one to tell Naomi that you are going to enlist?"

Johnny shook his head. No, he didn't want to do that. He really didn't want to go fight; he just felt he should do his duty. There was nothing Johnny had ever wanted to do except become a newspaper reporter. He and Aunt Naomi had planned on it all of his life. That was a dream they'd both lived for.

Chapter Thirty

The Fourth of July came in the nick of time. There'd been too much worry and too much gossip. Each year on the Fourth of July, the people brought their picnic baskets and their lawn chairs and set them up in the school parking lot, and the kids would set off firecrackers while waiting for dark. Then Abe Carver and Loncy Oppenmeier would set off rockets and roman candles, and anything else they could find that would shoot high and explode with a lot of noise and shower them with multi-colored sparks.

This year, Maureen Fitzroy, Marie Johnson, Matilda St. John and Naomi Hollister, the Tysen Special Events Committee, had decided to expand the festivities; it was the least they could do to remember the boys in Korea. Besides, there hadn't been anything in the way of entertainment since the pie supper, and the ladies were of a mind that since things had been a bit tense around town lately that everybody needed a lift. After giving a good deal of thought to it, they had decided on a Fourth of July Parade. "Who wouldn't love a parade?" Matilda enthused, "the pageantry, the music, the excitement." She looked around the group in Marie Johnson's living room for confirmation. They all nodded; it was true: most everybody loved a parade.

So it was decided, and the planning began. Marie thought it would be right nice if the children decorated their bicycles and wagons and marched through town waving tiny flags; she could order three or four dozen through the store and donate them to the cause. The rest of the committee agreed that was very generous of Marie.

They decided the parade should begin at 4:00 p.m., followed by a picnic supper on the school grounds that evening and then, as soon as it got dark enough, Abe and Loncy could set off the fireworks. Doobie Pratt, who had won an Uncle Sam costume in a poker game at the Veteran's Hall in Meramec City one Fourth of July some years ago, was the logical candidate to lead the parade (if he stayed sober), and Walter Mueller, attired in the Minute Man costume Millie had made for him for the school play last year, could bring his musket and march behind Doobie. Walter would be followed by the Tonette Quartet, playing John Philip Sousa marches. The children, in double file, would follow the Tonette Quartet. The Boy Scouts, in full uniform, led by a flag bearer with a large American flag and a snare drummer to set the pace, would bring up the rear. The ladies decided they had come up with a perfect plan.

It was just as they were relaxing, having their tea and muffins, that Bertie Reardon appeared unannounced right in Marie's living room. Bertie said she knew they were meeting and had come up with a marvelous idea: she could decorate her car, open the rumble seat, dress up like the Statue of Liberty and ride in the parade. She thought it was just the thing to bring up the rear.

All the ladies put down their teacups except Matilda; she believed in holding onto one's cup; "tea" had saved the Empire, after all. Nobody spoke for a moment. Then the Special Events Committee began to talk among themselves.

"Well, I don't know," Maureen began; changes in plans were sometimes unsettling to Maureen, and the thought of Bertie as the Statue of Liberty wasn't something she had envisioned—ever. She turned to Naomi.

Naomi's tone was speculative. "We've never had a car...."

"We've never even had a float," Marie added.

"Don't you think a car could be kind of a float?" Bertie asked. "And they dress up and have floats in St. Louis at the Veiled Prophet's Parade."

"Well, yes," Maureen began.

"And Tom Jr. has taught Bunny to drive right well. Tom Sr. will ride with her in the front seat in case she needs help. I've got it all planned."

The ladies could see that. They didn't quite know what to say.

"About the Statue of Liberty...," Naomi began.

"Oh, don't worry your head about that, Naomi. I've already made the costume out of old bed sheets, and I've made me a crown just like hers. It looks right nice, even if I say so myself." Bertie was never one not to say so herself.

Matilda, having sipped her way through an evaluation of the situation, said, "I think that we should be open to having Bertie's car. We'll have Uncle Sam, a Minute Man and the Statue of Liberty. It sounds festive."

They looked round at one another for a few seconds, still skeptical.

"Well," Naomi began, looking at the shine in Bertie's eyes, "it might add a little something extra. And it would be different from anything we've ever had."

They all agreed that was true.

"It would sort of be like a float," Maureen said. They were beginning to accept the idea, even if most of them weren't as enthusiastic as Matilda.

"Of course, it would," Matilda said,

Marie nodded in agreement. "I guess it couldn't hurt anything."

So, it was decided. Bertie could float her car in the Fourth of July Parade.

Bertie was so beside herself when they agreed, she did a bit of an Irish jig right there in the middle of the living room, setting the porcelain figurines left to Marie by her grandmother scooting across the coffee table. Three women held their breath, and Marie gasped, but Bertie, grabbed the figurines just before they leaped over the edge to their certain doom. "I just know it will be a Fourth of July everybody will remember," she promised, as she set the figurines carefully back in their places.

On the Fourth, the parking lot was full of cars and trucks at Johnson's Store, and the lot limit was being pushed at both taverns, trucks beds hanging over the edge of the blacktop. Wendell kept the store open on the Fourth because most everyone would want a cold soda pop and a packet of peanuts or a Baby Ruth while they watched the parade. On the porch of the store, there were two benches, one that ran the length of the porch and one at the end, to form an "L." Before or after shopping on any day, the men, mostly, would sit there, chew a little tobacco or have a cigarette, and pass the time of day. On the Fourth of July, it was a natural place to gather.

There wasn't a porch or a lawn without people. Even Eugene Proutty over at the Funeral Parlor had set up chairs and was serving lemonade. Russell and Matt, who were already installed on the front porch of the hotel, saw that Busby, Helen, and little Grace Howard had taken seats at Eugene's along with Hope and Alice, each holding a big glass of lemonade.

By 3:30, Maureen and the rest of the committee members were corralling children in the road beside Johnson's Store. Bicycles, tricycles and red wagons were jockeying to get to the front of the line. There must have been thirty kids from toddlers to the younger teenagers set to go, each with red, white, and blue crepe paper through their wheels and flowing from their handlebars. Doobie was right on time, top hat and all, looking almost sober. Walter, clad in his Minute Man costume with musket in hand, fell into place behind Doobie. The Tonette Quartet was trying to squeeze into position behind Walter, while their heels were being nipped by the tricycles. Maureen finally got the children into line, convincing them that they would all be seen; there was no need to try to push to the front. She had even hinted that those closer to the back could break away after the parade to get to the ice cream freezers sooner than the ones in the front.

They were just about assembled when Matt spotted the Reardon's car coming down the spur road in front of the filling station. Bunny was driving, her hands in a death grip on the wheel. The front of the car was draped with an American flag, and a stuffed eagle on loan from Gene Proutty, who kept it in his office at the funeral parlor, served as a hood ornament. Tom Sr. was sitting on the passenger side of the coupe attired in a black suit coat, top hat and Abe Lincoln whiskers, all of which Bertie had neglected to mention.

Bertie was standing alone in the rumble seat, in bleached white bed sheets swathed around her Greek style. She held a cardboard torch up over her head with one hand, steadied herself against the car's back window with the other, and looked regally over the crowd. When Bunny pulled to a careful stop at the back of the procession, the crowd cheered. From the back of the group on Johnson's porch, Loncy Oppenmeier yelled, "Good job, Bertie. It's a beauty."

"And you don't look too bad yourself, Bert," Doobie yelled from the front of the line.

At that the crowd laughed and began to clap. Bertie stood more erect, her torch higher overhead, looking off toward Naomi's porch, where Naomi had come to join the men, and smiling broadly at Naomi.

Naomi waved to Bertie as she settled into her chair. "The woman drives me half crazy at times, but there's something about her I've just got to love," Naomi said.

Naomi was looking forward to today. The parade would give people something else to talk about other than what was going to happen at the Baptist Church. Naomi was grateful that folks didn't seem to be upset with her, even if Busby was.

Russell had seemed some better this morning. He said he wanted to get out on the porch early so he wouldn't miss a thing. Matt had taken him out about 2:30.

"It's better than a movie set," Russell said.

"It could do with some dancing," Matt told him, and Russell grinned. "On another day, I'd have helped you out."

"No, you wouldn't," Doc said. "Busby's over there to put the quietus on anything fun. Looks like we're on different sides of the track, doesn't it?"

"Well, there's nothing today that he can object to," Naomi said. "There's not a dance step among the lot of them." She waved her hand in a broad sweep, taking in the entirety of the parade group.

"Which way they marching?" Russell asked Naomi.

"They're going to march past the funeral parlor and George Wilson's on down to B Street and cross the tracks at the far end of town and turn and march back down in front of us; then they'll cross the tracks right here, ending at Johnson's Store where they started." East of town at B Street, the main track ran straight for a mile and a quarter before disappearing over the horizon; west of town, on past the hotel, it ran straight for only a short quarter mile; then the track curved quickly out of sight.

Johnny and Ray arrived just as the parade got underway. They'd been over at the school helping to set up the fireworks.

Maureen signaled, the scout drummer began his rat-a-tat-tat, and Doobie led off, looking right smart. He waved at the children who watched along the way, and shook hands now and again with the adults who were holding onto them. He even doffed his hat to the ladies.

Walter Mueller carried his musket over his shoulder and marched right along. Millie was out on the porch sitting in the swing, one ear tuned to the telephone board, but she didn't think many calls would be coming through. Naomi called over to her. "You did a nice job with that costume, Millie. Walter looks like a real Minute Man."

Millie blushed nicely. "I am proud of it, if I do say so myself," she called back.

Behind him the Tonette Quartet played, *The Stars and Stripes Forever*, and they were generally on key. The children didn't worry about staying in line, but they did keep to the road with the help of some adults who were standing by to watch. The tricyclers pedaled with fury for minutes at a time and stopped to suck their thumbs; then they had to be urged on by their parents. The bicyclers made figure eights showing off their cycling skill, and the children pulling wagons were just happy to be there.

The Boy Scouts, almost in step to the rhythm, followed the children; then along came the Reardons. Bunny stared straight ahead in solemn concentration, hands still clenched on the steering wheel. Tom leaned out of the car window and raised his hat, his whiskers slipping slightly to one side, but managing to stay attached at his ears. Bertie stood, tall and glorious, torch above her head in her right hand, steadying herself on the back of the cab with her left hand. It was her moment; she strove to look noble, to stand with dignity. She was the Statue of Liberty, the symbol of the country, the pride of Tysen, Missouri, on this Fourth of July, 1950.

As the parade moved past, the crowd joined in the color and the noise. They reached B Street and turned right to cross the tracks. Bunny slowly bumped her way across. They made another right and began their march past the feed store, the Talk of Tysen Café, the Wright place and the Jensen's, the post office and the telephone exchange, coming in front of the hotel. Doobie made a deep bow and swept his hat in front of Naomi. Walter saluted Millie, and she blushed again. The Tonette Quartet played, *America, the Beautiful*, and the Boys Scouts were actually marching in unison. Bertie turned loose of the back of the seat for a quick wave at the group on Naomi's porch, but Bunny hit a chug hole, and Bertie had to grab on tightly, righting herself. But never for a moment had she lost her poise. Bertie was winning the day.

The planning committee, scattered here and there along the parade route, was thrilled to a person at how well the parade had gone. It was a triumph. They could be justly proud. The parade turned right beyond the hotel to cross back over the tracks to make their way back to Johnson's Store. People were waving from the porch and clapping as they returned.

Children swarmed off bicycles and tricycles and out of wagons and were dispersing toward Johnson's porch to get to the ice cream freezers that would be standing in puddles of melted ice and salt. Doobie and Walter had joined the group of men who'd come out of the tavern to watch the parade. Walter was showing off his musket to some of the men, and Doobie made a quick duck inside for a beer.

Everyone had crossed the tracks except the tail end of the Boy Scout Troop and the Reardons when Tom happened to look to the west and saw that the arm on the signal pole was down, and the red light was on. Tom Reardon, old railroad man that he was, knew that in a matter of minutes a freight train would be coming round the bend from the west. With all their planning, the committee had not checked the train schedule. Bertie, above all people, should have been the one to call this to their attention; but in all her excitement, trains were the last thing on her mind.

Tom shouted at Bunny to put on the brakes. Bunny froze to the steering wheel and braked hard, forgetting to step on the clutch. The little car dipped forward, jerked, and stalled directly on the railroad tracks. Bertie, unaware of what was happening inside the car, was thrown forward. Her crown went flying to the ground behind her into the street. It was all she could do to hold onto her torch. When she turned to see what had happened to her crown, she lost her grip and went tumbling back into the rumble seat.

Matt said, "What in heaven's name is going on out there?"

"Looks like Bunny stalled the car on the tracks," Doc said. "I wonder what ever possessed her to throw on the brakes like that?"

People had begun to notice across the way, and some were stopping to point toward the stalled car. Just then from some distance they could hear the faint blast of a train whistle. Inside the car, Tom was shouting at Bunny, "Start the car, you blasted female; don't you have any brains? Don't just sit there; try to turn the engine over. There's a train coming down the track. Do you want to get us all killed?"

Bunny finally remembered to step on the clutch, but couldn't remember how to turn the engine on. She just kept pushing on the gas pedal. "Push the starter button, damn it. Push the button," Tom was shouting.

Bertie got to her feet, saw the red light, and leaned down to yell in to Tom. "There's a train coming. Get my car off this track, you old fool."

"Damn it, I know there's a train coming, but I can't get this stupid daughter of yours to start the car."

Bunny was crying. "I'm trying, Mama. I'm trying. I just can't start it."

"Try harder, Bunny," Bertie yelled at her. "Try harder."

"The damn thing's flooded now," Tom yelled at Bunny. "You'll never get it started." By this time, everyone had stopped in their paces to see what was happening. People were coming out of the tavern to watch.

Bunny kept grinding away, trying to get the engine to start.

Tom heard the whistle of the train and knew it was just around the bend. "It's no use, Bunny; get out of the car," he shouted. "That train will be coming around the corner at any minute."

Bertie yelled, "Bunny, don't you move. Keep trying. Keep trying."

"Don't you do it, Bertie Jr.," a name Tom rarely called her. "We aren't going to try to start this car. It's not worth it to get ourselves killed. You get on out now with me." And Bunny slid out of the front seat, head down, not looking at her mother.

"Now, Bertie climb down out of there," Tom ordered.

"I'm not coming," Bertie yelled at him. "This is my car, and I'm not going anywhere."

A slow moving freight train came round the corner from the west. "Bertie," Tom yelled up at her, "you're gonna get yourself killed. That train is coming straight down the track right at you."

"I tell you I'm not going anywhere; I'm gonna die in this car. It's the only thing that belongs to me." Bertie stood up again with all the aplomb she could muster.

"You crazy old woman," Tom screamed. He turned to Bunny. "We've got to get her out of there," he yelled. "Help me pull her out." The two of them began pulling at Bertie, and Bertie held on for dear life to the inside of the rumble seat. The Reardons pulled, and Bertie held on, and the train kept coming toward them, its whistle blowing for all it was worth. With one great tug, the two of them finally pulled Bertie free, and they all fell in the road in a tumble. Tom grabbed both of Bertie's arms, pulled them up over her head and dragged her away from the track with Bunny following. They had just moved out of range when the slow moving freight hit the little car and tossed it end over end like a pinwheel. It crumpled like an accordion and landed just off the track near the hotel. The train puffed its way onward without stopping.

Later, people would remark on why nobody had moved to help; they had all just stood there watching. Doc had said that all they had to do was put it in neutral and push it off the track, any fool knew that.

But at the moment it happened, Naomi was not concerned about the car. "Oh, Blessed Lord, poor Bertie. Just look at her." Bertie looked dirty and defeated. She was the picture of a dream gone awry.

Naomi called, "Bring her up on the porch, Bunny." Tom and Bunny had righted Bertie and got her to her feet, but Bertie pushed Tom away. "Get away from me you son-of-a-bitch," she shouted. "You've destroyed it all." She began to sob heavily into the front of her bed sheets. "Oh, Blessed Jesus, this man is my ruination." Tom looked at Bertie and then at Bunny, and shook his head. "I'll never understand the woman," he said, and turned and walked away from them, passing the car, crossing the tracks, and going straight into the tavern.

Matt and Doc made room for Bertie and Bunny. Both women were crying; Bunny was embarrassed and ashamed. Bertie, though, saw all her plans to have some status, to have people look up to her, to be recognized as something other than the station mistress were gone. Life looked bleak.

Naomi held Bertie's hand while Johnny was sent in to get lemonade for Bertie and Bunny. Except for Russell, the other men moved off the porch to go examine the car and help move the carcass to the side of the road.

"My car's gone, Naomi. My beautiful car is gone." Her shoulders were slumped, her chin on her chest. Bunny hunkered down in the chair next to Russell and didn't look up.

"I know, honey. I know," Naomi consoled, patting her hand.

"What ever will I do now?" she asked without looking up.

"It'll work out somehow," Naomi said, without believing a word of it.

"No, it won't. How can it?" The tears poured down her cheeks through lines made by winter cold and summer glare.

Johnny came back with two glasses of lemonade, handed them to Naomi and went off as quickly as he could to join the men.

"Here, Bertie, take a drink of lemonade; it'll help calm you," Naomi told her.

Bertie shook her head. "I couldn't get it down just now."

Naomi put a glass on the porch floor beside Bertie and carried the other glass to Bunny, who took it between both hands and looked into it as though it might hold the secret of how she could escape to a place where nobody would know her.

Naomi looked at Russell as though for help, and he raised his shoulders in a don't-ask-me shrug. After all, he, too, was a man; he just couldn't escape to the street.

"It's all my fault, Momma," Bunny said. "I'm so sorry."

"It's not your fault, baby. It's your daddy's fault; he's the one that was telling you what to do. You just did what you were told," Bertie said between hiccoughs. "I shoulda left him years ago."

"Oh, Momma, don't say that."

"It's the truth, Bunny. I should. Most everything bad that has happened to us your daddy brought on. Now, he's gone and wrecked my car, and I'll never have another one."

"Momma, daddy didn't wreck the car; he just got scared when he saw the train coming."

Bertie had to admit Bunny was right about that. It was also true that she, Bertie, hadn't checked the train schedules. She was the one who'd disgraced them all. She swabbed at her eyes again with her abused toga. Her armpits hurt from being dragged by Tom. She just wanted to go home and hide, and Bertie had never run from anything in her life. The fight was gone out of her, and she didn't see how she could ever get it back. "It is my fault, Naomi. I'm the one didn't check the train schedules. I really messed up and ruined the whole parade."

"Bertie, the only thing that is ruined is your car. The parade went real well, and your car made all the difference."

"I'll say," Russell muttered from behind closed eyelids. Naomi had thought he was asleep. She nudged his foot with her shoe, and he grinned without opening his eyes.

"Just look over there, Naomi," Bertie said, looking over toward Johnson's Store. "I've got to get through all those people before I can get to my house and close the door."

Naomi had to admit it would be like running a gauntlet. There were quite a few men over there just waiting to torment her. They loved teasing Bertie at anytime, and she usually gave as good as she got. But today, Naomi knew that she just didn't have it in her.

"Well, it won't help to stay here," Bertie said. "Come on, Bunny, we're going home." She gathered her toga around her with one hand and took Bunny by the other and started down off the front porch, holding her head as high as she could. Across the track, Maureen, Marie and Matilda had been standing in a clump watching and talking among themselves. "Jesus, Mary and Joseph, I'm going to have to face the three 'M's," Bertie sighed.

Naomi had seen them standing there, looking over toward the hotel. Just what they were saying she couldn't imagine. She watched as the two Reardon women walked over the railroad tracks, one with head high, one with her chin on her chest. Poor things, Naomi thought.

As Bertie and Bunny approached the group, Maureen separated herself and came in their direction. Well, here it comes, Bertie thought.

"Bertie," Maureen said, putting her hand on her shoulder, "would you like to join the Tysen Garden Society?"

Chapter Thirty-One

The pain woke Russell about six a.m. There was a half-filled glass of water on his bedside table, and the bottle of codeine tablets was near it, lying on its side, half a dozen tablets spewing out of it. Naomi had left the lid off so he wouldn't have to fumble with it, but he'd upset the bottle in the night with the back of his hand and had to go chasing two white pills, clutching at them several times before he retrieved them and ate them out of his hand, chewing them for what he hoped was quicker relief; then chased them with a large swallow of water.

At six it was light outside in late July. The heat hadn't begun yet, and the breeze pushing at the light, frothy white curtains at the windows was fresh from the south. Russell plucked up two pills from the table, almost reached for a third, then decided against it. Doc had told him to take more when he needed them or to take them more often, but he wanted to hold out as long as he could.

The cancer was on the move. The wheelchair hiding in the corner of his room with his light robe across its arms was an instantaneous reminder, even before he tried to move his weakening limbs. Sometimes, when he awoke in the night or before anyone began to stir in the mornings, he swore he could feel the cancer pushing its way along his arteries and veins, drilling tiny holes into his bones, taking bites of his organs. It was there all right; he knew he couldn't stop it. All he could do was hold out against it for as long as possible.

As he waited for the drugs to dull the pain, he reminded himself there were still things he wanted to see about. He wanted to see Johnny off to Mizzou; he wanted to see Ray get Alice away from Webster and Sample, and he wanted to know that sweet Hope would be all right even living with Busby Howard. That was a big one, he knew, but he did believe in miracles. In spite of Busby. Hadn't he been able to come home? Hadn't they taken him in, Naomi, Matt, and, finally, Johnny, and cared for him, reclaimed him as one of their own? What was that if it wasn't just short of a miracle?

There were things he knew he wouldn't live to see, couldn't live to see, but if he could just hang on through the end of August when things would have to be settled because time called for it, Russell thought leaving them all would be easier. Sometimes, time is on our side, Russell thought. Not mine, maybe, but theirs.

He heard the alarm clock go off in Naomi's room and knew it was 6:15 without moving his head to look at his own clock. He heard her door open and her step lightly pass his door on her way to the bathroom. Then the bathroom door closed. Russell waited for the toilet to flush, and listened for the water tap to spit twice, as it always did, before the swoosh of it hit against the bottom of the basin. Above him, the floor creaked in Matt's room, and Matt, too, made his way toward the bathroom upstairs. Naomi would be coming to check on him soon.

Life was on its feet at the hotel. Another day had begun in the house where he was born, and he was still here to be a part of it. Even with the pain, that was a blessing.

Chapter Thirty-Two

As the summer lolled its way into late July, Evelyn Tolney began to come back to her old self; in fact, she looked better than her old self since she had had all that bed rest and good care, and Webster hadn't been shouting at her. She was able to speak, even though some words were hard for her to get her tongue around, and she was getting around the house with the walker Doc had brought by. Alice could even take her out on little drives.

On his last visit, Doc told Evelyn that he expected her to be as right as rain, but after he settled Evelyn on the front porch out of earshot, Doc stopped Webster, who was on his way out of the kitchen, and told both Webster and Alice that Evelyn would be fine, but she had to be kept quiet and she shouldn't be upset. Webster looked at Doc like he didn't know what Doc was talking about. "Ain't no upsets 'round here," he told Doc. "Everything 'round here is going along just fine." He grabbed his old, straw hat off the hook by the kitchen door. "I can't worry about this none; I've got work to do," he said. "Alice here will take care of her mother. That's her job."

"It's your job, too, Webster," Doc told him, but Webster acted as though Doc hadn't said a word, jammed his hat on his head with one hand, pushed the screen door open with the other and left without so much as a "goodbye."

As they watched Webster rattle his thin frame toward his old blue truck, Doc said, "Your daddy is a bullheaded jackass, Alice."

"I know, Doc," Alice said, sighing. "I sure do wish he wasn't."

Doc did, too; but he could practically hear Webster braying as he turned over the engine and gunned it into a cough, followed by a raspy whine. After Webster drove through the gate, leaving it standing open behind him, Doc looked toward the porch where he could see Evelyn holding a coffee cup with both hands. He said, "Alice, honey, I want you to be very careful. Your daddy could find out about your meeting Ray."

Alice's cheeks stung pink. "Meeting Ray?" Her breath caught. "What do you mean, Doc?"

"I mean I don't want your daddy to know that you go walking in the woods around lunchtime, sometimes alone and sometimes with Hope. And Ray heads into the woods from over by the sawmill, sometimes alone and sometimes with Johnny. Now, it doesn't take much to figure out that the four of you are meeting in the woods, probably at Flat Rock."

Alice, who had been sitting at the table stood up quickly, then sat back down again, holding the edge of the table for support. "How long have you known?"

"I've seen you two or three times, and Matt has seen you far more because he's delivering mail every day. It didn't take much to put it together."

Alice felt herself shake. "Does anybody else know?"

"Matt, of course, and Naomi and Russell. None of us will be telling anybody, but it's just a matter of time. You know nothing stays secret around here long. Somebody else is bound to see you."

"But we were being so careful," Alice told him.

Doc covered her hand with his. "I don't mean to scare you, honey. Just be more careful and tell Hope to do the same."

She nodded, biting her lip.

After Doc left, Alice stayed in the kitchen, staring out the screen door. They'd been living all summer, she and Ray, Johnny and Hope, as though August were years away. Hope refused to talk about September when Johnny would leave. All she had said to Alice was that she wouldn't have any life then, so why talk about it now.

Alice walked out on the side porch; the air smelled like rain. Even in the heat, she shivered; Ray's mother was killed in a summer storm. She searched the horizon for clouds which she found just raising their heads far off to the North.

Her eighteenth birthday was in less than three weeks, and what she hadn't told Ray was that lately Sample kept hovering closer and closer. He seemed to settle easier and easier into his chair at the dinner table or on the front porch. She did her best just to ignore him, big as he was. It wasn't hard with Ray so much on her mind. Sample had quit bringing gifts. He hadn't brought anything since the dress material. She thought maybe he'd forgotten about it.

Then one night last week he asked her if she'd made her dress yet. Alice was startled by the question, and she didn't know just how to answer. Her papa and Sample were looking at her.

"It's about time you got it done, ain't it? You might have a need to wear it sometime," Sample said, leaning back in his chair and looking right at her. He wasn't smiling.

She had turned away toward the stove and stirred a pot of stew that didn't need stirring. The extra material was in the spare room where they kept the sewing machine.

Alice had put it into the sewing chest. She hadn't thought of it since.

"Mine's finished," Evelyn told Sample, trying to redirect his attention. "Alice did a right nice job on it. 'Course I haven't had a chance to wear it yet."

He nodded at her to indicate he'd heard and kept his eyes on Alice.

Alice decided the first chance she got she'd get rid of the material completely. She didn't want to look at it again; she didn't even want to touch it. She didn't want anything that came from Sample Forney.

She knew the only reason her papa hadn't pressured her lately was because he did not want Evelyn's care to fall to him until Evelyn was well enough to take care of herself. Alice knew, too, that Webster was depending on the fact that Sample wasn't going anywhere. Not when he'd set his eyes on Alice with that lust-to-own look in them.

One thing Alice knew for sure: She'd rather be dead than married to Sample Forney.

The day after Doc warned her, Alice left the house after lunch feeling she was being watched. She carefully gazed off down the road, north and south, and listened for any sound off in the distance, a car engine, or gravel crunching. She listened her way across the pasture to the place where the path entered the woods, then turned around and strained her eyes to look up and down the road again. Nothing moved.

When she was sure the woods hid her, she bolted like a frightened doe to Flat Rock and sat down to catch her breath, run a comb through her hair, and wait for Ray. By the time she saw him coming, she had worried herself into a tizzy. She blurted out as soon as he reached her what Doc had said yesterday. Ray had listened while his forehead did that little dance that brought his eyebrows almost together.

He took a deep breath, "Well, it's time for us to do something about this, honey."

She nodded.

"I've been thinking about this, Alice. You'll be eighteen on August 8th; that's just a little more than two weeks. We need to do something then, that very day. I want you to marry me as soon as we can get a license. They can't stop us if they don't know about it, and after it's done, there won't be anything they can do. Will you do it? Will you marry me that day?"

"Oh, Ray, I want to marry you more than anything; I'd do it today, this very minute." She stopped, swallowing hard. "But I keep worrying about Momma and her having another stroke," she said softly.

He put his hands on her shoulders and looked into her eyes. "Alice, sweetheart, you got to believe me. I've told you over and over again, you didn't give your momma that stroke. You didn't give her the illness; you didn't treat her badly; you didn't bring her out that night when she should have been home in bed. You know all that."

Alice wished she could believe him.

"Your daddy acted up because of himself, not us. He got angry because he wasn't having things his way. You can't control what your daddy does."

"You should see Papa around the house; he acts like he's got a business deal all sewed up. He goes around talking about his new land, and Sample just sits there looking satisfied." Her eyes were stinging with first tears. "And the worst part is," she began to sob, "the worst part is that I know," she snuffed in a wet breath, "I know I'm the trade off my own papa's made to get what he wants, and he doesn't even care." The sobs came in gasps.

Ray put his arms around her. "Alice, nobody is going to be using you as trade. They'd have to come right through me to do that." He squeezed her against him, her face wetting the front of his shirt that always smelled to her like morning air and starch. "But the fact that he'd try to do it should be enough to make you certain that you've got to get away. You can't spend your life saving your momma."

"But I worry about her; you know that I do."

"I want you to listen to me." He put his finger under her chin and lifted her face to his. "I'm going to take care of your momma. She's always going to have a place to live: she can even live with us if she wants to—as long as she doesn't bring Webster."

Alice knew that Ray was joking—but not really.

"And she'll have good food and clothes and medical care. I'll treat her like my own momma; I promise you that, Alice."

"What if she won't come?"

"Then she won't come. But there's no way short of shooting us that he can keep us away from her, and after Sample and his property have gone back home, Webster will need us, and he'll know it. Webster's never gonna want to take care of things on his own. I've thought about this every night, honey. And you know your daddy, and you know I'm right."

She slowly nodded. "You're right," she said. Her papa would want help after Sample left him. "You don't think Papa will take it out on Momma?"

"He'd be foolish to try that when he'll need our help, and I don't think you're giving your momma credit. She's not fought him much in the past, but I think this time is different. After it's done, I think your momma's going to be so glad you got away she won't be having a stroke. Have you ever thought of that?"

Alice hadn't. And she wanted to believe that was true, or she would never be free from her papa. "But what about Sample?"

"What about him?"

"He'll make trouble. He's not going to be quiet about it. As soon as he finds out, he'll be roaring mad."

"You let me worry about Sample. You'll be my wife, Alice. I'll take care of you." He felt her relax against him. He wiped her face dry with his sleeve. He always wore long sleeves when he worked at the mill. "You haven't really said it, Alice. Will you go with me to get the license on your birthday? Will you marry me?"

"Oh, yes," she told him. "I'll marry you; I'll marry you."

After kissing her soundly, Ray said, "Now, sit down here with me and let's eat lunch. I'm starved." Ray finished his sandwich and half of hers. Alice was too excited and a little frightened; she wasn't really hungry. Besides, she liked watching Ray eat.

Ray said, tossing his waxed paper into the sack, "The only thing about eloping is that you won't have a church wedding like you always wanted. Will that bother you a whole lot?"

"If I had a choice," she said, looking off through the trees, "I'd be married at the church with Hope as my bridesmaid, all dressed up in a beautiful, white wedding dress. You in a new blue suit, looking so handsome."

"I doubt Busby Howard would marry me to anybody. He'd probably consider it a sin,"

Alice had to smile. "He probably would. I wish we could have some of the people we love with us, though."

Ray thought for a minute. "Maybe they could come with us to the Justice of the Peace over at the county seat. Who do you want to come?"

"I'd like Johnny and Hope, and Naomi and Matt, and your daddy. And I sure would love it if Mary Jo could come. I know Momma and Papa won't be there."

"Well, no, they won't, but I'll see what I can do about the others. I'm going to make you happy, Alice; I promise you that." Ray held Alice as the afternoon sun fell through the trees.

Finally, Alice said, sitting straight up, "Oh, Ray, I forgot about Johnny and Hope. What do you suppose will happen to them?"

Ray sat up beside her, shook his head and frowned. "We can tell them what Doc said, and they'll have to decide for themselves. There's not much we can do. John is leaving, so it's going to be easier on him, though I don't know how Hope will take it."

"She'll be happy for us; I know she will."

Ray smiled at this girl who had won his heart and changed his life and decided not to tell her he wasn't sure that was so.

Chapter Thirty-Three

Johnny and Doobie were straining against the handles of their cant hooks to roll a log onto the loading table for its trolley ride back and forth through the whirring saw-blade, when Ray drove his truck though the gate and parked it at the side of the mill. Ray never walked from the mill when he went to see Alice; he drove down the road around the bend and hid the truck in the woods on an old logging road.

Joe Mueller was clearing the area around the saw of scraps of bark and slab wood that had broken off and fallen to the ground during the morning cut, a job done only when the diesel was off and the saw was still. "Where you been, boy?" Doobie teased Ray. "We're here working our tail ends off, and you're off lolly-gagging somewhere." The Muellers grinned at him, and Johnny echoed Doobie, "Yeah, man, where you been?"

"Just doing business, boys. Somebody has to be the brains around here. You four sure don't have any."

"Come spell me a while so I can head over to the john, will ya?" Doobie asked him.

"I'll spell you," Ray told him. "Just don't stay to read the whole Sears Roebuck Catalog. I never know whether you moon over the women or the tractors."

"Moon over the tractors, Doob," Hance said. "They've got more staying power."

"Yeah, but they ain't got as much spark," Doobie responded as he headed off toward the two-holer set back at the woods.

"He's got you there, Hance," Joe told his brother. Then called after Doobie, "You been sparked any lately?"

The four of them laughed. Doobie lifted an arm and waved over his head, but he didn't look back.

"Let's get back to it, boys," Ray directed, and flipped on the switch that awakened the saw. It moved from a gentle swoosh to a high-pitched whine, and the men took their places.

Under the sound of the diesel and the saw, Johnny asked, "Did you see her?"

Ray nodded. "We need to talk later. Meet me down at the river after work."

"Everything okay?" Johnny wanted to know.

"Not everything," Ray told him.

When Ray pulled his truck onto the riverbank beside Harris Ford, Johnny was sitting on a large rock near the water. The river rushed down stream, spilling over boulders, smelling clean and blue-wet. Johnny watched Ray walk over the gravelly bank toward him. When they were kids, they ran over the rocks and gravel barefooted, heading toward the cold, pulsing water. Their feet must have been leather. Now, Ray's work boots crunched on the gravel, and he stepped around the big rocks.

Ray sat on the boulder beside Johnny and shook out a couple cigarettes, lighting a kitchen match with a flick of his thumb; he held it first to Johnny's cigarette, then his own. They both inhaled, exhaled, and watched the smoke move like two small clouds over the water.

"River's down some," Ray said.

"Yep," Johnny responded. "Alice okay?"

"Yeah, she's fine. Just worried some."

"What's she worried about?"

"Doc came by today to look in on Evelyn."

"She doing all right?"

"She's coming along, but Doc said to be careful not to upset her."

Johnny nodded, waiting.

"You need to know that Doc told Alice that he and Matt knew we were all meeting over by Flat Rock."

Johnny swung his head around in surprise. "How'd he know that?"

"He's seen Alice and Hope heading into the woods, and so has Matt."

"Matt never said anything, but then he wouldn't." Johnny looked at the ash at the end of his cigarette. "Aunt Naomi know?"

"Yeah," Ray said, "she knows."

Johnny said after a minute. "They won't tell anybody."

"That's not what Doc's worried about."

"What is he worried about?"

"If he and Matt have seen us, somebody else is bound to before long. Doc is worried about it. He don't want us to have any more trouble."

"Neither do we. But we're not going to be meeting much longer. I'll be leaving right after Labor Day for school. We can just be more careful."

"We're already as careful as we can be; you know that." Ray flipped his cigarette in the rushing water. "John, Alice and I decided today we're going to get married right after her birthday. We've got to do something right away; the pressure from Webster will just keep getting worse. I half expect Sample to be waiting outside the kitchen door the morning of her birthday."

"I wouldn't put it past him."

"We're going to get our blood tests on her birthday, and we'll have that three-day waiting period for the license. So we'll get married the first weekend after that."

Johnny said slowly, "That's only two and a half to three weeks from now."

Ray nodded. They were both quiet, Ray waiting for Johnny to take in what that meant for all of them. Finally, Ray said, "I've got to get her away from there, John; you know that."

"I know you do," Johnny told him. Then he smiled and stuck his hand out to shake Ray's, "I'm happy for you; I really am. I think it's great; it couldn't happen to better people."

They grinned at each other, sitting there on a rock just across the river from the spot where Ray had taught Johnny to swim. Then, because neither of them knew how to break the handshake which held all their friendship, Ray slapped Johnny on the shoulder, and they pulled apart.

"You got another cigarette," Johnny asked. He was thinking about Hope, but he didn't want to bring her up just yet.

Ray shook out two more, and they smoked a few minutes in silence.

"So, you'll be an old married man here shortly," Johnny said.

"And you'll be heading out to become the next Pulitzer winning reporter."

"I'm going to do my best," Johnny told him.

The late afternoon sun was hot in July, but the breeze off the water always kept the air cool there at the Ford.

Johnny asked, "What are you going to do about Webster and Sample? You know how stirred up they're going to be. You ready for that?"

"If I can marry Alice, I'm ready for anything." From the look on Ray's face, Johnny knew that he meant it. Ray said, "I'm not worried about Webster; he'll threaten a lot, mouth off a lot."

"What about Sample? He may come after you."

"What's he going to do once we're married?"

"I don't know, just keep an eye out. He's not a man to give up easily. I just hope you can get married before anybody finds out anything."

"That's why we decided to do it right away." Ray looked at him. "Now, what are you planning to do about Hope?"

Johnny shook his head. "I don't know." The blue water in front of them swirled by, rewashing small pebbles on the shallow bottom.

"It's going to be hard on her once you leave. You're going off toward something you want. She's staying here with Busby. I wouldn't wish that on anybody. What does Hope say?"

"She doesn't talk about it. We've both sort of been trying to forget it. It's not like you and Alice. I've got to leave for Mizzou; I can't marry Hope."

"If you could, would you marry her?"

"I've never felt about any girl the way I feel about Hope." He hesitated. "It's just that I don't want to get married to anybody anytime soon. You know I've got plans to be a reporter. Aunt Naomi and I have saved for that for years."

"I know that, John," Ray said. "Does Hope know how much that means to you?"

"I've told her, but I'm not sure. She can't come to Mizzou to go to college when she graduates next year because Busby is dead set on her going to the Baptist College in Bolivar. She goes Baptist or she goes no where."

"Does she want to go there?"

"No, she hates it. Her cousin told her four kids got expelled for dancing last term. And they're expected to attend revivals five and six times a year. They even have to go with the student preachers down to the town square where they preach on street corners every Saturday."

"Why do they have to do that?"

"To sing I guess."

"Out on the square?"

'"Yep."

"It sure beats all. Want another cigarette?"

"Sure. Ever hear of a reporter who doesn't smoke?"

"I don't know why I thought you'd ever fit in with the Howards," Ray said, lighting their cigarettes, "especially when you keep the wrong friends."

"Nothing wrong with my friends," Johnny grinned. "Besides, when you're a reporter, you've got to mix with all kinds."

"Just trying to hold up my end," Ray said.

"And you're doing a bang up job of it," Johnny told him.

The river moved on under them.

"It's not going to be easy to tell Hope," Ray said.

"No, it won't. I sure will miss her, Ray. Don't think I won't."

Ray nodded, his cigarette bobbing at the corner of his mouth.

They looked out over the water. After a bit Ray said, "Good day for fishing."

"Yeah," Johnny said. "A good day for fishing."

Chapter Thirty-Four

Naomi, Matt, and Doc were sitting on the front porch after dinner. Russell was asleep; he'd had to be in bed earlier and earlier the last week or so.

"He's failing pretty quickly now, isn't he, Doc?" Naomi asked.

"I keep telling him to up his pain medication," Doc said, "but he doesn't want to do it. He said he'd keep upping the codeine, but he wanted to hold off on the morphine as long as he could. I told him that wouldn't be for much longer."

"He's not ready to go yet," Naomi said. "I think he's waiting on Johnny."

"Why do you think he's waiting for Johnny, sweetheart?" Matt asked.

"Maybe if he sees Johnny go off to the University, he'll see a part of himself going with him."

"Gives him a kind of immortality, I guess," Doc said.

"Johnny is his brother's son," Naomi said.

"Johnny is your son, Naomi, and Russell knows that," Matt said, taking her hand. "He knows because you married him you have Johnny; he gave you a son, even if he wasn't here to see you raise him. I believe he's waiting to be sure you are both happy."

"I guess so," Naomi said. "I hadn't thought of that."

Doc said, "I think you've hit the nail on the head, Matthew."

They sat in silence, listening to the cicadas whirring in the background that seemed to agree with Matt.

Doc viewed his empty glass and stood up. "It's getting late, folks, and I have to be at the hospital early in the morning."

Neither Naomi nor Matt tried to stop him. "We'll see you tomorrow evening," Matt said.

Doc rose. "I don't like Russell's color. See if you can get him to eat a little more, Naomi. It doesn't matter what, just as long as he can keep it down."

"I'll make soup; he'll like that. Supper's at six," Naomi added as a matter of course.

Doc waved over his head as he made his way down the steps and out to his car. He slowly backed out of the driveway and drove toward home.

"Want some tea?" Naomi asked Matt.

"No, but I would like to talk some. Let's go sit in the swing." They moved in unison to the end of the porch and settled into the old swing, almost disappearing in the shadows. The only light on the porch came through the front door and the kitchen window. Matt drew her close against him and set the swing to moving with the toe of his shoe. "With everything that's been going on, we've not done any talking about you and me."

"No," Naomi agreed, "we haven't. It hasn't seemed like the time for it somehow."

"I think it's time now," Matt said. "Naomi, just looking at Russell and what little time he's got left has made me even more certain that what I'm about to say is right. Not everybody gets a chance to love somebody a second time, and you know that I truly loved Beth Lynn."

"I know that Matt. I don't believe I ever loved Russell the way that you loved her."

"Whether you did or you didn't really isn't important. What is important now is that we've found each other. Because I want you to be my wife, and the sooner, the better."

"Matt," Naomi began.

"Wait, I'm not through. I want you to know that I'm not dancing on Russell's grave, but we both know that it's just a matter of weeks; he can't hold out longer than that. It's just that after he goes, I want us to be married as soon as possible. I don't think it's disrespectful. In fact, I'd think he'd agree. We've come to be friends, pretty good friends, in this time. He's a part of our family: yours and mine, and Johnny's."

There was a glint of laughter in Naomi's eyes. "Are you going to ask Russell's permission?"

"No, but I will ask Johnny's. But first you have to tell me you'll marry me."

Naomi started to speak.

"Wait just one more minute. There's something else I have to say." He took a deep breath. "I love you, Naomi; I've loved you for a long time, longer than I knew. And you're my best friend. A man couldn't want more than that. I am the most blessed man on this earth." She lifted her head to meet his kiss. The sweetness of it as his lips swept lightly against hers, touched her heart, and as the kiss deepened, all of her that had been unused and painted over for all these years was filled with a warm, urgent rush she'd never felt with Russell. For the first time in her life, she knew what it was to want a man, want him right then and there, want him with an urgency that would have shocked her if she hadn't been so thrilled by it.

When Matt lifted his head, he said, "What I need to know is two things: do you love me, and will you marry me?"

The light caught the reflection from her hazel eyes, darkened to green, and Matt saw for the first time what he knew would make them both very happy people.

Naomi, still a little breathless, said, "Oh, I love you, and, of course, I'll marry you."

In one motion, Matt stood and lifted Naomi up from the swing in a bear hug that left them both feeling eighteen and wanting to move toward the bedroom. "How soon can we get married?"

"Not soon enough," Naomi said, laughing up into his face.

"Can't I move down to your bedroom?" Matt asked half seriously.

Naomi slapped him on his arm and laughed. "We can't move you in just yet, and we can't very well have a preacher standing by right after the funeral."

"No, of course not, but I think a week would be long enough. What do you think?" Matt asked, and he pulled her full length against his body.

"Maybe two at the most," Naomi said, putting her arms around him.

Ray's truck pulled around the corner from the spur road and stopped in front of the hotel. They'd quit parking in back for fear of waking Russell; it was too hard for him to get back to sleep sometimes. Ray and Johnny came up the front porch step in two strides. Naomi and Matt pulled apart and walked toward the boys.

"You two been doing some sparking?" Ray kidded.

"Looked like it to me," Johnny said.

Naomi blushed and Matt grinned.

"You boys don't worry about us," Matt said. "What have you been up to?"

"Ray's got some news for you," Johnny told them.

"What kind of news? Sit down and tell us about it," Naomi said. She and Matt arranged themselves in chairs and looked expectant.

Ray hesitated. Johnny said, "Tell them, Ray; you know you're busting to."

Ray sat down in the chair across from them, his back to the street. "I guess it's no news to you that I've been meeting Alice over near Flat Rock."

Naomi and Matt looked at each other before Matt carefully said, "No, it's no news."

"And I guess you know that Hope and I have been meeting once or twice a week," Johnny interjected.

"That, too," Naomi nodded. "Fact is, we've been worrying about the four of you. You know you can't keep anything quiet for long around here."

"That's what Doc told Alice yesterday," Ray told them. "And when Alice and I met today, we decided we had to do something about it as fast as we could."

"What are you going to do?" Naomi looked concerned.

Ray came out with it in a rush. "Alice and I are going to get our blood tests and license on her birthday and get married as soon as the tests get back." His face looked like Christmas morning.

"Oh, honey," Naomi said to Ray as she and Matt got out of their chairs in unison. Naomi hugged him, and Matt shook his hand. Naomi went on, "I'm so happy for you and Alice. I just know you were meant to be together."

"Congratulations, son," Matt said, patting him on the back.

"I want to hear all about it," Naomi told him. "Let me check on Russell, and then you can tell us."

Naomi went into the kitchen, and Matt said quietly to the boys, who had lowered themselves back into chairs, "You've done some thinking about how you'll do this, I take it."

"I have," Ray said, "we'll be real careful so nobody will know before hand."

Naomi came back out onto the porch. "Now," she said, "tell us all about it."

"I was just telling Matt that we'd have to be real careful until then, so we'll slip off separately and meet to apply for the license and get our blood tests over at the county seat, and as soon as we get the license back, we'll go back to the Justice of the Peace and get married. We'll have it all done before anybody can stop us."

"Webster will raise a ruckus," Naomi said.

Matt said, "Yes, but he's all blow. Course, I imagine he'll be blowing like a steam engine for a while. I'd be more careful about Sample. What are you planning to do about him?"

"Nothing. We'll be married; there won't be anything he can do."

"He can come after you," Matt said.

"What would be the point?" Ray asked. "He wouldn't have anything to gain by it."

"He'd have his pride to look out for. People around here think that he's managed to get an inside track. They half expect Alice to marry him just to keep peace in the family," Matt said.

"That's because they haven't figured out yet that Alice isn't like her mother," Ray said.

"You're right; she isn't," Naomi said; "the girl has more spunk. But I know she's got to be worried about her mother."

"She is worried," Ray agreed, "but we'll both take care of Evelyn. I won't let Webster make her miserable, even if I need to take her to live with us. And," he said to Matt, "as far as Sample goes, I can take care of him. You know I've been fighting all my life until I met Alice. I'm not proud of it anymore, but I've learned how to hold my own with just about any man."

Matt cautioned, "Sample's been known not to play by any rules to get what he wants."

"I'll be careful, you can count on it." Ray tilted his chair back until it leaned against the porch railing.

He looked more contented than Naomi had ever seen him.

"Okay, now," Naomi said, "since you are doing this soon, let's talk about your wedding. We don't want you getting married without us."

"We were thinking we'd ask you to come with us to the Justice of the Peace. John, here, you, Matt, Doc, Russell if…well, you know. Maybe Hope, if we can get her away some how. And my dad."

Naomi hadn't heard Ray call Jackson "dad" in years.

"We could do that if you want us to, but I think I have a better idea about where to get married," Naomi said, suddenly excited. "I think it would be right nice if you two got married here in the living room."

The men looked at her. Matt cleared his throat and said carefully, "Now, Naomi, much as you might like it, how in the world can they do that if they are going to keep it a secret?"

Naomi said, "We can do it in the early evening when most folks are home eating dinner. You know everybody in town eats about the same time. That's the one time that people keep their eyes on their plates more than they look out the window. I think if we do it right, it can work."

Ray was thinking his way through Naomi's plan. "That sounds real nice, and it sure would make Alice happy, but Busby wouldn't marry us, not that we'd want him to. And if another preacher came, people would see him and be talking before we could have the ceremony. I don't want the Tolneys or Sample or anybody else, for that matter, to know anything before she's my wife."

"Of course, you don't. But we won't have a preacher." Naomi's mind was going clickity-clack. "I'll bet you anything Doc could get Ronnie Wilkers who's the J.P. over at the county seat to come here to marry you."

"They have been friends for years," Matt said. He was in the mood for a wedding. "Doc brings him over to the Meramec to fish."

"See, there," Naomi said. "They could come wearing fishing clothes and change after they got here; nobody would be a bit wiser." Her mind had gone into full speed. "We could work it out about Jackson, too. I know we could do it."

Naomi was totally caught up in the moment. "I can make a wedding bouquet out of flowers from my garden, the roses are just beautiful now, and I'll make a wonderful dinner. I'll bake a big, white, three-tiered wedding cake and decorate it special. We'll play some beautiful records, whatever ones you and Alice want. I'll make it real, real nice. It'll be a day for all of us to remember." She looked at the three faces in turn, waiting to see what they'd say.

"What do you think, Matt?" Johnny asked. "You think we can?"

"It'll take some careful planning, but it just might work."

The boys could tell he'd already put his mind to it.

Ray said, "That sure would make Alice happy, and it sounds nice to me, too. What do you think, John?"

"I can't think of a better place."

Ray said, “Okay, we’ll plan it just that way, Naomi. I can’t thank you enough. You and Matt, too.”

“There’s no need for thanks, Ray; you’re my other boy.”

Ray lowered his head and fumbled getting a cigarette pack out of his pocket. “Well,” he mumbled, clearing his throat, “don’t think I don’t know what you’ve done for me.” Naomi reached over and patted his knee.

I knew I was right about that boy, Naomi thought, looking at Ray grown to manhood. Ray, who’d been without mother and brother, who’d been lost in so many ways to his father; and she wanted to put this moment of happiness under a bell jar in her kitchen for him to keep.

After a bit, Ray said, “I can’t wait to tell Alice, but since I can’t see her tonight, I guess I’d best be getting on home and putting myself to bed. My best man and I got a lot of lumber to saw tomorrow.” He grinned at Johnny.

“So I’m your best man,” Johnny grinned back at him.

“You’ve always been my best man,” Ray said. The two young men stood and hugged their ungainly hug that showed to anyone witnessing their deep affection.

“See you early in the morning,” Johnny said, and Ray nodded, touching his shoulder. He shook Matt’s hand again and hugged Naomi. “I love you, Naomi,” he said softly into her ear.

“I love you, too, honey. Sleep well.”

Ray drove away, stirring up spirals of dust behind his back wheels. They followed his taillights around the corner and out onto the blacktop as he turned left toward home.

“Johnny, you going to tell Hope tomorrow?” Naomi asked him.

“I won’t see her until Tuesday,” he said.

“This is going to be hard for her.” As happy as she was for Ray, Naomi’s heart felt heavy with her worry about Hope. She wished there were something she could do.

“Yes, ma’am. It is.” Johnny looked despondent.

“And it’s going to be hard for you,” Naomi said.

“But it’s worse for her. I’m the one who’s leaving; she’s the one who’s staying.”

“After you tell her, I’ll be here waiting for you when you get home,” Naomi told him. It was the most she could offer. She wondered if Helen would be there waiting for Hope.

Chapter Thirty-Five

Alice couldn't wait until Thursday to tell Hope that she and Ray were getting married. As soon as she'd finished the breakfast dishes and settled Evelyn on the porch, she filled half a bushel basket with peaches she'd picked yesterday and told her mother she was taking the peaches into Helen Howard for peach cobbler. She'd be back in an hour or so. Evelyn waved her off.

When she pulled up in front of the parsonage, Alice could see Hope with her mother through the screen door shelling peas. When the truck stopped, Hope looked out then came to open the screen, pushing it wide enough for Alice to easily pass through with the basket.

"Morning, Hope, morning Miss Helen," Alice said, setting the basket on the floor near the kitchen table. "I just dropped by because Momma wanted you to have these; she knows how much the preacher likes peach cobbler."

"Well, honey, that's right nice of you and your momma. Just look at these beautiful peaches, Hope, aren't they grand?"

"Yes, ma'am," Hope said, looking first at the peaches and then at Alice. It was a rare thing for Alice to come by the parsonage.

"Would you like some iced tea, honey?" Helen asked.

"Oh, no, thank you, Miss Helen. I have to get on over to Johnson's Store and get some sugar so I can bake a cobbler myself this afternoon. I was just wondering if Hope might walk over there with me, and we could get a soda pop? We wouldn't be gone long."

"Well," Helen said, looking at the clock over the refrigerator, "I don't see why not as long as you don't take too long. You'll need to be back here before your daddy comes home for lunch," she cautioned Hope.

"Oh, we won't take long, Momma," Hope said. "Just long enough to get a soda and talk a little."

"If I know you two, you'll have a soda and talk a lot," Helen laughed.

"We'll hurry," Alice said. Hope grabbed her purse, and the two of them left air trails as they shot out of the door.

"Tell me," Hope said, as soon as they were out of earshot.

"Let's wait till we get our sodas. I don't want to start and have to stop in the middle."

"Just tell me, is it good?"

"Yes, it's good," Alice said, and then stopped. "At least, most of it is. You'll see."

There was nothing like reaching into the old pop cooler that Wendell kept filled with large chunks of ice that would melt into freezing water around the icy bottles of Royal Crown Cola and Orange Crush, a Seven-Up or a Dr. Pepper scattered here and there among them. The arm went into the water to the elbow, sometimes above, with an exquisite chill that spread to the base of the skull and the tips of the toes.

They dried their arms on the towel Wendell hung fresh each morning on the ring on the front of the cooler, popped the top off in the opener attached to it, and pushed two straws through the foam and down into the chilled fizzing cola. Alice got five pounds of sugar, they spoke to Wendell and Marie for as long as good manners made it necessary, and left as casually as though they were just out for a stroll. They crossed the spur road, the tar under their feet sending up its hot-day biting smell, passed Harvey's Tavern, sucking in cold R.C., and reached the lawn in front of the Catholic Church.

"Let's sit on the steps; there's nobody in there," Alice said. The concrete of the porch was still cool, shaded by the large oaks in front of the white, frame church.

"Okay," Hope said. "Tell."

Alice took in a deep breath. "Ray and I are applying for a marriage license on my birthday," Alice said in one quick breath.

Hope blinked. The straws were lying against her lower lip; she'd stopped pulling on them. "What?"

"We're getting married."

"On your birthday?" The straw slipped back into the bottle.

"As soon as the tests come back. Isn't is wonderful?"

"Yes," Hope said, trying to sound happy. "I just wasn't expecting it so soon."

"We have to do it sooner than we thought," Alice said and told her about Doc Barnes, the words tumbling out of her mouth. Then she added, "If we're married, Papa and Sample, they can't do anything; it'll all be over. And Ray says we'll take care of Momma, and everything will work out, even with Papa—after a while, that is."

"That's so soon," Hope said again. She was staring out at the railroad tracks, not really seeing them. "Married, married, married," she kept hearing the word bounce from one side of her skull to the other.

"I knew you'd be happy for us, and I couldn't wait until tomorrow to tell you."

"Of course, I'm happy for you," Hope said, putting her arm around Alice's shoulder and kissing her on the cheek. Hope did mean that; she was happy for both of them. But she felt suddenly abandoned and wished with all her might she didn't feel that way. They sat there quietly for a minute before Hope took her arm away and asked, "Does Johnny know?"

"Yes, he knows. He'll tell you all about it tomorrow at lunch," Alice said. Then she stopped. "That's the only problem, Hope; Ray and Johnny think we shouldn't meet many more times because someone is bound to see us, like Doc says."

"The summer isn't over yet," Hope said with a soft, desperation in her voice. "It can't be over yet; we'll still have August."

"Ray says it's too risky to meet more than once or twice more; we'll do that just to get everything straight."

"That means I'll only see Johnny once or twice more."

"Maybe you and Johnny can work out something so that you can go on seeing each other until Labor Day."

"I just didn't think it would be so soon," Hope said again. The railroad tracks were shooting out glints of sunlight. Almost directly across the tracks sat the hotel, and Hope thought Johnny lived so close, so very close, just there on the other side of the tracks. There wasn't any way she could cross them if Alice and Ray got married. Johnny would be lost to her and so would Alice; her father would never let her near Alice if she married Ray. She knew Alice hadn't thought of that. Not yet.

"I didn't either, but you understand why, don't you?" Alice asked.

"Yes. I understand." Hope put the cola on the church step. "Our daddies won't let us be, will they?"

"No, not unless we can run away from them," Alice replied.

"I don't know where to run," Hope said, wanting to tell Alice that she'd wished again and again that she could run away with Johnny and get married and live at the hotel with Naomi while Johnny went off to school. Then, her father wouldn't have any say over her; she would have already slept with Johnny, and her father would expect her to stay with him because she would be a tainted woman.

"You can leave home after a year. You don't have to go to college. You could get a job in St. Louis like Mary Jo, and then you could wait for Johnny. That's what I'd do if I didn't have Ray; I'd go to St. Louis and live with Mary Jo," Alice said.

Hope saw the screen door open on the hotel porch, and Naomi pushed Russell out in his wheelchair. Even from here he looked very ill. His blanket was tucked in around him in the warm July heat. Naomi stopped the wheelchair at the shadiest end of the porch and put the brake on. When she looked up, she saw the girls sitting on the church steps and waved. Naomi knew, Hope thought. She also knew that Johnny wasn't like Ray; he wanted to travel the world and write stories. Johnny wouldn't be getting married. Hope knew it, too.

"Yes, maybe I could do that," Hope said, not believing it for a minute, and waved back at Naomi before Naomi went into the hotel.

Chapter Thirty-Six

Hope and Alice were sitting on the low bridge, their skirts hitched up under their tan legs, dangling them over the side so that the water could catch against their heels and ankles, making little wakes around them. Johnny had come by the Tolney farm late yesterday afternoon before Webster got home to tell Alice that he and Ray thought it was safer for Hope to come to Harris Ford. Ray would meet Alice on Friday in the woods, and they would make plans alone.

Alice got up as soon as she saw Johnny's truck coming down the gravel road and headed across the bridge to walk along the other bank, giving them some privacy. She waved at Johnny.

Hope was staring straight out before her at the water rushing pell-mell downstream, swirling around some boulders, leaping over others in a spray of blue light. Johnny took off his shoes and socks and left them on the gravel at the edge of the ford; then bent to roll up his jeans to mid-calf. Hope didn't turn to look at him even when he walked out on the weathered boards of the bridge and sat down beside her, putting his feet into the water near hers.

"You've heard it all?"

She nodded.

"I'm afraid Doc's right; it's just a matter of time until somebody will see us and blaze a path to the parsonage door."

She said, still not looking at him, "Probably."

"Maybe we could go on meeting at the Tolney's when Webster's not there. I don't think Evelyn would mind," Johnny said.

"No, that might call attention to Alice and Ray somehow," Hope said.

"I can't think of another place." Johnny was stumped. He'd thought and thought about it.

"I don't think there is another place," Hope said.

"Do you think it would do any good for me to talk to your daddy again? I'd do that if you thought there was any hope." Johnny reached for her hand, but she pulled away.

"There's no talking to Daddy. Not about us, not about anything."

The rushing water seemed to be pushing faster and louder against their feet. Neither of them said anything. Finally, Johnny said, "The time just kind of slipped up on us, didn't it?"

Hope nodded. She looked at Johnny out of the corner of her eye. "I'm happy for Alice and Ray," she said quietly.

"I am, too; I just wish there was something I could do so you'd be happy, Hope," he told her.

She wanted to shout at him: Oh, there is something. There is something. Don't you see it? I've thought about it, and thought about it, night after night. In fact, it's all I've thought about. We could run off and get married, and after we'd slept together nobody could break us up. Baptists don't get divorced. You could go away to college, and I could live with your Aunt Naomi until you graduated. That's what she wanted to shout, but she just kept looking at the water, clenching her jaws together, praying hard he'd say something, anything that might make it possible.

"Don't you think it'll be better when you leave for college?" he asked.

"The Baptist College?" A tinny little laugh fell out of her mouth. "As long as I have to attend a college where everybody knows Busby Howard and thinks he's just wonderful, I won't be getting away from him. How can I go there for four years? Four long years?"

The pale face she turned to him looked tired and empty. He felt suddenly older, and his heart hurt to look at her. Her hands were clenched in her lap, and when he reached again for one, it was limp and as cold as his own, but she let him take it.

"We'll write to each other. And we can meet at Thanksgiving and Christmas when I come home from the University."

"Thanksgiving and Christmas will be just like this. There won't be any place to go. Besides, where are we going to write to each other? I can't get mail here." She started to cry and before she knew what was happening, she heard herself say it: "Johnny, I want you to marry me.

If we were married, I'd be free. Daddy could never order me to do anything ever again because I'd be with you." It was out of her mouth, and there was no taking it back.

Johnny's tanned face lost some of its color. "Hope," he stammered, "I don't know what to say."

"Say something," she shouted at him.

Johnny had never heard Hope even raise her voice before. He struggled before he said, "I—I can't get married. It's too soon to get married." Any thoughts Johnny had had about marriage were always far off in the future. The university was always out there waiting for him, and beyond that were his dreams of traveling the world searching for news. Joe Pulitzer's top reporter; that's what he'd be.

He had wanted a girlfriend. Oh, yes, he had wanted Hope in a way he'd never wanted any girl, but he hadn't wanted a wife. Not yet. He wasn't ready for a wife.

"Hope, I love you, but Aunt Naomi and I have worked hard and long for this. I can't let her down." He paused for a minute; he couldn't put this on Aunt Naomi. "The truth is, I want this; I've always wanted this. But, please understand, it isn't that I don't love you."

"I don't want to understand," Hope said. "Don't you understand I need you to marry me? How else will I get away from him? I can't live there any longer."

Alice called to them from across the river as she walked back toward the bridge. "I've got to get back to Momma, guys. You about through?"

"Hope," Johnny said urgently, "I don't know what to do. I don't know how to make things work out for everybody."

Hope knew with certainty there was nothing Johnny was going to do, not now, not ever. She called to Alice, "We're ready; let's go back." She pulled her feet out of the water, and Johnny stood up and helped her to her feet. They started toward the truck, and he put his arm around her. She pushed it away.

When they reached the truck, Johnny said, "I'll try to think of some way for us to meet again; there has to be some way." He helped her in and shut the door for her. "Okay?"

She was looking straight ahead, out the windshield. Alice slipped into the driver's seat and started the engine.

"Okay, Hope?" he pleaded.

Hope said, "Let's go, Alice."

With a quick wave to him out of the driver's window, Alice pulled off, spewing bits of rock behind the back wheels.

Hope didn't even look back.

Chapter Thirty-Seven

In the weeks moving toward Alice's birthday, Naomi watched Russell fade slowly like an old photograph. This past week, they'd put his bed in the living room near the front windows. That way Naomi could check on him from the kitchen across the foyer when he was napping, and there was always a cross breeze there. He seemed more content in there even after the town fell dark and asleep, as though, for him, life was still up and moving. She began sleeping on the living room couch, seeing that he had his medicine or a bedpan, holding him when he had a coughing spell that doubled him near in two.

Sometimes, in the middle of the night she'd hear Russell talking, sometimes even heard a low chuckle. She knew it was the drugs, even though he took as few as he could. At first she could only grasp a word or two, but as the weeks went on, she realized that each night, Russell was having a party. He was meeting with the boys after work at the Tysen Hotel; he'd brought them home to Tysen with him. Russell began painting word pictures so vivid that Naomi watched with him as Gene Kelly and Doobie Pratt tap-danced in the kitchen, and Doc talked to Harry James. Johnny would play with Tommy Dorsey's trombone, and Naomi had danced around her kitchen table with Fred Astaire. It was a lovely party, and this time he took Naomi.

When morning came, he was back with them, wanting to know what time Johnny left for work or when Matt was coming home. After he'd eaten some tiny bit of scrambled egg and toast or had a glass of milk, he was ready to move out onto the front porch in his wheelchair. The night had moved far away.

It was August 1st, and Tysen was hot. The only two people who didn't seem to mind the heat were Ray and Alice; they were just happily waiting for August 8th when they would each drive alone to the county seat and apply for their marriage license. Alice drove into town at least twice a week for supplies, and she'd stop by the hotel for a visit with Naomi to talk wedding and leave messages for Ray. Ray came by every evening on the off chance Alice had made an extra run into town, and even if she hadn't, he was just glad to be where she had been.

Naomi told Matt that the two of them wouldn't have noticed if it were 110° in the shade. Matt said he knew just how they felt and slipped his arms around her waist from behind while she was standing at the sink running water over a colander of strawberries. She swatted at him with a dishtowel, and he kissed her on the back of the neck before happily going out to join Russell on the porch.

Settled on the porch, Russell read the paper and watched George Wilson across the tracks. George had begun hobbling off the porch and making his way to the edge of the track every day at 5:52. Then, he'd stand there close as he could while the Express went whooshing by.

"Matt, look over there at George," Russell said as Matt eased into his chair.

"What's he doing?"

"I think he's gearing up."

"What for?"

"To step out in front of the Express."

Matt stared hard at George who was sitting still as a monument, looking at the moment as if he'd never move anywhere again, much less walk in front of a train. "Now, why would you think he's going to do that?" Matt asked.

"I think it's cause his face is half gone," Russell said.

"He doesn't have to look at himself," Matt said. "Mary Lee took down all the mirrors except the one in the bathroom. She told Naomi so."

"I don't think it's the mirrors," Russell said. "I think it's looking at people looking at him. George sees it in their eyes, over and over again, all the fear and repulsion. I've seen enough of the fear in people's eyes myself. If you added repulsion to that, it'd be enough to make anybody want to walk in front of a train."

"Who wants to walk in front of a train?" Naomi asked, opening the screen door with her elbow, and carrying out a tray with lemonade and sugar cookies. Matt wondered if she ever thought about just coming out to sit down without thinking of what they might want to eat or drink.

"George over there," Russell said.

"Russell thinks George is going to commit suicide," Matt told her.

"He is," Russell said.

Naomi set the tray on the table between them with a doesn't-that-beat-all shake of her head. "Wherever did you get that idea, Russell?"

"I watch him everyday. When the train goes by and he watches it go round the bend, he looks over at me real steady-like. Like he's trying to find out if I know something he can't figure out since I'm closer to moving on to the other side than he is."

"I'd think that'd depend on just how soon he intends to do it," Matt said wryly.

"Matt," Naomi said, but only half-reprovingly.

Russell and Matt both laughed.

Naomi waved them both aside. "Well, just tell me this," she said, "if he's set on going, what's keeping him from it?"

"Don't know," Russell said, studying George. "Don't know if he knows. The time's just not right yet."

"Maybe it's too hot for him," Matt suggested before swallowing a large, long drink of lemonade.

"Could be," Russell agreed. "People get real touchy about heat when they're dying."

"I would think so," Matt said. "You never know which direction you might be heading."

They both laughed.

"You two ought to be ashamed of yourselves talking this way," Naomi said, but they noticed there was a twitch at the corner of her mouth. "Poor George," she said looking across the tracks as if her gaze alone could stop him. "You can't be right, Russell."

"Just wait and see, Naomi," Russell told her. "Matt, you remember when old man Hankins hung himself?"

"Remember? He raised the flag on the mailbox and left me a note saying, 'Postman, please find me hanging on the back porch. Thank you, R. T. Hankins'."

"At least he was right polite," Russell said. Naomi had noticed Russell's Missouri accent had come back in full bloom.

"Yep, that was right thoughtful of him," Matt said dryly. "I had to get Jackson Redeem to help me lift him down. Hankins weighed close to 200 lbs."

Russell commented, "Poor old Mrs. Bloom must have been easier to get off the back of her front door."

"Well, she was," Matt said. "She didn't weigh more than 90 lbs., and both the Puckett boys were there to put her in the back of their truck and bring her into Gene at the funeral parlor."

"Will you two stop it," Naomi didn't really ask. It was a statement. "I don't want to hear anymore of this. Here I am planning a wedding on one hand and trying to deal with a boy who is guilt-ridden because he feels he's let his girl down, and you two are determined to be gruesome."

"We didn't mean any harm, Naomi," Russell said, then quickly changed the subject. "Has Johnny seen Hope again?" he asked.

"Not since the river," Naomi sighed. "Hope told Alice it would be too difficult for her to get away from her daddy, but I think it's too difficult for her to see Johnny."

"Johnny isn't responsible for Busby," Matt said. "He needs to understand that."

"I think he does," Russell said. "He just hasn't come to terms with having Hope feel she's being left behind. That's a feeling I'm acquainted with." He glanced at Naomi.

"Hope can't expect Johnny to fix things for her," Naomi said. "She'll have to learn that." Naomi touched Russell's hand, and he turned his to squeeze hers lightly in gratitude. "I've told him that, but it's all very new, and he's hurting for her and himself, and he's lonely. It'll be better after he leaves for college."

"When does he leave?" Russell asked.

"The day after Labor Day," Naomi said.

"It'll be a hard four weeks for him," Russell said.

He's been watching the calendar, Naomi thought. "But he'll make it through," Naomi said, standing up. "Well, I've got dinner to make."

"I think I'll go over and say 'Hi' to George," Matt said.

"See if you can keep him from stepping in front of the train today," Naomi called over her shoulder.

"If not," Russell told him, "see if you can get him to wave to me before he goes."

Chapter Thirty-Eight

Webster was finishing the fried eggs and bacon he had each morning for breakfast when he announced to Alice he was giving her a birthday party. After all, she was going to be eighteen and a woman now, he said. Said it was only fitting. Said a party would give them a chance to thank all the people who had been so nice to him and her momma while her momma was sick. They could wish Alice a Happy Birthday at the same time.

Alice, who was dishing up oatmeal at the stove, stopped short and turned quickly to her mother. From the startled look on Evelyn's face, she knew no more about this than Alice.

"I-I don't know, Webster," Evelyn said.

"Evelyn, you just leave this to me." He went back to his breakfast.

"Webster," Evelyn tried again with more strength than Alice had seen in her for some time, "Maybe Alice doesn't want…."

"Evelyn, we're gonna have this party." He didn't look at her.

Evelyn swallowed hard and stared at him.

Alice said, "Papa, Momma's doing much better, but she still can't do a lot of things. And I don't have time to get ready for a party. It's just a week 'til my birthday."

Webster kept his eyes on his plate. "Sample's got all that figured out." He held his cup out in her direction and took another bite of fried egg. "Pour me another cup of coffee while you're standing there at the stove."

"Sample's got what figured out?" Evelyn asked.

"He figured Alice could bake up some pies and a big cake, and he said he'd bring his housekeeper over to help her out. It won't be all that much trouble for her."

"Why is Sample planning Alice's party?" Evelyn asked. "Shouldn't we be the ones doing that?"

"'Cause Sample is paying for it," Webster said, wiping the egg off his plate with a piece of toast and popping it into his mouth.

Evelyn's face tightened. "Why is Sample paying for it?"

"Said he wanted to give Alice something for her birthday she'd always remember."

Alice broke in, "I don't want to remember anything from Sample, Papa. Tell him that."

"We're beholden to Sample, and it wouldn't be neighborly. Sample is dead set on paying for this party, and I wouldn't be one to deprive him of it." Her father put his coffee cup back in its saucer, picked up his straw hat, and started for the door. "We're having a party," he said, and slammed the screen door as he went out.

"Momma," Alice choked out, "what'll I do?"

"I'll talk to him later," Evelyn told Alice who was beginning to cry. "Don't go getting all upset. We'll work out something."

Alice turned back toward the stove and started to clean out the oatmeal pan, tears still sliding down her face. She knew her momma would try, but Alice didn't hold out much hope; her papa had made up his mind. Alice knew Sample would not be paying for her party if he didn't think he was going to get something from it, and she also knew Sample thought that something was going to be her.

Evelyn did talk to Webster that day at lunch, but the best she could do was get him to have the party on Saturday, the 12th. She convinced him more people would come if they had it on Saturday afternoon. It would give Alice an extra day.

Webster certainly wanted people to come. He wanted everybody in Tysen to witness the fact that his daughter was going to marry Sample Forney. Webster planned to announce it right after Alice cut her birthday cake. That, in Webster's mind, would raise his status.

Sample came that night, and Webster made Alice and Evelyn come sit out on the front porch with them after dinner while the men talked about the party. Alice sat on the porch steps, leaning against the pillar apart from the chairs and never said a word unless somebody asked her a question. Sample didn't speak to her; he just watched. She could see him out of the corner of her eye. Alice never looked at him straight on; she was afraid she'd see that look of ownership. She knew he thought she was bought and paid for like a blue ribbon cow. She got through the evening by telling herself again and again, Just wait, Alice, just wait. And after that night, she counted off the days like those on an Advent Calendar, reminding herself each night when she got into bed that one more had gone by. One day closer to marrying Ray.

Alice made trips into town as often as she could on some errand that would give her time to stop by Naomi's and see how the wedding plans were coming. On Thursday afternoon, just a week and two days before the wedding, Alice stopped by to tell Naomi what her papa was up to.

"What am I to do, Naomi? Let Momma think it's all going to happen?"

"Now," Naomi said, "don't worry; everything is going to be just fine. I'll go out to see how your momma is doing; I was planning to anyway. I'll have a little talk with her. Right now, I want you to come in the bedroom with me; I have a surprise for you."

They walked down the hall to Naomi's bedroom.

"Shut your eyes a minute," Naomi said before she led her through the door.

Alice shut her eyes, and when she opened them, there, on the bed, was a white eyelet, ankle-length dress, made to come off the shoulders. A blue silk sash was tied in a bow at its waist. Beside the dress was a pair of white high-heeled pumps and a tiny blue silk purse.

"Oh, Naomi," Alice held the dress in front of her and looked into the mirror on Naomi's dresser, "I didn't think I'd have a wedding dress. And it's perfect. It's just perfect."

Naomi told her, "Wait a minute; there's one more thing to set it off." Naomi lifted a hatbox down from the top of the closet and brought out a white eyelet pillbox hat with a tiny veil that would cover Alice's face.

Naomi crowned her with the hat and pulled the veil over her face. "There," Naomi said, standing back to admire her, "aren't you the beautiful bride."

Alice's tears touched the mesh of her veil. "I don't know how to thank you."

Naomi took Alice's hat off, saying, "Now, stop that, child; we can't have you messing up your veil. We just wanted to make you happy. The dress is from Matt and me, the hat is from Johnny, and the purse is from Russell."

"You all are so good to me," Alice said, laying the dress on the bed and running her fingers over it, smoothing out wrinkles where there were none. "It's all just beautiful." Alice's face saddened. "I just wish Momma could see it."

"Take my word for it, Alice, your momma will see this dress. I'm going to take care of that."

"How, Naomi?"

"Don't ask too many questions, child. Just take my word."

Alice nodded and added wistfully, "I wish Hope could see it, too."

"I'm afraid I'm not going to be able to do anything about that, honey, but I'm sure she's thinking about you and your wedding day. Now, quit worrying, child. Go home and do something that keeps your hands and your mind busy. Everything is in order. Just be happy."

Alice decided to take Naomi's advice. The next morning she launched into cleaning the house, closets and pantries, drawers, chests and stored boxes. Evelyn crocheted in her chair in the corner of the kitchen beside the wood stove they used for heat when the weather turned cool. The chair stayed there summer and winter; it was a cozy out-of-the-way spot. From there, she watched her daughter move in and out of the kitchen, going from room to room, and she hadn't missed the bounce in Alice's step as she worked, in spite of Webster's announcement. Evelyn knew full well that Sample Forney wasn't making her Alice's eyes shine. But she knew to keep her own counsel.

Alice left her mother's sewing room until last, making the room ready for Evelyn when she felt up to sewing again. She moved the sewing machine in front of the windows so Evelyn could look out at the flowers in the front yard and see who was coming up the drive when people came. She had vacuumed and polished to a shine, almost finishing, when she spied her grandmother's old traveling trunk in the closet. It was there Evelyn kept her material, all the feed sacks she was collecting until she had enough that matched to make a dress. It needs to be sorted out, Alice thought.

She opened the lid and lifted out the top layer of cloth, and there it was, buried under some laundered feed sacks where she'd put it, the blue material Sample had bought for her to make a dress. Alice had stuck it there so she wouldn't have to look at it. Clenching her jaw and narrowing her eyes, Alice thought, there isn't going to be any dress, and she said aloud without knowing it, "Papa and Sample, there isn't going to be any party."

She lifted the material from the chest, held at it at arm's length, and decided to get rid of it. How? She could cut it into pieces and bury it. Or, better yet, she could burn it. There was the wood stove in the kitchen. All she needed was some old newspapers for kindling. It shouldn't take long to burn, and the stove would be cool by the time papa came home from working at Sample's. She'd do it when momma went up for a nap after lunch. Evelyn was able to move up and down the stairs now; she just had to take her time.

After lunch, Alice washed the dishes and set them to dry in the rack on the drain, swept the kitchen floor and side porch, and waited for her mother to drop into a deep sleep. Evelyn usually slept for an hour or more. Doc said the longer the better.

Gathering the material and the scissors from the sewing room, she brought them into the kitchen, and, laying the material on the table, cut it quickly into four pieces, leaving them in a soft heap on the table. She scrunched up several pieces of newspaper and stuck them one at a time into the stove.

Alice opened the damper on the stovepipe and put in the first piece of cloth. She took a kitchen match from the box that hung on the wall behind the stove, struck it, and held it to the newspaper, watching the smoke curl out from the sides of the shiny, blue cotton, which caught fire as though it had been waiting for the flame. When the first piece was in full blaze, she put the second on the poker and shoved it into the fire, sighing with satisfaction. The material wisped away into smoke and ash and swirled up the chimney.

She reached for another piece, placed it on the poker, and turned to the stove. Intent on the blaze, she didn't hear the screen door open or the heavy footsteps over the sill. It was his voice, sounding like low thunder before a summer storm, that made her jump. The material slid off the poker and fell to the floor.

He was filling up the doorway, larger than she'd ever remembered. His face was pulled tight, and he was staring first at the fire, then at the flow of blue cotton covering her sandaled feet. He growled, "What are you doing, girl? Just what do you think you are doing? I paid for that dress."

Alice tried to step back, but her feet were tangled in the cloth. The poker dropped beside her. She was in the kitchen alone with Sample whose eyes were agate hard, and his big hands were clenching and unclenching. He smelled of earth and sweat, and he moved closer. "Answer me," he demanded.

For the first time, Alice was afraid of Sample Forney. She disliked Sample, was repulsed by him, and disgusted by him, but she'd never been afraid of him. Until now.

"It isn't a dress," Alice said finally, her throat felt so dry she could barely speak.

"What do you mean, it isn't a dress?" Sample demanded.

"I never made a dress," Alice said, reaching down to untangle her feet from the cloth. When she did, Sample moved toward her, pushing her aside with his shoulder. He slammed the stove door shut with one hand and jerked the cotton from around her feet. Alice lost her balance and fell back against the table.

"You're burning my gift," he said, shaking the material in her face. "You can't do that." He threw it past her at the table. "I own this material. I own it just the way I'm going to own you."

"You're not going to own me. Not now, not ever."

"I am; your daddy promised."

"I didn't promise. I've never promised you anything."

"Your daddy is a smart man. He knows what I can do."

"My poppa knows what you can give him; he just used me in the bargain."

"Well, it's a bargain that's set."

"I'm not going to marry you. I wouldn't marry you ever even if there was no one else to marry."

Sample looked at her a long minute. "You telling me there is someone else for you to marry?"

"I didn't say that." Alice had slipped; there was fear in her eyes.

"You said 'even if there was no one else to marry'; that's what you said. I ain't stupid, Alice. I didn't make a fortune being stupid."

"I don't want your money, Sample. I don't want anything from you except for you to leave and never come back." Her back was hurting badly where she'd hit the table, but she pressed back against it to get away from him.

"That's not going to happen. You're daddy will see to it. I'll see to it." He leaned over, pressing his body against hers, bending her back harder onto the table.

The weight of his body on hers made her want to scream for her mother. She could feel the scissors under her right wrist. If she had to, she would stab him. "My papa's not going to stop me either," she hissed at him.

"Stop you? Stop you from what?" Suddenly, he straightened up and stepped back. "You're thinking about Redeem. You're thinking that after you're eighteen that drunken Redeem will be hanging around, and you can go running around with him again." He grabbed her by the shoulders and began shaking her. "God damn you, Alice, I was going to treat you good, give you things," he shook harder and harder, and Alice could feel the table beating against her back. "And look what you're doing! You're trying to spoil it all." Sample inhaled and lifted Alice up by her shoulders, holding her off the floor so he could stare her in the eyes. "It ain't over yet, little girl. What I want, I get, and whether you like it or not, I want you." He threw her back against the table. "It may just be with Ray Redeem gone, you'll be changing your mind," he said, moving toward the door.

Alice, pain shooting through her neck, shouted at his retreating back, "I'll never change my mind, and Ray will never leave me."

"We'll see about that," Sample roared back. He jumped into his truck, and Alice moved painfully away from the table to watch him drive out of their gate and head south toward the Redeems. Ray, she thought, he's going after Ray. Then she sighed with relief, remembering that Ray wouldn't be alone at the mill.

Chapter Thirty-Nine

Ray had sent Johnny and Doobie to deliver a load of railroad ties. The Mueller brothers had gone to their uncle's funeral in Meramec City, and there wasn't much left to do until Monday when they had to start cutting that order for the new feed store going up in Havana. Jackson was itching to try out his new .225 rifle with a 10-power scope. Something had been carrying off their chickens for the last month, and Jackson had finally found fox hair with some chicken feathers caught in the chicken wire where the fox had crawled under the fence with the dead bird in its mouth. Ray told him to go on. Doobie and Johnny had filled the skidway with logs before they left, and he could finish the 2x4s Albert St. John had ordered.

Ray used a cant hook as easily as he moved his arm, cinching the log in a single movement and rolling it onto the trolley that would carry it down the track to the saw for a flat cut. He locked the log into place and moved to the far end of the track to turn on the diesel. The quiet struck him; he was used to the loud rattle and clack of the diesel idling; then, the roaring grind of the saw or the bantering of the men. He wasn't often alone at the mill.

He turned the key and pushed the starter button, and the diesel came to life. He moved over to the saw and pulled the lever that started the blade whirring. That's more like it, he thought, and moved back to the waiting log, pulling the lever that sent it down for the first cut that would saw the slab of bark from its side. Moving back and forth the length of the log, Ray fell into a rhythm that he'd known all his life.

He didn't hear Sample's truck; the diesel and the saw were too loud. It was the fighter's sense that something was coming at him that made him look up. Sample was some twenty feet away, moving as though he were propelled. His fists were clenched, and he was breathing hard. Ray thought, he knows. Somehow, he knows.

"God damn you, Redeem," Sample shouted. "Stay away from Alice Tolney."

Ray shouted back, "Don't be giving me any orders, Sample."

"I am giving you orders. Alice is mine. She don't belong to no one else." Sample had moved so close to Ray, Ray could feel his breath when he shouted.

"Alice don't belong to you. Now get out of here; I got work to do," Ray shouted back.

"I told you to stay away from her." Sample's face was getting redder and redder. "I won't be telling you again."

"I said get out of here, Sample." Ray turned back toward the saw.

"Didn't you hear me?" Sample grabbed Ray's shoulder, pulling him around toward him. "Alice is mine."

Ray threw up his arm and knocked Sample's hand away. "Alice isn't yours. She never was, and she never will be." He shoved Sample backward. "Now, get in your truck and get the hell off my property, and stay away from Alice."

Sample turned as if to leave, but swung around and caught Ray with a hard blow on his right temple. Ray staggered back against the diesel. He pushed himself away and came straight at Sample with his fists up. Just before he reached him, Ray lowered his head and butted Sample backwards, knocking him to the ground.

Sample came up almost as quickly as he went down, covered in sawdust with a broken piece of 2x4 in his hand. He swung at Ray; Ray ducked and punched Sample hard in the gut, moving him only a step or two back. Ray had fought men as big as Sample, but he knew when his fist struck Sample's middle he'd never fought any as solid. And Sample was five inches taller and fifty pounds heavier than Ray. When Sample came at him again, Ray tried to side step, but Sample swung the 2x4 catching Ray across his side; Ray knew when he went down his ribs were broken; he'd had it happen before.

When Ray came up, he went for Sample's kneecap with his foot. With a "God damn," Sample went down, and Ray was on top of him, pummeling his face and head with both fists. Sample was able to jab hard at Ray's left eye, and his knuckles caught Ray's forehead hard enough to gash it. The blood began trickling down Ray's temple.

When Ray hit Sample again, he felt Sample's nose give. At that blow, Sample hoisted up like a whale and rolled Ray off him, kicking Ray's side, his foot connecting with Ray's broken ribs. Sample's nose was to the side, and blood was oozing from cuts above his eyebrow and on his cheek. His right eye was beginning to swell. Ray was trying to roll out of Sample's reach, but Sample picked up the 2x4 and put a foot on Ray's stomach. "All right," he said, "you going to stay away from Alice?"

Ray's lips were cut and swollen; he shook his head, no, and said, "I'm going to marry her. You can't stop it."

"I can if I kill you," he said.

"Then kill me, you son of a bitch. You'll have to kill me to stop me. And even if you kill me, she won't have you."

"She'll have me. She'll by God have me," Sample roared, and he swung the 2x4, catching Ray across the forearm Ray had automatically raised to protect himself. They both heard it break. Ray tried to roll away, but Sample advanced and brought the 2x4 down squarely on Ray's head. Sample thought he'd done it, he'd killed him, but he could see the rise and fall of Ray's chest. "You hard-headed bastard," he shouted at Ray, "I'll make sure you're dead."

He didn't see or hear Jackson Redeem running toward him, shouting as he came, from the edge of the woods behind the mill.

Jackson had come out of the woods just as Sample lifted Ray's limp body and moved toward the log. "Sample," he shouted, "Sample," even though he knew Sample couldn't hear him. Ray sagged over Sample's shoulder like the dead fox over Jackson's own. "Sample," he shouted again and began running toward the mill, the fox sliding to the ground. "Blessed Lord," he prayed, "don't let him hurt my son. My only son." He saw Sample drape Ray's body over the log and ran harder, continuing his prayer. When Sample straightened Ray's body so it laid out flat, Jackson stopped, raised his rifle and put the cross hairs of the scope on Sample's head. "Sample," he shouted one last time, and Sample heard and turned. Jackson's rifle was pointed at his forehead. "I'm going to kill him, Jackson; you can't stop me," and he reached for the lever that would send the log toward the saw.

Jackson knew the Sixth Commandment. "Thou Shalt Not Kill," he heard as clearly as Moses had on Mt. Sinai. Then, just as clearly, he remembered Ray saying, "When you fight, you go for something vital, not fatal." Jackson lowered the cross hairs to the crotch of Sample's overalls and squeezed the trigger twice. Sample screamed and crumpled before he could hear the first shot, and by the time he could have heard it, he'd passed out.

Jackson dropped his rifle and ran to Ray. Ray was still breathing, and he moaned when Jackson lifted him down and laid him in the sawdust beside the log trolley. "Thank you, Jesus," Jackson offered up.

Doobie pulled the truck into the yard as Jackson was moving toward Sample. "Help me over here," he shouted. Johnny and Doobie jumped out of the truck, doors flying open on either side of the cab, and ran toward Jackson.

"God Almighty, Jackson, what's happened?" Doobie shouted.

"Johnny, see to Ray. Watch to see if he's breathing all right. Doobie turn off the diesel while I cut Sample's overalls off him so I can judge how bad he's hurt."

A red ooze was forming a pool under Sample at the crotch; he was still unconscious.

"He's breathing okay, Jackson," Johnny called, "and his pulse seems steady." Johnny had watched Doc often enough of late to know what he was doing.

"Keep a close eye on him, son," Jackson told him.

"I've got him," Johnny said.

Doobie had come back and was looking over Jackson's shoulder as Jackson slit the legs of Sample's overalls with his pocket knife and pulled them open.

"God Almighty, Jackson," Doobie said, "you shot most of his pecker off."

"He's lucky he's still got enough to pee with," Jackson muttered, kneeling down by Sample. "Check the water cooler, Doobie; see if there's any ice left. I've got to get this blood stopped."

Jackson used his neckerchief to tie a tight tourniquet around the three inches of penis left to Sample Forney and wrapped the rest of the scarf around it to cushion it. Below the tourniquet, attached only by a few ragged strings of bloody tissue, dangled what was once the legendary prick.

One of the hollow point bullets had also taken off the bottom of his left testicle, and when Doobie came back with a large chunk of ice, Jackson placed the ice on the mangled skin. "Get a shovel full of sawdust, Doob, and I'll pack this ice with it to keep it from melting as soon as I get him on the truck."

Doobie came back with the sawdust and put in on the truck bed. "Now," Jackson ordered, "grab those horse blankets in the tool shed. We'll make them a bed in the back of the truck." Doobie went for the blankets in the shed beside the mill, and Jackson went to Johnny to help him lift Ray. "John, I want you to drive; Doobie and I'll stay in the back with the two of them."

Johnny nodded. Jackson took Ray securely under his shoulders, and Johnny lifted Ray's legs. Doobie was ahead of them with the blankets, and they laid him in carefully, using extra blankets under his head and one to cover him. The three of them went to get Sample, Jackson at his head and Doobie and Johnny at either side. Sample moaned, but didn't come to.

"Think he'll die, Jackson?" Doobie asked.

"No," Jackson said, "he won't die. He hasn't lost enough blood to die."

"He may die of shock when he sees his pecker shot off," Doobie said. Jackson ignored him. "There ain't no way Doc's gonna be able to save that." Doobie went on talking to himself. "No way."

They slid Sample in beside Ray, readjusted the ice, and packed it with sawdust. "Sit there beside Sample, Doobie. Put a blanket under his head and cover him. I'll take care of Ray. Johnny, drive as careful as you can, but hurry."

Johnny jumped into the front seat and moved the truck over the ruts as gently as he could, and when he had all four tires on the blacktop, he pushed the gas to the floorboard, heading for town and on to the hospital. He prayed as he drove, Dear God, please don't let Ray die. Please don't let Ray die. He was passing the "Welcome to Tysen" sign before he remembered to include Sample, too.

They were passing the hotel and slowing for the railroad tracks, when Jackson caught sight of Naomi bringing Russell out onto the front porch. "Naomi," Jackson shouted, "Call Doc Barnes to meet us at the hospital. Ray's hurt bad, and so's Sample."

When Johnny felt the back tires cross the tracks, he waved an arm out of the cab window and pushed the gas pedal to the floor.

Naomi left Russell in his wheel chair sitting in the middle of the porch and ran for the phone. Naomi's first call went to Doc Barnes, and her second to Alice. "Alice, bring your momma and come to the hotel. Ray and Sample have both been hurt bad. I'll take care of Evelyn while you go to the hospital."

Alice didn't stop to ask questions, she just gathered up her momma. "Momma, Ray's been hurt bad, and I have to go to the hospital." Evelyn looked at her daughter's pale face and said, "Of course, you do." She picked up her purse, climbed into the truck with Alice's help. "Don't drive too fast, sweetheart," she admonished, "you won't get there any quicker, and we all want you safe."

"Yes, ma'am," Alice said. Neither spoke another word until they reached the hotel.

One call to Doc Barnes and all of Tysen got the news through the party lines that Ray and Sample were both badly hurt. One call to Alice and all of Tysen wondered whose hand it was Alice Tolney was rushing to hold.

It would not be until evening when Doobie settled onto his accustomed bar stool at Harvey's Tavern that the people of Tysen learned that Jackson Redeem had shot off most of Sample Forney's pecker.

Chapter Forty

Naomi and Evelyn sat in the kitchen drinking hot tea and waiting for a call from the hospital. Russell was dozing in his hospital bed in the living room. Sitting in his wheelchair for any length of time had begun to wear him out. Naomi had her eye on him through the archway. He was sleeping more and more since he'd been forced to take morphine for pain.

"Russell's fading pretty fast, isn't he?" Evelyn asked softly.

Naomi nodded. "He's finally given in to taking morphine, but he won't take it often. He's dead set on seeing Johnny get off to school."

"I remember Russell was always strong-willed, even when we was children."

"He still is," Naomi chuckled, checking the rise and fall of the light blanket she kept over him even in this heat.

"You're a good woman, Naomi, to take Russell in and care for him after what his leaving and all."

"It isn't goodness, Evelyn; it's just what has to be done."

"People don't always do what has to be done." Evelyn looked down at her cold cup of tea. "I haven't."

Naomi didn't say anything; she just reached over and put her hand over Evelyn's.

"This stroke almost killed me, and when I got to where I could, it made me do some hard thinking. I'd come so close to dying; I saw things different than before. Lying in that bed at home day after day and watching Alice, listening to her and Hope plan and dream when they thought I was asleep, I knew I had to make some changes. I didn't know how I would do it, but I knew there had to be a way." She looked up at Naomi. "I know I've never been a strong woman, but I swear to you, I wouldn't have let Webster force her to marry Sample Forney. I'd have stopped him somehow."

"Who are you stopping, Evelyn?" Matt asked. "Need any help?" He'd come in quietly so as not to disturb Russell. Both women looked up startled, but just for a second. Matt and Evelyn had been in the same class through school, and they liked each other. He'd always thought she'd deserved much better than Webster Tolney.

Evelyn blushed, but she smiled at him. "I may, Matt."

"Matt," Naomi interrupted, "there's been a bad accident." She told him what little she knew.

"Do you want me to drive over to the hospital?" he asked.

"I wish you would," Naomi said.

"So do I," Evelyn said, softly.

Matt looked surprised. Naomi said, "Go on; I'll tell you about it later."

Evelyn said, "Matt, will you please tell Alice to come here and not go straight home?"

Matt was puzzled, but he said, "I'll tell her."

"Don't forget now." Evelyn was biting her lower lip.

"I won't forget, and I'll call as soon as I know anything." Matt kissed Naomi on the cheek. It was a reflex, and he decided to kiss Evelyn's cheek, too, to smooth everything out.

Naomi asked, "Why don't you just call and tell me you're on your way home if everything is all right? That way we don't have to broadcast it on the party line."

"Right," he said, slipping quietly out the front screen door and going to get his car which was parked beside the post office.

They were quiet for a few minutes; then Naomi roused herself. "Would you like a cold glass of tea?" she asked. "Here we sit drinking hot tea on a hot day."

"There's something soothing in hot tea," Evelyn said, "even in August."

There was truth in that, Naomi knew. "We'd move out onto the porch, but there'd be people coming to ask questions."

"In here is just fine," Evelyn told her.

Naomi placed their iced tea and a plate of cookies on the table. It was busy work; neither of them bothered with the cookies.

"Naomi, could Alice stay here with you until the wedding? I don't want her to have to be around her daddy until I can straighten things out."

Naomi could feel her face jerk in surprise. "You know about the wedding?"

"Yes, I know," she said. "I've heard the girls one day when they thought I was asleep. You believe Ray's a good boy, don't you, Naomi?"

"He is a good boy, Evelyn. He's been in this house as much as his own, and I love him almost as much as I do Johnny." She took both of Evelyn's hands in hers. "He loves Alice so much he's about to burst with it. He'll be good to her, and he'll provide for her. He'll take good care of you, too; he's told me that. He said you could live with them if you wanted to; if you didn't, he'd see you had everything you needed. You can believe him, Evelyn. I've never known him not to keep his word."

"That makes me rest easy," Evelyn said, "Oh, not because of me. I just don't want Alice living the life I've lived. I want her to have some say in her life and someone she can talk to. Someone who'll provide for her and not always be scheming to make himself important."

"He'll do all that, honey. I want you to know I was coming out this very afternoon to tell you this," Naomi said.

"I believe you," Evelyn said, "and thank you for helping my girl."

Naomi squeezed Evelyn's hand; "Let's just say a prayer that the two of them will have a long and happy life together." The women bowed their heads, and Naomi offered up a simple plea for Ray's recovery.

"Now," Naomi said, sliding the plate toward Evelyn, "let's have a cookie."

Chapter Forty-One

At the hospital, Doc Barnes had his hands full. He'd sent Ray off to be x-rayed and told Dora Mae, the nurse on duty, to call Doc Whiteside. Doc figured Jimmy Whiteside was fishing at his pond, which he always did on his day off, but his wife would go fetch him. He'd be mad, but mad or not, Doc needed help. Ray had a concussion, and Doc didn't know how bad it was. Doc also knew at least three of Ray's ribs were broken, and he wanted to be sure one of them wasn't poking into a lung. And his left arm needed to be set as soon as possible.

Right now, though, Doc had to get to Sample into surgery. When they'd first brought them in and Doc lifted away the sawdust and undid the tourniquet, he found nine inches of penis dangling by shreds of tissue and skin and a mangled left testicle. If Sample had had the good sense to wear underpants, Doc thought, he might not have lost quite so much. He had lost some blood, but Jackson's tourniquet and the ice had done their job. Doc could fix him up. He needed to get at it right away, but he wanted Ray in good hands. Next to himself, he could trust Jimmy Whiteside more than any doctor he knew.

While they took Ray off to x-ray, Jackson called the sheriff. That's what you did when you shot somebody. He, Johnny and Doobie had just sat down in the waiting room when Alice came running down the hall and through the doors. "Jackson, is Ray all right?" she asked, breathlessly. She'd run all the way from the parking lot, and now she collapsed on the imitation leather sofa beside Johnny.

Jackson and Doobie were sitting in straight chairs close by. Jackson told her, "He's still unconscious, but Doc Whiteside is doing everything he can."

"Where's Doc Barnes?" she asked.

"In the operating room working on Sample," Johnny said.

"What happened to Sample?" She looked first at Johnny and then at Jackson.

Doobie started to speak, but Jackson gave him a look. "I shot him," Jackson told her without explaining the bullet's location, "but he's going to be all right. Doc just has to sew him up some."

Alice started to cry. "It's all my fault. Sample was so angry when he left my house, and I knew he was heading for the mill, but I thought with everybody there Sample wouldn't be able to hurt him."

"We was all gone; Ray was by himself," Doobie told her.

Johnny interrupted. "Sample came to your house in the middle of the day? Why?"

"I don't know. I just looked up, and there he was, standing there in the doorway." She looked at a loss. "I'm the one set him off. I was burning some dress material he brought to my house for me, and I wanted to get rid of it, and he saw what I was doing. Then, he started shouting at me and told me I couldn't burn gifts he gave me because I belonged to him, and I told him I'd never marry him, that I loved Ray, and he said I'd never have Ray and jumped in his truck still shouting at me, and, and…," she began sobbing.

Johnny put his arm around her. "It's going to be all right," he said as he held her. He looked at Jackson. "Ray was going to tell you this evening, but you need some explanation now, so I don't think Ray would mind. He and Alice are planning on getting married next week, right after Alice's birthday. They've been keeping it a secret because of Sample and Webster."

"They're getting married?" Doobie asked. "Didn't nobody know a thing." Doobie was astonished that any bit of information could get past him and was slightly miffed.

"That was the idea, Doob. They didn't want anybody to know," Johnny said.

Jackson looked at the girl who lifted her tear-washed face from Johnny's shoulder to see how Jackson had taken the news about her marrying his son.

She said, "We were planning on telling you, Jackson, before we did it; honest we were. I'm so sorry I said anything to Sample; I just couldn't help it. I'd never do anything to hurt Ray."

"Sample's the one did the beating," Jackson said. "You couldn't have stopped him once he made up his mind."

"I didn't know he'd be coming to the farm in the middle of the day. He never came without Papa." She wiped her eyes on some Kleenex she'd found in her purse and took a deep breath. "My papa is dead set on keeping Ray and me apart. He wants me to marry Sample because Sample has all that land, and he'll give some to Papa if I marry him." She took a deep breath. "Jackson, I can't marry anybody but Ray; I love Ray more than anything in the world." Her eyes begged him to understand.

Jackson looked into those eyes, filled with pain and love and hope, and for the first time since Loretta died, he felt his rusty heart begin to open. "I see that," he said gruffly. "Now, don't fret. We'll see to Ray, and then we'll work things out somehow."

It was another thirty minutes before Doc Whiteside came into the waiting room. The four of them stood up to hear the news. Doc put his hand on Jackson's shoulder. "He's regained consciousness," he said. "He's got himself a good size concussion, but he knows who he is and where he is. We'll keep him overnight for observation, but you can probably take him home tomorrow. We've taped his ribs, set his left arm, and put some stitches into that deep cut above his eye and the one on his cheek. He's going to be mighty sore young man for a week or two, but he's a mighty lucky one.

"I think he'll want to see you as soon as they get him settled in a room. Should be about thirty minutes. Your name wouldn't be Alice by any chance, would it, young lady?"

"Yes, sir," she said and blushed.

"I wouldn't be going anywhere until I saw that young man of yours; he seems mighty anxious to see you."

Jackson shook his hand and thanked him. Doc Whiteside waved at them and hurried out the door.

Jackson bowed his head and said aloud, "Thank you, Lord, for saving my son." Johnny and Alice echoed, "Amen." Doobie nodded.

The sheriff, Clarkson Ford, came into the waiting room just as they sat down again. He asked Jackson what had happened. Jackson told him, and Doobie and Johnny added what they could about what they'd seen when they got there. Clarkson asked Jackson if he wanted to press charges against Sample. Sample Forney might be the richest man in the county, but nobody in his right mind would doubt the word of Jackson

Redeem. Jackson said he'd let the sheriff know after he and Sample had a talk about some things. Clarkson said that would be fine and that he was going to have a talk with Sample himself.

Busby Howard, Bible in his right hand, came into the waiting room as the sheriff was leaving. "Brother Jackson," he said, ignoring the others, and putting his free hand on Jackson's shoulder, "I came to pray with you."

"I've been praying, Preacher; I haven't stopped praying since it happened. I've been praying for my boy. You here to pray for my boy?" Jackson was steely-eyed.

Busby stuttered, "I'm here to pray for you in your suffering."

"My boy's the one suffering. He's the one Sample beat and tried to saw in two."

Alice gasped. Johnny said softly, "It's all over now, Alice. Ray will explain it to you in a bit."

"You here to pray for him?" Jackson asked again.

"Of course, I'll pray for him. I pray for sinners."

Jackson looked down at the floor; he seemed to be studying the tile between his feet; then, he lifted his head and looked in Busby's eyes. "For a good many years now, I've heard you take my boy to task from your pulpit, and I've sat there and just let it roll on off me 'cause I guess I wasn't really taking it in. I haven't been taking in a lot of things for a lot of years. If I had been, I'd have called you on it right then and there and walked on out of that church the way my son did that night.

"Now, here's what I want you to understand, and I'm not asking you, I'm telling you: Quit attacking my boy, or I'll never set foot in that church again."

"You can't tell me what to preach, Jackson. Only God does that."

"I'm not telling you what to preach; I'm telling you not to use my boy as your whipping post in your sermons. As far as God telling you what to preach, I'm not so sure anymore that you can tell what God wants. I think it's mostly what Busby Howard wants. Now, if you want to pray for somebody, you'd best be praying for Sample Forney; he's going to need it," Jackson finished.

"He sure as blazes is," Doobie couldn't resist saying. Jackson hushed him with another look.

"I'll pray for Brother Sample, and I'll pray for you, too. It's a prideful man who doesn't think he needs the prayers of another," Busby replied. "Since I'm not wanted here, I'll take the Lord's work to others who do want me." Busby turned on his heel to leave and bumped smack into Matt who'd just arrived. "You're blocking the door," Busby huffed at Matt.

"One of us is," said Matt. Busby stepped around him and turned right, heading toward the lobby.

"Looks like he's not going to wait to talk to Sample," Doobie commented with a smile.

"What's happened?" Matt asked, and Johnny told him.

They decided that Johnny and Doobie would ride home with Matt as soon as Johnny had seen Ray. Alice would come home a little later to pick up Evelyn, and Jackson had his truck so he'd come when he was ready.

Matt went out to the lobby to use the phone to call Naomi, and through the swinging glass doors, he could see Busby sitting in his car, staring out the windshield. He must have a plateful to mull over, Matt thought, as the phone was ringing, but when Naomi answered, he forgot about Busby, and by the time Matt hung up, Busby was headed back to Tysen.

Matt dropped Doobie off at Harvey's Tavern, and he and Johnny drove across the tracks to the hotel where three anxious people were waiting to hear from them. Johnny told them everything right down to the leftover length of Sample's penis and the talk Jackson had with the Sheriff.

"You're sure they'll both be all right?" Naomi asked.

"Considering the facts, I don't know if Sample will ever be all right," Matt said.

Russell, who was sitting at the table in his wheelchair threw back his head and started to laugh. His laughter came first from his belly and then pushed outward filling the rest of his body, growing and growing until it was totally consuming. And as they watched him, they joined, one by one, in this joyous relief of prayer and of irony.

When Sample didn't come back from town, Webster knew he'd have to walk home. It was only two miles from Sample's place to his if he cut across the fields; by road it was four. He was put out at the thought. He didn't relish walking home anytime, much less after a hard day's work, and he couldn't figure out why Sample wasn't there to get him. Sample was counting off days until Alice's birthday, and it wasn't like him to miss dinner at Webster's.

By the time he'd reached his own place, he was flat out angry. When he opened the screen door, he saw the kitchen was empty, and there was no food on the stove. "Alice?" he called. "Evelyn? Where the hell are you? Where's dinner? What's going on?" There was no sound in the house. He went to the front porch and saw the truck was gone. He checked the bedroom upstairs; the bed was made up, and there was no sign of Evelyn. He'd never found the house empty when he got home from work. He didn't know what to do or where to look.

He decided to call Sample's house to see if he'd come back from town and find out what had kept him. Wanda Puckett, Sample's housekeeper, answered. "Oh, Webster," she cried, "isn't it awful?"

"Isn't what awful?"

"About Sample being shot and in the hospital, and Ray Redeem being hurt so bad."

"Sample's been shot? Is he alive?"

"He's alive, but I don't know yet how he's doing. I suppose somebody will call when they know. If you hear anything, will you call me?" Wanda asked.

Webster asked without answering her, "You don't happen to know where Alice and Evelyn are, do you?"

"They're at Naomi's. At least, Evelyn is. I heard Alice is at the hospital. She went there as soon as Naomi called her."

Webster hung up on her and called Naomi's number. When Matt answered, Webster didn't even bother with a greeting. "I want to talk to Evelyn."

"She just sat down to eat, Web. She'll call you soon."

"I want her home now."

"Just hold your horses, Webster. Let the woman eat her dinner."

"Her dinner, hell; what about my dinner?"

"You've got a stove there, Webster. Cook something."

"Put her on the phone, Matt."

"I'll have her call you as soon as we're finished," Matt told him and hung up.

Webster let the receiver fall and stared at the phone. If Naomi had called Alice, she wasn't reporting on Sample; she had to be calling about Ray. That son-of-a-bitch Ray Redeem. Alice was there with him. Webster kicked the wall so hard his boot toe made a hole in the plaster, and he had to pull his foot away.

"God damn it," he shouted. "God damn it to hell." He might not know what had happened, but he knew in his bones that one more time, one damn more time, he wouldn't get what he'd planned for, and what he worked for, and what was his by rights.

Webster Tolney sat down at his kitchen table, put his face in his hands, and sobbed.

Chapter Forty-Three

After Matt and Johnny had eaten, Naomi settled Russell in his bed and came back to the kitchen table where the men were keeping Evelyn company.

"I've asked Naomi a big favor," Evelyn said, looking at Johnny and Matt, "and she's agreed that Alice can stay here until the wedding."

"The wedding?" Johnny asked, looking at Naomi.

"She knows all about it, honey," Naomi told him and gave him that look that said just wait and I'll explain it all later.

"I don't want her to come home just yet. I don't want her there until Webster thinks over what I have to tell him."

This was a first. Evelyn had never, as far as they knew, given Webster anything to think over. There was a moment's silence.

Matt asked, "You going to be all right out there?"

"I'll be all right," Evelyn told him.

"You're welcome to stay here; we've got two vacant rooms upstairs, one for Alice and another for you," Naomi told her.

"No, thank you, Naomi. You've done enough; you've helped more than you know."

"Well, the offer stands anytime you want it or need it, and I'll come out and get you and bring you in to see her as often as you want. Webster doesn't slow me down a bit," Naomi told her.

Evelyn smiled. "I don't know anybody can slow you down, Naomi. I just wish I had your gumption."

"You've got more gumption than you know; you're going to be just fine, honey," Naomi said

The door opened and Alice floated in. She began telling them even before she got to the table, "Ray's awake and talking, and he's probably coming home tomorrow. Isn't it wonderful?"

"It's wonderful," Evelyn replied. Alice hugged her mother. "Oh, and Doc says Sample will be okay, too."

"We're all glad Jackson didn't kill Sample, but we're even more happy that Sample didn't kill Ray. Now, you need something to eat," Naomi said.

"I think I'm too happy to eat," Alice said.

"Well, then, why don't you take your momma back to my bedroom, and you two can have a little talk. I think there's something back there you might be waiting to show her, and I'll fix you a plate while you do that. You may feel more like eating when you come back."

When Alice had led Evelyn down the hall to the bedroom, Naomi asked Matt, "You think she'll be all right alone with Webster?"

"I'll see to it before I leave her," Matt said.

Johnny looked as though he was asleep in his chair. "Sweetheart," Naomi said, "you've had a big day. Go on to bed now and sleep late. There won't be any work at the mill tomorrow."

Johnny put his arms around her.

"See, honey, things have a way of working out."

"Not all the time, Aunt Naomi," he said, thinking of Hope. She hugged him tightly. "No, not all the time, but we have to just wait and see." He gave her a parting squeeze and went slowly up the stairs to his bedroom.

Naomi poured Matt another cup of coffee and sank into the chair beside him, saying, "Well, I never in all my days."

Matt said, "You're right about that, sweetheart."

Chapter Forty-Four

When Busby Howard left the hospital, he drove directly to his office at the church. Nobody would be there that late in the afternoon, and he didn't want to go home to work. He had a sermon to write, and he didn't want to stop and talk to Helen or the girls. And Hope— Hope had begun turning her back on him, leaving the room as soon as he came in. She had actually begun acting as if he was in the wrong. He knew he had measured out a just punishment to Hope, and justice was more important than mercy.

Right now, he didn't have time for them. Jackson Redeem had lit a fire under him. Jackson of all people. He just couldn't believe it. Here he, Busby, had gone to offer his hand in prayer, and Jackson turned on him. Turned on him right there in front of all those people. Well, Jackson couldn't tell him what to preach or what not to preach, who to use and who not to use in a sermon. That was his to decide. After all, it was still his church.

The door to the church office creaked, and Busby sighed. When were they going to fix that? The office felt stuffy. He'd shut the window when he left last night; it had looked like rain. He hung his suit coat on the hook on the office door, loosened his tie, rolled up his sleeves, and went directly to the window to wrestle it open; that needed fixing, too.

Across the parking lot, Charlie Clark was standing at the tree line, not moving. He just stood there looking at the church building, looking at Busby. It was the third time this week Busby had seen him. Busby didn't have time to call Wyman to come get him; he had work to do. He'd call later.

He settled at his desk. Busby needed a sermon that would proclaim—yes, that was the word, "proclaim"—to all the members that their Preacher was unjustly under attack. He had planned on preaching on the Sermon on the Mount; he opened his Bible to Matthew 5, to begin, but his mind went back to Jackson. Jackson Redeem had been his rock to lean on when others were more faint of heart. Jackson, who was solid in his faith, never swerving to left or right, never letting people get in the way; he had always admired Jackson for that. Now, Jackson, at this late date, had turned on him in favor of his son. To think he'd do that even after Busby had chastised his very own daughter in front of the entire congregation. Well, he'd show them all who was the better Christian. After this sermon, the congregation would see the Light.

He looked down at Matthew 5:3 in his King James Version of the Bible and began reading:

> *3 Blessed are the poor in spirit: for theirs is the kingdom of heaven.*
> *4 Blessed are they who mourn: for they shall be comforted.*
> *5 Blessed are the meek: for they shall inherit the earth.*
> *6 Blessed are they which do hunger and thirst after righteousness: for they shall be filled.*
> *7 Blessed are the merciful: for they shall obtain mercy.*
> *8 Blessed are the pure in heart: for they shall see God.*
> *9 Blessed are the peacemakers: for they shall be called the children of God.*

Nothing Busby had just read would make the point he sorely needed to make. When he had chosen this text, he hadn't known what would happen between Sample and Ray, and he certainly couldn't have known what would befall him at the hospital with Jackson. He'd read on, and if nothing touched his heart, he'd find another topic.

> *10 Blessed are they which are persecuted for righteousness' sake: for theirs is the* kingdom of heaven.

Thank you, Jesus, Busby thought, Verse 10 is my text. The Lord has shown it to me, and the congregation will know I'm the persecuted one.

Busby marked his passages and jotted the notes he wanted to use. He never wrote out a sermon; he left if to the Holy Spirit to direct him. Men who wrote out sermons and studied too much didn't depend on a direct communication with the Lord.

It was growing dark when he pushed back the desk chair. He shuffled his notes together and placed them in his Bible; he'd look over them again Sunday morning just as a refresher. He straightened his tie and rolled down his sleeves as he moved to close the window. Charlie was walking across the parking lot, coming toward the office steps. What on earth is he doing? Busby wondered. What does he want in here? The man is crazy as a coot. And as strong as a bull, he remembered. Charlie had beaten up his father and his brother more than once, though it hadn't happened since they brought him home from the asylum.

Before Busby could get to his coat, he could hear Charlie coming up the steps. "Preacher," he called, "you in there?" Busby didn't answer; he was wondering how he could defend himself against Charlie. "Preacher, you in your office?" Charlie called again. The door creaked open, and Charlie filled the doorway.

"What do you want, Charlie? You're not supposed to be here," Busby told him.

"You have to do something for me, Preacher," Charlie said, coming into the office.

Busby backed up a few steps until he felt his desk behind him. He felt frightened, but he said forcefully, "I've got to get home to dinner; you go on home now."

Charlie placed himself in front of Busby. "You can't go home. You have to help me first."

"I'm going home, Charlie; now get out of my way," Busby said, trying to step out and around Charlie.

"No, Preacher, no," Charlie cried and shoved Busby back against the desk.

"Let me go, Charlie. Let me go right now." Charlie's weight pressed him against the desk. Busby's arms were behind him, his palms flat against the desk, holding himself up.

"You gotta listen, Preacher. You gotta listen. I can't let you go until you hear what I've got to say."

Busby was too frightened to really hear anything. "Let me go, Charlie; I'm warning you."

"No, Preacher, no." Charlie pushed so hard that Busby's arms collapsed and as he fell back across the desk his head hit the desk lamp with a whack.

Busby's whole day fell in on him: Sample, Ray, Jackson's betrayal, and now this. His right hand had fallen on the large polished rock he kept on his desk as a paper weight. His rock. His reminder of Peter. For in Matthew 16:18, Jesus said:

That thou art Peter, and on this rock I will build my church; and the gates of hell shall not prevail against it.

Closing his fingers around the rock, he brought up his arm with all the strength he could muster and hit Charlie Clark in the temple.

Charlie looked at him like a child who'd asked for a drink of water and had been slapped. He never looked away from Busby as his knees buckled, and the blood began to spout from the side of his head, "Why did you do that, Preacher?" he asked.

His hand clutched Busby's Bible as he fell, and the notes came fluttering to the floor. "I came to be saved, Preacher. I came to be saved. I don't want to be crazy no more. Ain't it your job to save sinners?"

He slumped backwards, his arms flung straight out to his sides, the blood making a halo on the floor around his head. "I need to be saved."

"Oh, my Dear Lord," Busby cried as he finally understood what it was Charlie had wanted.

"I wanted you to listen, Preacher," Charlie said, his eyes glazing over.

Charlie was lying at his feet, growing paler as the blood continued to flow from the crushed side of his temple, his hand still grasping Busby's Bible. Busby couldn't move; he just stood there watching the blood seep into the frayed carpet that was under his desk.

"Busby? Busby?" Helen called from the hall. "Are you in your office?"

He didn't hear her; he just stood there frozen.

She came through the door saying, "It was getting so late I came over to check on you. I was afraid you might have fallen asleep or something." She saw Busby's back and then the rock in his hand before her eyes dropped to Charlie. Her hand flew to her mouth. "Oh, my dear Lord in Heaven, Busby, what have you done?"

She moved to Charlie without even thinking and knelt beside him, putting her ear to his chest. She looked up at Busby, "He's breathing, but just barely. Don't just stand there, Busby, call Doc Barnes." Busby just looked at her. "He's at the hotel with Naomi; I just saw his car." Busby didn't move. She jerked on his pants leg. "Busby, move; do you hear me? Move," she said and gave his leg a shove.

"He wanted to be saved," he muttered, still standing there.

Helen wasn't listening. "Busby," she almost shouted, "I've got to stop this blood; now get yourself to the telephone and call Doc." She tore the front of her skirt to the waistband, tore it across and then down. She slid Charlie's head on her lap and pressed as hard as she could with the material. "Please, dear Lord," she prayed, "don't let this man die. Don't let him die."

Busby called the hotel. When Naomi answered, he said without thinking to identify himself, "Naomi, there's been an accident here in the church office. Send Doc over as fast as he can get here. Charlie Clark may be dying."

When Doc came running into the office less than five minutes later, Busby still had the receiver in his hand, the rock was beside the phone. Helen was softly crooning to Charlie, "Doc's on his way, Charlie. Doc's on his way. Just lie real still now."

Doc knelt beside Helen and put his stethoscope to Charlie's chest.

"How is he, Doc?" Helen asked, her face pale with concern.

Doc shook his head. "He's bad," he told her. He looked up at Busby. "Call his folks; don't just stand there."

"What should I tell them?" Busby asked.

"Damn it, man, what's wrong with you? Tell them the truth, tell them he's dying. I don't know if he'll live until they get here, but you don't need to tell them that."

Busby called the Clarks. When Wyman answered, he said, "Wyman, there's been an accident here in the church office. Bring Charlene, Charlie's in a bad way. And Doc says to hurry."

Doc was applying a large gauze pad to Charlie's wound. Just as he was finishing, Charlie opened his eyes and put a hand on Doc's arm. He whispered, "I came to be saved, Doc. Am I saved now?"

Doc's face flooded with pain. He took Charlie's hand and leaned close to his ear, "You're saved now, Charlie. You won't have to live with this sickness anymore. Everything is all right now, you sleep."

Charlie smiled at Doc, clutched Busby's Bible to his chest, and let out his final breath.

"Poor sick soul," Doc said, closing Charlie's eyes, "May the Good Lord welcome you home."

Helen was weeping and used the torn tail of her slip to wipe her eyes.

Doc hoisted himself up from the floor. He took the torn skirt out of Helen's hands, helped her to her feet, and pillowed the bloody skirt under Charlie's head.

Busby was sitting at his desk, looking like somebody trying to understand a nightmare. Doc helped Helen into a chair in front of the desk, "Sit here, honey, you've had a terrible shock."

She just nodded. The tears wouldn't stop.

Doc sat in the other chair across from Busby. He took in the papers scattered by Busby's desk and the rock tinged with blood beside the telephone. "What in God's name happened here?" he asked Busby.

"Charlie tried to kill me," Busby said.

Doc eyed the rock, "Why did Charlie want to kill you?"

"I don't know why," Busby said. "He's crazy. He's been watching me for weeks now from the edge of the woods, and tonight he came for me. Came right into the office."

"What did he do that made you think he wanted to kill you?"

"He pushed me back against the desk and wouldn't let me move, kept saying I had to do something for him."

"Did he attack you?" Doc asked.

"He wouldn't let me move; he had me wedged down on my desk. I didn't know what he was going to do. I had to do something, didn't I? I just couldn't stay there."

"What did you do?"

"I had my hand on my paperweight, and I hit him with it. Hit him to get him off me. He just kept talking and wouldn't let me move."

"Did you try to talk to him?" Doc asked.

"How do you talk to a crazy man? He didn't want to talk anyway; he kept telling me he wanted me to listen. It wasn't 'til after I hit him he said he came to be saved."

"You could have tried listening, man. Isn't that part of your calling? Talking to people, listening to people?"

"I couldn't save a crazy man."

Doc closed his eyes and exhaled deeply. When he opened them, he looked at Busby. "When did you come to believe that you could save anybody?" He pointed toward the Bible Charlie held tightly. "Where in that book does it say that you, Busby Howard, can save anybody? And where does it say that you can choose the people who come to you for help, crazy or not? Didn't Jesus cast out demons? And didn't he say, 'Whosoever has done it unto the least of these?" Doc leaned forward toward Busby. "When, I ask you, when, you egotistical son of two asses, did you decide you were God?"

Before Busby could open his mouth, the Clarks came running into the office.

Charlene ran to Charlie, fell to the floor, and took his head in her arms. She looked a question at Doc who got up and stood behind her. "He's gone, Charlene." Doc put his hands on her shoulders.

Charlene rocked Charlie in her arms; her tears ran down her face and fell onto his, splattering into the blood. Wyman took off his hat, came to take Doc's place behind her, and wept so hard his shoulders shook. No one said anything, their silence speaking their grief.

Finally, Charlene said, "I know it's probably better, him being so sick and all, but lately he'd seemed so much better, I'd begun to hope."

"He had been better lately," Wyman said, looking at his dead son, resting for the last time in his mother's lap. "He's been an awful burden at times, but no matter what, he was our son, and we loved him."

"Of course, you did, Wyman," Doc said. "Charlie's been sick a long time, and the two of you should take comfort in the fact that you always took care of him. He knew that." Doc paused for a minute, "And I can tell you this, he was as sane as we are when he died. He didn't come here to do harm; he came here to be saved by the preacher."

They both looked to Busby. "That why he came, Preacher?"

Before Busby could answer, Doc said, "Look there in his arms, he's holding Busby's Bible."

"Thank you, Jesus," Charlene said. "I hadn't even noticed." She looked at the Bible as though it was a piece of the Cross—and, for her, it was. "Oh, what Glory; our boy will rest with the Lord."

Wyman said, "Preacher, I'll never be able to thank you for what you've done."

Doc interrupted, "You both need to know that Busby thought he was being attacked, and he hit Charlie with that rock out of fear. That's how Charlie was killed."

"Well, we know you would never hurt Charlie unless you thought he was going to hurt you," Wyman said. "That's not the kind of man you are. We just thank the Lord that you were able to guide him through Heaven's gate. That's the important thing."

"Amen," Charlene said.

Doc said, "Why don't you two go on home, and I'll call Gene Proutty and have him come and take care of things. You can talk with Gene tomorrow and decide about the funeral."

The Clarks nodded and prepared to go.

Helen, who had moved to a chair at the far side of the office, got up and hugged each of them as they left, saying, "God be with you both."

There was silence in the room until the sound of the Clark's truck faded away. Helen looked at Busby as though she'd never seen him before. For the first time since Busby had convinced Helen to share his dream, Helen saw her husband clearly. And to her confusion, embarrassment, and pain, she did not like the man she saw. She did not like him at all.

Doc asked, "Helen, honey, do you feel all right to drive home?"

"I can drive, Doc. I've got to get home and change and tend to the girls."

Doc put his arm around her. "Take two aspirin when you get home, will you? You'll sleep better."

"I will, thank you." She looked down at her torn skirt and the blood soaked carpet beneath Charlies's head. "Is it ever going to be possible to clean up all this blood?" she asked, and turned to leave without waiting for an answer.

Doc called Gene Proutty and asked him to get in touch with the Sheriff. Doc knew this would be put down as an accident, but he wanted to have it taken care of tonight. The Clarks would claim Busby was a hero, and, other than Doc, Helen and Busby, who would know what happened in this room?

"Do you have something to cover him with until Gene gets here?" he asked Busby.

Busby motioned to a closet to his right. "There's a blanket on the shelf. I use it when it's cold in here."

Doc covered the body and said, "I'm going to wait outside until Gene gets here. You can go home whenever you're ready."

Busby nodded and Doc went out to his car.

Sitting in the parking lot just outside the open window of the office, Doc could see Busby sitting at his desk. The night was cooling off, and the cicadas were in full orchestra. An owl answered them from the woods. Then, just as Doc leaned back against the seat to adjust his bad leg, he heard a howl that came through the office window, seeming to magnify as it spread into the evening air. Busby Howard, his head lifted to the ceiling, howling like a soul in the hell he preached about, cried out into the night. When at last the howl stopped, Doc looked through the window to see Busby tearing at his hair, and crying, "Oh, God, God, God."

Doc wasn't sure if what he heard was a prayer or a curse.

Chapter Forty-Five

At 4:00 in the morning, Doc Barnes was called back to the hospital. Mae Ellen Elwell had been the nurse with Sample when he'd come to in recovery. She'd given him a piece of ice to suck on and patted his arm while she told him how lucky he was that Doc Barnes had been able to save one testicle and three inches of his penis; she thought that would make him happy. It had taken two orderlies and three nurses to restrain him, and Mae Ellen told them she wouldn't go back into his room even if he suffered a stroke and died. They'd kept him sedated until Doc got there, and Doc went in with an orderly and a nurse in case they had a repeat performance.

"Sample, can you hear me?" Doc asked him.

Sample mumbled, "Yeah."

"Try to wake up. We've got to talk," Doc said.

"I'm awake," he mumbled again.

"Not enough," Doc said. "Come on; try to get your eyes open." He turned to the nurse. "See if you can give him some water, please, Connie."

Connie West, an old army nurse who hadn't been afraid of Hitler so she sure as shooting wasn't afraid of Sample Forney, laid a hypodermic needle on the bedside table. "See this," she said, "you act up, and this is going straight into your butt." Then she jammed a straw between his lips and ordered, "Drink this, and when you're finished, I'm going to wash your face. So keep your mouth shut while I do, or I'll shove it full of soap." Sample eyed the hypodermic while she swabbed his face and continued with her litany. "Dang fool. I've seen men with limbs shot off not taking on the way you are. You act as though you're missing something important." He tried to jerk his face away, but he was still weak, and Connie was an expert.

"Scaring little girls like Mae Ellen; you ought to be ashamed." Sample glared at her and made a growling sound, but she held his face firmly in the crook of her arm and scrubbed it dry with a towel. When she released his head, she stepped away from the bed and picked up the hypodermic, eyeing Sample the whole time. "There you are, Doc."

"Thank you, Connie," Doc said, moving to the side of Sample's bed. He began again. "Do you understand what's happened?"

"Yeah, Doc, I understand," he said in his low flat voice.

"Sample," Doc said, putting a hand on his shoulder, "I know you're upset; any man would be, but this is something you're going to come to terms with."

"The hell you say," Sample said, raising himself up and throwing a punch that hooked Doc under the chin and knocked him on his backside into the chair nearby; then he tried to climb out of bed to hit Doc again, but got twisted up in the sheets and his I.V. line.

Doc told the orderly, "Strap him down, Frank. I'm not having any of his nonsense, and I won't have him hurting the staff."

Sample turned the air blue with curses while Frank secured him with straps to the bed. Doc rubbed his jaw and ordered Connie to sedate him as soon as the straps were tight enough.

"I told you, you stubborn mule," Connie said. She smartly flipped him over, slapped his butt with an alcohol swab, and followed that by jabbing the needle with precision and force into the fleshiest part of it. Sample muttered curses all the while, but he finally grew quieter.

Doc said loudly into his ear before he drifted off, "I'll be back later, and when I come, I want you to understand that I'm not putting up with any more of this crap. One word out of you, and I'll keep you doped up for a week." Doc marched out of the room, leaving Sample to drift off with Doc's words floating over him like a cloud.

Some three hours later, Sample, still strapped down, woke to an empty room. He could move his head, but not his body. He was clear-headed enough to know shouting wouldn't get him anything except another knockout shot. A nurse he hadn't seen before stuck her head just inside the door and asked him if he wanted some ice. He nodded his head. She came cautiously across the room and stood as far away as possible while she shakily spoon-fed him three teaspoons of ice chips.

"Take these straps off," he ordered gruffly when his mouth felt less cottony.

"Only Dr. Barnes can order those removed, Mr. Forney." The nurse looked uncomfortable, and she kept her distance from the bed. "I'm sorry," she offered.

"Then get on out of here," he told her, and she gladly hurried out of the room.

Sample was left on his own, looking at the ceiling. Here he was strapped to a hospital bed with most of his pecker shot off.

He'd gone out to see Alice to tell her they were getting married after her birthday and that he planned to announce it at her party. He'd bought his first wedding ring, a shiny gold one, and he had it in his pocket to show her. She'd been right nice lately, and she seemed happy, smiling all the time. He hadn't seen any reason to wait. Webster had wanted him to, but he never listened to Webster, and there was no reason to start then.

So he'd gone. And there she was, standing at the heating stove burning something in the middle of an August day. The firelight lit her in the dim room, and she looked beautiful. And happy. What was it she was burning that made her look like that? He looked down to see what she was shoving into the fire, and there it was. Alice was burning the dress material that he'd bought because it had matched her eyes. She was sticking it in the stove on the end of a poker like it was something she didn't want to touch.

He felt the flame leaped out at him and caused a fire in his gut. He'd been so stupid. So stupid. Because of her. He'd wanted to strike her. He'd stepped toward her, and that's when she saw him. Her face went white with surprise and something else he couldn't name. He'd wanted to pick up the poker she'd dropped at the sight of him and beat her with it. He actually moved toward it, but he couldn't do it. He couldn't beat Alice. Not Alice.

He had shaken her and held her down against the table, and when she was looking up at him, he knew what he'd seen in her eyes. Alice was repulsed by him, and she had shivered under his touch and had tried to pull away. He'd released her and shouted at her. But even then, at that moment, he couldn't stop wanting her.

He'd always been able to get the things he wanted. He'd, by God, have Alice Tolney whether she wanted him or not, he'd thought. After all, he'd earned her. Hadn't he paid $100 for her pie?

Hadn't he sat there night after night at the Tolney's and waited? He'd never laid a hand on her, even knowing that she was going to be his. He'd brought her presents and talked nice to her momma. Hell, he was giving Webster right good land for her. He'd done more than he thought any woman was worth.

Before her, it had never occurred to him to think about trying to make a woman happy. He'd owned the land and the livestock; why would women be different? You married them so they could be yours to use whatever way you needed. Women had their place. But not Alice; she was going to be different, and she never even saw that. And she was burning his gift like trash. Like trash. No woman, not even Alice, could do that.

That's when he'd told her he already owned her. He'd closed his ears to what she'd said, and he'd gone after Ray Redeem. He hadn't planned to kill him; he'd just wanted to crush him so Ray would know that Alice would never belong to him. But Ray had said Sample would have to kill him to stop him, and in that moment, Sample had believed it was the only way to have Alice.

Now, there he was lying in this bed with most of his manhood shot away. He wouldn't be able to have any woman, let alone Alice. He was the man with one ball and a stub of a pecker. She'd laugh at him. Any woman would laugh at him. He drifted off to sleep, seeing a chorus of women pointing at him, saying, "Sample Forney got his pecker shot off. He's not the biggest man in the county now." The laughter echoed around in his head as he dropped into a deeper sleep.

When Doc came back to Sample's room in the late afternoon, he found Sample dozing. He settled himself in a chair beside the bed just out of reach.

"Doc?" Sample asked, rousing and trying to focus. "That you?"

"Yes, it's me."

Sample's eyes fixed on Doc's face. "Doc, you've ruined me. You've damn well ruined me."

"I did no such thing. I saved as much as possible, but I had to take off your left testicle; there was no way to repair it."

"You could've sewed my pecker back on."

"I couldn't sew it back on; it was too mangled. Those hollow point bullets spread out. I left you three inches of penis, which is as much as some men have to begin with, and as far as I can tell, you'll probably be able to do more than just pee out of it. Time will tell. You're just damn lucky Jackson didn't put a bullet through your brain. I would've if you'd tried to saw my son in two."

Neither of them had heard the door open, but Jackson had slipped in and was standing just inside the room. His voice came over the top of Doc's head. "I will put a bullet through your brain, Sample, if you come anywhere near my son or Alice Tolney. You have my word on it." With that, Jackson slipped out and left as quietly as he'd come in.

The door swung shut, and Doc and Sample were left staring at it. "There's a man who means just what he says," Doc said, turning back to Sample.

"I'm not afraid of Jackson Redeem," Sample declared.

"Nobody's asking you to be afraid. I'm just telling you that if you want to live, you'll do what he says. You're not a stupid man, Sample. Nobody's ever claimed that; you're known for your good business sense and your fairness with men. But everybody knows how you've treated women, and nobody's ever admired you for that."

"I don't give a damn what anybody thinks." Sample looked away from Doc.

"Of course, you do, you've got to do business with these people, and you have to hire them to work that big farm of yours; you can't do it on your own. You need the help, and now that everybody knows you're not able to treat women like cattle any more, I would imagine that should help your business dealings. Women will feel easier around you, and if you think that women don't influence their husbands, you've got another think coming."

"Why wouldn't they feel easier with my pecker gone?" He gave a low, angry laugh. "What woman would want me now, Doc, now that I'm ruined?"

"Hell, Sample, what woman wanted you before? You've bought women or traded for them from men too greedy or too stupid to act decently, and the women were too dumb or too frightened to know how to fight back. You could try treating women with some respect; they're not cattle, for God's sake."

"I only know how to act the way I act. I can't do no better."

"Well, you damn well better learn to do better," Doc said. "Hell, Sample, you haven't lost your business or your farm; you've just lost the end of your penis. Now, quit thinking your pecker is your life, and get on with living. Right now, get some rest. I'll be in later this afternoon." Doc got up to leave.

"I heard Alice was here," Sample said.

Doc could see it cost him to say it. "She was here to see Ray, Sample. Alice doesn't love you; she never has. Webster was after something, and he was willing to trade his own child for it and let you think she was willing. You two can't force a woman into your life like that. Hell, man, slavery was abolished."

"I never wanted Alice as a slave," Sample countered.

Doc studied him for several long seconds. "Maybe you didn't, Sample. But the next time you decide on a woman, you'd best be talking to her about it, not some male in her family who's looking to get ahead himself. You don't barter for a woman, not if you're ever going to be happy. Take some time while you're here to think it over." Doc got up and began moving toward the door.

"I want to get out of here tomorrow," Sample said.

"That's not going to happen; you're going to need special nurses for a while."

"How much longer am I going to be here? I've got things to do."

Doc moved toward the door. He said over his shoulder as he left, "I'd say ten days or two weeks should just about do it."

He walked off down the hall smiling to himself.

Chapter Forty-Six

Johnson's Store was humming with business and buzzing with gossip. It was August 11th, and Ray Redeem and Alice Tolney were getting married tomorrow in Naomi Hollister's backyard. Party lines had forwarded the message Naomi left at the telephone exchange: "All friends of the bride and the groom are invited to Ray and Alice's wedding. Ceremony, Saturday at 6:00 p.m. at the hotel. Bring a dish and a gift."

Bertie Reardon posted signs in the post office and on the side of the railroad station that faced the street. She knew it wasn't policy, but thought the railroad and the U.S. Post Office should make an exception for this wedding. The Johnsons had one up in the front window of their store, too.

Inside Johnson's and outside on the porch, the same gossipy questions swirled. Didn't Eugene do a fine job with Charlie's funeral? It was a right nice turnout, wasn't it? Most everybody in town was there. And wasn't it neighborly of Reverend Fair West to come over from the Methodist Church to fill in for Busby? Is Busby's stomach flu any better? He just can't seem to rid himself of it since he accidentally killed poor Charlie, can he?

Will Webster be at the wedding? Nobody's seen him since the fight at the sawmill; he sure is staying close to home. Evelyn is getting out and about a lot, isn't she? She must be glad to have both her girls together there at Naomi's. She's been there everyday. I wish I'd been a fly on the wall when she had her say with Webster. Did you hear Matt's Presbyterian minister from Havana is going to marry Ray and Alice?

Doc, who had gone into Johnson's for a R.C. Cola, had to straighten out some of the stories that had circulated concerning Sample. Yes,

Sample still had enough equipment to operate. No, he wasn't receiving visitors, not even his children. Yes, he would have to stay until the 15th or 16th of the month. No, Jackson hadn't come to the hospital to kill Sample; if he'd wanted to kill him, he would have done it at the mill. Yes, Jackson had told Busby he'd leave the church if Busby ever preached about Ray again. No, he didn't know how Busby felt about that; they'd have to ask Busby when Busby was feeling better. No, he didn't know how many others were leaving the church; they'd have to ask Busby that, too.

Across the tracks at the hotel, the ladies of The Tysen Garden Society had finished setting up tables for the food and rows of folding chairs in the backyard; they'd bring the freshly laundered linen table cloths and napkins tomorrow. Everybody wanted to pitch in. Matt and Johnny had built an archway for the bride and groom to stand under to take their vows. In the morning, Naomi and Maureen Fitzroy would cover it with the flowers that the Garden Society ladies would bring by early.

Matilda St. John had brought the cut crystal punch bowl she'd used at her own wedding with fifty matching crystal cups. The set had to be moved to Naomi's bedroom and was taking up the entire top of Naomi's dresser and part of the floor beside it. There were wedding gifts all around Russell in the living room, and there was no more room in the kitchen for anything except the wedding cake Naomi was baking.

Naomi had the kitchen to herself, thank heavens. Russell was sleeping. She could see through the archway how small he looked; he hardly made a mound under the light sheet she kept over him. She checked on the rise and fall of his chest as she would a baby's to make sure at night he was still breathing. As weak as he was, he still managed to sit up part of the day. He had to use more morphine, but he said he'd decided not to die; there was too much happening around here. The man certainly had a will.

Evelyn was resting up in Mary Jo's room. Mary Jo and Johnny had gone with Alice and Ray to get the results of their blood test and pick up the new blue suits Ray and Johnny had bought in Havana. Matt wouldn't be home for at least two hours. Naomi could get two more layers into the oven and sit down for a spell. This cake had to be perfect: seven layers high, light as a feather, and topped with cream cheese icing that, Doc said, could make the angels sing.

She closed the oven door carefully to keep the cake from falling and laid the potholders on the sink to the side. She turned and stopped short;

Helen Howard was standing next to the table, tears running down her face. "Naomi," she said, "I didn't know where else to go."

Naomi helped her into a chair and reached for a box of Kleenex in the cupboard, putting it on the table in front of her. Helen tried to speak, but couldn't; the tears came surging down her face and clogged her throat. They'd been damned up for so long. She doubled into a ball and sobbed.

"You just sit right there for a bit, and when you feel better, you can tell me all about it," Naomi said, taking a soiled Kleenex out of Helen's limp hands and replacing it with a fresh one. Gradually, the tears came less and less, and, finally, Helen lifted her swollen, blotchy face and blew her nose.

"I'm so sorry; I didn't mean to break down like that."

"Don't you worry about that," Naomi told her, going to the refrigerator for some cold water. "You've been through a terrible time what with Charlie's death, and all. I don't know how you've held up so well."

"I just had to talk to somebody. You were the only one I could think of."

Naomi handed her the glass of water. "Now, tell me what's happened."

When Helen began, her words, like her tears, were a flood. "It's Hope, Naomi, and it's my fault. I should have done something. I should have helped her through this more." Her tone grew hard. "I'm just so used to keeping everything in hand for Busby. You know how Busby can fill up rooms, and he takes over lives, and I've helped him, with hardly a word to the contrary. I should have paid more attention." Then, her voice softened again, "There she's been, my Hope, my sweet, sweet girl, cleaning, and sewing, and staying in her room reading, never going anywhere except to church and band practice. All the time with her heart breaking, knowing that Alice and Ray were getting married, and she couldn't be there. Especially knowing that she couldn't be there with Johnny. Oh, how I've let her down," she sobbed.

Naomi was becoming frightened. "Has something happened to Hope?"

"She," Helen paused for a moment, the words hard to say, "didn't come home from band practice last night."

"What do you mean she didn't come home?"

"She ran off with Billy Easton."

"She what?" Naomi didn't understand.

"She's married; she eloped with Billy Easton. They drove to East St. Louis because they don't have to get blood tests in Illinois. They didn't come home until this morning about four a.m. The two of them, babies, standing in the living room, holding hands, looking so scared and young, waiting for Busby. He came out of the bedroom, and before he could say a word, Hope told him that they were married, and they'd already slept together, and there wasn't a thing he could do about it. She was leaving his house, and nobody was ever going to order her around again. She told him, 'You're the meanest man I've ever met, and I hate what you've done to me. I'm a good person, a good person, and, in all my life, you never heard me; you never even saw me'."

"Oh, Helen, that poor child."

"She had to get away; she just had to. She couldn't wait another year," Helen sobbed.

"What did Busby say to her?" Naomi asked.

"He said if she felt that way, he didn't want her under his roof ever again. Then, he turned and walked off to the bedroom and shut the door. We sat down and talked for a while. Billy was so sweet with her and me. He told me he'd always loved her; he just never thought he stood a chance.

"I told them not to go, that it was my house, too, but they left to stay at Billy's folks. I don't blame them; why should they put up with Busby?

"After they'd gone, I stayed up the rest of the night. Oh, Naomi, what's going to happen to her?"

"Billy's a good boy, Helen," Naomi said, wondering herself what would happen to her. "He'll take care of her."

"I know he is, but they're so young. They told me last night that Hope is going to live with him and his folks until he leaves for college, and she's going to finish high school in Springfield and get a part time job to help support them."

"She'll be better off in Springfield with Billy than spending another year under Busby's roof." Naomi couldn't hold her anger in. "She doesn't need to be around a father who treats her like some sinner. That girl is as sweet and pure as they come. Busby doesn't need to hound her anymore. With Billy, she's got a chance of a future. I know he's your husband, Helen, but that's the way I feel about it."

Helen said, "Busby and I have hardly said a word to each other since the night he had the—accident—with Charlie Clark. I haven't known how to talk to him about it." She looked at Naomi, "I really didn't want to; that's the Lord's own truth. I just didn't want to hear what he had to say. He stays in bed most of the time, claiming he's sick. He hasn't spoken a word this morning. Not even to ask where Hope went." Helen stopped to sip some water. She looked like she wanted to say something else, but didn't know how to go about it.

"How about a cup of coffee? You need some more time just to sit here and rest."

"That would be good, and, yes, I am tired." She slumped into her chair as she waited for Naomi to bring her the coffee, drank half of it, straightened a bit, and then began slowly to speak. "Busby's been acting real strange."

"What's he been doing?" Naomi asked.

"He keeps getting out of bed to look for his Bible. He wanders from room to room, then goes back to bed again. In an hour or so, he's back at it."

"He doesn't know where he left it?"

"Oh, he knows. Charlie Clark was holding it when he died. In fact, they buried him with it."

"I saw the Bible Charlie was holding, but I didn't know it was Busby's."

"Charlie just grabbed it when he fell and wouldn't let go of it," Helen told her. "Busby's taken to mumbling to himself all the time. I can hear him even when I'm in the kitchen. It's like he's arguing with Charlie, telling Charlie he has to give him his Bible back. If he doesn't have *his* Bible, he says he can't preach because his Bible is the one God wrote in. It's not making any sense, Naomi."

"Honey, Busby hasn't made sense for some time now, but this sounds serious. Maybe Doc should have a look at him."

"He says he doesn't want Doc near him. Besides, he says, it's just a summer cold. Then he goes off mumbling again." She hesitated, staring for a moment at the cream in her coffee; then said, "Naomi, I don't think I can stay with Busby anymore. I can't have him treating Grace the way he's treated Hope; I won't have him break the hearts of both my girls. I don't know what to do but leave him." She watched Naomi for her reaction.

Naomi knew what it would mean for Helen to leave Busby; nobody would call a divorced man to a Baptist pulpit. She prayed she'd say the right thing. "You don't have to stay with Busby, honey. You need to do what's best for you and Grace."

"I'm worried though. I'm afraid I'm going do something that's a sin. You know what the Bible says about divorce."

"The Bible was written a long time ago, Helen, and not one of those men ever had to put up with Busby Howard," Naomi said. "Now, that's a test for a true saint." She smiled at Helen, who almost smiled back. "You take your time and talk to the Lord about it. You make up your own mind; do what your heart and prayer tell you to do; don't let Busby do it for you."

Helen put her arms around Naomi and hugged her tight. "That's good advice," Helen said, drying her eyes. "You're a good friend, Naomi Hollister; I'm proud to know you."

Naomi's eyes were tearing now.

"I wish I could be at the wedding, but I'm going to take Grace over to Meramec City for dinner with a friend of mine, try to keep her occupied and away from Busby."

"We'll all miss you; just you keep that in mind," Naomi said.

"You won't say anything until after the wedding? I don't want to spoil their wedding day with our troubles, and I don't want Johnny to be any unhappier than he already is."

"I won't say a thing, and thank you for thinking of Johnny."

"Johnny's a good boy, Naomi. This will be hard for him."

"It will be hard for Johnny, but he isn't the one who's had to go through what Hope has. She's a sweet, dear girl, and if things had been different, I would have been so happy if she and Johnny had gotten together."

Helen nodded. "I know; she loves you, too."

"You and the girls always have a place to stay here. You're not alone. People in this town love you; don't you ever forget it."

"I won't. Thank you, Naomi; I couldn't have gotten through the day without you."

"Oh, honey, that's what friends are for." Naomi encircled her in a tight hug. "Come back after the wedding. I promise to save you some cake."

Helen put her arm around Naomi as they walked outside into the fresh breeze. They stood on the porch like that for a minute.

"She's going to be all right with Billy; I know she is," Naomi said.

Helen nodded. "I pray you're right."

Naomi watched as Helen walked off the steps, head high, not caring who saw her leaving the front porch of the hotel. Naomi took a deep breath before she went back to the kitchen. She smelled change in the air.

Chapter Forty-Seven

An August day had never been more beautiful than the day Alice Tolney married Ray Redeem. The tables were laden with hams and baked turkey, with casseroles, and fresh cooked vegetables. There was corn on the cob and tomatoes that tasted of the sun. There were fresh baked breads and sweet rolls, corn relish and pickled beets. And flowers: everywhere you looked there were bouquets of flowers. Naomi's backyard, always a beauty, had been transformed into a floral extravaganza.

Tysen had turned out in all its glory. Women were in their finest summer dresses, and the men were wearing ties. Bertie Reardon had actually had her hair done at the beauty parlor in Meramec City, and Doobie wore a suit. Until that moment, no one in Tysen knew he owned one. Even more surprising was Jackson Redeem; he wore a smile, and that's something not many people remembered seeing him wear either. In fact, several people remarked that Jackson was still a fine looking man with a smile on his face.

The face that wasn't smiling was the one that Webster Tolney wore when he stepped down from his truck. Folks in the backyard nudged each other and watched as Ray went over to help Evelyn down. He told her how pretty she looked in her new blue dress and that Alice was waiting for her inside in the upstairs bedroom with Mary Jo. Then he walked around the truck to Webster.

"Webster," he said.

"Ray," Webster responded.

"Let's take a little walk, just you and me," Ray said.

Webster nodded, and the assembled guests watched them walk down the road behind Naomi's toward the post office. Some fifteen minutes later as they came back, Webster was talking to Ray as easily as if he did it every day. When they got to the edge of the yard, Doc, who was sitting in the yard swing out near the road, heard Ray say, "Well, we'll just have to see about that Webster. Today, let's just think about how nice it is to have Mary Jo here with her momma and you on our wedding day."

"I think it's right nice, Ray; I do. My girls have always been downright important to me." He patted Ray on the back with ownership and started off toward a group of men who were gathered around the coffee pot, but turned back to say, "Don't you forget what we was talking about back there."

"If I do, Webster, you just remind me," Ray told him.

"You can count on it," Webster said.

Ray joined Johnny who was drinking a Coca Cola and handed Ray one. "We sure are handsome devils in these blue suits," Ray said.

"I especially like the way your jacket sleeve is split at the seam to show off your cast," Johnny said.

"I make a striking figure, don't I?"

"You do, indeed, my good man," Johnny said, trying to imitate Cary Grant. "Now tell me what you said to Webster to make him come around so quickly."

"Evelyn's the one who straightened him out. I don't know what she said and neither does Alice. Evelyn said that was between the two of them. I just told him how much business a lumber mill could do in a year. Strangest thing, the man developed a liking for me and the lumber business right on the spot, especially now that his daughter is going to be a member of the family and all." They both laughed.

"Don't you sorta wish he falls under a plow?" Johnny asked.

"Too much to be hoped for," Ray answered. The two of them touched their coke bottles in a salute.

Across the yard, Webster poured himself a cup of coffee, and said to Doobie, "A fine day for a wedding, ain't it?"

Doobie said, "It is at that," and toasted Bertie Reardon, who was talking flowers with Maureen, with his pocket flask.

And it was, by all accounts, the finest wedding Tysen had ever beheld. Everybody said so. Matilda called it a lawn wedding delight, Marie

Johnson said that James Patterson, the Presbyterian minister, did a right nice wedding, the best she'd ever heard; there wasn't a doubt that Alice was the most beautiful bride they'd ever seen and Ray the happiest groom. Mary Jo and Webster didn't get close enough to fight, and blessing of blessings, nobody said a word about the Howards. Only Alice had said to Naomi when she came down from the bedroom with her mother and Mary Jo, looking wedding-picture perfect in her beautiful dress, "I wish Hope was here today."

"We all do, sweetheart," Naomi said, and it was all she could do to keep the tears from coming. "But there isn't anything we can do about it. This is your day; you enjoy it."

Now, in the dusk, Naomi stood on the back steps looking out over the guests who were eating cake and drinking pink punch out of Matilda's cut crystal cups. Doc and James Patterson were on their third piece of cake. Doc had just motioned to his plate and James's and held up three fingers for her to see.

Naomi liked James Patterson. She'd decided, listening to his sweet words of grace, as he spoke to Alice and Ray, that the business of the First Baptist Church was no longer hers. There was too much left-over pain sitting in her pew. It was at that moment she decided to become a Presbyterian.

Across the yard, Johnny and Mary Jo were laughing with Alice and Ray. She'd have to tell him about Hope, but not until tomorrow. Tomorrow would be the day for that. And tomorrow or the tomorrow after that would be the day for Jackson and Busby to fight out whatever they had to fight out between them. There'd be another day for gossip about Busby and about Hope, for the people of Tysen would certainly do that. The church was in turmoil, and Busby Howard was the one stirring the pot, and with Hope's revolt, even the diehards would have to face it.

Matt wheeled Russell over to where she stood. "It's time we took Russell in," he said. He was nodding in his wheelchair, and Naomi automatically tucked in the light blanket that she had put over his thin legs. Here she was with these two men she loved. Yes, she loved Russell, too. They'd had their years together. There would be another day very soon for watching Russell take his last breath, for telling him she loved him, for kissing him goodbye. Another day for sending Johnny off to his dreams. And there would be another day for her to begin the next page of living.

"You know, Matt, this wedding would have been completely perfect if we'd just been able to dance."

"We'll dance at our wedding; it won't be too late," he said,

"Amen," Russell said softly, not lifting his head.